BLURB

Ava Thompson has at long last surrendered to her true love, Jasper White, and this time, there's no going back.

They're both determined to forget their rocky past and focus on their promise to be together forever. However, with Ava living in New York, and Jasper in L.A., their future is held in the balance on where to call home.

So what's the compromise?

Ava doesn't want to leave, and Jasper doesn't want to stay. They've reached an impasse in their relationship and Ava soon realizes that for them to be together, one of them will have to give up their dreams for good.

But who? And more importantly, what happens when one of them sacrifices their dreams for the other? Whatever choice is made, Ava knows they'll both lose.

Adding to the heartache are two new players who are set on breaking up the ill-fated pair for good.

Do Jasper and Ava have the strength to survive this final test of love?

WHITE

International Bestselling Author

MONICA JAMES

WHITE

Follow me on:
authormonicajames.com

OTHER BOOKS BY MONICA JAMES

THE I SURRENDER SERIES

I Surrender

Surrender to Me

Surrendered

White

SOMETHING LIKE NORMAL SERIES

Something like Normal

Something like Redemption

Something like Love

A HARD LOVE ROMANCE

Dirty Dix

Wicked Dix

The Hunt

MEMORIES FROM YESTERDAY

Forgetting You, Forgetting Me

Forgetting You, Remembering Me

SINS OF THE HEART

Absinthe of the Heart

Defiance of the Heart

ALL THE PRETTY THINGS TRILOGY

Bad Saint

Fallen Saint

Forever My Saint

The Devil's Crown-Part One (Spin-Off)

The Devil's Crown-Part Two (Spin-Off)

THE MONSTERS WITHIN DUET

Bullseye

Blowback

DELIVER US FROM EVIL TRILOGY

Thy Kingdom Come

Into Temptation

Deliver Us From Evil

IN LOVE AND WAR

North of the Stars

Fall of the Stars

REVENGE IS SWEET SERIES

Crybaby

HEART MEMORY TRANSFER DUET

Heart Sick

Love Sick

KISS OR KILL DUET

Bad For You

Kill For You

LOVE HARD

Love Hard

Love Harder

STANDALONE

Mr. Write

Chase the Butterflies

Beyond the Roses

Someone Else's Shadow

Like a Boss

CHAPTER ONE
Conquest

"This...is your wake-up call."

"No, I don't want to," I groan, my eyes shut tight. "I'm not even awake. This, right here"—I blindly gesture to my torso in a sweeping motion — "is an illusion. See? I'm actually still asleep." I bury my head into the pillow, faking sleep.

Sadly, my staged snores don't convince my chuckling fiancé, Jasper White. "You're the world's worst actress, baby. Please don't give up your day job any time soon."

His truthful yet cheeky response has me opening my eyes in mock horror. "Well, *your* day job is the reason why I'm so tired," I gripe, throwing an arm over my face as the early morning sun burns my corneas.

So, it's been about a month since I surrendered, and let me tell you, what a month it's been. The night Jasper and I *finally* got our shit together was the greatest night of my life. I remember as if it was only yesterday—Jasper on his knees before me, sopping wet, declaring I was his forever and a day. Our love affair has been one you read about in books, and our journey, it's been bumpy, to say the least.

I can proudly say we've conquered distance, time, miscommunication, groupies, psychotic exes x2, a batshit crazy evil mother, insecurities, my whining, et cetera, et cetera, but most of all, we've conquered each other. And that, by far, is the greatest conquest of all.

We've both promised one another to focus on the future and forget the past, because our future together is all that matters. I just want to bask in our proverbial honeymoon and enjoy our reunion. Enjoy being together once again. And by together, I mean emotionally *and* physically.

Jasper has put my mind at ease and assured me he didn't sleep with anyone while we were apart. I did the same. We have so much to discuss, but for the minute, this stillness will do. It makes me happy to know that even after a year apart, our love is still as strong as it once was.

I'm still living in New York, and Jasper in L.A., but he's more here than he is there, as being separated sucks.

The year apart was beneficial for each of us. We both grew and discovered who we were and what we wanted. It goes without saying we wanted one another, but this time around, there's no breaking up or going backward. The stunning diamond on my finger is proof of that.

I am absolutely in love with my engagement ring, and the thought has me extending my arm out in front of me and looking at my beauty for the first time today. Jasper sees my obvious appraisal and laughs.

"You know, I'm starting to think you love that ring more than you love me," he says with a fake pout, his supple lips looking extra delicious with the staged movement.

I chuckle at his adorability and wiggle my finger so

the early morning light reflects off the perfected planes. "Don't be ridiculous," I reply, staring at Jasper's declaration of love.

Jasper breathes out a premature breath of relief as I add with a grin, "I love you both the same."

He bursts into laughter, his husky voice doing amazing things to my much awakened body. But as I look over at my clock, I see that if I don't get my ass into gear, I'll be late for work. It shouldn't matter of course, seeing as I'm the boss, but I really can't afford to be tardy because today is really important, as I'm interviewing all day long.

The reason why I'm looking for a new staff member is because Jasper and I have been invited to Jeremy's holiday home in Chicago for his 50th birthday party. The gathering is to take place over the course of a weekend, and I wouldn't miss it for the world. However, two of my best senior employees are on leave, and my assistant manager, Faith, is in the hospital, banged up with three fractured ribs, two broken legs, and a ruptured spleen, thanks to a taxi driver who looked left instead of right.

So it goes without saying I'm ridiculously short-staffed, and now is really not the best time to take leave. But with no other choice, I need to interview for the assistant manager's role because I don't know how long Faith will be out of action.

I'm really looking forward to meeting the Blackwood clan for Jeremy's party, which is taking place in a couple weeks' time. When I say clan, I mean *clan*, as Jasper went from having no family to having an endless amount of people in his extended family of aunts, uncles, cousins, second cousins, grandparents, a farmyard of animals, and more importantly, a younger half-brother he never knew about.

Jasper has Stephen, but sadly, there's no happy reunion in sight for those two anytime soon. Jasper hopes that one day his big brother will come around, but I guess knowing your mom is The Antichrist incarnate warrants you a little time to digest your thoughts. But like I said, Jasper has an entire bunch of people who, thanks to his wonderful dad, has become his family overnight.

Apart from Jeremy, I've yet to meet his nearest and dearest, and it's time to change that. I can't wait to get to know them because anyone who puts a smile on my boyfriend, sorry, fiancé's face, is my new best friend. Well, second best friend, seeing as my current best friend would string anyone up by the short and curlies if they dare try and take her place.

I really, really miss Veronica, and as much as I love New York and running my own restaurant, which has been my dream since I was five years old, I really miss L.A. Someone once told me you go to Hollywood to make movies, and you go to New York to make money. I never really understood what that meant until living in both cities and experiencing the excitement which goes on in both places.

I love the hustle and bustle of New York, but my heart will always be lost in the City of Angels. I mean, how could it not? It brought me my own personal angel. So to me, L.A. is my heaven.

But sadly, being the manager of an elite restaurant that doesn't run itself means I'm stuck in New York.

Metropolis got the respectable reputation it has because I put my heart and soul into its success, and in turn, it's now the hottest place to dine in NYC. But the thing is, now that I've started, I can't stop. It's only been a year, and I know the best is yet to come.

I want to see Metropolis grow, and like all buildings in NYC, I want to build up. My dream is to see Metropolis continue to flourish in the direction of the fine dining experience that it is, but afterwards, instead of patrons going home, I want the elegance to continue upstairs where a cool piano bar and lounge will be readily available for those who aren't ready to call it a night.

I guess this dream was inspired by my personal muse, Mr. Jasper White.

After seeing Jasper perform that night on the piano, the vision of him and I pulling this off has become more of a reality and less of a dream because I want this to happen. I *know* it can happen.

I've looked into everything, but sadly, Jasper wasn't too keen on the idea when I mentioned it in passing. I didn't press because I didn't want to ruin our reunion.

I know he would never stand in the way of my dreams, and would support me no matter what, but I know his heart will always lie in L.A. He loves it here, and he's only here for me. I think deep down, he's wishing that I'll find the right person to fill my shoes, because that person will ultimately send me back home.

So that's the plan. I'm to find a new assistant manager, and eventually, leave my baby in their very capable hands. But the mere thought of not being here leaves a big open gash in my heart. But home is where the heart is, and my heart is with Jasper. No dream is worth losing him over—not again.

Therefore, I'll go into these interviews with an open mind and not fault the interviewees on their dress sense, what color pen they used to fill out the application form, or if their surname starts with the letters A-Z. I just need to come to terms with the fact that I can't have my New York cheesecake and eat it, too.

Jasper is enough of a dream come true and without him, my life is incomplete.

Going away to Jeremy's is a brilliant test to a see how I'll survive being away from my baby, and to also see if I can actually do this and quit a job I so love to do. I know it makes sense, and I know eventually I'll end up moving back to L.A. I mean, my friends, my family, my cat, are all there—I just wish I could pack Metropolis up and take it with me.

"...And then I said, 'I'm engaged,' and she's all like, 'I don't care, I wanna touch it.'"

"Touch what?" I bark quickly, whipping my head towards Jasper and meeting his amused cerulean eyes.

"Oh, so you were listening?" he mocks.

"Just 'cause I'm not looking at you doesn't mean I'm not listening," I reply with a smirk.

"You're such a multi-tasker," he teases, propping himself up on an elbow.

"Yup, I'm the queen of doing two things at once." The moment the words leave my lips, I instantly regret them, as Jasper's mouth tips up into a dimpled smile.

"Oh, really? Would you be willing to test this theory out?"

"That all depends," I rebuke, my chest beginning to rise.

"On what?"

"On what you propose I test it out on," I reply, my voice turning hoarse, turned on by Jasper's obvious innuendo.

I watch with interest, anticipating Jasper's next move because I have a feeling it's one I'm going to like a lot.

One minute I'm lying on my side, and the next, I'm on my back with Jasper laying on top of me, balancing his full weight on his hands. "I can think of a few things," he huskily replies, his gaze dropping to my scarcely covered chest.

"Oh yeah? Care to share your thoughts?"

"I would rather show you," he replies. I smile, preferring that option also.

I take a moment to appreciate the man before me—the man I've loved from the first moment I saw him.

I run my fingers through his trademark tousled hair, and then trace the perfect brow above his bright blue eyes, the eyes that have seen my beauty even when I didn't. Drawing a line down the slope of his perfect nose, I linger on his mouth, brushing over the scar which shouts to the world what a fighter he truly is. His stubble tickles my finger, and the only way to resolve that is to slip it into his parted, delicious mouth. I outline his full lips and then slowly seek refuge inside. My body warms the instant I feel his tongue wrap around my pointer.

His eyes never leave mine as he sucks the tip lightly, but it's enough to leave me panting, my heart rate increasing to a deafening staccato. If I don't remove my finger, I know where this is headed, but I'm quite enjoying my exploration of Jasper, and I'm not halfway done with the tour.

With great difficulty, I remove my pointer and sweep my thumb along his chiseled, hardened jaw. Working my way lower, I trace down the curve of his neck as he willingly extends backwards, completely trusting me and allowing me full access to his body.

Admiring the wonderful sight before me, I decide to stop at his Adam's apple along the way. I reach for his ball chain necklace and finger the ring I gave him for his birthday. The inscription, 'Surrendered,' looks back at me, and I can't help but smile, as that single phrase is so true.

As my gaze drops to my new favorite part of Jasper White, a shiver passes through me and I bite my lip to stop my moan of approval. Just when I thought my rock god couldn't get any hotter, Jasper has now upped the ante by adding a hint of ink to his deliciously hot body.

My name stares back at me from his left inner upper arm, the cursive font making my name look beautiful and classic. Jasper watches as I trace the letters over and over. He smiles.

"I think you need to add to this," I casually say, and Jasper raises a brow. "Just above my name...it doesn't have to be big or anything," I backtrack while Jasper chuckles.

"Let's hear it."

"Well, it could say, 'Property of...Ava?'" I suggest, only half joking.

Jasper shakes his head, laughing at my idiocy.

"What? I think it'll be cute," I offer as an explanation to my madness.

"Cute? It'll make me look like a lost sweater," he replies while tickling my sides.

Giggling, I squirm out of his clutches, and he thankfully stops. "It's just an idea to keep those groupie whores away," I say, and Jasper pulls back, faking shock.

"My, my. Ava Thompson, soon to be White. You kiss your mother with that mouth?"

I can't help but laugh. "I also kiss you with it. And White? Who said I'm going to be changing my name?"

Whether we get married today, tomorrow, or never—it won't matter, because nothing will come between us ever again.

"You know you're just itching to be Ava White, I mean, who wouldn't?" I playfully slap him on the arm.

Jasper turns sober as he says, "But in all seriousness, no one needs to know who I'm the property of…"

Just as I'm about to smack him again, he adds, "This," and he picks up my hand, gesturing to my ring. "This is enough to show the entire world that I belong to you, and you belong to me."

As touched as I am by his heartfelt confession, I can't help but reply, "Yeah, well, too bad you can't take my hand with you when you go on tour and bitch slap Delilah Rose's face with it," I say, scowling the moment I mention her name.

"Baby," Jasper says, his lips pulling into a thin line. "We've talked about this."

"I know. I just hate her. And her perfect face." I snicker under my breath.

"You could always come with me…" he suggests. He's been bugging me to go with him on his six-week

European tour, which is to take place in a few weeks' time.

Passengers of Ego have dominated the charts and their record label has organized for them to go on their first international tour, which is brilliant, but sadly, they'll be touring with Roses.

Delilah Rose is the lead singer of the punk band, Roses, and she's also Jasper's ex...whatever. I know it's in the past, and she's no longer a threat, but I still hate her and wish she caught laryngitis and pulled out of the tour.

I trust Jasper. She's the one I don't trust.

However, focusing on his earlier question, I reply, "I wish I could, but I can't. Metropolis is probably going to fall apart without me for the three days we're gone. Can you imagine what would happen in six weeks?"

"That's why you're going to find the perfect Ava fill-in today, and then—" But he pauses, not finishing his original thought.

"And then what?" I ask, even though I know what he meant to say.

"Then you can come home. I miss you, baby," he confesses.

Even though I'm grateful he told me the truth, I lower my eyes, because the truth sucks.

Jasper reads my disappointment instantly, and sighs. "Hey, I know this is important to you, but I just want to go back to L.A. and start building our life together. We've wasted enough time, and it's time I make an honest woman out of you."

I smile, deciding to think about his serious statement *after* I have my coffee. "I kind of like living in sin," I reply, tracing his jaw line with my fingertip. "I mean, what if we become the typical, boring married couple, who ends up living by rules and routine?" I blanch as I have another thought. "What if we turn into my parents?"

Jasper's deep chuckle rumbles low in his chest, which hits me where it hurts...oh so good. "That'll never be us," he affirms, his body picking up on my sudden awakening.

"And why's that?" I ask, the breath catching in my throat when he tongues his lower lip.

"Because I'm a rule breaker," he cheekily whispers.

"You are?" I say in mock horror.

"Yup. Right this second," he says in a scheming tone, cupping his mouth. "I'm not wearing any underwear—that's how much of a rule breaker I am. I laugh in the face of routine."

I can't help but giggle at his goofiness.

"But do you wanna know how much of a rebel I *really* am?" he asks, his eyes suddenly turning dark.

I nod, gasping as Jasper runs a hand up my leg.

"Jasper," I whimper, his fingers inching higher up my thigh.

"Yes?" he replies smugly, his touch spreading goose bumps from head to toe.

"I'm going to be...oh god..." I moan when he sweeps his fingers over the front of my sleep shorts. "Late for work," I manage to choke out a second later.

In response, Jasper lowers his lips to mine and licks the seam of my mouth, deliriously slow. "See, I told you I'm a rebel. But do you really wanna see me live life on the edge?" he asks, his fingers skating around where I desperately want them to be.

"Yes," I beg, raising my hips in silent pleading, succumbing to his touch.

Jasper chuckles, owning my body with a single touch alone. "Hold on, baby, because when I break the rules, I make sure to break them all. Are you ready to break them with me?"

I nod, incapable of speech, and for the next two hours, we break every rule there is—over and over again.

CHAPTER TWO
Heat in the Kitchen

Thanks to Jasper's rule breaking, I'm now running forty-five minutes late for work. I would usually be in a panic, as I like to get there early to prep for lunch. But the three mind-blowing orgasms Jasper gave me have me walking on cloud nine. Even after a year apart, his touch is still as raw as it was the first moment he touched me.

"Morning, Ava," chirps Sara, one of my chefs as I walk into the kitchen.

"Morning. Sorry I'm late," I reply, reaching for my apron.

"It's okay," she says with a dimpled smile. "You're the boss. You're allowed to be late every now and again." She leans forward and whispers, "And due to the fact, your top is inside out, I dare say you being late is thanks to that stud of a fiancé of yours."

My cheeks instantly redden, and I quickly reach for the back of my shirt to feel the tag is indeed hanging on the outside. "You caught me," I reply, matching her tone. "But don't tell anyone."

"Wouldn't say a word," she replies, her rosy cheeks glowing in mischief. "Nor will I imagine all the ways in which he's made you late," she adds with a chuckle when I playfully smack her on the arm.

"You're so bad," I reply over my shoulder as I make my way to the bathroom.

"It's not my fault. Blame him for being so hot!" she shouts. "And that hotness is amplified due to the fact he's a rock star."

I laugh and shake my head because she's right. Jasper *is* exceptionally hot, and I don't blame girls for forgetting to use their mouth filter when in his presence, or talking about him. But to me, Jasper is just...Jasper, but to others, he is their 'rock god.' But that's the nice thing about New York, everyone is so busy doing their own thing, no one really cares if a celebrity is walking amongst them.

Sara is harmless, as she reminds me so very much of V. I have no issues with her blatantly checking Jasper out when he comes to visit, but it's the other girls—girls like Delilah I have an issue with. There is nothing innocent about her, and her intent to cause trouble between Jasper and I, worries me.

She's constantly texting him with trivial band shit and asking for his advice, seeing as Jasper has 'made it.' He tells me I have nothing to worry about, but I wouldn't trust her to save my life. Girls like her prey on anything that doesn't belong to them. They want what they can't have, and now that I'm wearing Jasper's ring, it's more of a challenge than ever.

Brushing those thoughts aside, as they've totally ruined my high, I slip off my shirt and make myself a little more presentable before I face my first interviewee. As I peer into the mirror, I see my appearance resembles how

I feel—totally unexcited at the prospect of finding someone who could fill my shoes.

Hearing Jasper say the words I knew to be true was hard to digest. Yes, L.A. is my home, but am I ready to pack up just yet? Am I ready to leave all this behind? It scares me I can't answer that with conviction.

"Ava?" Sara asks as she knocks on the door, thankfully interrupting my thoughts.

"I'll be right out," I reply, tying up my hair in a loose ponytail.

"Okay." She waits a second before she asks, "Um, Ava...the fish supplier is here with like a dozen crates of salmon. Did we order that many?"

"A dozen?" I ask, just in case I've misheard her, as there's surely some mistake.

But there is no mistake as she replies, "Yeah. We're drowning in fish at the moment."

Sighing, I fasten my apron and give my reflection a quick pep talk before opening the door to face a puzzled Sara.

She passes me the order sheet for the week and scratches her head with a pen. "I've gone over this twice, and I can't see us featuring salmon on our menu any time this week to require such a huge order of fish. Or am I totally blind?" she asks, and I quickly scan through the list.

She's right. This is obviously an error on my supplier's end, and now I have the fun of telling the poor delivery man.

"Great," I reply, holding the clipboard to my chest and taking a deep breath. "Giovanni is going to be pissed.

This is the second order this month his staff have messed up. Luckily last time it was product we were able to return. But fresh salmon…" I shake my head. "We have no space for that much seafood."

"I know," Sara replies, biting her lip. "Good luck," she adds, giving me a thumbs up.

"Thanks. I need it," I reply, making my way toward the back door.

As I see my other chef, Paulo, arguing with the red-faced delivery man who is tossing the crates onto the ground, I know this is going to be a long day.

Giovanni Bruno, the biggest and best seafood supplier in New York, was very apologetic over the phone. He said one of his girls admitted she read our order wrong and just assumed we wanted that much salmon, so she went ahead and processed our order without checking. We couldn't return the stock, seeing as the rude delivery driver sped off the minute the last crate hit the ground, and Giovanni couldn't make the pick up till after four. So that means I'm now stuck with twelve crates of fresh salmon. But on the plus side, Giovanni gave jame a great price for the sought after fish.

Metropolis is chaotic due to the half price salmon we've advertised, and there's currently a line extending around the block. I'm ecstatic we're booked solid, but I'm also run off my feet, thanks to being short-staffed. It wouldn't normally be an issue, but my genius idea of contacting every office in a fifty-mile radius has backfired, and I'm now snowed under with hungry patrons.

"Where is the lemon wedges to go with my brown sugar-cured salmon for table nine?" I ask Paulo, who is surrounded by white dockets.

"Thirty seconds!" he shouts, and I nod.

"Sara, is Melanie okay up front? How long a wait is it?" I ask, frantically garnishing my dish.

"She said roughly twenty minutes," she replies, working on the mini apple crumble desserts.

"Shit," I curse, wiping down the plates and placing them onto the serving tray.

As I look out into the sea of hungry faces, I know I need another chef. Paulo and I are run off our feet, and due to the last-minute menu change, he's still trying to get the hang of my quinoa salad recipe. Sara is on the other counter, prepping anything that isn't seafood, so between us three, we're working our asses off.

"Ava!" calls out Helen, my number one waitress as she rushes into the kitchen, hands filled with dirty dishes.

"Yes," I reply, reaching for the dockets to see what tables are next.

"There is some Michel to see you."

"Who?" I ask as I squint, attempting to decipher Helen's messy handwriting. "I have no idea who that is," I add when she remains quiet.

"He said he's here for the job," she explains, dunking the dishes into the sink.

"I've cancelled all interviews for the day," I reply, looking at the clock. "Paulo, where's my wedges?"

"Thirty seconds!" he replies, rushing between counters as he opens the oven door.

"You said that thirty seconds ago," I reply, tongue in cheek.

I realize Helen is still standing, waiting for my answer. "Grab his details and I'll contact him tomorrow," I say over my shoulder as Paulo and I dance our way around one another and onto different work stations.

"Okie dokie," she chirps, pulling out the pen from her apron pocket. "Oh, table fifteen left. They said they've waited for forty-five minutes."

"Crap." I huff, but am thankful when I see Paulo serve up the wedges to eight different plates. "C'mon guys, we're losing paying customers," I say with a clap of my hands, hoping to encourage them to move quicker, not that that's possible, as we're all moving faster than Superman.

"Sorry, Chef!" both Sara and Paulo pipe up in unison.

"It's okay. I know you're trying your hardest. If we weren't down so many staff members, we'd be fine," I reply, frying up a new batch of salmon.

"Owww!" yelps Sara as a plate drops, shattering the moment it hits the floor.

Spinning around to see what the commotion is about, I'm faced with Sara clutching her bleeding hand to her chest, while my salmon sits tangled amongst the shards of broken porcelain.

"Are you okay?" I ask, side stepping the ruined meal and rushing over to Sara.

"I'm all right. I stupidly cut my hand while peeling the apples. I'm so sorry, Ava," she says as I reach for a dish cloth.

"It's totally fine. Let me look." I gesture with my chin to her cradled hand.

When she uncurls her fingers, I see a clean cut across her palm. "It doesn't look too deep, but I won't take my chances. Run it under some water, get it cleaned up, and then march your butt to a doctor to get it checked out."

"I can't leave you," she rebukes, frowning.

"Well, I can't have you bleeding into my food," I reply, turning on the faucet and yanking her hand underneath.

The kitchen door barges open, and in comes Kia with a tower of dirty plates. "Oh boss, they're getting rowdy out there." As she dumps them into the sink, she sees the bedlam around her and wisely reaches for a broom.

"Ava, I've got five tables ready to go," Paulo says, rushing over to the stove to save my burning salmon.

Helen is instantly garnishing and wiping down the plates for her section, and I do the rest. "You okay to hold the fort while I get these orders out?" I ask Paulo.

"Yes, Chef!"

"Can it, wise ass," I reply with a grin, gathering my orders and shouldering open the door.

Not looking where I'm going, I bump straight into a solid brick wall of flesh. "Shit! I'm so sorry," I quickly apologize, my hands clutching the tray as I almost dropped my cargo.

Looking up, I see the amused face of a handsome stranger.

"No problem." He chuckles, gripping my upper arms, kindly attempting to steady me. "Do you need a hand?" he asks, peering down at my loaded tray.

"Oh no, it's okay," I reply with a smile. "I can't have a guest helping me out. No matter how desperate I look." I cringe when I realize how that sounded, and my handsome stranger smirks.

"You don't look desperate at all," he replies with a slight French accent, his grey eyes scanning down my body.

"Well, um...thanks," I reply, unsure how to respond to this man unashamedly flirting with me. "Anyway, I better get these out. I have hungry mouths to feed," I explain, looking down at his fingers, which are still attached to my biceps.

"Oh, right," he says, quickly removing his hands, appearing embarrassed.

I attempt to pass him but stop dead in my tracks when he says, "Did you use Persian feta?"

"How did you know that?" I ask over my shoulder, raising an eyebrow.

"I'm Michel. I saw your advertisement online, and I know it's not really protocol to just turn up announced, but I really, really want this job. So I thought instead of waiting for you to call, I'd call you," he adds with a dimpled smile, his accent becoming thicker.

"Well, I'm impressed by your determination, but now is not a good time. Maybe you could come back tomorrow when I'm less..." I look around my restaurant. "Less insane?" I finish.

Michel laughs. "Tell your chef to let the quinoa rest after cooking it for twenty minutes. It'll give it time to soak up the last bit of liquid, and also allows the starches to firm up. This will stop it from being too gluggy," he whispers, looking down at my plate.

"How did you know that?" I ask, because he's right yet again.

"My mom's a chef," he evenly explains.

"Oh, awesome! Would I know who she is?" I ask, intrigued.

"Maybe. My mom is...Adelia Dupont," he confesses, his accent rolling off his tongue flawlessly.

My mouth drops open. "*Maybe?* Oh my god! You're Michel *Dupont?* As in, you're the son of the world's most famous, brilliant, legendary chef? Your mom is like the French version of Martha Stewart! And you said you were her son?" I ask, just in case I've misheard him.

Michel nods, brushing a piece of hair which escaped from his short man bun behind his ear. "Guilty as charged."

"Holy shit!" I cry, unable to believe a Dupont is standing in my restaurant. "I don't believe it."

As I hear people grumble around me, I remember their food isn't going to serve, or cook itself. "Okay, you've got my attention. Show me what you've got. I'm down one chef. Do you think you can fill in?"

Michel smirks, his dark eyes twinkling in excitement. "I'll start on the crumble." He winks before rolling up his sleeves and making his way into the kitchen.

Looking down at my tray, I realize I don't have that dish on there and Michel recognized it from smell alone.

Well, now I'm really impressed.

CHAPTER
THREE
Always

After the most frantic lunch rush I've ever experienced, I finally have five minutes to sit down and regroup.

Looking over at Michel, who is happily helping Helen clear the tables, I know he totally saved my ass today. And it wasn't just his skills in the kitchen. It was everything. He fit right in and even got along with the alpha Paulo, who usually scares off anyone who dares enter his work area. But after fifteen minutes of seeing Michel work, I think Paulo was thankful to have another set of skilled hands to help him out.

I've gone over his résumé and I won't lie, it's damn impressive. If anything, he's *over* qualified to work here. He could be running his own business, no expense spared, thanks to his billionaire mother. That fact alone is the sole reason why I'm not jumping out of my seat in excitement and offering him the job. Until I know what his motive is for working here, I'm keeping my cards close to my chest.

"Michel?" I call out, and he stops chuckling with Helen as he looks up to meet my gaze.

"Yes?"

"Wanna have that interview now?" I ask, holding up his résumé.

"*Absolument*," he replies with a smile.

I can see Helen totally checking out his ass as he walks away from her. Not that I can blame her, because he is incredibly attractive, not that I'm checking him out. But any female with eyes would appreciate that full head of lush brown hair, piercing grey eyes, and amazing bone structure. Combined with his dominating height, muscular frame, and not to mention that French accent, Michel must be one popular boy with the ladies.

But I'm sure he's accustomed to girls going gaga over him because he's played off Helen's advances like a total pro.

"How'd I do, boss?" he asks, tongue in cheek, while pulling up a seat.

"Look, your credentials are amazing, and honestly, I would be stupid not to hire you," I confess, waving his resume.

"But?"

"But," I reply. "I can't help but wonder why you want to work here."

Michel grins, and I quickly backtrack. "Okay, that came out entirely wrong. What I meant was, the position I'm hiring for, it's for the assistant manager's role, and maybe one day manager, if circumstances change," I add, feeling my throat close over. "I mean, with your experience and reputation, you could open your own Metropolis."

"Ava, I'm honored you think so highly of me, I really

am. But I think you mean my *mother's* reputation," he says, casually leaning back in his chair.

"I didn't mean..."

But he waves me off with a strained smile. "It's fine. I'm used to my surname being a curse."

"A curse?" I ask, incredulous. "The Dupont name is hardly a curse. I mean, it's legendary."

"Legendary to some. But not to me," he replies, running a hand through his shaggy hair.

"I mean no disrespect, but how so?" I ask, not quite understanding his line of reasoning.

"When you've grown up your entire life in the spotlight, and it's just expected for you to follow in your parents' footsteps, it grows old pretty quickly," he explains, meeting my intrigued gaze. "I want to make it on my own because someone believed in *me*, and not my name. I—"

"You're hired," I quickly say, cutting him off.

Michel pulls back, looking at me like I've gone mad. "*Excusez-moi?*" he says, and I can't help but laugh.

"You're hired," I repeat. "There is nothing I respect more than a hard-working, honest employee, and you tick all those boxes. And some extra ones, too."

Michel looks overjoyed, and it takes a moment before he speaks. "Thank you so much for believing in me. You won't regret your decision. I promise."

"I know I won't," I reply, and that's what scares me.

I can't believe I'm home from work at 7 p.m. on a Monday night.

Michel said he had everything under control, and after showing him the ropes, I tend to believe him. He's a fast learner, knows his way around the kitchen, and the staff love him. I really couldn't ask for a better employee. So why am I not overjoyed and relieved?

I know the reason is because Michel is manager material, and give him six months, and he could take over my role with his eyes closed. But that's a good thing, right? That's what I hired him for. I just gotta keep reminding myself of that fact.

Shaking those thoughts aside, I quietly insert the key into my apartment door, as I want to surprise Jasper. I briefly told him over the phone that I had hired Michel, but didn't go into details. At the time, I didn't know if Michel was capable of running the show, but with Denise on dinner duty, I knew he was in good hands.

Opening the door softly, I peer my head around the doorjamb to see if Jasper is anywhere in sight. I can't see him, but as I hear the shower running, I know where he'll be. I slip off my shoes and dump my bag and coat on the sofa and tip-toe to the bathroom, excited to catch Jasper unaware.

Slowly opening the door a fraction, I sneak my way into the steamy bathroom, the mist thick from Jasper's scorching shower. The radio is tuned into some rock station, and the heavy water spray splashing against the tiles drowns out my racing heart. I stop a few feet away, as I need to absorb the sight of pure perfection before me.

Jasper's back is turned, and the first thing my eyes fall to is his firm, supple ass. Feeling like a total pervert however, I move my gaze up higher and appreciate his narrow waist, which supports an impressive, muscular upper body. As he turns and reaches for the shampoo, his toned obliques ripple with the movement and I have to remind myself to breathe, because I just caught a glimpse of his toned V.

Thanks to his new gym workout, his biceps are the size of my head, and when he lifts his arms to wash his tousled hair, I know I need to touch every inch of that toned, muscular flesh—with my tongue.

When "Pour Some Sugar On Me" by Def Leppard comes on the radio and Jasper starts singing along in his deep, sensual voice, still oblivious to my presence, I quickly yank off my tee and jeans. When he belts out the chorus, teasing me with images of pouring sugar on him and making him hot, sticky and sweet, I slip out of my bra and underwear immediately, ready to join in for the second verse.

Stepping over his boots, jeans, and Jimmy Hendrix tee, I creep towards the shower door, hoping to remain undetected. I ease open the screen door and am thankful my fiancé has a fair set of lungs on him as he sings loudly, his eyes closed as he conditions his hair.

Pouncing on him the moment the door closes behind me, I wrap my arms around his waist and poorly join in with his singing. Jasper's body freezes for a second, but instantly sags against mine as he interlaces our fingers.

As he sings huskily about sugar, and whether I take one lump or two, his mischievous words have my body shivering in yearning. Untangling our fingers and sliding a hand down his hardened abs to come to rest at the junction between his thighs, I reply, "I'd say one huge lump."

My bold words have Jasper's semi-hard length eagerly nudging my hand. "I think you should come home early every day," he gasps when I rub over his tip.

Reaching for the soap, I lather up a foamy handful and use the sandalwood wash as the ideal lubrication. "Well…I think you should just come," I purr.

Jasper groans low in his throat. "That was so hot. I'm so hard for you, baby."

"I know," I whisper, lightly squeezing his swelling length.

The control I have over Jasper is empowering, and gives me a surge of sexual confidence. "Turn around," I command, and Jasper complies without delay.

A breath catches in my throat when I'm confronted by his straining arousal. He's enormously perfect, and my mouth involuntarily waters. Dropping to both knees, I lick my bottom lip while flicking my eyes upward, meeting Jasper's heated gaze.

I watch with fascination as beads of water cascade down his wet body. The droplets glide between his defined pecs, and slip over his ripped six pack. I hungrily stare at one large bead as it rolls down his taut V and into his groin. Before I can stop myself, I lunge forward, trapping the droplet between my lips.

Jasper hisses the moment I suck his soft flesh into my mouth. His skin smells and tastes so good, and I can't help myself as I take more of him into my mouth, sucking harder.

"Fuck, baby." He lightly threads his hands through my hair.

I wrap my hands around his slender waist for support and continue sucking and softly biting until I'm satisfied I've left a hickey the size of Texas. Unable to help myself, I glide my hand around and stop when it comes to rest at his firm butt cheek. Giving it a gentle squeeze, Jasper groans low in his throat and spreads his legs wider, silently begging me to put him out of his misery.

With my hand still squeezing and palming his ass, I use the other to rest it against his straining upper thigh and bend forward, stopping inches away from his arousal. Regardless of how many times I've been with Jasper this way, his size, stamina, but most of all, his passion for me always leaves me speechless. To him, I'm the most beautiful girl in the world, and I've never felt so loved, so wanted than I do when we're like this, vulnerable to one another in the most primitive way possible.

"I love you," I whisper, raising my eyes to meet his.

"And I love you," he replies, softly brushing away a damp tendril of hair from my cheek. "But love doesn't even seem like a sufficient word anymore. I fucking worship you. Without you, I'm nothing."

"You're everything," I correct, because he is. "You're my everything."

Before he has time to refute me in true Jasper fashion, I close the distance between us and take him deep into my mouth. I would usually start out slow, but I can't help myself and need to consume my man this second.

Jasper's hands tighten in my hair, and I relish in the fact he wants this as much as I do. I try my hardest to take in his entire length, but I'm lucky to get halfway down without needing to pull back before I gag.

"Baby, that feels incredible," he pants, fisting my hair in his palm.

That's all the encouragement I need and I bob back down, relaxing my throat and taking him in deeper.

"Fuck." He pumps his hips forward, before quickly pulling back when he hits the back of my throat.

"Sorry," he breathlessly apologizes. I hold on tight, not wanting him to move an inch.

I start bobbing my head faster, creating a vacuum with my mouth. The pressure hollows my cheeks and forces me to draw deep breaths in through my nose. We fall in sync with one another, just like we used to, and the year apart feels like nothing but a dream.

"Ava... oh, fuck," Jasper moans, his hips now moving in concert with my fast rhythm.

His firm ass flexes under my fingertips and I push down on it, savoring in his passion. The move sends Jasper wild and as I raise my gaze. I whimper around him when I see how unrestrained he looks with his head thrown back and eyes squeezed tight. His tense abs ripple with each thrust, and as I catch a glimpse of my name on his arm, an inexplicable ferocity passes over me and I bury myself deeper into the valley between his thighs.

Jasper's fingers tighten in my hair, softly maneuvering how fast and how deep to go. But I don't need direction because I'm ready to bring this home. I walk my fingers up to his crotch, and pull my head back a fraction so I can slip my hand around his base. The warm water acts as the perfect lubrication and I begin stroking him, the rhythm of my hand matching my mouth.

He's close, I can feel it. So I pull my lips back, exposing more of his flesh and work him over thoroughly with my fist. I pump up and down, my mouth sucking him harder, and with a deep, sated groan, Jasper quickly attempts to pull his hips away. But I hold on tight, as I want him in my mouth when he explodes.

With a loud curse, he propels forward and spills his release down my throat. I swallow it all, and before the last tremor wrecks his body, he lifts me up by my arms and spins me around, so I'm flush against the shower wall.

I don't have time to question his motives because he makes his intentions crystal clear when he reaches around my waist and pops my hip backward so he has access to my soaked entrance. With skilled fingers, he slides his pointer along my folds, testing and teasing me until finally he slips inside me while I moan at the delicious intrusion.

"I can never get enough of you," Jasper whispers into my ear, his words warm against my wet cheeks.

"Good," I reply in a breathy moan, while Jasper chuckles.

He works his finger deeper into me. I don't need any prepping because I was ready to burst the moment I saw Jasper wet and nude.

"More," I shamelessly demand, on the verge of begging.

Thankfully, he senses my need and inserts another finger, stretching me impossibly wide. I buck backward, my ass brushing over Jasper's crotch. A breath hitches in my throat when I feel he's ready for round two.

"Told you," he says when he hears my amazement at him being ready to go so soon after he just came.

I wish I could reply, but the only thing coming out of my mouth is breathy moans and impassioned whimpers. My release is so close, but Jasper skirts around where I want him to be because I know he wants to feel me explode around him, and not his hand.

"Jasper," I plead, thrusting my hips backward, rubbing over his straining length.

"Baby," he smugly says, but I know he's not unaffected by my pleas.

"Please," I beg, not caring how desperate I sound as he fingers me deeply.

"Please what?"

"Please...fuck me," I reply, unashamed by my crassness because all I care about is coming.

"Holy shit, you ruin me," Jasper growls, dragging his teeth along the side of my arched neck, and latching onto my throat.

The moment he bites me, he flicks over my throbbing center and I explode with a loud, thunderous scream. My release is long, loud, and earth shattering, but I know this is only a taste of what's to come.

My entire body is shaking and I don't think it'll stop anytime soon, but that's not a deterrent for Jasper, who softly kicks my legs apart, spreading me wide. He gently removes his fingers and just as I'm about to cry at the loss, he inserts himself into me, filling me whole.

We both moan at the connection, and I push my hips backward, while Jasper drives his hips into me. The force propels me forward, so I place both hands on the shower wall for support as Jasper's strikes are brutal—exactly what I need. He anchors me by placing both hands low on my hips as he increases the speed and ferocity of his strokes.

"I... love... you," he says between intermittent breaths. "You own me. You destroy me. I want...no need," he growls. "You...with me...always."

"Always," I breathlessly cry, my body seconds away from coming.

"Always," he repeats, driving into me with one final, hard thrust that has us both coming in deafening, unrestricted screams.

My orgasm lasts for what seems like minutes, and if not for Jasper's firm grip around my waist, I no doubt would have fallen into an ungraceful heap on the ground.

But that's Jasper—he's always holding on tight, making sure to never let me go.

CHAPTER FOUR

Unplanned

I arrive at Metropolis early the next morning, not really knowing what to expect.

I have no regrets leaving early, as my sated body is still humming with the memories of Jasper's kisses and touch. But I am a little anxious to know how last night went without me being there. I really hope it went by without a hitch, but a small part of me hopes it was a complete disaster.

Unlocking the door, I switch on the lights as its still dark out. Taking a quick look around, I see that everything looks to be in order. The tables all are prepped for today's lunch rush, and nothing looks to be broken. I breathe out a sigh of relief, but that breath is short lived when I smell something burning.

"Shit!" I curse while running towards the kitchen like a bat outta hell.

I shoulder open the door and am ready to dive for the fire extinguisher but freeze when I see Michel fanning a smoking saucepan with a cloth as he turns off the stove.

"*C'est vraiment des conneries!*"

I have no idea what he just said, but it doesn't sound good. "Michel?" I ask. "What are you doing here?"

He spins around, completely surprised he has

company. "Oh, Ava. *Excusez-moi*," he says, brushing a hand against his damp brow. "I hope you don't mind me being here so early. Denise left early as we had a slow night, so I offered to lock up. She mentioned you came in at the crack of dawn, so I wanted to surprise you with breakfast, to say thanks for hiring me. But now I've gone and almost burned down your kitchen," he explains, pulling a guilty face.

I can't help but laugh at his expression, which radiates nothing but genuine concern. "It's fine, don't worry about it," I say with a wave of my hand.

Standing up on tippy toes to look over his shoulder at the burned mess, I ask, "What were you making?"

"*Pain au chocolat.* It was going well until I thought I'd be fancy and try something different and add a dipping sauce."

"Oh." I sigh in understanding, as it's a common mistake to stray from a traditional recipe.

Looking at the leftover ingredients, I smile. "Shall we try again?"

Michel smirks. "That sounds like a good idea. But this time, you can show me how it's done."

"I'm embarrassed, Ava. You totally out cooked me at a meal that's meant to be my signature dish, seeing as I'm French."

I can't help but laugh as I sip my coffee. "Please, it was beginners' luck," I humbly reply.

Thankfully, Michel doesn't argue, and I find myself being completely relaxed in his company. I've only known him for less than twenty-four hours, but it feels like I've known him for years. We have a lot in common, and there's an unspoken respect between us, which I know will come in handy when cooking alongside one another in the future. I really am lucky to have him here and for the first time in forever, the possibility of leaving Metropolis doesn't make me gag, as I know my baby will be in good hands.

Michel's phone ringing has me returning to the here and now, and I give him a nod when he looks at me apologetically. The moment he sees who's calling however, he groans.

Before I have time to question what's wrong, he picks up the phone. "*Bonjour, Maman.*"

My eyes widen in excitement as I register the fact that Michel is talking to his mom, in my restaurant. But as Michel shakes his head and rolls his eyes at me, I think it's safe to say the excitement is one sided.

After some heated French words, their meaning totally going over my head, I decide to give Michel some privacy and call Jasper. I stand and hold up a finger, indicating I'll be gone for a minute.

He mouths, "Sorry," while once again rolling his eyes.

I wave his apology off, feeling a touch sorry for him because I can hear his mom yelling at him in French. Giving him a sympathetic smile, I make my way into the kitchen to call Jasper.

"Mornin', baby."

His husky, sleep laden voice triggers a chain reaction of goose bumps to spread out over my entire body, and I bite my lip to stifle my moan.

"Stop biting your lip," he softly reprimands, and my lip instantly pops free.

"I wasn't," I reply, looking around me to ensure he's not hiding in my pantry. When the coast is clear, I ask, "Whatcha up to today?"

"Just working on some new stuff for the album. I've got a Skype date with Lucas at 11."

I can't help but laugh. "Another date? Holy moly, the neighbors will start talking."

Jasper chuckles, and I can hear him walk through the apartment. "What can I say, I miss his ugly ass."

I sigh, knowing this is a topic we'll eventually have to discuss.

"Hey, I miss yours more though," he says, picking up on my distress.

"Are you calling my butt ugly?" I playfully tease, leaning against the counter.

Jasper hums low in his throat. "Baby, don't tease me, especially when the subject matter is your butt."

"Why?" I ask, suddenly feeling heated.

"Because now, all I can think about it your butt and how it drives me crazy when you wear those tight blue jeans," he replies without delay.

Looking down, I see I'm wearing the ones he's referring to, but I decide to play dumb. "Which ones?"

"The ones with the small rip on the top of your left thigh," he says, his voice dropping an octave.

"Oh right, *those* ones." I pick at a loose thread in the tear.

"Yup, those ones," he confirms. "So...are you wearing them now?" he asks with a slight pause.

"Yes." I feel my cheeks heat.

Jasper groans. "Are you wearing anything underneath?"

"Jasper!" I quietly scold, but my sudden breathlessness reveals how much I like this conversation.

"You so aren't," he replies, and I blush because he's right.

I don't know how long Michel will be, but I can't help myself as I timidly ask, "So, um...what are you wearing?"

As I hear Jasper's breathing deepen, I clench my thighs together, the sound doing incredible things to my awakened body.

"You're killing me, Ava," he says, groaning louder this time. "I just had a shower, but I think I need another. And this time, it'll be a cold one."

"This is good practice for when you're away."

Jasper groans, but this time around, it's not a happy sound. "So you don't think you'll be able to come on tour? I thought you said this Michel was a godsend."

At that precise moment, Michel walks in, looking flustered and annoyed.

"Michel *is* a godsend," I say, looking at him with a smile, and he happily returns it. "It's just...let's see how things go while I'm away for Jeremy's 50th. Speaking of, have you decided what you want to get him?" I ask, needing to change the subject.

"Not really." Jasper sighs, and I know he's fisting his

hair in frustration. "What do you get someone who has everything?"

I've got a few ideas up my sleeve—ideas I don't plan on telling Jasper until he sees it for himself when I give it to Jeremy.

"You'll think of something," I encourage, as I know Jasper is slightly nervous spending the weekend with all of his family gathered in the one place.

He's met most of his extended family, but sadly, not his stepbrother, the one person Jasper wants to meet.

"And besides," I add when he remains quiet. "He has you. That's the best present. Like ever."

Jasper chuckles, but it doesn't quite reach his voice. "Thanks, baby."

As I look at Michel who is patiently waiting for me to get off the phone, I say, "I better go."

"Okay. Have a good day. I love you."

"I love you, too," I reply, and notice Michel's eyes widen a fraction.

I heed no attention to his odd response because Jasper surprises me by saying, "Oh, and by the way...I'm not wearing anything underneath my jeans, either."

A breath gets caught in my chest and I clear my throat, afraid I'm about to choke. "You're mean," I whisper, and hang up to Jasper laughing quietly in my ear.

"Sorry." I place the phone in my pocket.

"It's okay," Michel replies with a nod. "Boyfriend?" he asks, and I smile.

"Fiancé," I reply, pulling the silver chain out from under my sweater, which has my engagement ring dangling off the end of it.

"Oh. I didn't know you were engaged." His eyes focus on my ring.

"Yeah, just newly," I reply, mesmerized how my diamond catches the light.

"Well, he's a lucky a guy."

I shake my head slowly. "I'm the lucky one," I reply in a faraway voice, my gaze still glued to my ring.

Remembering where I am however, I quickly tuck the chain back underneath my sweater, and ask, "So what about you? Anyone special in your life?"

Michel scoffs, and I raise an eyebrow.

"With a mother like mine," he explains, "it's hard to find a girlfriend who lives up to her high expectations. And it's also hard to find someone who actually likes my mom. And besides, any girlfriend who would put up with my mother, and her judgmental ways"—he pulls a face—"I really would question their mental stability. I did have someone, but she turned out to be as crazy as my mom."

I can't help but giggle. "Oh, c'mon, she can't be *that* bad?"

I refuse to believe the woman I idolize, the woman who inspired me to start cooking, is such an ogre. I mean, Adelia Dupont is my rock star. Sad, but true.

However, when Michel raises both eyebrows, I think I'm about to change my mind. "Oh yes, she can. Actually, that's the reason why she called."

"What do you mean?" I ask, totally puzzled.

"Well, somehow, although it shouldn't surprise me, Mother has found out I'm working here."

"Oh," I reply, elated she knows where *here* is.

"So," Michel says with pause. "She decided it would be *fun* if she came to visit."

"Oh, that'll be fun, right?" I nod in encouragement.

He smirks, shaking his head. "No, you don't understand. When I say visit, I mean visit *here*, as in Metropolis."

"What?" I gasp, almost choking on my tongue.

"I know, I'm sorry, Ava. I told her no, but well—"

"No," I interrupt, "I'm not angry. I'm honored," I clarify with a smile.

"Honored?" Michel asks, looking at me like I've lost my mind.

"Yes. I know you don't see eye to eye with her, but I'm a big fan of hers, and to have her here, even just to check out where you work, is pretty amazing."

"That's not why she's coming," he quickly says.

"Oh?"

"*Oui*, she's coming here to eat. But she's bringing the Food Network with her," he says, making a pained face.

"What?" I ask, almost gagging. "When?"

"Um...in four days," he replies softly.

"Four days?" I wheeze. "Oh my god! I'm not ready. There are so many things I have to do. I don't have a menu put together for serving someone like your mom. And not to mention, I would want Metropolis to have a total makeover. And—" My panic attack is cut short when Michel places his hand on my arm.

"I'll tell her not to come. I'm sorry. I know it's a lot of pressure, I just thought this would be great exposure for Metropolis as she's got a whole segment mapped out for her culinary experience at New York's finest 'food *boutique.'* Her words, not mine. But I'll call her right now and tell her no," he says, reaching into his pocket for his cell.

But this time, I'm the one who interrupts him. "Are you insane? Of course she has to come. I just don't know how I'm going to pull this off in four days."

"If it's any consolation, I'll help. I have an advantage, as I know what she likes. And I also got you into this mess, so I sort of owe you," he sheepishly says.

"It would be an honor to work alongside you. And this isn't a mess; it's an opportunity of a lifetime. Thank you, Michel. This is really incredible," I say, still astonished that this is actually happening.

"Don't thank me just yet." He chuckles. "So, shall we?" he asks, offering me his arm.

Looping my arm through his, I nod. "We so shall."

"So you really think we go for lamb for the main course? I mean, maybe we could go for something a little more filling? Steak, maybe?" I ask, sipping my wine and looking over my scribbled notes on my notepad.

"*Oui*, my mother eats like a sparrow. She'll probably take one bite and be full," Michel replies, retying his thick hair.

"Okay," I say with a sigh. "You know best."

We've been at Metropolis for hours after closing time,

and we're still no closer in deciding what to prepare for Adelia's visit. I never thought I would be so nervous preparing a meal for someone, but I am, because Adelia is not just *a* someone, she's *the* someone.

I glance over at Michel, who's scratching his full beard, deep in thought. He's looking over his scribbled handwriting, appearing just as stressed as me. But having him on my team is a huge relief. Not only does he know his mother better than anyone, he's also full of brilliant, inventive ideas. We're on the same page when it comes to how prepare different dishes, and I'm not afraid to admit, I've learned a thing or two talking to him about his cooking experiences.

I have no doubt that whatever we create will be amazing, but I'm still incredibly nervous.

It must show. "Hey, it'll be okay," he says, reaching across the table and patting my arm lightly. "If it sucks, she'll blame me anyway, so don't worry."

Resting my pen against the notepad, I have the balls to ask something I've been dying to know. "Why don't you guys get along? I mean, I know all families have their issues, but I'm detecting something more here."

As Michel shuffles in his seat uncomfortably, I know I've struck a nerve.

"I'm sorry, that was really rude of me to ask. It's none of my business," I say, feeling like a nosy ass.

"*Non*, it's fine," he says, waving off my apology. "Honestly, I don't know why. My father left when I was five, and all I can remember is being miserable from then on. He was the fun one, and she, well, she was the not so fun one," he says with a shrug.

"I'm sorry." I love my parents, and I know how lucky I am to have their support no matter what.

"I guess when I got older, Mom just expected me to be a chef. I didn't really have much of a choice to do anything else. I sometimes wonder what I would have chosen if not for cooking," he says, tapping his lip in thought. "I don't regret it. I love what I do, but one can't help be curious, you know?"

I nod.

"Have you ever thought that? Or have you always known that you wanted to be a culinary genius?" Michel asks with a grin, while I scoff.

"Genius? Hardly. I guess I always knew. I remember when I was little, I used to watch my mom bake my favorite cookies, thinking how one day, I'd bake them for her. Two weeks later, I did just that," I confess, smiling as I think back to a fond memory.

"Mini genius at work." He chuckles when I throw my pen at him.

"I think I'll learn a lot from you, Ava Thompson," he says, my name rolling off his tongue with an exotic accent.

"I think we'll learn a lot from one another, and discover each other's strengths and weaknesses," I correct with a smile.

"I hope so," he replies, his warm eyes turning serious.

I don't know why, but I suddenly feel like we're talking about something else. My gut tells me I'll learn what that is all in good time.

CHAPTER FIVE
Favors

The next couple of days fly by in a blur.

I'm running on pure adrenalin, and I know once this is over, I'll sleep for a week. Michel and I have worked nonstop, planning and trialing a menu that would be fit for a queen. I've also been lucky enough to score some interior decorating tips from a friend of his. With her expert advice, I've given Metropolis a complete makeover, and I won't lie, it looks awesome.

This entire experience has really cemented the fact that Michel is a keeper, and I really enjoy working with him. Thanks to him, I actually think we can pull this off and come out on top.

Jasper has been incredibly supportive, and understands how important this is to me. He doesn't question me when I'm gone before he wakes. Nor does he get mad when I come home when he's sound asleep. He simply sends me encouraging text messages, or calls me to tell me how much he loves and misses me.

It's now the night before D-Day, and somehow, Michel has convinced me to go home while he deals with finalizing the last minute details with the producer of *Food Exposé*, who I was about to strangle. I understand she's trying to produce a TV show, but I can't have the camera crew set up shop in my kitchen while I'm trying to cook. If she said 'think out of the box' one more time, I was going to scream.

As the smell of something sweet hits my nostrils when I open my apartment door, I instantly forget about my stressful day.

"Honey, I'm home," I playfully say, tossing my keys into the bowl near the door as I slip off my Chucks.

The moment I duck my head into the kitchen, I smell something delicious—and I don't mean Jasper. I smell gooey chocolate.

"Are you baking?" I ask, walking into the kitchen and laughing when I see the mess Jasper has made.

"I'm trying," he replies, turning over his shoulder with a smirk. "I dunno how you make this look so easy. I've almost burned down the kitchen—twice—and it's a packet mix."

I chuckle as I roll up my sleeves and tie my hair into a high ponytail. Walking over to the mess he's made, I smile when I see he's been attempting to make brownies. "Are these for me?" I reach for the wooden spoon, but hold back my grin when it remains cemented in the mix bowl.

Jasper nods.

"I think you should stick to being a rock star," I tease.

"No arguments there," he says in agreement.

Reaching for the discarded brownie box, I turn it over to read what went wrong. As I'm studying step two, Jasper wraps his arms around my waist and rests his chin on my shoulder.

"So, Chef, where did I go wrong?"

His warm breath tickles my exposed neck, and I

suddenly find it hard to focus on anything other than his hard body pressed up against mine.

Jasper reads my body language instantly, and runs a finger along the sliver of exposed flesh between my jeans and sweater. "I've missed you, baby," he whispers, kissing the shell of my ear.

"I've missed you, too." I gasp when his finger flicks over the button of my jeans.

"You know, our bed has been awfully cold and lonely without you in it."

"I'm sorry," I say with a hitch when he flicks open my button.

"It's okay. It's just reinforced the fact that I can't live without you. It also reinforced the fact that being away from you for six weeks is going to be hell," he hoarsely says, his index finger tracing a line along the top of my underwear.

"Maybe I could come halfway through your tour?" I suggest, my eyes drooping shut as he dips his finger lower.

"It's better than the alternative of not seeing you at all," he replies, heating my awakened flesh.

"Oh god," I softly moan, a bundle of pleasure twisting wildly in my belly.

Jasper, ever being the tease, skims over where I need him to be, and just as I reach down to offer him a hand, my cell chimes loudly, jolting me from my perverted thoughts.

"Shit," I curse, my eyes snapping open.

At this point in time, answering my phone sounds like a god-awful idea, but with tomorrow's proceedings in mind, I know I have no choice. Jasper also understands my dilemma and gently slips his hand out of my jeans.

Sighing, I sadly reach into my pocket, but cock an eyebrow when I don't recognize the number flashing on the screen.

"Hello?" I say, and the moment I hear her voice, my stomach drops.

On the other end is the cellist I hired for tomorrow night's event. She was to play soft background music, which was to complement the planned black-tie event. Now I'm left without any entertainment because Belinda has just informed me she's broken her arm and won't be able to play.

"Oh, I'm so sorry to hear that," I say, while Jasper raises an eyebrow. I shake my head, defeated.

"No, it's okay," I sincerely say when she apologizes for the tenth time. "You just look after yourself. Okay, take care." I hang up, about ready to have a heart attack.

"What's happened?" Jasper asks as I toss my cell onto the counter.

"Belinda broke her arm," I groan, running a hand down my face.

"Oh shit," Jasper replies, as he was the one to recommend her because she is apparently Manhattan's best.

"You can say that again. I have no idea where I'm going to find a replace...ment," I say with a pause as I look at Jasper.

"Baby, if you want your evening to run smoothly, you'll stop looking at me like that. Cello isn't my thing," he wisely says, knowing what I'm thinking.

"No, but piano is."

"Hey, I offered my services, free of charge," he adds with a wink. "But you said Michel mentioned that the queen ogre hates the piano, and compares its sound to that of Lucifer's plaything."

I let out a laugh because this is in fact true. "I know, but she'll change her mind once she hears your voice. Lucifer's plaything will be overshadowed by your angelic voice. Please?" I add, interlacing my hands together. "I'm begging you. I'll do anything."

As Jasper cocks a dark brow, I know I'm in trouble. "Anything?" he asks, his lips tipping up into a lopsided smile.

"Yes, anything," I confirm, knowing I've won him over.

Pulling on my belt loops, he draws me forward and stops when we're toe to toe. "Okay. I'll make sure I cash in my favor chips ASAP. I can think of a few things," he adds with a grin, and I playfully smack his arm.

"Thank you, you pervert."

Jasper bends down and kisses the tip of my nose. "Begging or not, I still would have done it for you. I'll do anything for you, baby."

I smile because I know that's true, and that's what makes me the luckiest girl alive.

I t's now 3:30 p.m., and everything that could go wrong, has gone wrong.

"Michel," I groan, about ready to throw in the towel. "How do you propose we make one hundred lavender crème brulee without any eggs or lavender?"

"It's fine, Ava. Breathe," Michel says with a smile, placing both hands on my shoulders to calm me down. "I'll go down to the market and get what we need."

"Its 3:30. Do you forget we live in New York? Traffic is going to be hell. I can't believe Marcus' truck broke down. My produce is in there!" I say, frowning.

Michel gives my shoulders a reassuring squeeze. "It'll be okay. I'll get there in time. Just leave it to me. Start on the appetizers, and I'll be back before you know it. Okay?" he reiterates when I look at him doubtfully.

"Okay," I reply half-heartedly, and chuckle when he playfully shakes me. "Okay," I reply a little more optimistically.

"Good girl, *Cheri*," he says, but looks to be regretful the moment the words leave his lips.

I don't understand what the big deal is, so I shrug it off. "Make sure you get enough lavender bunches," I say, and Michel nods, thankfully looking less guilty.

Removing his hands from my shoulders, he smiles. "On it, boss."

His confidence has me feeling a touch better, but that confidence is shattered when I hear a curse, followed by something crashing in the kitchen.

I shake my head and Michel laughs.

"If that camera crew doesn't destroy my kitchen by the end of the night, it'll be nothing short of a miracle."

Michel continues chuckling, while I wave goodbye and face yet another disaster for the day.

Shouldering open to the door, I see Angus, cameraman number three on his knees, collecting pieces of my white chinaware. When he lifts his eyes to meet mine, he cowers, as I no doubt look livid.

"I'm so sorry," he apologizes quickly. "It was an accident." His hands are filled with my good china.

"It's fine." I sigh, reaching for the broom. "I got it." He stands up, gingerly handing me half a plate.

"Thanks," I say with a roll of my eyes.

The camera crew go about their merry way setting up in the area I've designated for them. After fruitless arguments with Yolanda, the producer and host, I've given up on the notion of having them set up in the restaurant only. They were here to stay, so we came to a compromise. I've agreed to them being in here, but they must stick to their nominated area. If they were to step outta that area, then they were going to have a pointy encounter with my knife. And I made sure they knew I wasn't kidding. I need my space, and I also need to keep my nerves under control, and having nine cameramen in my face was certainly not going to achieve that.

Yes, I understand what an amazing opportunity this is, but I would only jeopardize Metropolis' reputation if the head chef was a raving lunatic in the kitchen.

Just as I reach for the dust pan, a pair of hands wraps around my middle and squeezes me tight. "Rough day?"

"You wouldn't believe the half of it," I say with a sigh as I sag into Jasper's embrace.

"What can I do?" He kisses my cheek lightly.

"You can tell me the piano arrived in one piece and you haven't caught laryngitis," I reply, internally crossing my fingers.

"I'm healthy as an ox and yes, she's here in one piece. Are you sure it's okay to hire out the Bechstein? She's a little pricey, but she plays like a charm," Jasper explains, his voice betraying his excitement at playing such a beautiful piano.

Spinning around, I can't help but smile at his enthusiasm. "For the fifteenth time, yes, it's okay. I know it'll be worth every penny."

Jasper smirks, running a hand through his messy hair.

"I'm sorry to spring this on you. I haven't really given you much time to practice."

"Practice is for amateurs," he replies, tongue in cheek. "And besides, like all true artists, inspiration comes from beauty, and what's more beautiful than my hot fiancée, cooking up a storm?"

I smile, his kind words calming me down. "It's kinda cool us working together, right?"

Jasper nods. "It sure is."

I know this isn't really the time or the place, but I can't help myself as I say, "You know, this could be us every day."

"It could be," he replies, holding his cards close to his chest.

"But…" I prompt.

"But I think we should discuss this when you're not surrounded by potential weapons."

I half smile. "It was worth a try."

"Baby," Jasper says, rubbing my cheek. "Wherever

you want to go, or wherever you want to be, I'll be there, right with you. I belong by your side, wherever that may be. They say home is where the heart is. Well, you're my heart. So wherever you are...is my home."

I try not to melt at his sweetness.

"But let's get tonight and Jeremy's over with, and not to mention this damn tour, and then we can discuss our future. Okay? Whatever happens, it's our future. Together."

"Together," I repeat with a nod. "That sounds like a good plan."

Yolanda suddenly comes charging into the kitchen, interrupting our moment. "Why the hell is there a huge piano blocking my stage?"

However, she stops dead in her tracks when she sees Jasper. "Oh my god," she gasps, a hand poised over her heart. "You're Jasper White? From P.O.E.?"

Jasper nods, while I smile, so accustomed to this reaction.

"Holy crap, I'm a huge fan. 'Surrendered' is my all-time favorite song," she gushes, shoving her hand between us.

Jasper politely shakes it. "Thanks. This little beauty here was the inspiration behind it." He looks down at me with nothing but love in his blue eyes.

"Who? *Ava?*" she asks, her mouth hinging open in shock.

"Yes," he replies with a smile. "Every word was written for her."

I redden and lower my eyes because some of those words bring a bright blush to my cheeks.

"Oh, I didn't realize she was your girlfriend." Yolanda looks at me in disgust.

"Fiancée," Jasper corrects, reaching for my hand and stroking over my ring.

"Oh," she replies, and I almost laugh at her stunned expression.

"Well…congratulations. That's awesome." Not. "Are you here for support?" she asks, no doubt wondering why he's here.

"Oh no, I forgot to tell you. Jasper is totally saving my ass and replacing Belinda, who broke her arm. He'll be playing the piano." When she remains quiet, I add, "I hope that's okay?"

"Of course, it is!" she replies, clapping her hands. "This is brilliant. This will send our ratings through the roof." She squeals, while I blanch—like I needed any more pressure.

"What are you wearing tonight?" Yolanda asks, suddenly turning serious.

Jasper looks down at his ripped blue jeans, combat boots, and white V neck. "Um, this?"

Yolanda shakes her head in horror. "No star of mine will be seen in torn jeans."

Star of hers? Since when?

Just as I'm about to rebuke, she adds, "You want to look your best for Ava, right?"

Jasper nods. "Of course, I do."

"Jasper," I softly state, telling him he looks completely fine the way he is, and not to listen to this twit.

But he shakes his head. "I'll do anything for you, baby. Remember?"

I nod, but as touched as I am, I don't want him compromising his style and comfort for me. "I know, but you look perfect as is."

"Nonsense," Yolanda interrupts, latching onto Jasper's arm. "I've got the perfect outfit in mind." She drags him off toward my office, which she's taken over as her own.

As he throws me a quick wink over his shoulder, gesturing it's okay, I breathe a sigh of relief and for the hundredth time today, I realize how lucky I really am to belong to Jasper White.

CHAPTER SIX
Nightmare in Heels

It's now 6:15 p.m., and Michel has stuck true to his word and delivered the goods. Things are finally looking up and running relatively smoothly, considering the start to the day.

"Have you marinated the lamb?" I ask Michel as I chop my sixtieth potato.

"Yes, Chef," he says, his grey eyes twinkling in mischief. "The answer hasn't changed from when you asked it five minutes ago."

Sara looks over at us and chuckles, no doubt amused by our ongoing banter in the kitchen.

"Keep that up and your mom will be eating takeout," I reply jokingly.

But Michel shrugs like it's no big deal. "No skin off my nose. Let's make sure it's from that little takeaway shop on the corner of Fifth. I heard the last person who ate there went blind."

I stop chopping and look over at him, half stunned, half amused. "I honestly can't believe she's as bad as you say."

Over the past few days, Michel has given me an insight into what his childhood was like. The picture Adelia Dupont paints of herself is definitely not the one

Michel sees. According to Michel, she is overbearing, controlling, and thoughtless—and that's on a good day.

"No, she's worse," he replies with a smile, as if reading my thoughts.

"We'll see," I reply, as I want to make my own mind up before I join the Adelia Dupont haters.

"She can't be that bad," I add when Michel remains quiet. "I mean, she did a pretty okay job at raising you."

Michel raises an eyebrow. "Okay job? Well, thank you...I think."

I chuckle but don't elaborate, and Michel puts a hand over his heart. "Oh, *Mon Cheri*, you wound me so."

I can't help but break into fits of laughter as he stages an over-exaggerated hurt expression.

My laughter however is cut short when Yolanda announces her arrival by pushing open my door. "Ava Thompson, you are one lucky girl."

I spin around to face her, wondering what she's talking about, but she's the furthest thing from my mind when I see Jasper standing behind her. Yolanda may be an idiot, but she sure knows her way around an outfit.

Jasper's looks are beyond hot, and he looks like a runway model in whatever he wears, but now he looks fucking epic. He's in tight black jeans which hug all the right places perfectly, stylish black boots, a white close-fitting tee, and a black fitted jacket with attached grey hood. A grey slouchie beanie is sitting loosely on his head with wisps of his tousled brown locks sticking out from underneath.

"You're welcome," Yolanda says when I stand frozen, not hiding my approval of his looks.

Jasper smirks, his dimple hugging his right cheek. "So I don't look like a complete douche then?" he asks, pulling at the draw straw of his hood.

I shake my head animatedly. "No. You look amazing."

"Thanks, baby," Jasper says with a knowing smile, as I'm about five seconds away from combusting.

Michel clears his throat, reminding me that I'm not alone, and thoughts of defiling my hot fiancé are put on hold. "Michel, this is Jasper," I say, pointing to a suddenly scowling Jasper.

Ignoring his random response, I say, "Jasper, this is Michel," and turn to look at a scowling Michel.

I don't know if I'm reading into things, but I detect a mutual hatred passing between the two boys, which is absurd, seeing as they just met.

Thankfully, Yolanda's tactlessness decides to kick in, and she says, "Ava, you are *not* wearing *that,* are you?"

Looking down at my red Chucks, torn jeans and Ramones tee, I nod. "Um, yeah. I figure I'm behind the scenes, so it doesn't matter what I wear," I reply, still getting a weird vibe off Jasper.

No, no, no," she says, appalled. "The cameras are going to be filming your every move. You can't look like a homeless person while cooking for Adelia."

"She does not look like a homeless person," Michel says, quickly jumping to my defense.

"Thanks," I say, giving him a small smile.

However, when I hear Jasper grind down on his jawbone, I look at him, silently asking him to tell me what's gotten into him. But he gives nothing away.

Yolanda has either not picked up on the heat in the kitchen, or she simply doesn't care as she snaps, "I won't have you in ripped jeans on my show. Follow me." She beckons me with her finger as she brushes past a rigid looking Jasper and out the door.

I decide to humor her and follow, as I plan on dragging Jasper with me.

"I'll hold the fort until you return," Michel says, walking over to my work station.

"Thank you. I really appreciate it. I won't be long," I reply as I untie my apron.

"Of course, you won't. You look great to me, *Mon Cheri*," he says, shooting me a cheeky wink.

"Ava, can I have a word?" Jasper says suddenly, his tone clearly indicating he's pissed.

"Sure," I reply, still baffled by his hostility.

I give Michel a small smile, not wanting to let on something is wrong. Jasper holds the door open for me and I walk through it, turning to face him the moment he shuts it behind him.

"*Who* is that?" he asks, hooking a thumb behind him.

"Um, who's who?" I ask, confused.

"The dude who looks like the French version of Channing Tatum," he replies huffily.

"Michel?" I ask, taken aback.

"I don't know, I'm asking you," Jasper replies, crossing his arms over his chest.

"Jasper, I have no idea what you're talking about. It's not like you haven't heard me talking about him. I mean, I think that's all I've talked about since I hired him," I say innocently.

"Yeah, that's the problem," he replies, snappily.

When I continue looking at him like he's lost his mind, he elaborates. "So Michelle is a man?"

"Um, I'm going to go with yes. Are you high?" I joke, offering that as an explanation to his sudden insanity.

Jasper scoffs. "No, but I wish I was. I thought this life saver; this person who you have not stopped talking about was a *girl*."

"A girl?" I ask, pulling back. "Why the hell would you think that?"

"Oh, I dunno, maybe because his name is Michelle," he replies like I'm crazy.

"He's French, and it's Michel," I say, pronouncing it correctly.

"It's Michelle," he stubbornly counters. "And last I checked, Michelle is a girl's name."

"Who cares what his gender is—" But I stop, unable to keep the smile off my face. "Oh my god, you're jealous?" I accuse, while Jasper scoffs.

When I raise an eyebrow, he sighs, ripping the beanie off his head. "Okay, maybe a little. But you failed to mention your angel looked like Chris Hemsworth."

I can't help but laugh. "'Cause I never noticed."

Jasper pulls a disbelieving face and I chuckle. "Trust me, when I've got you for my fiancé, all other men pale in comparison. And besides, I would say he's more like Liam, and you know how much I hate Miley," I add, trying to lighten the mood.

Jasper's mouth thankfully turns up into a smile. "I'm sorry for going all alpha dog in there," he says, gesturing with his head toward the kitchen.

"It's fine. I kinda liked it." I take a step towards him and wrap my arms around his neck. "And besides, I know the feeling all too well."

"In my defense, my admirers don't look like Adonis reincarnate. Nor do they speak the language of love."

I open my mouth, not sure which comment to address first. "Firstly, your *stalkers* aren't exactly trolls; secondly, Delilah sings the language of love, and thirdly, admirer? Michel is my employee, not admirer—big difference."

"Have you heard what Delilah sings about?" Jasper says, raising an eyebrow. "I wouldn't exactly call *that* the language of love."

"No, I have not heard what she sings about because quite frankly I would rather dig out my eardrums with a fork. And don't change the subject," I say, poking him in the chest. "I have no idea why you think that of Michel because it's not that way. At all."

"Baby." Jasper smirks, pulling me close when I attempt to twist out of his embrace. "Trust me on this."

Just as I'm about to rebuke him, he places a finger over my lips to silence me. "We'll talk about this later."

"There's nothing to talk about," I stubbornly say from around his finger.

Jasper grins, shaking his head. "You're so stubborn."

"And that's why you love me," I reply as he removes his pointer.

When he hesitates, I playfully attempt to slap his arm, but he dodges my attack.

"I hate to break up this little love fest, but I've got a

show to run," shouts Yolanda, tapping her foot a few feet away.

"This isn't over," I whisper to Jasper, giving him a quick peck on the lips before facing my nightmare in heels.

"This isn't practical," I say to Yolanda as I attempt to untie the satin bow from around my waist.

"I don't care," snaps Yolanda, smacking my hand away. "You look stunning."

"I don't cook in silk," I reply. "Do you know what this dress will look like at the end of the night? Like a five-course disaster, that's what."

"Stop arguing," she replies, slapping my hand away when I make an attempt to tie up my hair.

"If you slap me more one time, you'll lose a finger," I warn, and she chuckles.

The only positive thing that has come out of this speedy makeover is Yolanda hasn't been a total bitch to me. For the past twenty minutes, she's fawned over Jasper and how she's been a fan since she heard 'Surrendered.'

"I still can't believe 'Surrendered' is about you," she says, putting away her makeup set.

"Gee, thanks," I reply, looking at my reflection in the mirror.

"I didn't mean it that way," she backtracks. "I just

meant, wow, Jasper White is your fiancé. I didn't even know he was engaged. I mean, I make it my business to know the happenings of the entertainment industry."

"Jasper isn't an industry, he's an artist," I snap, spinning around, my pleated skirt twirling with the movement.

Yolanda shrugs, going about packing up. "Like it or not, Jasper represents a brand name now. Passengers of Ego are starting to get more and more attention, and with Jasper being the front man, that attention will focus on him and his personal life. So that means you. Can you handle that?"

"What do you mean?" I ask, my head spinning.

"I mean, you can use the fact that Jasper's your fiancé to your advantage. Can you imagine what it'll do to Metropolis' reputation if people knew you were Jasper White's fiancée?" she explains, her eyes lighting up deviously.

"I'm not using Jasper that way," I gasp, shaking my head. "And besides, Metropolis already has a great reputation. And that's all thanks to me and my hard work."

Yolanda scoffs, running a hand through her auburn hair as she opens her compact to check her appearance. "Think outside the box, Ava. You're little league at the moment, but you could strike it big if an anonymous tip was sent to the *New York Times* or *Rolling Stone*."

"I would never do that to Jasper," I spit, hating that another person sees him as a money maker.

"You kinda already have," she says, reaching for her lipstick.

"What are you talking about?"

"Inviting him to play tonight will bring you much attention, and the googly eyes you two give one another is a dead giveaway you're involved," she explains, smacking her lips together to ensure her ruby lipstick is evenly spread. "I'm surprised the press hasn't caught wind of this sooner."

"What? *Googly eyes?*" I ask, as I have never heard such rubbish.

"Oh, please. You can smell your happiness a mile away. Let's just hope you don't have any skeletons in your closet. Otherwise, the media will have a field day."

I blanch at her comment. Skeletons? Jasper and I have enough damn skeletons to fill a cemetery.

When Yolanda sees my reaction, she shrugs and snaps her compact shut. "You may as well play on it. You could be the next Java!"

"Huh? Coffee?" I ask, scrunching up my nose.

"Oh my god, have you been living under a rock? Brangelina, Kimye, Bennifer. Ring any bells?"

"Are you insane?" I ask, only half joking.

Yolanda ignores me as she continues on with her speech. "Java...it's definitely a winner, seeing as you're a chef. I'm definitely onto something here," she says, tapping her chin, deep in thought. "I could be the one who announced your tragic, yet poetic love affair to the world. Imagine what a breaking story like that could do to my career?" she declares, her face radiating greed. "And I'm guessing I'm the only person that knows the number one song on the charts at the moment was written about you. Oh god, I can see the headlines!"

My mouth is hanging open, and if I could curse this

bitch out, I would. At the moment, however, I'm stunned she came up with this devious plan in the span of thirty seconds. There's no way I'll allow her to use Jasper and myself this way. We are no one's stepping stones, and we most definitely are not headlines.

Thankfully finding my voice, I take a step towards a glowing Yolanda. "Listen here, you..." A knock at the door stops my rant.

"Um, Ava, it's Sara. Sorry to interrupt, but Adelia and her entourage are here. Should I tell them to wait?"

Glaring at Yolanda, I reply, "No, it's fine, Sara. I'll be out in a minute."

"Okay," Sara replies, no doubt hearing the irritation in my tone.

I take a calming breath, but it's in vain, as my temper has reached boiling point. "Leave Jasper out of this," I say, warning Yolanda. "Otherwise, New Yorkers will be waking up to another headline, and that'll be you having to surgically remove my foot from your ass!"

Yolanda gasps, while I internally thank V for teaching me such good manners.

"Oh, and by the way," I say, angrily yanking the hair tie from my wrist and tying up my hair into a messy bun. "I'm the boss around here, not you. Got it?"

"Loud and clear," she replies, narrowing her eyes.

"Good. And another thing," I add, kicking off the ridiculous wedges she insisted I wear. "Stay outta my kitchen. And stay away from my fiancé."

"Careful, Ava. With a bad attitude like that, people just may think you've ridden Jasper's fame train to get where you are. Or is that what you've secretly done?" she sneers, cocking her head to the side, daring me to rebuke her claims.

There is only one phrase a soulless parasite like this will understand. Stepping towards her, her mammoth frame towering over mine, I spit out, "Fuck you."

I don't wait around for a response as I yank open the door and storm through my restaurant in search of Jasper.

During my rampage, I meet Michel's confused stare, but I don't have time to address the issue why I'm tearing through my restaurant, bare footed and hair coming undone, because I have other pressing issues on hand.

As much as I hate what Yolanda insinuated, she's right. The press will have a field day if they unearth me being linked to Jasper, and if Yolanda doesn't get there first, the media will no doubt fabricate some story that I indeed rode on Jasper's coattails to get to where I am—which is a total lie.

Both Jasper and I are in the position that we're in thanks to hard work and determination, and I'll be damned if anyone accuses me of riding on anyone's coat-tails. I'll also be damned if I allow Yolanda to use mine and Jasper's engagement as her stepping stone to boost her career.

The reason I hadn't thought of this sooner was because Jasper and I have been holed up in our own personal bubble, where no one exists but us. But now I think I've gone and fucked all that up.

"Jasper," I say, just under a scream when I see him sitting at the piano.

"Hey baby," he replies, not lifting his eyes from the sheet music as he writes something in the bar lines. "I was thinking of adding in 'Apologize' by One Republic. What do you think? It's my way of saying sorry for being such an ass."

"You need to leave," I whisper, cutting him off.

"Okay, I won't play it then," he says with a smirk as he raises his eyes.

However, the moment he sees me leaning an arm against the piano as I put on my Chucks, he pales. "What's happened?" he asks, jumping up and rushing to my side. "Is everything all right?"

"No, everything is not all right." I huff, blowing my hair off face as it's slipped free from my bun.

"Talk to me," he presses, reaching for my arm.

"No, don't," I say, subtly pulling away from his hand.

"Ava," he sternly counters. "What the hell is going on?"

Looking over his shoulder to where I see Michel lingering, I whisper, "We can't be seen together because I make googly eyes at you."

Jasper raises an eyebrow, totally confused.

"Look, Yolanda wants to make us into Java," I say, adding to his confusion.

Jasper pulls in his lips, making a puzzled face. "She wants to make us a coffee?" he asks, scratching his head.

This conversation would be quite comical if I wasn't moments away from having an anxiety attack. "Forget about Java," I say, shaking my head. "Yolanda is an immoral bitch who wants to use our relationship to boost her status. She also thinks I should use our engagement, use you, to boost Metropolis' reputation. Or worse yet, that's what I've already done," I explain, gasping for air.

Jasper softly grabs my upper arms and pulls me close. "Take a deep breath, calm down, and please explain to me in English what the hell that means."

I do as he says because quite frankly I'm moments away from having a breakdown. "Jasper, Yolanda wants me to use you and our engagement to boost Metropolis' popularity. She also suggested that I've gotten where I have by riding your coattails."

"Why the hell would she say that?" he implores, dropping his hands and fisting his hair.

"'Cause you're the hottest thing since sliced bread," I snap, frustrated by his denial of being hot shit.

He scoffs. "I'm me, baby, and you're you. You've worked damn hard to get Metro on the map, and it'll be a cold day in hell when I allow some B-grade reality TV host taint your hard work."

"Where are you going?" I ask, latching onto his arm as he stalks past me.

"To give that woman a piece of my mind."

"No, no," I say, tightening my grip. "Not now. Adelia is here," I whisper from the side of my mouth, while looking over his shoulder.

Jasper subtly peers behind him and turns back with a frown. "I thought she'd be taller."

I know he's trying to lighten the mood, but I can't stop thinking about what a media circus this will be if the press got wind of Jasper and I being engaged. They've already linked him to every female on the planet, so what happens when we're actually seen together?

Our uncomplicated life just got way complicated, and it's all my fault.

"What's going to happen when everyone finds out we're together?" I ask, hating that I've allowed Yolanda to ruin my big break.

Jasper places both hands on my cheeks, drawing our foreheads together. "Who cares," he whispers.

"But it might be bad for your career. I mean, the illusion of a single rock star, who girls secretly hope for one sexy, sweaty night with, is far more appealing than the reality that their rock star is engaged, and is in no way available to them."

"Engaged or not, I would never be available to them anyway," Jasper affirms. When I remain silent, he roughly adds, "The only person I'm available to is you."

I can't help but smile. "Yeah, but your career—"

"Screw my career," he says, putting me at arm's length. "If my band stops me from declaring to the world I'm yours, then I'll quit. You're all that matters to me. We've been through so much, baby, and you've stuck by me, through thick and thin. All of this means nothing without you."

I close my eyes, his words like a salve to my blistering mind.

"But if you think being linked to me is going to taint your career, or the evening, then I'll leave," he sadly says.

My eyes pop open and I pull out of his grip, as I know he means every word. "No. Don't go. In the words of someone wise, screw my career. I don't want you to be a secret, and I don't want to be yours."

Jasper nods, a look of relief passing over his perfect features. "No more secrets. We've had enough to last us a lifetime."

"Amen." I smile in agreement, wrapping my arms around him.

"I don't want to break up the happy couple, but I've got a TV show to run," Yolanda says, her words dripping in sarcasm.

I quickly pull away from Jasper as I turn to look at the witch. Jasper locks his hands around my waist. "Awesome. I was actually just telling Ava I've worked on a new number for tonight," he says, his eyes levelling with hers.

Yolanda gushes the moment he addresses her, and I frown, as we most definitely were not taking about that.

"Oh, yeah? What's it called?" She leans against the piano, making sure to flash some leg in the process.

"I actually wrote it for you," he replies, letting me go.

I stiffen up, not sure where he's going with this.

"Really?" she purrs, licking her lips.

"Yes, really. It's called"—he advances forward so he's inches away from her face—"'Stay the fuck away from my fiancée; otherwise you'll be looking for a new job.'"

Yolanda pulls back horrified, while I can't help but smile smugly at her.

"I like that song," I say to Jasper, who is still glaring at Yolanda.

"Me too," he finally says, staring Yolanda down. Giving me a quick kiss on the forehead, he adds, "Go do your thing, baby. I'll be watching all night."

"Okay," I reply, standing on tippy toes to kiss his lips. "I love you."

"I love you, too."

I leave him and rush over to Michel, who is standing

awkwardly off to the side. "Sorry," I say. "I had to take out the trash."

Michel doesn't address my bitchy jab, and simply nods. "You ready to meet Mother?"

Looking down at my beautiful blue dress and red Chucks, I laugh. "No. But what other choice do I have?"

"None." Michel confirms what I know to be true.

"Let's get this over with." I sigh, wishing I didn't resemble a madwoman when first meeting Adelia Dupont, but I'll try my best to own the crazy.

"If it's any consolation, the red shoes really bring out the blue in your dress," he says with a wink as we make our way towards his mother and her posse.

"Ha, funny," I whisper, but smile, as his humor cheers me up.

"*Maman*, it's my pleasure to introduce you to the brilliant Ava Thompson," Michel says. Adelia gracefully turns to face us.

However, the moment her grey eyes meet mine, I catch a glimpse of the stern woman Michel has told me all about. She quickly hides her disapproval and smiles. "*Cheri*, the pleasure is all mine. I can hardly wait to see what I'm in for this evening," she says, stepping forward and kissing both my cheeks.

"It's lovely to meet you, Adelia," I say, choosing to ignore her sarcastic comment. "I'm a huge fan. To have you here is simply a dream come true."

Adelia smiles, her Tiffany bracelets jingling as she brushes away a stray piece of brown hair. "I can imagine," she arrogantly replies, and my childhood dreams of one day growing up and being like Adelia Dupont have just exploded into a ball of fiery flames.

Michel picks up on his mother's snippiness, but sadly, he doesn't look too surprised. "*Maman*, please follow Denise to your table. Ava and I are ready to commence whenever you are."

Adelia nods. "Very well. Let me do a quick wardrobe check. Speaking of, Michel get a haircut, you look like a *voyou*," she says, curling her lip in disgust.

Michel's hair is long, but it's stylish. The trend is man buns and beards at the moment, and Michel can pull off both perfectly.

When we remain silent, she ignores her snippy comment like it never happened and says, "I look forward to trying your dishes, Ava. Michel has sung nothing but your praises."

I look to Michel, who looks pissed that his mother called him a vo-whatever, and timidly smile. "Well, tonight is a joint collaboration. My dishes are also Michel's," I explain, not wanting to take all the glory.

"In that case, I'm all the more intrigued." She gives me a forced smile before calling out to Yolanda.

The moment she's out of earshot, I let out a breath of relief. I look at Michel and he simply shrugs.

"I told you."

Yes, he did, but I was hoping he was wrong. Sadly, he wasn't.

CHAPTER SEVEN

Ava, You Got Me on My Knees

"Okay, so we cut to you after I've done Adelia's introduction. Got it?"

"Yes," I reply, unable to make eye contact with Yolanda, as I'm afraid I'll use my frying pan as a weapon.

"Now remember, this isn't live to air, but I want you to pretend like it is. I want this edited and screened as soon as possible, and the only way that's going to happen is if you guys don't screw up," Yolanda says, looking around at my staff, her eyes landing on me.

"Let's get this over with," I mumble under my breath, but I know she's heard me.

"Right. It's showtime. I think we'll start with a close-up shot of Jasper playing," she states, baiting me.

It works.

I lift my eyes, meeting her smug gaze. "Don't touch anything," I say, meaning every single word.

"Don't worry, Ava, I'll be sure not to break anything," she replies, and I know we're both speaking in innuendoes. This time however, I don't take the bait and simply continue preparing my appetizer.

Two of the cameramen follow her out and I unclench my jaw the moment she leaves. "This night can't end soon enough," I say to Michel, who stops chopping the garlic.

"I should have also warned you about Yolanda. Working with my mother for two years has a certain effect on people," he explains, wiping his hands on his apron.

"Oh, I don't think you mother is to blame for her attitude. I think 'bitch' is part of her DNA," I quickly reply, not caring who heard me.

Michel and a few of my employee's chuckle into their palms, and I'm surprised when the cameramen do the same. No doubt they agree with me.

I take this moment to put on my big girl panties and give my team a much-needed pep talk. "Guys." Eight heads turn my way. They're waiting for further instruction from Yolanda, so before they have to go out there and face the music, I say, "C'mon over here, let's huddle."

Sara stops midstride and looks at me like I've lost my mind. Actually, they all do.

"Get over here," I persist, extending both arms.

Michel is the first to budge and walks over, looping his arm over mine. The others thankfully follow, and before long, we're all huddled in a circle, bent low.

"Whatever happens tonight, remember that I'm proud of you all. No matter what that tyrant Yolanda says, you do what you've done time and time again—you rock this place. Smile, be courteous, and have fun. This is a once in a lifetime opportunity, and I'm so happy to be sharing it with you," I say, suddenly getting emotional. "Now, go do me proud," I conclude, looking at each of my employees with a smile.

"Yes, Chef!" they yell in unison, and their enthusiasm is music to my ears.

We break apart like a basketball team before a big game, and in a way, we're all pumped and ready to win.

"You did good, Chef," Michel says, playfully bumping me with his shoulder as we walk to our stations.

Giving him a small smile, I nod. "Thanks. Let's rock this place."

"Sara, if I hear you sigh one more time, I'll gag you," I warn with a chuckle.

"I can't help it. It's so unfair listening to that," she says, pointing to the door, "and not being able to see it."

By *that*, she means Jasper.

We're halfway through the evening and without jinxing it, I think the night has been a success. Everyone has been on their A-game and the food has been well received. The guests, who are thrilled to be part of a live audience, are having a ball, and I can't help but think Michel was right. Adelia's spotlight on Metropolis will do big things for my baby. I just gotta get through dessert, and then I'm home free.

I'm surprised I've kept my cool, but as I hear Jasper sing 'You Found Me' by The Fray, I know he's the reason I haven't gone batshit crazy. Just hearing his voice has been enough of a motivator to solider on. Especially when his song choices seem to give me the musical support I need to get through the night. Sadly, I haven't had a chance to catch him in action as I've been stuck back here in the kitchen. But the girls have told me the crowd, and—surprise, surprise—Adelia, love him.

Yolanda comes charging in like she owns the place, and I tell myself it's nearly over. "Adelia is ready for dessert."

"Awesome," I reply, disinterested as I reach for the lavender crème brulee.

I settle them onto a tray and pass them to Helen, but Yolanda stops me. "Adelia wants you to bring it out to her."

"Why?" I ask, as she hasn't said boo to me all night.

"Well," Yolanda replies huffily, looking unimpressed with my defiance. "This is the final dish, and it'll make good television, that's why."

I look over at Michel who gives me a sympathetic smile. "Fine. But I'm not changing," I stubbornly state, looking down at my original outfit of torn jeans and Chucks, as I threw Yolanda's outfit where it belonged—in the trash.

"Suit yourself." She snickers, curling her lip in revulsion when she gazes down at my appearance.

I yank off my apron, as it's splattered with every food group under the sun, and shrug into my 3/4 sleeve, white chef shirt with Metropolis' logo embroidered on the front. Taking a deep breath, I grab the tray off the counter and look at Michel. "I want you to come out with me. You've worked just as hard as I have. You deserve the recognition, too."

"Are you sure?" he asks, appearing taken aback at the offer.

"I'm sure," I reply with a nod as I touch his arm in assurance.

Michel smiles, his dimples making a surprise appearance. "Thank you, Ava."

"Thank *you*," I reply, referring to him making this possible.

Michel quickly removes his apron and runs a hand through his thick hair. He gives me a small nod to indicate he's ready. Yolanda gives us a quick rundown and before I know it, we're walking towards Adelia, every camera in the room focusing on us.

I glance over at Jasper, who is softly playing 'Strong' by London Grammar. I can't help but smile as this is one of my favorite songs, and I know Jasper is playing it to help calm my nerves. His intense eyes are focused on me and he gives me a reassuring nod, no doubt sensing my anxiety. The gesture instantly calms me. I straighten my spine and put my game face on.

Adelia looks like a queen sitting at the head of the table, surrounded by her posse of fans. Her inquisitive eyes meet mine, and as she smiles broadly, I know this is entirely for the cameras. I take a small breath before placing the dish in front of her.

"*Merci*, Ava," she says, her accent thicker than when

we spoke without the cameras rolling. *"Charmant."* She leans forward and smells the dessert.

Again, I know this is for show. But I smile and nod. "I hope you enjoy it," I reply, and move next to Michel, who is standing a few feet away.

Adelia barely acknowledges her son as she daintily picks up her spoon, her little finger extended outward. She taps on the caramelized top and raises an eyebrow, while I suddenly feel like I'm on *Master Chef.*

I look to Michel who mouths, "We've got this."

I smile because he's right.

The moment Adelia spoons out a small portion of brulee, the rich smell of vanilla and lavender permeates the air, and I know she's impressed. She takes a measured bite, and it seems she's attempting to distinguish all the flavors in the dish.

After she swallows and wipes her mouth with a napkin, she looks up at me and smiles. There is a pregnant pause before she claps her hands. *"Très magnifique. Cheri.* You are going to be the next big thing."

I can't believe my ears because this time, I believe her actions aren't for show and she actually means every single word. "Th-thank you," I stutter, taking a step forward. "But this wasn't a solo effort." I look behind me at Michel.

Adelia looks over my shoulder at her son, who is standing tall and proud. I'm expecting some kind of recognition, but instead, I'm stunned at what she nastily says.

"I've taught Michel everything he knows, and I know I haven't taught him this."

For a moment I stand stunned, incredulous to what she just said. But once my brain kicks in that the cameras are still rolling and patrons are staring at me, waiting for some kind of kooky rebuttal, I open my mouth to protest.

Michel subtly bends sideways and whispers, "Don't bother."

I meet his wounded gaze and shake my head, unable to allow her to insult her son that way, and in front of an audience, no less.

"I—" I'm rudely cut off by Adelia, who abruptly stands and sweeps her hand out to the customers. "*Bon appétit.*"

The crowd claps loudly, drowning out my defense, and I know any further conversation is off the table. The cameras pan to the guests who are happily eating and chatting amongst themselves, totally forgetting who I am.

"Thanks for trying," Michel says into my ear.

I frown, still infuriated with Adelia's insolence as I watch her obliviously flutter about, chatting to her fans. "She's wrong. She said she's taught you everything you know—well, I know for a fact that's incorrect because your modesty and kindness was *definitely* not learned from her."

Michel's eyes widen and he waits a second before bursting into fits of laughter. I can't help but join him, losing myself in the moment and the craziness of the past few days, but when Michel throws his arms around me and draws me in for a loose hug, I'm aware of two things. Number one is that Yolanda and Adelia are looking at me with matching expressions of 'what the fuck,' but both are articulated for entirely different reasons. Yolanda's sinister smile reveals 'headlines,' while Adelia sees me as a threat. But they pale in comparison to when I glance over at Jasper, who looks about five seconds away from losing his shit as he eyeballs Michel.

I quickly unfold myself from Michel's embrace, who looks a little hurt by the rejection. I give him a small smile before returning my gaze to Jasper, who has thankfully remained seated and stopped with the daggers, but he still looks pissed. However, when his mouth tips up into a wicked smile, I know he's about to express his feelings like the true artist he is—and that's through song.

"To end things off," Yolanda says, batting her fake eyelashes to the cameras, while I try not to gag. "We have the world's *hottest* artist performing 'Grenade' by Bruno Mars. I'm Yolanda Fey. Thank you for watching, and *Bon appétit*," she concludes, spreading her hand towards Jasper.

The cameras follow her motion and pan to Jasper, who still hasn't broken eye contact with me. "Actually," he roughly says, leaning forward into the microphone. "I've decided to play something else. Ava," he declares pointedly, giving me a sultry smirk, while I blanch. "This is for you."

Before Yolanda can call cut, Jasper's skillful fingers brush over the keys and the distinguishable tune of 'Layla' by Eric Clapton can be recognized by all. I stand and stare, not getting why he would choose this song for me until he gets to the chorus.

He sings passionately and genuinely, changing each 'Layla' to 'Ava,' and although I know everyone, including

Yolanda, is staring at me, I don't care. Each and every time Jasper sings, a little part of me dies and goes to heaven, and everyone, everything, doesn't exist, and now is no exception.

The crowd sways and sings along to his beautiful voice, as he's totally worked them under his musical spell, but I know this song is for me and for me only. And Jasper makes that clear when he sings the chorus, as he almost begs me to 'ease his worried mind' over Michel, no doubt.

I can feel Michel clam up near me, and I don't understand why. I ignore the niggling feeling that Jasper may be right about him, and focus on my man.

I shake my head at Jasper, unable to wipe the smile off my face as I mouth, "I love you."

Jasper continues singing, never missing a beat, but I can see my words haven't gone unnoticed by him as his entire demeanor changes and he turns into Jerry Lee fucking Lewis. The crowd 'oohh' and 'ahh,' appreciating the true musical genius in front of them as Jasper wraps up his version of a classic song. The crowd goes wild, me included, as I bounce on the spot in excitement, clapping loudly.

Jasper rewards me with a heart stopping wink, and if we were attempting to keep our relationship out of the limelight, well, we've just gone and blown it. But I don't care. It doesn't faze me when I run over to Jasper and throw my arms around him, burying my face into the crook of his neck as he lifts me off the ground. Nor does it faze me when he smashes his lips to mine, rewarding me with a near pornographic kiss. Nothing fazes me because if anyone had any doubts to who I am to Jasper, he's now made it clear—and I couldn't be happier.

CHAPTER
EIGHT
Smile for the Camera

I wake to the best feeling in the world. I wake in the arms of Jasper White.

I take a moment to recollect my thoughts because the past few days have been a whirlwind of events.

Once the cameras stopped rolling, I was surprised when Adelia gave me her business card. She seemed to genuinely enjoy her meal and said I had potential. I happily accepted her compliment, but was thankful when she and her entourage finally left.

Yolanda stuck around, trying to butter up Jasper for an exclusive interview, but he politely declined and made clear his decision would never change. Like ever.

So all in all, the night was a success, except for Michel and Jasper's random dislike for one another, which was even more evident when Jasper offered to help clean up. Michel was quiet and not his usual, cheerful self, and Jasper was possessive, hovering any chance he got.

I don't understand what's gotten into the both of them, as I haven't misled either. Whatever issues they have amongst themselves, they'll just have to get over it because both are here to stay. I would have thought

Jasper would be happy I found Michel, seeing as he'll be the one to send me home.

But after last night, the thought of leaving all this behind leaves an even bigger question mark over my future because I'm not ready to go. I want to stick to my dream of seeing Metropolis grow, and I want that growth to be with Jasper. He totally looked at home on stage and owned the crowd—as usual. But this is my dream, not his, as I know his dream is to play with his band members in front of the world.

So what's the compromise? I don't want to leave, and Jasper doesn't want to stay. We've reached an impasse in our relationship and I realize to be together, one of us will have to give up their dreams. But who? And more importantly, what happens when one of us sacrifices our dreams for the other? My career is no more important than Jasper's, so who wins here? Sadly, I think whatever choice is made, we'll both lose.

"Whatcha thinking?" asks a husky sounding Jasper.

His voice startles me from my heavy thoughts and I decide to be honest, seeing as we've put it off for long enough. "I was just thinking about last night," I reply, meeting his crystal clear, blue eyes.

"What about it?" he asks, shuffling closer so we're almost nose to nose.

"I liked working with you," I explain. "I just...I don't how we're going to do this."

"Do what?" he asks, his brow crinkling in confusion.

"Come to a compromise where we're both happy. I know you hate it here, and it makes sense for you to go back to L.A."

"But..." he pushes.

"But it doesn't for me," I reply, lowering my eyes.

"Hey," he coos, raising my chin with two fingers. "The only thing that makes sense is for me to be where you are. I meant it when I said all of this means nothing without you."

"I know," I reply, leaning into his touch as he strokes my cheek.

"You know," he says with a smile, "I could buy you your own Metropolis in L.A."

Jasper is referring to the million dollars he inherited from Jeremy. The million dollars his mother wanted to steal from him. The thought of that dragon turns my stomach, and I want nothing to do with it.

"No," I say with a firm shake of my head. "That money is yours."

"Ours," he quickly corrects.

"I can't just take it, Jasper," I reply, and I mean it.

"Can't or won't?" he asks, running a hand through his hair. "I'm trying here, baby, but it sounds like your mind is set."

"It's not. I've just worked so hard. Leaving when I'm not ready feels like I'm cheating," I explain, wishing I felt differently.

"I know." He sighs, blowing out a frustrated breath.

"So, what do we do? Live in separate states?" I suggest, totally joking.

Jasper raises an unimpressed brow. "That's not even funny. We'll figure something out. Could you maybe reconsider the option of borrowing the money, and starting afresh in L.A.?

I nod half-heartedly. "I can do that." Although, my gut tells me there would be no point.

As Jasper's dimpled smirk challenges my half-assed reply, I respond a little more convincingly, "I promise."

"Thank you," he replies, placing a light kiss on my forehead.

"So...while we're on the topic, why do you hate Michel?" I ask while playing with the ring hanging from Jasper's necklace.

Jasper chuckles, his deep voice doing amazing things to my body. "Way to ruin my morning," he says, and I know he's dead serious.

I wait for him to rely, but he merely shrugs. "Why do you hate Delilah?"

I pull back, so not expecting his response. "Firstly, way to ruin my week," I say with a frown. "And secondly, there aren't enough hours in a day to explain why I hate her. But at the forefront, the fact she's trouble and she's hot for you is a good reason why."

Jasper raises his brow, pulling a smug face.

"For the tenth time, Michel is *not* hot for me, and he's hardly trouble. Delilah, on the other hand, is a conniving, soulless whore," I state, my teeth clenching at the mere mention of her.

Jasper laughs while attempting to pull me close. I resist however, as I want to get to the bottom of his hostility towards Michel.

"I—" But Jasper silences me by placing his mouth over mine.

"Just be careful around this guy," he says, his lips tickling mine. "I don't trust him."

I open my mouth, ready to protest, but when Jasper nudges his tongue against mine, I totally forget we were even talking.

Kissing Jasper always feels like the first time, and I can never get enough, especially when he does that *thing* with his tongue—the thing he's doing right now. The moment however is ruined when I remember Delilah has experienced the same thing.

"Oh, and another reason why I hate her..." I say, quickly pulling away. Jasper's lips are still pursed, and I can't help but smile at his stunned expression. "...is because she knows about the *thing* you do with your tongue."

Jasper pulls back, looking completely lost. "What thing?"

"Don't play dumb, you know, the *thing*," I say with an encouraging nod.

"No, I don't know." He scrunches up his face.

"You really don't know?" I ask, shocked.

Jasper shakes his head, his messy hair slipping into his eyes. "No idea. Care to enlighten me?"

All thoughts of Delilah are long forgotten when I scan down his hardened chest. Is it possible that my fiancé, my rock god, has no idea of the things he's capable of? As he continues staring at me, waiting for my reply, I know that it's very possible.

Things just got so fun. "It's probably best I show you," I cheekily reply, licking my lower lip.

Jasper follows the movement and nods quickly. "I like this plan."

Before I have time to react, he rolls on top of me, his

body weight cocooning me in a bubble of pure bliss. Sadly, my bubble bursts when Jasper's phone sounds loudly on the bedside table.

"Just ignore it," he says, which comes out muffled, as he's trailing kisses down my chin.

Thankfully, the incessant thing quits ringing and I can focus on Jasper's lips, which are fluttering over my racing pulse. I'm really getting into it, and if the imminent bulge which is deliciously poking me between the legs is anything to go by, so is Jasper. But I jolt in surprise when his cell sounds once again.

"Ignore it," he repeats against my throat.

"It might be...important," I gasp when he nicks my skin.

"Nothing is more important than this," he bluntly replies, kissing in the valley of my breasts.

Sadly, the caller doesn't agree, and when the phone sounds for the third time, Jasper gives in with an annoyed sigh. Reaching over to his bedside table, he picks up his cell. "This better be important," he says, not even looking at the screen to see who it is.

The moment he hears who's on the other end however, he smirks. "Hell-" But he can't finish his sentence, seeing as the other person is chewing his ear off.

"-o," he concludes after thirty seconds of verbal bashing.

I wonder who's on the other end, as Jasper hasn't been able to get a word in sideways.

A full minute passes before he passes me the phone. "It's V," he states with a grin.

I should have known. "V?" I ask, as I sit up against the headboard.

Jasper nods, sitting up beside me.

"Hello?" I say, wondering why she called Jasper's phone instead of mine.

"Don't you answer your cell?" she barks, while I hear Jasper chuckle.

"Well, hello to you, too. Good to see you woke up on the right side of the bed this morning," I reply, unable to wipe the grin off my face as I've missed her so much.

"I haven't been to bed thanks to your niece being the damn Energizer Bunny. I'm convinced she's part demon. No normal child should have this much energy, right?" she says, and I can just imagine her scratching her head in question.

Before I can reply, I hear a loud thud, and V yelling in the distance. "Put that down, you little monster! Lucas, can you please control your child?"

I can't help but smile as I look over at Jasper. He's smirking, as he can no doubt hear V screaming at his drummer.

"Come here, baby. Mommy forgot to take her meds this morning," Lucas says, and I stifle a giggle behind my hand.

"Sorry about that," V says, picking up the phone she dropped. "Seriously, Ava, stay single, life is way less complicated when you don't have two babies to look after."

"Love you too, Honey," Lucas says in the background, while I hear Cara coo.

"So infuriating, yet...so, so hot," she mumbles under her breath.

I clear my throat, as I know she's currently eye fucking the hell outta her husband. "So, what's up?" I ask. "Why did you call me on Jasper's phone?"

"'Cause I've been trying your cell all morning," she replies with a huff.

"Oh, it's on silent," I say, remembering I muted it last night.

"Have you seen *juicygoss.com?*"

"Um, no," I reply as I crinkle my nose in confusion. "Why? I don't even know what that is."

"Because I hate to break up your little honeymoon, but you and Jasper are today's news, that's why," she replies with a sigh.

"What?" I gasp, my back instantly straightening.

"Who the hell is Foody Fey? And why is she calling you Java?" she asks as I hear her fingers click over the keys on her laptop.

I groan, and Jasper leans forward, his eyes searching mine. I gesture with my head to my iPad on the floor, and he quickly jumps up to get it.

"What did she say?" I ask, dreading V's answer.

"It's probably best if you read it yourself."

Shit, this can't be good. I type in the web address and choke the moment I see the picture I'm greeted with.

"Well, on the plus side, Indie's nose job looks hideous. What did you break it with? A brick?" V asks, popping her gum.

"V, I gotta go." I wheeze when I stare into the eyes of

the devil. "I'll call you later, okay? Thanks for the heads up."

"You got it, babe. Oh, and Ava?" she adds, while my eyes scan down the article detailing mine and Jasper's relationship.

"Uh ha," I vaguely reply, feeling my heart rise into my throat.

"I knew you before you were famous, just remember that," she teases, which is exactly what I needed.

"Goodbye, Veronica," I say with a smile before hanging up.

Jasper is leaning over me, madly reading the article on Yolanda's blog. Even though she has used a lame alias, I know it's her. I mean, who else would claim they had the scoop of the century? Not to mention, she goes on to describe mine and Jasper's relationship in great detail. Details she obviously learned from seeing us together last night, and details we told her, like how 'Surrendered' was written for me. If that isn't proof enough, then the Java bomb pretty much seals the deal.

The things she says are quite flattering, until her 'inside scoop' also includes an interview with Indie Scott. "How the hell did she get this online so quickly?" I ask, my skin crawling when I read Indie's responses to Yolanda's personal questions.

Jasper shrugs, shaking his head in disbelief. "I'm so sorry, baby. I underestimated her. I underestimated them both."

I can hear his teeth clench when he gets to the interview with Indie, who of course has painted me as some boyfriend stealing, heavy-fisted psycho.

"She can't get away with this," he animatedly says, jumping out of bed and angrily stepping into his jeans.

"Who? Yolanda? Or Indie?" I ask, hating that after all this time, I have to bring up the mega bitch's name.

"Both," Jasper barks, running a hand down his face.

"What are you doing?" I ask as he reaches for his cell.

"I'm going to make things right. They both need to be put in their place. Did you read the shit on there?" Jasper implores, pointing to my iPad.

I now know what Yolanda meant when she mentioned skeletons in my closet. By publishing this blog post, it looks like she just went and set them all free.

"I know." I sigh, reading over the part where Yolanda suggests I'm a home-wrecking whore. "Well, the good thing is she can't attack Metropolis because that would contradict Adelia's opinion and undermine her. I'm sure Adelia wouldn't stand for that."

"So she's settled for attacking you personally?" Jasper retorts while pacing the room.

"Oh!" I say, holding up my finger. "She does say my skills in the kitchen are professional, unique, and heartfelt."

"Read the next paragraph," he directs, running a hand through his hair.

"That bitch!" I curse as I read aloud, "Too bad these skills cannot be applied to her personal life."

"I'm going to kill Indie," he snarls, furiously searching though his phone.

"Do *not* call her," I screech, jumping up like the bed is on fire. "That's exactly what she wants. Just ignore this. I mean, how many people read blogs? I didn't even know what a blog was until I googled it," I confess, placing my hand over his to still his irate fingers.

Jasper raises a brow, but thankfully smiles. "Baby, not everyone lives in the dark ages like you do. You're the only person I know who still uses a diary."

"Ha, funny," I reply, relieved we're joking.

Jasper sighs and loops his hands low on my waist, drawing me to him. "So, I guess the cat's outta the bag. You're now officially stuck with me."

"I wouldn't have it any other way," I reply, running a hand through his messy locks. "I don't care that everyone knows. Do you?"

Jasper smirks, and the sight makes all the troubles from the morning disappear. "The only thing I care about is you. Our relationship was never a secret because I didn't think it was that exciting to make today's top news."

I open my mouth in faux horror, and Jasper laughs. "You know what I mean," he explains, and I nod because I do.

"It'll be fine," I say, wrapping my arms around his neck. "We'll be yesterday's news soon enough."

Jasper nods, pulling me into his chest and resting his chin atop my head. "Yeah, you're right," he replies half-heartedly, as we both know this is just the beginning.

The moment I round the corner and see a line of reporters and P.O.E. fans outside the doors of Metropolis, I know I'm in trouble. I try and turn around, but sadly, I'm spotted by an enthusiastic fan.

"There she is!"

With no other choice, I push my sunglasses higher up my nose and charge towards the entrance with my head bowed. "Excuse me," I say, pushing past the noisy crowd as I try to get to my front door.

"Ava, who is Indie Scott?"

"Is it true you slept with Jasper White to boost your popularity?"

"Are you pregnant with his twins?"

"Did you bribe Adelia Dupont to eat at Metropolis?"

These are only some of the absurd questions that are yelled at me as I frantically attempt to unlock the door. I keep my head lowered, but the constant flashing from the cameras blind me and my fingers fumble as I try to get the key into the lock.

"Oh my god, that's Jasper White's girlfriend!" a girl beside me says as she creepily touches my arm.

"Lucky bitch," another snarls.

"I thought he'd go for someone taller."

"And prettier," another bimbo pipes up, which has my blood boiling.

Thankfully, I get my key into the lock and barge into my restaurant, slamming and locking the door shut behind me. The camera flashes continue sparking, taking last minute shots of me as I run towards the safety of the kitchen.

I sag against the kitchen door, and take a moment to

compose myself and catch my breath. What the fuck was that? That was full blown paparazzi shit, and I didn't like it. Little ole me is sure as shit not interesting enough to make headlines—but looks like I was mistaken.

Pulling out my phone from my back pocket, I quickly dial Jasper.

"Hey baby, everything okay?"

"Can we go to Jeremy's early?" I say, getting straight to the point.

"Um, yeah, of course. But why?"

"It appears good news travels fast," I reply, afraid to look outside.

"Shit," Jasper curses under his breath. "Are you all right?"

"I'll survive," I reply with a sigh. "I just wanna get away. And besides, this will give me the kick in the pants I need to slowly detox myself off Metropolis."

"Baby," Jasper refutes, but I cut him off.

"No, Jasper, you're right. L.A. is my home. I just need time to get used to the idea."

"Okay." He sighs after a minute of silence. "I'll come get you."

"No, it's probably best you stay away. I don't think the paparazzi or your fans will be leaving any time soon."

"That bad?" he says, shocked.

"Worse," I reply, shuddering when remembering the bombardment outside.

"Fuck."

I think Yolanda just opened a can of celebrity worms, and I'm so not ready to face the vultures any time soon.

CHAPTER NINE
Getaway

"Ladies and gentlemen, the captain has turned off the Fasten Seat Belt sign so you may now move around the cabin. In a few moments, the flight attendants will be passing around the cabin to offer you hot or cold beverages. Now, sit back, relax, and enjoy the flight. Thank you."

I squash down all the unpleasant memories which flood my brain when I hear the dreaded air hostess's announcement. I've got enough on my mind, and I don't need any unwanted nostalgia to add to the shit pile.

"Baby, you're giving me motion sickness with all your fidgeting," Jasper says with a chuckle.

"Sorry," I quickly apologize. With a sigh, I brush the tiny pieces of torn napkin into a neat pile on my tray table.

"Are you nervous to see Jeremy?" Jasper asks, still attempting to decode my erratic behavior.

Flying to Chicago and leaving behind the media circus in New York may seem a little irresponsible, but I acted on a whim. Sadly, I'm now second guessing my decision. I called Sara, Helen, and Michel before I left, letting them know I'll be outta town for a week and while

I'm gone, I was handing manager duties over to them. They were surprised at my sudden decision to take a break and I must confess, I too, was also surprised at my spontaneity. But I needed to get away.

I was telling Jasper the truth when I told him I would think about setting up shop in L.A. This is the perfect opportunity to see how many days I'll last without going stir crazy. So far however, things don't look promising.

"No, I'm not nervous about to seeing Jeremy," I reply.

"Good, because you know he loves you," he says, reaching for my hand and stilling my fingers from twirling the charm bracelet he gave me many Christmases ago. "So, if you're not worried about seeing Jeremy, then what's up? Are you having second thoughts about leaving?"

"I don't know. Maybe?" I shamefully reply, turning to look into his gentle eyes. "I guess now that I'm not getting attacked by the paparazzi and can think straight, everything has just hit home. The past year has been crazy, Jasper," I say, and he nods.

"Now that I'm away from Metropolis and really thinking about your offer, I think I'm just, I dunno, scared of the unknown. While we were apart, Metropolis was my life, my savior, and being away from it..." I pause, trying to find the right words. "It's like being away from your child for the first time." I know it's a poor analogy, but it's the only one I can think of that fits the situation.

Reality blows.

Jasper thankfully nods, and seems to look relieved at my honesty. "You do realize if Metropolis was a dude, I would have kicked his ass by now," he says with a dimpled smirk.

I chuckle at his comment, relieved he's making jokes.

But he turns serious, knowing this is something we will have to eventually discuss. "Ava, I know the past year was about discovering who we both were, but I'm back now, and I'm not going anywhere. I'm hoping I can take Metropolis' place," he concludes, his sincerity touching me.

"You *are* my life, Jasper," I press, placing my hand against his cheek. "No one, or nothing, will ever take your place. I'm just worried, that's all."

Jasper seems to weigh up my reply before he responds. "Metro is in good hands."

I pull back, stunned. "I thought you hated Michel. And his hands."

Jasper shrugs, running his fingertips down my arm. "I don't hate him, I just hate when his hands and *eyes* are all over you."

"Jasper," I scold, shaking my head. "His hands and eyes were *not* all over me."

Jasper cocks a daring brow. "I'm not going to discuss this with you again. Actually, I propose to make this week a Jasper and Ava week only. Everyone else can go to hell," he says, his eyes twinkling in rebellion.

"That might be difficult seeing as we'll be surrounded by your family," I reply, a breath hitching in my throat when his tongue sweeps out to wet his bottom lip.

"Do I need to sing you into submission?" he asks, leaning in closer, his heady fragrance overwhelming me.

"Yes, please," I reply with a playful nod. "I like being submissive to you."

My cheeky response has the desired effect and Jasper leans in even closer, growling low in his throat. As he nuzzles the length of my neck and lays a single kiss over my racing pulse, I press my legs together and remind myself I'm on a plane full of people.

"You said you were going to—" I gasp when Jasper softly bites my neck. "Going to sing to me," I manage to say, barely able to contain my desire.

"What do you want to hear?" His breath is warm against my ear.

"Anything you sing will be perfect," I reply, closing my eyes and sagging into him.

He takes a few seconds before he counts down and starts softly singing 'Kiss Me' by Ed Sheeran. It's perfect.

My body reacts how it usually does when I hear Jasper sing, I swoon. The lyrics seem to encompass everything I'm feeling, and I don't think he could have chosen a better song to convey everything that has happened to us.

Jasper singing for my ears only is one of the most erotic experiences of my life. The way he expresses each word so passionately shows me he feels everything I'm feeling, too. He brushes the hair draped over my shoulder to one side and as he sings the chorus, he places a soft kiss against my skin. My eyes are still closed, and there's something so safe, so innocent about being blind to him and using his voice as the only guide to tether me to the universe.

Just as he starts singing the second verse, the air stewardess stops by our seats and clears her throat. My eyes instantly pop open and I look into my lap, thinking I may have forgotten to fasten my seatbelt, but I see that it's fastened.

"Sorry to intrude," the perfectly groomed brunette says. "But do you think I could get your autograph?" she asks, producing a white napkin and a pen. "I'm a big fan."

I hear Jasper sigh softly, but he politely nods and reaches for the pen as I scoot back in my seat. "Of course. Do you want me to make it out to anyone?"

"Could you make it out to Carly, please?"

"No worries," he kindly replies, resting the napkin on the chair in front of him as he signs his name.

I can feel Carly looking at me, so I give her a stiff smile in acknowledgment.

"I read the post on Foody Fey's blog," she says, looking around the plane to ensure no one needs her services.

I keep my face masked, unsure of what to say as I feel Jasper freeze up beside me.

She must be able to read my discomfort because she smirks. "That Indie," she says, and then pauses. "What a bitch," she concludes softly from behind her hand.

This time, my smile spreads into a genuine one. "Yeah, she really is."

"Here you go," Jasper says, handing the attendant her autographed napkin.

"Thank you so much," she gushes, holding the napkin like it's made of gold.

"No problem. Oh, and by the way," Jasper says, leaning over me while the air hostess draws in closer.

"Indie *is* a bitch. Please feel free to tell anyone you've heard it from the source."

I pull back, stunned. He plants a kiss on my cheek and the air stewardess coos, placing a hand over her heart. "You two are really cute together."

Jasper chuckles and shakes his head. "She's the cute one in our relationship. Feel free to also share that with anyone you know."

The hostess smiles and quickly darts off to no doubt tell her colleagues the scoop. I turn to look at Jasper.

"For the record," I say, unable to wipe the smile from my face. "You're adorable."

"I do what I can," he replies, tongue in cheek.

His calmness towards this entire situation settles me down because I know whatever happens, Jasper will always have my back.

It's dark by the time we get to Jeremy's cabin in the woods. As we head up the long, windy driveway, surrounded by nothing but green trees and nothingness, I know I've made the right choice to leave. Living in a concrete jungle has made me really appreciate the vast forest, and I sigh in relief.

Jasper places a hand on my knee, his eyes concentrating on the driveway ahead of him. "I'm really looking forward to it just being you and me."

"Me too," I reply, looking over at him, resting back

against the headrest. The events of the past week, make that year, have been exhausting, and this is exactly what I need to get my brain in check.

Jasper parks our rented car over near the double garage. The moment he switches off the engine, Jeremy opens the front door and bounces down the stairs, no doubt overjoyed to see Jasper. The year we were apart, Jasper stayed with Jeremy in Chicago and really got to know his dad. He established a solid, healthy relationship with his father and as Jasper eagerly unbuckles his seatbelt, I can see he can't wait to pick up where they left off.

"Son," Jeremy says as he stands by the door, patiently waiting for him to exit.

"Hey, Dad." Tears prick my eyes when I watch father and son affectionately embrace. The exchange lasts only for a few seconds, but it's enough to have me dabbing at my eyes.

Jasper opens my door and ducks his head into the car. "Are you going to sit in there all night?" he asks with a playful smirk. Thankfully, he doesn't address the issue of what a cry baby I am.

As I make an attempt to unbuckle my seatbelt, Jasper reaches over me and unfastens it. The action engulfs me in his musky, woody signature fragrance, and I stifle my moan. He turns to face me and his blue eyes smolder when he sees the desire reflected in mine. Suddenly, the reality of us being here, miles away from anyone, or anything sinks in, and I can't wait to get inside to check out our room.

"I've got you all to myself for one whole week. Whatever will we do?" Jasper huskily asks.

"I think the question is what *won't* we do?"

Jasper's tongue darts out to wet his lower lip before he swoops forward and kisses me.

The intensity takes my breath away and has me curling my toes in bliss. Sadly he pulls away all too quickly, and I'm left panting and incredibly turned on. When I remember that my future father-in-law is just outside, grabbing our bags from the trunk, I refrain from reaching for the collar of Jasper's shirt, and going in for round two.

"Dad, you remember Ava," Jasper playfully says as he offers me his hand.

Slipping my fingers into his, I quickly step out of the car and come face to face with the handsome Jeremy Blackwood. I can't help but think how unfair it is that some men seem to get better with age, while some women have to resort to fillers and Botox to remain youthful and age free.

"How could I forget," he says, his cerulean eyes shining under the moonlight. "Come give your father-in-law a hug," he adds with a dimpled smile, reminding me so much of Jasper.

"Hi, Jeremy." I step into his open arms. "It's so good to see you again."

"You too," he replies, pulling me out at arm's length. "Let me take a good look at the girl who willingly puts up with my son."

I cover my mouth to mute my laugh while Jasper sighs. "We've only been here for two minutes and already with the dad jokes. This is going to be a long week."

Jeremy laughs at his son's playfulness and I can't

wipe the smile from my face when I see how happy Jasper is.

"Come on, I'll show you two to your room," Jeremy says, slapping Jasper on the arm teasingly.

Jasper shoulders his backpack while Jeremy does the same to mine. "Thanks for letting us crash," Jasper says as we ascend the wooden stairs.

"No problem. It's nice to have the company," he replies, holding the front door open for us.

The moment I step inside, I feel like I'm transported into a rustic resort in the woods. The double story home is modern and contemporary. There are huge bay windows everywhere, which I can imagine would light up the house beautifully in the daylight. The rooms are huge, open spaces, decorated with an urban touch.

"Your room is upstairs," Jeremy says, as he ascends the oak staircase. We follow closely behind while I gawk at my astounding surroundings. The place is really beautiful.

Jasper's hand sits snugly in mine and I give it a gentle squeeze when Jeremy stops in front of a door, which I presume is ours.

"My room is down the hall." He looks to the left. "If you need anything, please let me know."

"Thanks, Dad," Jasper happily says, and I still can't get my head around him referring so comfortably to Jeremy in this way.

The carefree, relaxed look suits Jasper, and I suddenly can't wait to spend the entire week together. Jasper must be able to sense my excitement. "We'll just unpack and come down in a bit."

"No hurry," Jeremy replies with a smile. I hope he can't read my very perverted thoughts concerning his son.

He passes Jasper my bag. "Well, make yourselves at home." He reaches out and clasps Jasper affectionately on the arm. "I'm so glad you're here, son."

"Me too," Jasper replies with a nod.

Jeremy seems to not want to let him go, and once again, the love for his son has me feeling sentimental. I subtly wipe my eyes, while Jeremy clears his throat before removing his hand. "Okay, I'll be in the study if you need me." He gives me a tight hug before making his way downstairs.

Jasper chuckles while shaking his head at me. "You're such a girl."

I open my mouth, faking offense, and make a move to slap him playfully on the arm, but he dodges my attack and darts into our room.

"Holy shit," I gasp when I see the monster of a bedroom in front of me.

The room is decorated in warm shades of mocha, and set off with subtle undertones of coffee, with a splash of midnight black.

"This bedroom is the entire size of our apartment," I say, turning in a full circle to take in the full beauty of this glorious room.

"You like it?" Jasper asks, wrapping his arms around my waist when I stop spinning in awe.

"I love it!" I correct. He laughs as he rests his chin in the groove of my neck.

"So..." he says hoarsely, turning me slightly so we're facing the humongous bed.

"So…" I parrot, feeling a warmth beginning to spread from head to toe.

"You know…you have way too many clothes on. Allow me to remedy that," he whispers, unbuttoning the top button of my coat.

I shiver at his bold words and actions, and my arousal spurs Jasper on.

He unfastens my coat and slips it from my shoulders so I'm standing in my blue babydoll dress. The neckline is low, so Jasper slithers his fingers upward toward the collar, tracing the lace frill before dipping two fingers inside. He bypasses my bra and goes straight in for the kill, palming my heavy breast into his warm palm. We both moan at the delicious contact, and I lean backward, resting my head against his shoulder, and pushing more of myself into his hand.

"You drive me fucking crazy," he says breathlessly into my ear.

He rubs over my erect nipple, and I bite my lip to smother my moan.

"We…can't," I pant, my ass gently grinding against Jasper's growing erection.

"Why not?"

"Because, Jeremy. He'll hear us," I manage to get out.

"Then he'll have to mute us out because I can't keep my hands off of you," he replies, his words ringing passionate and true.

That's all the fight I have left in me and I nod, because all I can think about is how I want Jasper's hands to travel further south. He reads my desperation and with the one hand still heatedly palming my breast, he uses the other to bunch up my skirt and slip his hand underneath. He wastes no time and pushes aside my thong, slipping two fingers inside.

He's greeted with my arousal and hisses the moment he touches my heat. "I can't wait," he passionately states, pushing two fingers inside me and stretching me wide.

He pumps into me furiously while I buck into his strokes, approaching a loud, steady release, but he surprises me when he abruptly removes his hands from my body and pushes me up against the wall. In one quick movement, he yanks up my skirt and rips my underwear clean off. I hear the frantic sound of his belt buckle unfastening and then his jeans hitting the floor.

"When I'm with you, I lose all control. I love you...so fucking much," he breathlessly says, before thrusting into me with a wild, satiated groan.

I'm pushed up the wall with the fierce impalement, but it's exactly what I need. He wraps both hands around my waist to steady me, and then, he starts moving.

With each brutal strike, my body undulates, ready to come.

"Let go, baby." I splay both hands in front of me for support before I fall down.

His husky voice, deep intakes of breath, and rough, desperate actions drive me over the edge, and I come so loudly and violently my entire body trembles from head to toe. I'm sated beyond belief but as Jasper continues pumping into me, I know we've only just begun.

He tightens his grip around my waist while guiding my hips to meet his increasing strokes. The other slides around to my front and begins playing with center.

"Oh god," I moan as Jasper softly bites the side of my neck.

I'm sticky and about ready to combust again, but would I trade this feeling?

Hell no.

"Being with you this way compares to nothing else," Jasper confesses, his breath brushing against my cheek as I rest my forehead against the wall.

I can only whimper in response, as I doubt anything coherent would pass through my parted lips.

"Every day, I thank the moment you walked into that bar. I was ruined from that moment forward. I was yours, and you were mine. Tell me you're mine," he says, circling my clit harder and faster.

I sag, and if not for Jasper's firm grip, I would have tumbled to the floor.

"Tell me, baby," he presses, sucking on my neck while my eyes roll into the back of my head.

"I'm...yours!" I breathlessly scream. "I was yours from the moment I saw you."

"Yeah, you were," he groans, his hips driving into me faster. "You'll always be mine." With one final thrust, he comes with a loud moan.

I follow closely behind when his skillful fingers rub over my core and bring me to an earth-shattering climax. We're both breathless, our hearts racing out of control, but I can't wipe the satisfied smile off my face.

The moment he pulls out, I hug the wall, afraid I'm about to collapse, but Jasper's firm grip never wavers, and he pulls me against his chest as we both bask in our post-orgasmic bliss.

"I love you," I sleepily say while Jasper kisses over my racing pulse.

"I love you, too," he replies, his tone just as exhausted as mine. "I now know what to get Jeremy for his birthday."

"What?" I ask, catching my breath.

"Some earplugs," he smugly replies, while I blanch, realizing we weren't exactly quiet.

"Oh god, I'm so embarrassed." I look over my shoulder to see a proud Jasper.

"Don't be," he says, kissing the tip of my nose. "It's kinda nice being caught making out with your girlfriend by a parent who actually gives a shit."

I give him a gentle nod, totally understanding what he means. I decide to let him bask in his parental rebellion and ignore my shame.

"Well, looks like we better stock up on those earplugs then."

Coming here was the best thing for the both of us, and I plan on enjoying every minute.

"I'm going to take a bath," I say, turning around.

Jasper smirks and reaches forward, running the back of his knuckle down my cheek. "Give me ten, and I'll come join you."

"Make it five," I cheekily counter.

Jasper eagerly nods. "I'm just going to duck out for a smoke."

"Okay. I love you," I say, standing up on tippy toes to kiss his plump lips.

Jasper groans when I nip his bottom lip, but I pull away before things get too heated once again.

"Keep the water warm for me."

"Hurry back," I reply as I reach for the hem of my dress and lift it over my head.

"You're a damn tease," he says, shaking his head, his eyes zeroing in on my naked core.

"No, I'm just giving you a preview of what'll be waiting for you when you return," I boldly reply.

As I turn toward the bathroom, Jasper smacks me lightly on the butt. I yelp in surprise and he chuckles as he heads out the door. Taking off my bra and dropping it to the floor, I make my way into the bathroom and squeal in excitement when I see the size of the tub. Nothing has ever looked this good.

I turn on the faucets and sit on the edge of the bath, searching through the different jars of body salts and bath bombs. I pick a lychee and black tea scented bubble bath and pour a generous amount in, while running my hand backward and forward through the water. I can't wait to jump in. I watch in delight as the bubbles begin growing as the water level rises.

The longer I spend out here, the more I come to value my decision. I know in a way I'm running away from my problems, but they'll be there when I return home whether home be in New York or L.A.

Deciding to give my brain the night off, I turn off the water when the bubbles are almost overflowing the edge. The hot water has created a beautiful scented thick mist, and I can't wait to sink inside.

When the door opens, I smile as Jasper stuck true to his word and is back in five. "Back so soon?" I say, standing up and turning to face the door.

However, the face staring smugly back at me is not that of my fiancé, but that of a complete stranger—somehow, he appears to be familiar. As his mouth tips up into a dimpled, lopsided grin, I know the reason behind his familiarity is because I've seen that grin reflected on the face...of his brother.

CHAPTER TEN
Family Reunion

"Ahhh! Get out!" Covering up my pink bits with both hands, I attempt to reach for a towel hanging off the rack with my foot.

My smiling assailant does nothing of the sort however, and he casually leans against the doorjamb, crossing his arms across his broad chest. "Hi, I'm Kris. Please don't tell me you're my new mom?" he says tongue in cheek as he totally checks me out.

"Get out!" I repeat, beyond mortified.

When he makes it clear he has no intention of leaving, I turn my back because my hands are doing a poor job of acting as a makeshift shield against his prying eyes. Using one hand to cover my ass, I use the other to reach for the towel, which I quickly wrap around me.

"Ah, c'mon, you're not going to tell me who you are?" he asks, the humor clear in his tone.

"I'm five seconds away from screaming at the top of my lungs, that's who I am," I warn as I spin around, but he has the gall to laugh.

"What the fuck?" Jasper snarls as he barges in through the door, his eyes widening in shock.

"Who the fuck are you?" both boys say at the same time.

Now standing beside one another, there's no denying the similarities between them, but I'll analyze that later because right now, I'm holding onto the modest towel for dear life.

"I'm the person who's about to kick your ass if you don't get out of here," Jasper sneers as he quickly steps in front of me, shielding me from snooping eyes.

Just when I thought things couldn't get any more embarrassing, Jeremy steps into the bathroom, taking in the bedlam before him. "Kris, what are you doing in here? Get out!" Jeremy says angrily.

I sink further behind Jasper, wishing the damn towel would swallow me whole.

"Oh, Ava, pardon me," Jeremy quickly says, covering his eyes when he sees me red as a beet.

"It's fine," I say, trying my best to use Jasper as my shield.

"We'll talk once Ava gets dressed," Jeremy says, and I nod in concurrence as that sounds like a brilliant idea.

Kris however, doesn't agree. "That's a shame, as I was really enjoying the show," he sarcastically says, baiting Jasper as he stands on tippy toes to look over his shoulder, hopeful to get another eyeful.

It works. I hear Jasper grind down on his jawbone. I don't even want to imagine the look on his face.

"Kris, stop being such a smart aleck." Jeremy sighs.

"Why?" he counters, and I pick up on a slight British accent.

"Because he's your brother," Jeremy softly replies.

Jasper's spine straightens when he hears who this peeping Tom is.

"So who's the girl?" Kris asks, choosing to ignore the fact he's just met his brother.

"The *girl*," Jasper sneers, crossing his arms over his chest, "is mine."

This is about to explode in the worse possible way, and if I wasn't half naked, I would try and diffuse the situation. But sadly, I have to watch from the sidelines until I can get dressed.

"Oh. Well, she's got a great rack. Kudos to you, *bro*," he sarcastically says with a snicker, while I squeak in embarrassment. "And her bare pu—"

"Kris! Get downstairs. Now," Jeremy says, his tone stern when Jasper takes a step forward, about to no doubt punch the living hell out of his sibling.

"Yes, *Father*." The word *father* has never sounded so dirty. "It was a pleasure meeting you, Ava. Thanks for giving me some very vivid images which I plan on revisiting later tonight," Kris says with a wink as he leans to the left to look around Jasper's rigid frame.

I blanch and tighten the towel around my body, but I may as well be naked under his insinuating stare. I can't see Jasper's face but I think it's safe to say the look isn't pleasant.

"Catch ya 'round, big bro," Kris spits. He then shoves past Jeremy, who looks utterly embarrassed. "I'm so sorry, son," he says when Kris leaves. "I didn't know he was coming home early."

"It's fine," Jasper says, his shoulders hunched.

"Ava, my apologies again," Jeremy says, still avoiding looking in my general direction.

"It's okay, Jeremy," I reply, because this isn't his fault.

"I really am sorry, Jasper. That wasn't how I wanted you two to meet." The remorse is clear in his voice.

"Don't sweat it. You're not the one who should be apologizing," Jasper replies, running a hand through his hair.

Jeremy nods and softly closes the door behind him. When the coast is clear, Jasper slowly turns around to face me. He looks absolutely livid, and I recoil because I've never seen him this mad.

"Well, that was embarrassing," I say, trying to lighten the mood.

It sadly doesn't work. "How much did he see?" he asks, looking at the small towel barely covering my body.

I could lie, but I have a feeling Jasper knows he saw it all. "He got the entire show. Front row, center," I reply, feeling totally embarrassed as I scrunch up my face.

Jasper clenches his jaw, and his nostrils flare in rage.

"It's okay," I quickly say. "He's family." That probably makes this situation even worse.

Jasper angrily shakes his head, his eyes incensed. "That"—he growls, hooking his thumb behind him—"is *not* my family."

I nod, knowing this is an argument not worth having.

As we descend the staircase hand in hand, I know this will go one of two ways. Judging by the way Jasper is latching onto my hand and has remained deathly quiet for the past hour, I'm putting my money on it going horribly.

I've tried to be encouraging, but Jasper seems to have taken an instant dislike to his half-brother, Kris. I must admit, he's also rubbed me the wrong way. I flinch when I realize how that comment could be construed after today.

As we reach the bottom step, we hear Jeremy having a stern word with Kris in the living room. "He has every right to be here, and I will not allow you to disrespect him, or his fiancée in my home."

"Well, he being here is disrespecting me," Kris angrily retorts.

"Why on earth would you say that?"

"Because I don't want him here. He's *not* my brother, nor will he ever be. Just because you want to play happy families, doesn't mean I do. As far as I'm concerned, he can go back to whatever trailer park he came from," Kris cruelly concludes.

Jasper charges toward the doorjamb, but I latch onto his bicep to stop his retreat. As much as Kris deserves the living hell beaten out of him, I don't want Jasper to ruin any chance they may have of getting along once they've both cooled down, and gotten used to the idea of being under the same roof as each other.

Thankfully, Jasper listens but he pulls out of my grip and storms towards the front door, slamming it shut behind him. Jeremy comes running out and his face drops when he sees me standing in the foyer.

"Did he hear?"

I nod, feeling awful, as this isn't Jeremy's fault.

"Damn it." He sighs, running a hand through his salt and pepper hair. "Should I go after him?"

I know Jasper, and he'll want to be alone to vent and express his anger in four letter words. "Just give him some time to cool down."

"I feel terrible, Ava. Kris got kicked out of Cambridge, that's why he's home early," Jeremy explains, looking disappointed.

"Oh," I reply, realizing that explains the accent I picked up on earlier.

"He's been living over there for five years with his mother."

I nod, remaining silent, as I'm too busy thinking about Kris' mother. I never gave much thought to Jeremy's ex-wife. I knew he was once married, but Jasper mentioned Jeremy didn't like to speak about her. I decide to leave the topic alone for now and go look for Jasper.

"I'm going to find Jasper. See if he's calmed down," I say, hating to see Jeremy so upset.

He nods. "Please tell him he's always welcome in my home. You both are."

"Thank you, that means a lot to the both of us," I reply, giving Jeremy a small smile.

Jeremy returns the gesture, but it doesn't quite reach his eyes. "Please tell him I'm sorry. Kris *will* be apologizing for his unacceptable behavior."

"It's okay, Jeremy," I say, wanting to calm his worries. "Jasper knows Kris' opinion isn't shared by you."

"I know, I just—" he says, pausing and taking a deep

breath. "I just don't want to lose him, Ava. I've just gotten him back, and I know how hard a time he has trusting people. I would hate for this event to undo all the progress we've made."

"It won't." I place my hand on his arm. "Jasper knows you love him. I think Kris is the one who needs the reassurance," I say, as I think that may be the reason behind his bitterness.

"Yes, you're right." He sighs, resting his hand over mine. "My son is so lucky to have you in his life."

"I'm the lucky one," I reply, sounding like a broken record.

Jeremy leans forward, and a gesture so like Jasper's, he places a kiss on my brow. "Tell him if he wants to talk, I'll be in my room."

I nod and excuse myself.

It's quite dark out when I open the front door, and I realize I probably should have grabbed a flashlight so I can see. Instead I reach into my pocket and use the light on my phone.

"Jasper," I call out, the cold March evening chilling my skin.

Looking from left to right I can't see him, so I descend the stairs and take a left towards the garage. "Jasper," I call out again, but still nothing.

He probably wants to be left alone, but I can't leave him to stew on his own. Jeremy was right. Jasper doesn't trust too many people, and I would hate for his bratty brother's comment to ruin the progress he and Jeremy have made.

The moment I smell a trace of cigarette smoke on the

light breeze, I know I've found him. I round the corner and see him leaning up against the garage wall with one boot resting against the bricks.

"Hey," I say, and he turns to look at me from under his hood.

"Hey yourself," he replies, taking a drag of his smoke while lowering his gaze.

"Are you all right?" I ask, slowly walking towards him and turning off the flashlight on my phone.

The full moon is the only light we have, but I see him shrug. "I'm okay," he replies, flicking his cigarette onto the ground.

"Do you wanna talk about it?" I ask, standing a few feet away from him.

"Not really," he blankly replies. "I mean, what's there to say?"

"Jeremy is mortified you heard what they were talking about. He said to say sorry."

"He's got nothing to be sorry for," Jasper replies, kicking off the wall.

"Jasper." I sigh, hating how miserable he looks.

"Baby, it's fine," he says, cutting me off as he walks towards me. "I'm a big boy. I'm not going to let some spoiled brat ruin my week with you. Yes, meeting my half-brother went down as the suckiest in history, but I've been through worse, right? I mean, my mom pretended she actually gave a shit about me, when in reality she was just after my money."

I flinch at the memory and I automatically reach out to touch his arm. "Don't let her ruin this place. She's in the past, Jasper. This right here," I say, resting my hand against his stubbled cheek. "This is our future."

He nods, his clear eyes meeting mine. "I love you. As long as I've got you, everything else can fall into place around us."

"I'm not going anywhere," I say, drawing out foreheads together.

Jasper rubs his nose against mine and lays a soft kiss against my lips. "So looks like our week just got a whole lot more interesting."

"Like we need any more excitement," I reply with a sigh. "When did our lives get so complicated?"

Jasper smirks, and the sight is pure heaven. "It was complicated from the moment you said hello."

My cheeks flush at the memory of falling over my feet when I first met him.

Jasper chuckles, his deep laugh resonating low in my body. "You were already falling head over in heels in love with me."

"Good to see your modesty is in check today," I say, playfully slapping him on the arm.

"Thank you," Jasper says as he catches my hand in his.

"For what?" I ask, confused.

"For being here with me."

"There's no place I would rather be."

And I mean every single word.

CHAPTER ELEVEN
Changes

I wake alone.

Jolting up, I brush my messy hair off my face and quickly scan the room for Jasper. He's nowhere in sight. I don't hear the shower running, therefore, he's probably not upstairs. Quickly jumping out of bed and throwing on some clothes, I race to the window and draw back the curtains to look outside.

After he calmed down last night, we went back to our room and fell asleep, both emotionally drained from the events of the day. He promised he was okay, and that he would talk to Jeremy in the morning, and maybe try to talk to Kris.

I haven't heard any yelling, so it's safe to assume he's not yet spoken to Kris, but I wonder if he's spoken to Jeremy. Jeremy was so hurt about Kris' bad manners—I can't help but feel sorry for him. Deep down, I think Jeremy was hoping both boys would meet and be best buds. Sadly, I don't see that happening any time soon. I really wish that wasn't the case, as Jasper's happiness is so important to me, and I wish life could be easy for him, just this once.

As he jogs out of the woods looking flustered and

breathless, all thoughts are put on hold and I take a moment to admire the man in front of me. His white t-shirt sticks to his hardened chest, highlighting all the muscled planes and rocky contours he's been blessed with. His tousled hair is damp at the brows, and as he runs a hand through it, messing it up further, I bite my lip, suppressing my moan.

Jasper is pure perfection, but as I see his cerulean jewels light up when Jeremy walks over to him with a bottle of water in hand, I know his beauty runs skin deep. He's beautiful on the inside and out, and I wish his brother would see that internal beauty, because he's missing out on getting to know the best person in the world.

I watch their exchange, and from Jasper's serious expression, I have no doubt he's listening to Jeremy apologize for Kris' behavior. I've snooped long enough and decide to take a shower before Jasper comes up and hogs all the hot water.

Twenty minutes later, I'm showered and dressed, but Jasper still hasn't made an appearance, so I decide to go look for him. Just as I close our bedroom door and turn around, I bump directly into Kris.

"Oh, I'm sorry. I wasn't watching where I was going," I say, looking down at his hand, which grabs my bicep to stop me from falling on my ass.

"It's cool," he says, his accent smooth as silk.

He thankfully releases the grip on my arm, and I smile, suddenly not knowing what to say. A part of me wants to yell at him, scold him out for being so rude to

Jasper. But the rational part knows that won't accomplish anything—it sucks being the adult.

"So, Jeremy said you go to Cambridge. That's pretty awesome," I say, making small talk, unable to get over the physical similarities between Jasper and Kris.

When Kris turns his lip up in disgust, looking bitter and unkind, I can't help but wonder, how can two people who look so alike, be so different inside?

"Not really. It's just my father's way of making up for what a shitty dad he was. Look around you," he says, sweeping his hand out in front of him. "Jeremy thinks money can buy love."

I stare, my mouth agape, as I can't imagine Jeremy being anything but a wonderful dad.

"Sorry to disappoint you, love, but Jeremy isn't the person you believe him to be. He got my mom pregnant, and then he did a runner, leaving her to raise me on her own. She was seventeen, by the way," he adds, his stormy blue eyes narrowing.

"What? No." I shake my head. If what he's saying is true, then Jeremy had sex with a minor, because he would have been well in his twenties.

"How old are you?"

"I'm twenty. Trying to figure out the math, aren't you?" he says with a broad grin.

It's all too complicated, but there's roughly seven years between Kris and Jasper. I remember Jeremy telling me that after he gave up hope in ever seeing Jasper again, he moved to Europe. So this is where he must have met Kris' mom. Maybe in England? That might explain Kris' weird accent.

"Where's your mom now?" I ask, unable to keep the interest from my voice.

Kris' cocky mask slips. "Dead," he blankly replies.

"What?" I gasp, a hand falling over my heart. "I'm so sorry."

"Don't be. Both my parents were complete failures, and I don't expect my *brother* to be any different," he replies, pronouncing brother like it's acid on his tongue.

His response angers me, and I can't help myself as I lash out. "Jasper is *not* a failure," I say heatedly. "If only you got to know him, you'd see he's the kindest, most loyal, generous person you'll ever meet."

Kris scoffs, running a hand through his shaggy, light brown hair. "So he's got you wrapped around his little finger, too?"

"Excuse me?" I spit, taking a step backward. "I love Jasper."

"Well, that's too bad for you, because you'll fast learn that this family brings nothing but misery and disappointment to all those around them."

"That's not true. I know Jasper." I furiously shake my head.

"You may think you know him, but money has a funny way of changing people. It can buy so many people's love. Money controls people and people who have money, well..." he says, suggesting Jasper is controlling and buying my love. "My door is always open, love," he whispers, giving me a wink.

Refraining from smacking his smug face, I spit out, "Firstly, I am *not* your love, and secondly, close your door, because I'm not interested in anything you have to offer."

"We'll see," he arrogantly retorts.

I don't even justify his response with a reply, and simply turn my back before I say something I'm bound to regret.

After my little chat with Kris, I'm in the worst possible mood. Jasper tries to coax me downstairs, but I just want to be by myself. He knows something is up, but he doesn't push and has left me to think about what Kris said.

Yes, money changes people, but only if you let it. Jasper still wears the same ripped jeans and scuffed boots I met him in, for Pete's sake. He hasn't gone out and purchased me lavish, expensive things. Nor has he tried to buy my love like Kris wrongly suggests. He's still the same Jasper I fell in love with four years ago.

But thinking back to Jasper's comment about buying me a Metropolis in L.A. has put stupid, irrational thoughts in my head. Jasper isn't trying to control me. He's trying to keep us together. I need to stop being ridiculous, and there's only one way for that to happen.

"V, talk some sense into me," I plead as my friend answers the phone.

"You know, I should start charging you by the minute."

I can't help but laugh as her humor instantly lightens my mood.

"What's going on? Where are you?"

"Well, after your revelation yesterday, I freaked out, thanks to the paparazzi turning up on my doorstep, so we jumped on a plane and flew to Chicago," I reply, picking at a loose thread on the comforter.

V is silent for a moment, which is never a good sign. "Hold up, you're in Chicago? When normal people freak out, Ava, they usually go to a local bar, drink themselves silly, and dance the night away to Taylor Swift. They don't end up in Chicago. Why are you there?"

"Well, it's Jeremy's 50th this weekend, so I figured—"

"You'd dance to Taylor Swift over there?" she finishes for me.

"No," I chuckle, lying down on the bed. "I needed to get away."

"So, what's the problem?"

"The problem is Jasper's brother." I sigh.

"What the hell? Why? Oh no, what did you do? Your hormones went into overdrive when you saw him, didn't they? It's those damn blue eyes," she says, and I can picture her shaking her head.

"No! Oh my god, who do you think I am?" I ask, half smiling.

"A very lucky girl," she says in a faraway voice.

"Veronica, focus," I say, snapping my fingers.

"Sorry. So, what's wrong?" she asks, back on track.

"Well, he's a total pig. And he saw me naked."

V bursts out laughing.

"This isn't funny."

"It kinda is," she retorts, still laughing.

"Please explain to me how you're finding this funny."

"So what, he's a pig. All men are. I still haven't forgiven Lucas for giving me stretch marks," she says, only half-jokingly.

I groan. "So not helping."

"Just see him naked, and all is even," she suggests. I can't tell if she's teasing or not.

I rub my forehead, feeling a headache approaching.

V must be able to sense my dilemma because she turns serious and bossy. "Ava, stop being an idiot. Whatever this little jerkwad said to plant whatever issues in your head, you need to stop paying attention to them. Go out there, tackle your hot fiancé, and slap him on the ass for me."

"He said money changes people. That it'll change Jasper. I've been so happy, wrapped up in our reunion, have I missed the signs that he's changed?" I rebuke, needing to get this off my chest.

V bursts out laughing once again. "This is Jasper you're talking about. I don't think I've ever seen him wear a piece of clothing without a hole in it."

I can't help but smile. "I know, but he did say he wants to buy me a Metropolis in L.A."

"And?"

"And, I dunno. Is that a controlling thing to do?" I ask, scratching my brow, feeling utterly stupid.

"Um, no...it's a nice thing to do. I'm lucky if Lucas buys me a damn drink these days," she replies with a huff.

"You're right, I'm being stupid. I don't know why I've let him get to me."

"'Cause you're obviously making up excuses to why

you shouldn't come home," she replies with complete accuracy.

"Am I that obvious?"

"No, I just know you. You're too stubborn to leave until you're ready to go, which isn't a bad thing."

"I'm really confused, V. One minute I'm ready to leave, and the next, I'm losing my shit and acting like a nut job."

"Stop over thinking, Ava. That's always been your problem."

I nod, because this isn't the first time I've been told this. "You're right."

"Of course, I'm right. Just enjoy your time away, and deal with it when you get back to New York," she wisely says.

"Okay. Thanks, V. I miss you."

"I miss you too, babe. Life sucks without you here. But as long as you're happy, then so am I."

That's the million-dollar question. Where will I be happiest?

"I love you," I say, hating we have to say goodbye so soon.

"I love you, too."

I hang up feeling much better, as I knew I would. There doesn't seem to be a solution in sight. So what'll be, will be, and stressing over it won't change a thing. Besides, I've got other pressing matters to deal with, like how we're going to survive the week without Jasper and Kris murdering one another.

I've sulked long enough, so I decide to find Jasper and

apologize for being such a loon. As I make my way down-stairs, I hear Kris chatting to someone on the phone. I bypass him quietly, as I don't want a repeat conversation, now or ever.

Making my way outside, I see Jasper sitting under a tree, playing his guitar. His aviators sit atop his head, brushing his long bangs off his face. He's in ripped jeans, a tank, and his feet are bare, which totally contradicts Kris' absurd money changes people speech. He's still the same Jasper I knew and loved a year ago.

As I get closer, I see he has the leather-bound journal I gave him for Christmas resting on the grass beside him.

"Hey," I say when I come to a stop at his feet.

"Hey," he replies, looking up at me with one eye squinted to keep out the sun.

"Whatcha doing?" I take a seat near him.

"Just writing."

Casually peering over him, I try and catch a glimpse of his notes. He smirks and quickly closes the notebook, while I pout.

"You can read it once it's done," he says like the true perfectionist that he is.

"It better be about me."

Jasper shakes his head, his smile mischievous. "When aren't my songs about you? You possess my every waking thought. And dreams," he adds with a wink.

I smile, ashamed I listened to Kris' nonsense. Speaking of the troublemaker..."So, have you spoken to Kris?"

"Nope," he replies, his smile replaced by a frown.

"Are you going to?"

"Nope."

"Jasper…"

He drowns me out by strumming his guitar.

"Don't worry your pretty little mind

Come here, and I'll show you a good time…"

I place my hand over his to stop him from playing his ridiculous song. "You can't sing your way outta this one."

"I can always try," he replies with a shrug.

I laugh. "Just be the bigger one, Jasper. Try and remember what it was like to be twenty."

"How do you know he's twenty?" he asks, his curiosity piqued.

"Well…" I pause, picking a blade of grass. "He told me."

"When?" he asks, his brow crinkling.

"This morning," I reply, trying to forget what else he told me.

"So he's the reason why you've been hiding all day?"

I nod.

"What else did he have to say for himself?" Jasper asks, drumming his finger against his guitar.

"Well, he said his mom is dead," I reply, deciding to leave out the not so nice things he had to say about Jasper.

"Dead?" he says, stunned, as he places the guitar on the grass. "Jeremy never mentioned that."

"It's probably not the first thing he wanted to bring up in conversation after years of being apart."

Jasper nods. "That's true. What else did he say?"

What else *didn't* he say, that's more the question. "Why don't you ask him?" I say with a smile.

"I would much rather you tell me." He surprises me by wrapping his hands around my waist and pulls me onto his lap.

I yelp, but oblige by straddling him. "He said Jeremy was an awful father," I say softly, wrapping my arms around his neck.

Jasper pulls back, horrified. "No way. I don't believe that."

"Neither do I. I dare say there's no love lost between them. Well, on Kris' behalf, anyway."

"I don't want to hear anymore." Jasper shakes his head.

"Okay," I say, as I wasn't too keen on telling him about Kris' statement about money changing people, and by people, I mean Jasper.

"Can you do me a favor?" he asks, looking up at me with his big blue eyes.

"You got it," I reply, toying with the stray hairs at his nape.

"Stay away from him," he says, pulling in his lip.

"Jasper..." I protest.

"Ava, please, for me. It's taking every ounce of my self-control to not beat the smug smile off his face for seeing you naked," he says, his jaw clenching.

"It was for a split second," I interrupt, trying to play it off.

But Jasper won't have a bar of it. "A split second too long."

He reaches for my hands, which are looped behind his neck, and interlaces our fingers together, playing with my ring.

"Okay, I'll do it for you," I say, "but for Jeremy's sake, I think you should at least try to get to know your bro—" I don't finish my sentence because Jasper's tightened jaw reveals that referring to Kris as his brother may result in World War Three.

His cell suddenly chimes, saving us from a conversation that was doomed from the beginning. "It's Delilah." Jasper pulls a confused face.

"Oh, lucky you," I sarcastically say, attempting to get off his lap.

His hand darts out and grabs my upper arm, stopping me from moving a muscle. "Hello," he says, not at all impressed to be speaking to her.

"Hi, handsome." I can hear her loud and clear, seeing as I'm inches away from the phone.

"What do you want?" Jasper asks bluntly.

"Oh," she says, sounding taken aback by his hostility. "I...um, did you have the tour schedule for when we're in Germany?"

I roll my eyes when I hear her pathetic lie, and Jasper smirks. "Not on me, but I can email it to you if you like?"

"That would be great," she replies, her enthusiasm a little too eager for my liking. "So, it sucks about the no partners on tour rule, right?"

Her comment has both my brows rising in alarm. This was a little fact I didn't know about. I wasn't planning on being there for the entire tour, but at least part of it. So this means I'll be without Jasper for six whole weeks.

Well, today can just blow me.

Jasper must be able to read my disappointment

because he shakes his head and caresses my cheek. "Well, lucky for me, I make my own rules."

"Oh?" she says, no doubt pissed.

"Yup. I would go stir crazy without my girl there, so for the sanity of my band members and crew, she'll be coming with."

I'm unable to wipe the smile from my face. Well, that is until Delilah boldly retorts, "A little crazy isn't a bad thing."

I let out a frustrated sigh, and my fingers itch to reach out and pry the phone from Jasper's hand.

"It is when you're miles away from your girl," he quickly replies.

"I would even volunteer to go crazy with you," she says, her tone dripping with seduction.

"Thanks for the offer, but no. The only crazy thing is the thought of being away from Ava for six weeks," Jasper says, looking at me sincerely.

"Well, let me know if you change your mind," she replies. I can hear the bitterness behind her words.

"I won't. So, I'll send you the tour schedule when I get a chance," he says, winding up their conversation.

"Oh, okay," she replies, sounding disappointed her ploy to lure Jasper over to the dark side didn't work.

"Catch ya round." He hangs up before she has a chance to reply.

He tosses his phone onto the grass and wraps both hands low on my waist.

"So, I can't come on tour with you?" I ask, not seeing the point of pretending I wasn't eavesdropping.

"What big ears you have," Jasper retorts cheekily in a high pitched voice.

I can't help but laugh at his lame impersonation of Little Red Riding Hood. "I really don't like her," I say for the hundredth time.

"I know," he replies with a sigh. "But it's business. I don't get to choose who comes on tour, the label does."

"I know," I reply, as this is a conversation we've had many times before.

"You'll just have to kick her ass when you come with," he says, testing the waters.

"I'm not sure how long I'll be able to tag along, but I'll definitely be there for some of the tour," I reply sincerely.

"You promise?"

"You bet your ass I promise. I plan on being your personal bodyguard."

"Ava, what big teeth you have," he says in his high pitched tone once again.

I cuddle into him with a chuckle. "You're a goofball."

"Sorry to interrupt," Jeremy says a moment later.

I untangle myself from Jasper's arms and give Jeremy an embarrassed smile as I sit on the grass.

"What's up, Dad?" Jasper asks. I'm glad he hasn't let Kris sour his relationship with Jeremy.

"I have to go out tonight for a tedious business dinner I completely forgot about. I'm so sorry," he says, shaking his head.

"Don't worry about it. We're the ones who crashed your week. Go do what you have to do. Ava and I can entertain ourselves," Jasper says, his heated tone making me blush.

Jeremy smiles, thankfully not commenting on his son's cheek. "I still feel awful. I won't be late."

"It's fine. Go out," Jasper says, reassuring Jeremy.

"Are you sure things will be okay while I'm gone?" he asks, and by *things,* he means will Jasper kill Kris while he's gone?

Jasper nods. "I'm sure. And besides, I may take my beautiful fiancée out for dinner, too."

I smile, as that sounds like an awesome idea. I would love to see Chicago.

"What a wonderful idea. Did you want to take the Ferrari?" Jeremy asks, nodding in encouragement.

My mouth hangs open, as I didn't know people actually drove Ferraris. I thought they were only for show.

"It's okay, we've got the rental car," Jasper says, shaking his head.

"I insist," Jeremy presses. "Nothing like seeing the Windy City from the front seat of a Ferrari."

His comment has Kris' remark ringing loudly in my ears. But I quickly snuff it out, as he's only trying to be nice.

Before I can object, Jasper nods. "Okay. You drive a hard bargain, but I'm sold. Baby?" he says, looking at me excitedly.

Is this what Kris was talking about? Is Jeremy trying to buy Jasper's love?

As I look at an excited Jasper, I know Jeremy is doing nothing of the sort. Jeremy has Jasper's love, and nothing about it was bought. It was earned.

"So, is it red?"

Both Jeremy and Jasper smile.

Jeremy's smile suddenly dies down as he rubs the back of this neck. "I've told Kris, no parties. So if he disobeys my request, please feel free to break it up."

Jasper nods, his smile also disappearing. "It'll be my pleasure."

I internally cross my fingers that it doesn't come to that, because if it does, I have a feeling heads will roll.

CHAPTER TWELVE

Broken Pieces

"I'm so full." I brace my hands on my bloated belly.

Jasper glances over with a smile as he zips in and out of traffic, totally loving his new speedy toy. "I said you'd regret that third piece of pie."

"I know," I mumble. "You should have stopped me."

"I like where my bits 'n pieces are, thank you very much," he replies with a smirk.

Jasper and I have had a lovely day sightseeing. After cramming in some of the more popular tourist landmarks, we ate at a lovely restaurant downtown, where I couldn't help myself and ate almost everything in sight.

As Jasper takes a sharp left, I groan. "Oh god, I'm pregnant with a food baby," I say, but quickly shut my lips when I realize what I stupidly just said.

Sensing Jasper tense up beside me, I kick myself for saying something which is totally inappropriate, seeing as the fact I thought I had a real baby inside of me, but in fact didn't, was the reason why we broke up.

"Shit, sorry," I quickly apologize, looking over at him sheepishly. "I wasn't thinking."

"It's fine," he replies, not meeting my eyes. "It's in the past. Remember, we've both agreed that's where it stays.

No dredging up memories we both don't want to remember."

I nod. "Okay." But I still feel like shit bringing it up. Maybe we should have spoken about this sooner?

The car is quiet for a little while, the low hum of the engine filling the sudden uncomfortable silence.

When Jasper breaks it however, I wish it was still silent. "Maybe one day we could put a real baby in there," he says, his eyes never wavering from the road.

I don't know what to say. We've discussed the mistaken pregnancy, and although Jasper says he forgives me, I know he still wishes the pregnancy was real.

I do, too. But I want to focus on us before we go adding another to the equation, especially since I don't know where I want to live.

"Maybe one day," I say, as I know Jasper is awaiting my reply.

"But not before I marry you, right?" he asks, finally meeting my eyes.

I have no idea where this has come from. "Is everything okay?"

"Yeah," he replies, nodding. "I was just thinking aloud, that's all."

"Well, did you wanna think aloud some more?" I say, needing to get inside his head.

Jasper sighs, and I automatically think the worst. "I just wanted to know where you see us in five years."

Five years? Wow. I was just getting used to us being back together for five weeks. Is the honeymoon over already?

I think about his question seriously because honestly,

I don't know. "I'm just getting used to having you back in my life, Jasper. The year apart was the worst year of my life. But it was also the best," I confess, knowing how cruel that sounds.

Before I have time to finish, Jasper finally turns to look at me. "The best?"

"Yes," I reply honestly. "Look at everything I…no, we accomplished while apart. Yes, it sucked that we weren't together, but you never left my mind or heart. I did all of it for you. I fucked up so badly, I needed to redeem myself, but I also needed to find out who I was, and what I wanted."

"And what do you want?" he asks, raising an inquisitive brow.

This isn't a trick question. "You, Jasper. I want you. That has never changed. From the moment I met you, I've wanted you. I just needed to be worthy of that want," I reply, reaching out and placing my hand on his arm.

"You are worthy," Jasper rebukes. "I told you I've forgiven you. I fucked up, too. We both did."

"I know." I nod. "But what I did—" I'm unable to think about how I hurt Jasper without wanting to cry.

"Baby," he coos. "I thought we agreed to leave the past where it belongs? It takes sadness to know happiness, and I think we've experienced enough sadness to last us a lifetime." He places his hand over mine.

"You're right," I say with a sniff. "Sorry. I guess when things start going well for us, I'm just waiting for a shit storm to roll on in and rain on us."

"Old habits die hard," he replies, indicating to turn

onto Jeremy's property. "But we're going to change that, right?"

I nod, feeling a new sense of hope radiate through me. "Yes. Nothing but sunshine and happy days ahead," I reply as we head up the driveway, only to be confronted by a naked man holding a beer bottle.

"What the hell?" Jasper says as I cover my eyes in shock.

"Please tell me it was just a shadow," I say, but the loud music is a sure sign I indeed saw what I thought I did.

"If only," he says, beeping the horn and winding down his window. "Move outta the way!"

I part my fingers, hoping I don't see any more naked men. Thankfully everyone seems clothed, but I don't know what's worse; being confronted by a huge crowd of half clothed college kids, or one naked man. "I think I liked it better when I had my eyes closed," I mumble under my breath, watching the kids stare and whistle at our car.

Jasper thankfully navigates the Ferrari into the garage without running anyone over. He's out before I can unbuckle my belt.

"Holy shit, that's that dude from that band," a blond guy says, nudging his oblivious friend.

"What band? Thirty Seconds to Mars?" he asks, looking at Jasper.

"No, dumbass. Passengers of Ego."

"Fuck me! *That's* Jasper White?"

Conversations such as this are what I'm greeted with as I exit the car and quickly chase after Jasper, but I pay no attention to them as I'm too busy trying to keep my eyes on him. He's charging through the swarm of people, fists clenched.

"Jasper!" I call after him, but it falls on deaf ears, as Eminem is drowning out my pleas.

I watch as he hurls himself up the steps two at a time and barges through the front door.

"Shit," I curse, quickening my step and rushing up the steps.

The moment I step inside, I'm hit with the smell of beer, weed, and vomit, and if that isn't enough, the half-naked girl straddling the staircase banister is enough to make me wanna barf. I stand on tippy toes, hoping to catch a glimpse of Jasper, but I can't see anything, thanks to the few hundred people jammed inside.

As I push my way through the crowd, my butt gets smacked way too many times to count, and I'm asked by five different guys if they can see my boobs, but I ignore these imbeciles as I see Jasper speaking animatedly to Kris.

"Pardon me!" I yell, using my hands as a tool to push my way through the crowd.

Thankfully, the swarm must be able to read my desperation and let me through. The moment I get within earshot, I know I have to separate Jasper and Kris this second, as they're moments away from brawling.

"Get these people out of here now. This isn't a damn fraternity!" Jasper yells, poking Kris in the chest.

"Make me," he snarls, inches from Jasper's face.

"Stop being such a disrespectful little shit. Whatever issues you have with me, take it out on me. Don't trash

Jeremy's home to spite him, or me," Jasper says, running a hand through his hair.

"Better I take my issues out on this house than on you," he replies, his eyes narrowing.

"I'd like to see you try," Jasper says, his lip curling into a sinister scowl.

"Stop it!" I yell, jumping in between them.

"Hello, love. Couldn't stay away?" Kris says, taking a step towards me.

Rolling my eyes, I place a hand on his chest to stop his advance. "In your dreams."

"Oh yes, you've certainly been in them," he replies, his seedy tone making me feel very uncomfortable.

Jasper snarls, and I extend my hand out behind me to stop his retreat. "Don't, Jasper. He's only trying to upset you," I say, my eyes locked with Kris' cocky gaze.

I'm standing between both boys, my hands pressed against their chests, keeping them from killing one another. I have no doubt Kris did this to get a rise out of Jeremy, and it takes all my willpower to stop myself from reaching out and smacking him in the teeth.

"Let's go upstairs, Jasper." My back is still turned to him, as I refuse to take my eyes off Kris. When he doesn't reply, I press, "Jasper?"

I can feel his heart pounding against my hand, and it angers me that Kris has gotten to him in this way. But I'll deal with that later.

Thankfully, Jasper's harsh breathing steadies, and he sighs. "Fine. Let's go."

"Looks like I was wrong, love," Kris says while I blanch. "Looks like you're the one who's in control." He leans close and whispers his mistaken observations into my ear.

I pull back horrified, and can't bite my tongue a second longer. "I feel sorry for you if you really think that's how people work. Love isn't about control; it's about respect, something you know nothing about. But with an attitude like yours, it doesn't surprise me you think that way because the only love you'll ever get is from the friends and whores you buy."

Kris' stormy eyes widen and I know I've struck a nerve, but I'm sick of this little brat's temper tantrums.

It stops now.

I don't wait for his smug reply and turn to face Jasper, who also stares at me, stunned by my outburst.

"Let's go."

Jasper nods, and I walk past him, charging up the stairs. I push aside anyone who stands in my way and when I get to our room, I sigh, thankful to be here. I open the door and discover a couple making out on our bed; my anger rises once again.

My anger however, pales in comparison to Jasper's. "Get. Out," he snarls between clenched teeth.

When the amorous couple continues playing tonsil hockey, ignoring Jasper's request, he reveals just how serious he is when he punches the wall forcefully.

"Out!" he yells, his punch echoing off the cabin walls.

His ferocity has them breaking apart and running out of the room terrified. The moment they're out the door, Jasper slams it shut and I jolt with the forceful impact. He begins pacing the room, fisting both hands in his hair.

I watch for a while, not sure what to do, but he's

giving me sea legs, so I sit on the edge of the bed, waiting for him to speak. When he doesn't, I do. "Jasper, you need to calm down. Give me your phone and I'll call Jeremy."

But he continues pacing. Thankfully, a moment later he reaches into his back pocket to pull out his phone. In the process however, I see that his hand is bleeding.

"Jasper," I gasp. "Your hand."

Jasper looks down at it and shrugs. "It's fine. It doesn't hurt."

"Either way, you're bleeding." I jump up and sprint to the bathroom to get a towel.

I run it under some water and head back to find Jasper standing at the window, looking at the bedlam below.

"Why is he such a dick?" he angrily asks—no guessing to whom he's referring.

"I really don't know," I reply, reaching for his injured hand.

He thankfully lets me attend to his wounds. Pressing the towel to his bleeding knuckles, I try and clean it as best as I can. "Do you wanna go home? We can come back in a few days for Jeremy's birthday. I just don't know how you'll survive the week without killing him," I say, half joking.

Jasper shakes his head, pulling his hand away. "No, I'm staying," he stubbornly replies. "And besides, we go back to New York and face a different kind of circus. What's the difference?"

When he flicks his fiery eyes to meet mine, I know

what his next question will be. "What did he say to you down there?"

I bite my lip, clutching the soiled towel in my hands. "I'm sorry," I say, suddenly feeling like I'm going to cry.

"Why are you sorry?" he asks, his gaze focused on my face.

"I dunno," I reply with a defeated shrug. "I just feel like whenever we're together, shit always hits the fan. You've only just come back into my life and things were going amazing because it was just us, but now that other people are involved, it's slowly falling apart. It's like the world doesn't want us to be together or something," I unhappily confess, my lower lip trembling.

"Hey, don't say that," he says, wiping away a stolen tear from my cheek.

"It's the truth," I press. "When you came back to me, I thought this is it. This time, no more drama, no more issues, but was I naive to think that? I mean, love should be easy, right?" More tears follow and before long, I'm crying in Jasper's arms.

"Baby, sshh, don't cry. All great loves have to withstand obstacles."

I scoff at his comment because our obstacles just keep on coming.

Jasper presses, enveloping me tighter against his chest. "Our love *is* easy; it's all the other factors that make it difficult. If it were just you and I, like it was when I first came to New York, then things would be simple. But life, Ava, it's not meant to be easy. It's a giant test, weeding out the fighters from the people who simply roll over and surrender. You've got to experience pain to appreciate pleasure, noise to appreciate silence, and absence to value presence. I'm sorry if you think our love is hard, but I call what we're doing living," he says, his earnest words filled with conviction.

I pull back, wiping away my tears. "I guess I thought you'd come back and things would be different."

"Things *are* different. We've both changed for the better," he says, his words reminding me of Kris's.

"*Have* you changed, Jasper?" I ask, afraid of his reply.

He pulls back, stunned and confused. "What do you mean? Why would you ask me that?" When I don't answer and lower my eyes, he heatedly asks, "What did he say to you?"

"He said that money changes people," I confess. "Has it changed you?"

"What?" he asks, aghast. "No, baby, no. I couldn't give a damn about the money. How could you believe him?"

"I don't, I didn't," I say, shaking my head. "I just...I guess you came back and we didn't really talk about us and what went wrong."

"I thought we agreed to focus on the future? I don't need to discuss how we screwed things up because I'll never make those mistakes ever again," he says passionately. "Is this because of Metro? We'll figure it out."

"It's not just that," I state, brushing my hair out of my face. "Are we naive to think our past won't affect our future? Have we just swept our problems under the rug? Is history repeating itself?"

Jasper stares at me, his face betraying how my words have wounded him. But I want to get everything out in the open because if we're to do this, there are no second chances this time around.

"I'll do whatever you want me to do." He reaches for my hand and presses it against his heart. "I'm still the same man who fell in love with you the night you walked into Little Sisters and changed my life forever."

"I know you are," I say, hating to see his pain. "But these past six weeks, they've been insane. I don't know how much more crazy I can handle."

"Ava," Jasper says, placing his hand over mine. "Please don't scare me. I can't handle this. Not again." He shakes his head and squeezes my fingers tight. "I'll do whatever you want."

His heartfelt plea reveals what I always knew to be true, no matter what our circumstances, Jasper will love me, through and through.

"Jasper, I'm sorry for being such an idiot. I think this is all too much. The year apart was so uneventful and boring, and I guess the past six weeks have just been so full on."

Jasper nods, his eyes turning soft. "I totally get that. If you want to leave, just say the word. I'll do anything for you, baby."

"I know. I'm sorry for my mini freak out." I feel incredibly silly, but I'm glad I got everything off my chest.

"Don't ever say you're sorry for telling me how you feel. We're in this together—a team. Team White and Thompson."

"You mean White," I correct with a smile.

Jasper smirks, my comment obviously making him

happy. "Hell, I'll hyphenate my name for you. I heard it's progressive."

I chuckle. "No, Ava White sounds perfect."

"It sure does," he replies, his smile warming my insides.

At that precise moment, we hear an out of tune guitar outside. My mouth drops open and Jasper closes his eyes for a split second before charging over to the window. Drawing back the curtain, he curses the moment he looks outside. "Son of a bitch."

"What's going on?" I rush over and stand near him.

What I see takes my breath away. Kris is standing in the middle of a human circle, people watching intently as he holds up something above his head.

"No," I gasp, as that *something* is Jasper's guitar.

"He has your guitar!" I obviously state, just in case he can't see what I can.

"I know," he replies calmly.

"You know? Why aren't you going down there to kick his ass?" I ask, my tone rising in anger.

"'Cause you know what? I'm over it," he replies, his fingers clasping around the curtain's lace edge.

"But you love that guitar. It's the first guitar you ever owned. It's your baby," I add, shocked at how calm he is.

"No," Jasper corrects, turning over his shoulder to look at me. "That would be you."

His kind words touch me, but I can't tear my eyes away from what Kris does next. "Sshh," he says, motioning with his hand for the untamed crowd to quieten down. "So, some of you may or may not know that my long lost brother is none other than Jasper White."

The crowd oohs and ahhs at his revelations, and I can't help but wonder where he's going with this. "This right here," he says, pumping his fist into the air and raising Jasper's guitar to the sky like a damn sacrifice, "is his guitar."

I hold my breath, unable to believe what I see next.

"Unluckily for him, I never liked guitar. Actually, I hate it," he states, his eyes rising upward, aware of us watching him. "And the fact that this guitar belongs to him—a person I loathe—you can imagine how much I despise this thing."

I gasp because he wouldn't dare.

"Welcome to the family, *brother*," he snarls, his eyes locked with Jasper's as he violently draws the guitar down, smashing it into a million pieces as it shatters against the cement.

"No!" I scream, my hand flying to my mouth.

"That's rock 'n roll." Kris snickers, holding the broken guitar neck in his hands while the crowd goes wild.

Jasper has remained motionless throughout this entire scene, so I turn to him, afraid of what he's about to do. But he surprises me as he severs Kris' stare and turns to me. "Let's go to bed."

"Bed?" I ask, looking at him like he's lost his mind. "Did you not just see what happened?"

"I saw."

"And you're so calm because...?" I ask, waiting for him to fill in the blanks.

"Because I'm being the bigger one, just like you asked me to. I'm also doing this for Jeremy."

"But your guitar," I press, as I know how much he cherished it.

"It's just a guitar, baby. Gives me an excuse to go guitar shopping," he says, trying to lighten the mood.

I know he's only saying this for my benefit, as he can have a new guitar at the drop of a hat, thanks to his endorsement. But no matter what new guitar he has had in the past, he always comes back to his old one—the first guitar he bought when he sixteen. And now that same guitar is sitting in a sad, broken heap at the feet of a psychopath.

"I love you, Jasper White," I say, stepping forward and placing my palm against his whiskered cheek. "He will never be half the man you are."

Jasper smiles, but the smile looks strained and tired.

I lower my hand and interlace our fingers, hinting he should follow me to the bed. He looks over his shoulder, no doubt to pay his respects to his guitar, before he lets the curtain go and follows my lead.

Sitting on the edge of the bed, I scurry backwards, taking Jasper with me as I slowly lay down. He softly lowers himself onto me and runs a hand through my hair.

"It'll get easier," he says, his beautiful eyes searching mine. "Just please don't leave me."

"I promise you I won't."

"Good," he replies, his tone akin to a whisper. "A broken guitar, I can deal with. But a broken heart," he says with a pause. "Not ever again."

I know exactly what he means. "I'm not going anywhere," I say, meaning every single word.

CHAPTER THIRTEEN
Common Ground

The next morning I wake, wishing last night was a horrible dream. But as I look in the corner where Jasper's guitar once sat, I know it was real. Too real and horrible to even digest.

Jasper is sound asleep beside me, thankfully sleeping after a restless night of tossing and turning. He most likely was replaying the awful image of his prized possession exploding into smithereens. Now that I'm awake, I can't go back to sleep, so I quietly slip out of bed and throw on some clothes before sneaking downstairs.

The house is quiet and I wonder if Jeremy had a chance to speak to Kris once he came home.

The moment I descend the staircase, I want to run back up because it looks like a bomb has exploded and in its wake, it left behind a trail of red and blue cups, chips, and pizza boxes. Groaning, I go into the kitchen to grab a roll of garbage bags and start on the cleanup.

After five bags of rubbish, which don't even make a dent, I decide to go outside and start the cleanup out there because I need the fresh air. I open the door and zone in on the area where Jasper's guitar was sacrificed to the gods of rock 'n roll.

I collect trash along the way, filling two bags before I

stop at the spot where Kris was being a right royal dick to his brother. I scour the floor for any last traces of Jasper's guitar, but sigh when all I see are splintered bits of wood. Nothing remains, which makes me hate Kris even more.

How could he do that? That was a downright malicious thing to do. I'm proud of Jasper for showing such restraint, because I don't think I could show that sort of control. The only good thing that came out of last night was that Jasper and I spoke about our future, and I got whatever stupid insecurities I had off my chest. Coming here is definitely testing us, but in a way, I'm glad we came.

"Good morning, Ava," Jeremy says, interrupting me from my thoughts.

Looking up from scanning the ground, I meet Jeremy's plagued eyes. "Morning, Jeremy. I would ask how you are, but I guess this mess answers for me," I say, gesturing to his ruined lawn.

Jeremy nods, looking far from impressed. "You don't have to do that." He points to the garbage bag I'm carrying. "You weren't the one who made the mess. "

"It's fine. I couldn't sleep anyway. Sorry we interrupted your business dinner," I say, referring to our phone call last night.

Jeremy waves me off. "Please, don't be silly. Yet again, Kris is the one who should be apologizing, not you. How's Jasper?"

Looking at the ground, I see a tiny piece of his broken fret board. "Well, seeing as his guitar got smashed to smithereens before his eyes, I'd say he's a little pissed."

"Oh no," Jeremy gasps, running a hand down his

exhausted face. "I'll buy him another, although, I'm guessing it was irreplaceable?"

"It was his first guitar," I reply, making a sad face.

"This day just keeps gets better and better."

"It's okay. I just don't understand what his problem is."

Jeremy shrugs. "He's never been this bad before."

"He's never acted out like this?" I ask, trying to understand his actions.

"Kris has always been a tough child. Maybe I spoiled him?" Jeremy suggests as a plausible excuse to his asshole behavior.

"Could it do with his mother passing?" I ask, remembering what Kris had said.

"Passing?" Jeremy asks, shocked. "That's what he told you?"

"Yes," I reply, confused.

Jeremy shakes his head. "His mother is very much alive, Ava. My son has always had a very vivid imagination."

That lying S.O.B. He looked me straight in the eye and lied to me. I should be infuriated, but I'm not. I actually feel sorry for him.

"I'm sorry for being personal, but do you still speak to Kris' mom?"

Jeremy sighs, and his somber expression answers my question for me. "I tried to be a good father, I really did. But losing Jasper, I just...no one could ever take his place. It was my fault for ever comparing the two. I thought I did a good job of covering up my feelings, but I guess Kris saw through my lies. I think he hated Jasper even before he knew he existed. It was hard to live up to the big brother who could do no wrong," he confesses with a frown.

"Kris would misbehave more and more because his bad behavior would get him the attention he so desperately craved. The more trouble he got into, the more money I threw his way. I'm not proud of my actions, Ava. I know money can't buy love, but what Danielle did to me, she ruined me. And because of this, Kris' mom, Edith, suffered as well. I just couldn't let go on my past."

"Yeah, well, Danielle has a history of doing that to people," I reply, unable to keep the bitterness from my tone.

"No one is to blame for Kris' bad behavior but me. My detachment is the reason he's tuned into a spoiled little brat."

"Kris is an adult, Jeremy. He knows right from wrong," I argue, refusing to stand by and allow him to take all the blame.

"I know," he says with an appreciative smile. "I just think if I was a better parent, a better husband, then Kris wouldn't act out the way that he has. He's never had someone he's had to share his toys with, and now that Jasper is here, I think he feels threatened. He sees himself as being the bad son, while Jasper is the favored one. I only told him about Jasper a few years ago, but deep down I think he knew something was missing from our family. He blames Jasper for me being a bad parent to him."

I nod because it makes sense. It's hard to live up to someone's ghost because in Jeremy's mind, Jasper was still the innocent three year old little boy Danielle used as a pawn in her sick game, and sadly, I don't think Jeremy ever let that image go. He forever felt like he let Jasper down, and couldn't move on, no matter how hard he tried.

"It'll be okay, Jeremy. Trust me," I say, suddenly struck with an ingenious thought. "I've got an idea."

Jeremy cocks his head to one side. "The last time you said that, I got my son back."

Giving him a small smile, I reply, "Well, here's hoping I can work my magic a second time around."

"**W**ake. Up," I say between kisses as I shower Jasper's face with my love.

"Hmm," he groans, his tone rough and hoarse.

"C'mon, lazy bones. Wake up," I repeat, kissing the tip of his nose.

"No, I think I'll stay asleep because at the moment, my dreams are coming true," he replies, a smirk painting his sinful lips, his eyes remaining shut tight.

"Well, it's your loss. You'll miss out on seeing me naked," I say nonchalantly.

At that precise moment, Jasper's eyes snap open and I chuckle. "Works every time. You're really too easy, White."

"Hey," he says, his bare shoulders rising in a carefree

shrug. "You naked and in my bed is my one weakness," he adds, looking down my tank.

My hands fly up to my chest and he laughs. "You're such a pervert."

He smirks, not denying my claims. "So, now that I'm awake, how 'bout you make good on your word and join me under the covers...with way less clothes on," he says, flicking the strap of my top off my shoulder.

I wiggle out of his reach, as he'll totally distract me otherwise. "So...I was talking to Jeremy," I say, attempting to sound casual.

Jasper doesn't buy it, of course. "Why do I have a feeling I'm not going to like what you're going to say next?"

"Just hear me out," I reply, sitting up against the headboard.

"Now I definitely know I'm in trouble."

I grin. "You know how you said you were being the bigger one last night?"

Jasper raises an eyebrow. "Yes," he replies, his tone suspicious.

"Well, how do you feel about continuing your mature streak?" I ask with an encouraging nod.

"What are you up to?"

"Just let me explain," I quickly say, afraid he'll say no before he even hears my plea.

"Let's hear it," he thankfully says.

"I'm not making any excuses for Kris, because his behavior has been inexcusable."

"Go on," Jasper encourages.

"But I think you'll really regret not knowing your

brother if you walk away without really trying to get to know him," I say in a rushed breath.

Jasper seems to ponder on my statement, and curiously asks, "What do you suggest?"

"Well, maybe you could find common ground."

"How do you propose I do that? I have no idea who he is, or what he likes. Well, apart from spying on my naked girlfriend, and destroying my guitar that is," he bitterly adds.

I choose to ignore his jab. "You're great with people, Jasper. Just try and talk to him."

"I *have* tried," he retorts, sitting up beside me. "Our conversations usually last for no longer than thirty seconds, and the entire time I'm trying to convince myself why killing him is a bad idea."

I bite my lip to stifle my laugh. "I'm not asking you to work miracles, just try and talk to him without the constant cursing and stink eyes. You know you'll regret it if you don't."

"When did you get so smart?" he says with a smirk.

"I learned it from you," I reply. "Jeremy mentioned Kris likes football. Maybe you could ask him to teach you how to play?" I suggest with a shrug.

Jasper looks at me like I've gone mad. "Just in case you've got your wires crossed, football is a sport, not a spa treatment."

"I know," I reply, playfully slapping his arm.

"Well, in that case, you know I don't do sports. Ever. Does this body look like it's built to be a quarterback?" he asks, sweeping his hand down his torso.

I follow the motion, hypnotized by his delicious

frame. "That body is capable of anything. Trust me, I know."

Jasper smirks, but I won't let his dimples distract me. "As sucky as this is, Kris is acting out because he feels threatened by you. Maybe if you show him you're a friend, not a threat, he'll lighten up with the crazy and start acting like a civilized human being."

"Fine," he grumbles, stubbornly folding his arms across his broad chest. "But don't expect me to play nice if he's shitting on my olive branch."

I smile, clapping in excitement. "Gross visuals aside, this is the first step towards getting to know your brother. I know you won't regret it."

"We'll see," he says, unconvinced.

"Hey, that attitude stays off the field," I say, giggling. My comment has my mind wandering to a happy place. "I can't wait to see you in uniform."

Jasper shakes his head, his messy hair flicking up in rebellion. "There's no way I'm wearing that getup. It's bad enough I have to chase after a small ball like a brainless buffoon. If I'm forced to partake in such barbaric rituals, then I'm not going to be wearing tights while doing it."

I can't stop the laugh that bursts free, and Jasper joins in while flipping me onto my back and holding me prisoner.

"You're so going to love being a jock," I tease, as Jasper is so far from being a jock, it's not even funny.

"I highly doubt that. Although," he adds, his eyes lightening up in mischief. "If you agree to be my personal cheerleader, pom poms and all, I may rethink my decision."

"You know, I always wanted to be on the cheer squad," I confess with a smile.

"Really?"

"Yeah, but V threatened to shove my pom poms where the sun don't shine if I did."

Jasper chuckles while kissing my cheek. "Well, now is the time to live out your dreams."

A breath gets caught in my throat when he kisses over my racing pulse, his lips leading lower and lower. As he kisses in the valley between my breasts, I eagerly say, "Go, team go."

CHAPTER FOURTEEN
Game On

"This is ridiculous," Jasper says under his breath.

"You promised." I give his hand a gentle squeeze.

"Well, if he pisses me off, we're outta here." He narrows his eyes when he sees Kris sitting by the breakfast counter, sipping a disgusting looking green juice.

"Just try," I press, and literally push him so he almost bumps into Kris.

When Kris sees us, a look of fear and then arrogance pass over his features. My fingers twitch to slap his face when I remember what he did to Jasper's guitar, but I remain impassive, otherwise, my whole common ground speech would be shot to hell.

"Ah, how'd you sleep? I hope we didn't keep you up," Kris quips, his dark sunglasses slipping down his nose as he looks at us.

Jasper's fingers tighten in mine. "Hi," he says, which comes out hoarse and strained. However, this is an improvement from 'fuck you, you smartass little turd,' which I'm sure is what Jasper would have preferred to say.

Kris looks confused by Jasper's passivity. He pulls in his lips and cocks his head to the side. "Sorry about your guitar." He sniggers, trying another tactic to piss Jasper off. "If it's any consolation, it was a piece of shit anyway. I did the world a favor by putting that piece of junk out of its misery."

Jasper lets out a loud, frustrated breath, and when I steal a glance at him, I have no doubt he's counting to five to stop himself from lashing out. "Whatever, man, I don't care. It's just a guitar," he says casually after a few moments of silence.

The shock is clearly evident on Kris' face, but he plays it off. "Yeah, I'm sure our father will buy you another. He definitely knows how to make all of life's troubles go away by writing out a check," he says, looking at me sharply.

Just as I'm about to tell him to go screw himself, Jasper laughs. I turn to look at him, ensuring he hasn't gone mad. "I don't need Jeremy to buy me anything. I stand on my own two feet, something which you currently know nothing about."

Kris scowls, and I internally groan. This was a bad idea.

However, when Jasper adds, "I'm surprised you're even able to sit straight. You look like shit." I know he means the literal sense; he's obviously nursing a nasty hangover.

Both Kris and my facial expressions are matching, both unbelieving that Jasper is making a joke.

"And if you're going to throw a party, at least listen to

some good music. You need to be introduced to Kurt Cobain and The Beatles."

My mouth couldn't drop any further, and by Kris' silence, I dare say he feels the same.

"I know who Kurt Cobain is," he defensively replies, sitting up straighter, proving to Jasper he's not hung over as he rips off his sunglasses.

"Oh, yeah? Wow, a tween knows some decent tunes, who would have thought?" Jasper says with a smirk.

"I am not a tween. And besides, you're an emo, I've heard your songs.

My heart is forever broken,

And you're the only cure,

I have surrendered to you,

Our love is eternally pure," Kris says, singing the chorus to 'Surrendered,' while mockingly putting his hand over his heart.

"That's 'Surrendered,'" I gasp, unable to help myself.

Kris stops singing. He looks embarrassed to be caught out knowing one of Jasper's songs. "Well, it's on the radio all the time. All annoying tunes get stuck in your head," he says, brushing it off.

Jasper smiles and it's the first genuine one he's had all morning. "Well, you can blame Ava for that one. She was stuck in my head for a year, so now everyone else has to suffer."

I open my mouth and a laughs breaks free—I wasn't expecting that. "Gee, I love you, too."

I can't believe my eyes when I see Kris smile, but I don't make a big deal about it because it's progress.

"So, you like Johns?" Jasper asks, gesturing to Kris' tee.

I'm assuming Johns is a football player, as Kris is wearing a big number eighteen on his white t-shirt.

"Yeah. You know him?" Kris asks, raising a suspicious eyebrow.

"I know of him. My bassist is obsessed with the stupid sport."

"Stupid? Have you ever played?" Kris asks, defending his passion.

"Does it look like I've ever played?" Jasper asks, looking down at his ripped jeans and scuffed Chucks.

"Good point," he replies. "You were probably too busy performing in every school play," he adds with a defiant smirk.

"You're looking at the best Romeo Montague Los Angeles High has ever seen. No one ever rocked those tights like I did," Jasper says with an overconfident shrug.

I'm watching in complete shock as this normal conversation pans out before my eyes, and if I didn't see it, then I wouldn't believe it. But as Jasper gives back just as good as he gets, he chips away at Kris' tough wall, brick by brick. I'm not expecting miracles, but this is a start—a good one.

"How about I teach you how the big boys play?" Kris asks, smugly cocking a brow.

"Show me what you've got...little boy," Jasper replies, arrogantly laughing.

"Game on."

"How did I get roped into playing?" I breathlessly say to Jasper as I tie my hair up into a loose bun.

He shrugs, rubbing the sweat off his brow. "It was your idea to find common ground. It's just too bad that ground is so hard when you fall face first into it." I playfully flip him off in response.

For the past forty-five minutes, Jasper, Kris, Jeremy, and I have been playing touch football, and it goes without saying I suck.

"I thought you two could bond over a ball, while I could bond over a glass of red and a trashy magazine," I huffily reply, shaking out my sore legs.

"Where's the fun in that?" Jasper replies, stretching his arms above his head. "And besides, you're my cheerleader."

"Cheerleaders usually cheer from the sidelines. Not getting their asses kicked by their fiancés."

Jasper laughs as he wraps his hands around my waist, pressing me up against his sweaty chest. "Suck it up, princess. I promise to massage out those tender spots tonight," he says with a promising wink.

That's all the encouragement I need to continue, and it also gives me an idea to make this game a little more interesting. Well, for me anyway. Lifting up the hem of his black tee, I rip it off his head and throw it to the sidelines. "There, much better. If you're going to beat my ass, at least you can be naked doing it."

"And you call me the pervert," he says, standing before me looking like a total god.

"Think of it as foreplay," I whisper, standing up on tippy toes and giving him a light kiss.

He tastes of the raspberry Gatorade he just drank, and I kiss him deeper, loving the taste.

"Break it up, you two," Kris says, running over to where we stand making out. "Ava, you do realize you're kissing the enemy, right?"

I have been teamed up with Jeremy, while Kris and Jasper are on the same team. So far, so good.

"I know," I say with a sigh. "He's just so pretty."

Jeremy chuckles, looking carefree and relaxed as he walks over to us. He no doubt is also relieved my plan hasn't nosedived. "Okay, you ready?" he asks me as I groan.

"No."

My plea goes unnoticed however, as all the boys jog out into the open field. I unenthusiastically trail behind, standing behind Jeremy, who has the ball.

"Red 24! Red 24! Hut! Hut! Hike!" he shouts, throwing me the ball.

I scream, elated that I've caught it, and start running like a madwoman. This is the first time I've caught the ball without dropping it, and I turn over my shoulder to laugh at Jasper and Kris. However, what I see is Jasper clutching his sides laughing, while Kris is doing the same.

"Wrong way! Ava, you're going the wrong way!"

Jeremy yells, which explains why the two brothers are currently laughing their asses off at my expense.

"Damn," I breathlessly curse and turn back around.

Jasper stops laughing and runs directly my way. Who would have thought he was so damn fast? I try and dodge him by shifting to the left, but he reads my plan of attack and tackles me to the ground. I fall hard, and Jasper falls with me.

"Get the ball!" I hear Kris yell out to Jasper, but Jasper ignores him as he brushes the hair out of my eyes.

"Sorry, baby," he apologetically says, bracing his full weight on his palms, suspending himself above me. "I didn't mean to tackle you so hard. I forgot how small you are. Are you all right?"

I can't help but smile at Jasper's concern. Right about now, I bet Kris wishes he was on Jeremy's team because Jasper and I are obviously incapable of being on opposing teams.

"I'm fine," I reply, assuring him with a nod. But my head spins with the action. "I think I might call it a day."

Jasper concurs, and I can't help myself as I trace a finger around his nipple. "I kinda like seeing you all sweaty and sporty," I confess, watching the way his smooth skin reacts to my touch. "Please don't stop on my account."

"If *you* don't stop, then we'll be playing a very different ball game," he cheekily says, licking his lower lip. His long hair falls over his face.

I open my mouth, shocked, but also a little turned on. Sadly, Kris interrupts our moment, his shadow blocking the sun from highlighting all the perfect planes on Jasper's chest.

"Ava, no offense, but you suck."

Turning to look at him, I chuckle. "None taken. I'm going to call it a day, but please, continue playing. I have a feeling I'll have more fun watching from the sidelines."

As I hear Jasper's small intake of breath, I place both hands against his chest, his heart racing under my palms. He begrudgingly rises, offering me his hand to help me stand.

"You game, bro?" Kris asks, and although it's a slip of the tongue, I can see Jasper beam at the mishap.

"You bet. It'll be fun to gang up on the old man," he replies, slapping Kris on the shoulder.

Poor Jeremy has no idea what he's in for.

After two hours of watching the boys fight over the ball, I decided to go upstairs and take a shower because I was covered in mud and sweat. I'm now sitting on the bed, propped up against a few dozen pillows, reading a book.

I can proudly say that today was a success. I'm not expecting a simple game of football to undo whatever issues Kris has with Jasper and Jeremy, but at least it's a start. Jasper showed Kris what an amazing person he is, and how he's not the enemy in this situation.

I don't ever remember seeing Jeremy so happy, not

even when he told Jasper he was his father. I guess the reason is because now he's claiming back both sons, not just one. Once I'm done reading about Mr. Darcy, I plan on making the boys a hearty dinner because they're probably famished from their vigorous day.

The door opens and I raise my eyes to see a dirty, sweaty, topless Jasper stroll in with flustered cheeks and wild, unkempt hair. The moment he rewards me with his trademark dimpled smirk, I inexplicably squeeze my thighs together, incredibly turned on by the amazing visual before me.

"Hi," I say, my tone breathless and flighty, betraying my sudden racing pulse.

Jasper's clear eyes scan down my body, stopping when he gets to the junction between my legs. I'm wearing short denim shorts, but I may as well be naked. I feel completely exposed under his penetrating stare. He closes the door behind him, and with two huge strides, he's standing at the foot of the bed, reaching out and latching onto my arm. He pulls me towards him and I come willingly, kneeling before him and pressing my chest to his. He smells of dirt, sweat and grass—a surprisingly heady combination which has my already interested libido clawing at the walls.

The air sizzles between us, and I anticipate Jasper's every move, as he has still not spoken a word. With his pointer finger, he slowly strokes down the side of my neck, dipping over my chin and tracing over the lace collar on my camisole. His sensual touch is sending me wild, and if he doesn't kiss me soon, I will take control.

Jasper reads my desperation loud and clear and I

don't know who lunges for whom first because the moment our lips touch, nothing else matters. I claw at his bare shoulders, my palms sliding over his damp skin, still moist from his brisk activities on the field. His eager fingers pull up the hem of my top and he pulls away for a split second—enough time to tear the garment off my head.

When our lips reconnect, Jasper sweeps his hands up my sides, walking his fingers to my breasts. I'm wearing a push-up bra, and he growls low in his throat when he palms both my breasts hungrily, pushing them together to get more in his hands. I drive my chest forward, needing faster and harder friction.

Jasper senses my longing. He violently breaks our kiss, thrusts both bra cups down, and latches onto my pearled nipple. I moan in absolute bliss as his warm, hungry mouth is exactly what I need. He rolls the other between his fingers, working both breasts over with a fierce desire. I feel my body beginning to grow slick with desire.

Frustrated with the lace in the way, he impatiently unhooks my bra. It snaps open and gives him full access to my chest. He switches from one breast to the other, tonguing and rubbing each nipple until I'm crying out in need. My knees are starting to get a cramp, and my body is shaking from fatigue and desire.

"Lie down," he softly commands, licking his lips as I eagerly obey.

His gaze sweeps down my body and stops once it lands on the button of my shorts. He places one knee on the mattress and bends forward, resting his hand by my head. With the other, he cups my neck and then slides his palm down the middle of my chest, leaving a trail of passion behind. He runs his finger along my waistband, and I shift my hips, frantic for him to take them off.

He gives into my silent plea and snaps open the button with a smile. His hair flicks forward as he bends down and kisses just below my navel. "You smell so good," he says, humming in delight.

I clutch at the comforter underneath me, raising my hips and moaning low in my throat. His touch is every-thing I want and need, but I'm greedy and I want more. Jasper gives in and with swift fingers, he unzips my shorts, pulling them down my legs. I have on my skimpy black underwear and he hisses the moment he sees them, as they barely cover a thing.

He lowers himself between my legs, and I spread them to accommodate his muscular form. Gently bending my right knee, he exposes me completely to his predatory stare. I'm panting and trembling, needing him to do something other than love me from afar. I cry in relief when he slips his fingers into my underwear.

Feeling how geared up I am to take things to the next level, Jasper says, his voice laden with craving, "Always so ready to go."

How can I not be? I mean, I have the hottest man on earth worshipping every inch of my body.

He's driving me crazy however, as he scoots around where I want him to be. "Jasper," I groan, latching onto his wrist and coaxing him to take things further.

He chuckles, enjoying me begging for what we both

want. "Yeah, baby?" he smugly says, inching his finger into me.

I gasp, the deep intrusion exactly what I need, but it's still not enough.

I'm still clutching Jasper's wrist, encouraging him to drive in deeper and touch my throbbing center, but as usual, he dances around my sweet spot. He skillfully slips out of my grip and before I can protest, he yanks my underwear to the side and lowers his mouth onto my core.

The action is so quick I yelp in surprise, but that yelp turns to a low guttural moan when he laps at my entrance in one long lick. Tossing my head back, I squeeze my eyes shut. The feeling is just too much.

He buries his head further into me and wraps his hand around my waist, pushing my hips forward so I'm shamefully riding his face. But my bashfulness can take a backseat, as my hormones are currently behind the wheel.

He licks where I want. Touches where I need. And sucks where I yearn.

Every time his tongue drives into me, he brings me closer and closer to the edge. I uncurl my fist and latch onto his soft hair, pressing his face deeper. The action sends Jasper wild and when he twirls his tongue in just the right way, I know I'm seconds away from coming.

A moment later, he sucks on my center and I cry out loudly. I quickly let go of his hair and shove my fist into my mouth to mute my screams. He's relentless and doesn't stop until he's drawn every last tremor from my body.

My insides are singing, my heart is pounding against my ribcage, and I don't know if I'll be able to walk for the next ten minutes, but it's exactly how things should be.

Opening one eye, I squint when the bright sunshine hits my pupils. I look down at Jasper, lying between my legs with a satisfied smile on his face.

"Thank you," I say, my voice hoarse thanks to my noisy vocal performance.

As I open the other eye, Jasper slides up my body, rolling onto his back beside me. I see that he's very affected by what we just did, and I tell my groggy brain it's now my turn to return the favor, but I seriously doubt I'll be able to move for the next thirty minutes.

"I promise I'll return the favor," I say with a yawn. "Just let me get the feeling back to my legs."

Jasper shakes his head, his rosy cheeks flushed with his desire. "Don't worry about it. That was all for you."

"Not that I'm complaining, but why?"

"Because you deserve it. Your ingenious plan actually worked, and Kris has yet to look at me with that murderous gleam in his eyes."

I laugh, but my entire body hurts and I know I'll be sore tomorrow, but it's so worth getting my ass whipped because the smile on Jasper's face makes anything worthwhile.

"Well, I'm glad. At least my ass whooping wasn't in vain," I say with a wink.

When Jasper smirks, I know I'm in trouble. "I have an ingenious plan of my own."

"Oh, yeah?" I ask, my body beginning to heat all over again.

"Yeah," he replies. "Flip round to your front."

I do as he asks, curious what this ingenious plan of his entails.

"Ooh, you did get an ass whooping." He runs a hand over my butt. "I promise I'll be gentle," he adds, sliding his finger up my torso and finding my parted mouth. "But this time," he huskily whispers. "Bite on this." He slips his finger into my mouth as he slithers down my body, nestling between my legs once more.

As I hear his belt being unbuckled, I can't help but think his ingenious plan is quite clever after all.

CHAPTER
FIFTEEN
Missing Home

The next few days pass by rather quickly. And thankfully, uneventfully.

After Jasper and Kris sorted out their differences on field, their union seemed to affect their off field behavior, as they weren't constantly trying to kill one another. Well, not all the time, anyway.

They still had their fair share of arguments, but they were the petty arguments most siblings have, like who's the coolest or better looking. All in all, the whole common ground idea has seemed to work and I couldn't be happier.

Now that I can focus on something other than Jasper and Kris wanting to throttle one another, I've decided to give Metropolis a call and see how it's going. I must admit, it's been nice to not worry about food orders, rosters, and menus, but I do miss it. Metropolis has been my home for the past year, and I'm curious to know if it's survived without me.

I don't know why, but I dial Michel instead of Sara. He answers on the third ring.

"Bonjour, Cheri."

"Hi, Michel," I reply, smiling when I hear his greeting. "How's it going? Do you miss me?"

Michel chuckles. "*Oui*, we miss you. It's not the same without you, but it's going well. The paparazzi have finally given up and things have returned to normal."

I let out a sigh of relief. "Oh, that's great news. You don't know how happy I am to hear you say that."

"I can imagine. When will you be back?" he asks as I hear him fiddling around with the pots and pans.

"Next Tuesday. Is that all right?"

"You're the boss, *Cheri*. If it's okay by you, then it's okay by me. We'll manage without you," he says, tongue in cheek.

I frown, hating how true his comment probably is.

"But only just," he adds, and I figure he must have been able to read my silence for what it was.

Jasper opens the door and peeks his head into the room. I give him a small wave and he nods when he sees I'm on the phone.

"Oh, I forgot to tell you. Yolanda called," Michel says, and I can hear the revulsion in his tone.

The moment I hear her name, my teeth clench. "And?" I ask, looking at Jasper, who raises an eyebrow.

"Well, she said that Metro's ep will be screening next Thursday evening."

"Oh, that's awesome. That's so soon," I reply, feeling nervous. Suddenly, I'm struck with an idea. "Do me a favor?"

"Of course."

"Let's close Metropolis early on Thursday. Can you let guests know? Maybe put up a sign, and also put a note on the website."

"I can do that. May I ask why?" Michel asks, most likely confused by my request.

"What better way to thank staff than by eating some amazing food, and drinking some even better wine, and watching Metropolis shine on the big screen? It'll be a little impromptu party to say thank you to everyone for working so hard. I mean, it was a joint effort," I explain with a smile as Jasper nods in agreement.

"Sounds like a wonderful idea. I'll let everyone know. I'll also see if we can hire a big screen," Michel adds cheekily.

"Not too big. I'm not interested in finding out if TV really does add ten pounds to your ass. And I'm guessing that'll be doubled on a big screen."

Michel chuckles. "Impossible. You could never look bad. In fact, a ten foot Ava could be dangerous to one's health."

I look at Jasper, who's leaning against the doorjamb, arms crossed. I know he can't hear my conversion, but my flushed cheeks have totally given me away.

"Well, er, thanks. I'll see you next week."I totally ignore his compliment. "If you need me...I mean," I say, quickly backtracking. "If you need my help, just let me know," I conclude, guiltily averting my eyes.

"Will do. See you next week," Michel says, acting normal.

Maybe I'm just reading into things. "Okay. See you next week."

Tossing my phone onto the bed, I meet Jasper's far from impressed gaze.

"So, how's your boyfriend?" he teases, his tone revealing he's thankfully joking.

"He's not my boyfriend," I reply, standing up and walking towards him. "That's your job."

Jasper clears his throat twice. "Boyfriend?"

I chuckle and wrap my arms around his neck. "Sorry. Fiancé."

"Better," he says with a smile, interlacing his hands around my waist.

"Michel said the episode with Adelia is airing next Thursday. I suggested closing Metro early and having a screening night with all the staff."

"Awesome idea," Jasper says with a nod. "You all deserve to unwind and watch what a great job you did."

I smile, fiddling with the chain around his neck. "I thought so, too. You're invited, of course. You were also part of making the magic happen."

Jasper smirks, his dimple hugging his whiskered cheek. "Why, thank you. I was planning on coming anyway, seeing as I'll be leaving for London the next day."

My smile instantly disappears as it slipped my mind that he was leaving so soon.

"Hey, none of that," he says, lifting the corner of my mouth with his pointer. "You'll come join me when you can, right?"

I nod. "Of course. I just got you back," I reply, hating the thought of being apart.

"And I'm back for good," he says. "Once I'm back, we can talk about what you want to do."

The big, fat elephant has returned and I lower my

eyes, as this topic doesn't seem to be getting any easier. All I know is I want to be with Jasper.

"Okay," I reply, seeing no point in ruining our time away with issues that don't seem to be resolvable any time soon.

"Up for a game of football?" Jasper asks, and I groan.

"You can't be serious? Did you not see my ass getting beaten?" I stupidly ask, blushing the moment the words leave my lips.

Jasper raises an eyebrow, and a sinful grin slowly spreads from cheek to cheek. "Oh, I saw," he replies, his tone full of seduction. "And I liked what I saw. A lot."

"Let's go play football," I say, rolling my eyes.

"After all this time, you're still so shy. I love that about you. Among many other things," he adds, his hand dipping to my butt.

I chuckle, dancing out of his clutches. "Let's go, Casanova."

Jasper laughs and latches onto my hand as we make our way downstairs. "You know, Kris was right. You do suck," he playfully says as we walk outside.

"Gee, don't hold back or anything," I reply, shielding my eyes as the sun is bright.

"Well, you know that you do. So to even things up, I thought we needed to add a few more players."

"Oh, that's just great. More people to witness my lack of ball skills," I reply, tongue in cheek.

"Ball skills are not the first words I want to hear out of my best friend's mouth, thank you very much," says a disgusted voice to my left.

If it wasn't for Jasper latching onto my hand, I would

have fallen flat on my face, as the voice I just heard cannot belong to the person who I think it belongs to.

"V?" I ask, whipping around.

But it is her. Veronica is standing before me, holding a football under her arm.

"Oh my god!" I scream, running over and throwing my arms around her. "What are you doing here?"

"Nice to see you, too," she replies, hugging me back just as hard. "I heard you're embarrassing us girls on the field, so it's time to even up the score."

I can't let go and tears instantly spring to my eyes. "I can't believe you're here. I've missed you so much."

V squeezes me tighter. "I've missed you too, babe."

After I've squished the hell out of her, I pull away, needing to look at my best friend to ensure she's real. Her bright pink bangs are now red, and the intense color seems to highlight the brightness of her brilliant green eyes. Her lip and nose piercings catch the sunshine, and as I look at her inner left arm, the word 'Cara' stares back at me in an elegant script.

"Yes, I copied your sappy fiancé." She rubs her bicep, stroking over her daughter's name.

I can't help but laugh as I hear Jasper scoffing behind me. "Veronica, you say the sweetest things."

Now that I'm not behaving like a crazy woman and can think relatively straight, I can't help but wonder why she's here. Not that I'm complaining, but where's Lucas and Cara? Has something happened?

"Oh god, is everything okay? Has something happened? Are Lucas and Cara okay?" I ask, barely taking a breath.

V smiles and places both hands on my arms. "Yes, Cara is perfect and Lucas is...well," she says, looking over my shoulder. "Lucas is still a pain in the ass."

"Hey, I heard that!"

"Lucas?" I gasp, turning behind and seeing his smiling face. "What the hell? You're here too?" I impolitely say, as that came out a lot ruder than I meant.

Lucas and Jasper laugh, and Jasper shakes his head at me. "Well, we can always leave if you don't want us here," Lucas playfully says, his scruffy hair falling into eyes.

"No!" I say, practically tackling Lucas to the ground.

"Jesus. J, you said she sucked at playing ball, but with a grip this tight, she'd be able to strangle her opponents to death," Lucas says, his breath winded.

I instantly loosen my grip around Lucas and pull away, embarrassed. "I'm so sorry. I'm just so excited you're here."

"We can see that," Jasper says, smiling from ear to ear.

Suddenly, his smug smile and relaxed demeanor makes me think he was behind this little reunion. "You did this?" I point my finger at him.

Jasper's cheeky smile disappears, and he defensively cups his privates. "Um, yes?" he says, phrasing his comment as a question, not knowing if that's the right answer or not.

But it is. It's the best answer I've heard all day.

"Jasper..." I say, taking a step towards him. "This is the nicest thing you've ever done for me."

"Ever?" he asks, his smug smile returning while I roll my eyes.

Before I can stop myself, I run over and throw myself into his arms. He catches me, letting out a loud chuckle. "So, you're happy?" he asks, rubbing my back as I bury my face into his neck.

"Happy? Happy doesn't even begin to describe how I'm feeling right now," I reply, tightening my arms around him.

"Good. Only the best for my girl." He kisses my head.

I still can't believe my best friends are here. What Jasper did was so incredibly thoughtful. I don't know why, but I won't question it because I'm so damn happy.

"Ahem," V says, clearing her throat. "Could you please keep the PDA to a minimum? I mean, children are present."

"What?" I gasp, letting Jasper go and spinning around. "Cara!"

When I see the apple of my best friend's eye grinning broadly in the arms of Jeremy, extending out her chubby little hands, demanding a cuddle, I lose all composure and burst into tears. This is all too much.

"Don't worry, Ava, she makes me cry, too," V whispers, cupping her mouth while I burst into a half laugh, half sob.

"Look at how big you've grown," I say to Cara, wiping away my tears.

Unable to tear my eyes away from the cherub in front of me, Jeremy smiles and hands me the bundle of joy. "She's demanding to see her Aunt Ava." Cara coos the moment I cuddle her.

"Oh, you're so squishy," I say, hugging her tight.

V laughs. "Are you calling my baby fat?" she asks, while I look at her, horrified.

"Don't listen to your momma." I cover Cara's ears. "Your momma is a crazy pants."

Everyone bursts out into fits of laughter, although, I dare say Lucas is the loudest as he probably agrees with me wholeheartedly.

"Yeah, well, this momma is hungry," V says, looping her arm through mine.

I hold onto Cara tightly while V chuckles. "She won't break, Ava. Trust me, I've tried."

Shaking my head, I look into Cara's big hazel eyes and sigh. "Yup, kiddo, your mom is a total crazy pants."

"So you're here for the entire week?" I ask V for the hundredth time.

"Yup," she replies around a mouthful of pretzels.

"I can't believe Jasper did this," I say, shaking my head.

"Why not? He loves you, you bonehead. And what better way to express that love than by flying your bestie over to come see you," she replies, making a mini pretzel tower on the counter.

"I know, but it's just so—"

"Jasper," she says, filling in the blanks.

I smile. "Yes, it so is."

V told me Jasper organized for her and Lucas to fly over and stay for Jeremy's birthday. Apparently Lucas was anxious about touring, and had been calling Jasper every day, freaking out that their tour was going to flop. Jasper was sick of him blowing up his phone, so he decided to fly him and V out to spend the week with us.

I know it wasn't his intention to do so, but now that we're all together, I'm more homesick than ever. And by home, I mean L.A.

"What's got you so serious?" V asks, interrupting my thoughts.

"I miss L.A.," I confess, watching Cara crawl around on the floor.

"Well, L.A. misses you," she replies, tying her long black hair into a ponytail. "Have you decided what you're going to do?"

"No," I glumly reply. "I'm kind of putting it off until I have to deal with it."

"When's your deadline?"

"After the boys get back from Europe," I reply, reaching for my water.

"How long do you plan on staying there? I mean, I know you don't want to leave. But the longer you leave it, the harder it'll be."

I nod, letting out a frustrated breath. "I know, you're totally right."

"But..." she says, waiting for me to continue.

"But, I just feel like I'm giving up before I'm ready to leave," I reply, hating that I sound like a broken record.

"I understand," she says with a nod.

"And?" I say, waiting for her sarcasm.

"And nothing," she replies with a shrug.

"That's it? You're not going to grill me?" I ask, raising an incredulous brow.

"There's nothing I can say that you haven't already told yourself," she wisely says. "This decision is yours and yours alone. You know I want you back home, but this is your life, your career. I know you won't make this decision lightly. So whatever choice you make, I'll support you." I stare at her like she's grown a second head.

"Well, thank you, V," I say, still waiting for her second head to emerge.

"I could tell you what a fucking idiot you are, but what would be the point?" she honestly says, revealing the true V I know and love.

"Phew," I say, mockingly wiping my head. "I thought you got all mature on me."

"As if, don't let that baby fool you," she says. She points at Cara, who is eating a pillow.

V shrugs and pops a grape in her mouth. "You'll figure it out, babe, just like you always do. No doubt you'll go the long way trying, but in the end, I know it'll work out."

I smile. Here's hoping she's right.

CHAPTER SIXTEEN
Games

"I'm going to need an extra seat to fly home, babe," V says to Lucas as she spoons up her second helping of grits.

We're all sitting around the breakfast table, surrounded by so much food I think I've died and gone to food heaven. As I look around the table, I can't help but think how perfect this is. Even Kris seems to have warmed to everyone, and doesn't scowl at Jasper every time he opens his mouth. Maybe things are looking up.

"So what do you plan on getting up to today?" Jeremy asks, looking at Jasper.

Jasper shrugs as he sips his coffee.

"Maybe we could have an acoustic jam?" Lucas suggests, oblivious to the fact that Jasper's guitar is no longer with us.

Kris quickly reaches for his juice, looking anywhere but at Jasper.

"Nah, man," Jasper says casually. "Let's take the day off. How 'bout I beat your ass at a game of ball?"

Reaching for his hand under the table, I give it a gentle squeeze. He could have been an ass and ratted Kris out, but instead he decided to derail the topic by choosing Lucas' one weakness—basketball.

"You're on, White," Lucas says, rubbing his hands together sinisterly.

"You game, Kris?"

Kris looks surprised that Jasper would include him, but he plays it off. "Sure, why not. I've got nothing better to do."

"Kris!" Jeremy says, his silverware smashing onto his plate as he throws them down. "I would appreciate you showing a little more gratitude to your brother."

"Dad," Jasper says, shaking his head. "It's fine."

I silently watch, afraid what's going to happen next. I thought the bonding over football smoothed out all issues, but looks like I was wrong.

"Whatever," Kris grumbles, rolling his eyes. "Thank you, King Jasper."

Jeremy huffs, bunching his napkin in his fist. "Kristopher..."

Kris kicks back his chair, standing abruptly. "Save the speech for someone who cares, Jeremy."

My mouth almost hits the table, as I'm surprised at his hostility. V stops shoveling eggs into her mouth and watches the exchange with interest.

"What did I miss?" she whispers, leaning into me.

"I have no idea," I reply, watching Kris leave the room "Because I must have missed it too."

I let out a breath of relief when I see Kris stroll down the stairs, dressed in sweats and a loose tee.

"What's his problem?" V asks, pushing down her shades as she watches Kris walk towards Jasper.

"I told you on the phone, he's a pig. But I thought things were getting better. I mean, he seemed to really warm to Jasper when they played football," I say, disappointed.

"So I take it he doesn't like Jasper? Or Jeremy?" she asks, sipping her Coke.

"I don't know. Jeremy thinks he acts out because he spoiled him. He also thinks he's to blame for his bad behavior."

"Kris is a grown man," V rebuts, which was my exact response to Jeremy.

"I know, I said the same thing to Jeremy. But Jeremy thinks Kris' bad behavior stems from him being a bad father."

"I don't believe that's even possible," V says, scoffing. "All I've seen Jeremy do is fawn over Jasper."

"I know, and that's the problem," I reply with a sigh.

V's mouth forms into an O of understanding. "Kris is jealous," she says, figuring it out.

"Yup, even before he knew who Jasper was, he hated him," I reply sadly.

"Well, that sucks for Jasper. He can't help that his mother is the Whore of Babylon," V says as she pops her gum.

I can't stop the loud laugh that rumbles from my chest, and V joins because Danielle is certainly that, amongst other things. It's just like old times. Jasper looks over and shakes his head, as I know he's given up on trying to decipher our foolishness.

After we've stopped cackling like mad women, we settle into our lounge chairs to watch our men play ball.

"So, what are the rules?" Kris asks, shaking out his legs.

"The rules are...try and keep up," Jasper smugly replies, turning his black baseball cap around.

"That won't be a problem. I have about ten years on you," he replies with a smart grin.

"Yeah, well, those ten years are going to come in handy, seeing as your partner is like a hundred years older than everyone," Jasper teases, looking at Jeremy as he walks down the stairs.

"No way," Kris says, shaking his head. "I'm not playing with him."

"Too bad, we need even teams. And besides, I think it'll be good for you two to be on the same team for once," Jasper replies, no longer talking about basketball.

"Whatever," Kris grumbles, running a hand through his thick hair. "Just try and keep up, old man," he adds when Jeremy stands beside him.

Jeremy smiles, but it doesn't quite reach his eyes.

"Okay, so the teams are, me and Lucas, and you and Kris," Jasper says to Jeremy, who happily nods.

The boys take their positions and Jasper stands center court, bouncing the ball with a cocky smile. "You ready to get your ass whipped, Dad?"

Jeremy smiles and this time, it reaches his entire face. "Give it your best shot, son."

Kris rolls his eyes. "Just pass the damn ball already."

Jasper laughs. "You asked for it."With a quick pass, he bounces the ball to Lucas, who shoots up the court like a pro.

V squeals and claps excitedly. "He may be a pain in my ass, but holy shit, he's worth it. Look at that package," she says, licking her lips as her eyes zero in on Lucas' junk.

"Um, no, I'll pass, thanks," I say, making a grossed out face. "And besides, I've got my own package to look at."

We both watch our boys excitedly, and I can't help but admire Jasper's agile body as he runs up the court, laughing as he rebounds the ball from Kris' lame goal attempt. A sliver of his hardened stomach is revealed as he jumps up, and I bite my lip to stop my moan of approval slipping free.

After ogling the boys for ten minutes, V and I put our tongues back in our mouths and settle into our lounges. "So, have you been online?" she asks, sipping her water.

"No," I reply, tying my hair up into a high bun. "I'm trying to avoid it for as long as I can."

"Why?"

Sparing no detail, I tell her about Yolanda and my ever so pleasant experience with her.

"This bitch sounds like trouble," she says, shaking her head after I'm done telling her my woes.

"She *is* trouble," I reply with a sigh. "I'm actually dreading the Metropolis episode."

"Why?"

I haven't told V about Michel because as far as I'm concerned, there's nothing to say. But Jasper seems to think otherwise.

"Well...there's this new guy at work. His name is Michel." V lowers her glasses to glare at me.

"No, no, it's nothing like that," I quickly say, my hands raised in surrender.

"Go on," she encourages, still frowning at me.

"He's the reason why Adelia was at Metropolis in the first place. He's her son," I explain, while V continues looking at me, awaiting more information.

"Anyway, Jasper seems to think he's, um, er..." I say, stumbling over my words because saying them aloud is ridiculous.

"This Michel better not have eyes for your... beignets," V states heatedly.

"My what?" I ask, but quickly realize what's she referring to as she's pointing at my chest. "V!" I scold, my hands flying up to cover my breasts.

"What?" she says. "I tend to agree with Jasper on this," she concludes, shaking her head.

"You haven't even heard me out," I say, rolling my eyes.

"Don't need to. Jasper is a better judge of character than you are and if he thinks this dude—" She leaves the sentence hanging, waiting for me to fill in the blanks.

"Has the hots for me," I finish for her, pulling a face.

"Then I believe him. You need to fire him, pronto."

"But I can't. He hasn't done anything wrong," I refute, as firing Michel is not even an option.

"I think his wandering eyes are a good enough reason as any," she stubbornly replies.

"He doesn't have—" But I don't finish my sentence because this topic isn't worth justifying as I seem to be the only person who doesn't think Michel is up to no good.

"What is it with people interfering with your happiness?" V asks, throwing her hands up in defeat. "First Delilah, now Michel. You guys better not break up again, Ava. This is your first and final warning; I'll break your legs if you do."

"I can assure you, Michel is nothing like that tramp," I reply, shifting away from her threats of violence.

"Uh huh," V says, unconvinced.

Just as I'm about to defend Michel, I hear raised voices coming from the court.

"That was out!" Kris yells, pointing to the boundary line.

"Nuh uh," Lucas replies, bouncing the ball around his back.

"It so was. You're cheating," Kris retorts, storming over to Lucas, who runs circles around him, untroubled.

V and I watch closely, not sure what's gotten into Kris, but as he storms over to Jasper, we both jump up, knowing it's time to intervene.

"Chill out, man," Jasper says calmly, his hands out to his sides. "It's only a game."

"Well, I don't play with cheaters," Kris replies angrily, pointing to the line. "That shot was clearly out!"

"Kris, calm down," Jeremy says, walking over to him. "Like Jasper said, it's only a game."

"Oh, typical. Side with the golden boy, as usual," he spits out, while both Jeremy and Jasper pull back, stunned.

"Mind your tongue," Jeremy says, looking appalled.

V and I wisely remain silent off to the side, only mediating if things get out of hand.

"Here then," Jasper says, passing the ball to Kris with a forceful throw.

He's taken off guard and the ball hits him square in the jaw. Everyone can see it's an accident, everyone except Kris. "You asshole!" He rubs his chin. "You did that on purpose."

"It was an accident. I'm sorry," Jasper says between clenched teeth as his patience is wearing thin.

Kris shakes his head angrily as he storms toward him. "Yeah, I'm sure it was."

"Walk it off, Kris," Jeremy says, arms extended as he stands in front of Jasper.

Kris stops dead in this tracks and glares at both men. "Whatever, this game is lame, anyways. I'm outta here." He shoulders past Jeremy, bumping into Jasper as he storms off court.

Jasper stands still, his chest rising and falling quickly, but he thankfully doesn't take off after Kris, demanding what the hell his problem is.

"He doesn't like to lose," Jeremy says as if to explain Kris' irrational behavior.

"With an attitude like that, that's all he'll be doing," Jasper replies, no longer referring to sports.

Jeremy doesn't reply, he simply nods because he knows Jasper is right. "Sorry, son."

"Again, not your fault," he replies, angrily walking off the court.

V looks at me and I shrug. "Great, like our lives weren't complicated enough."

CHAPTER SEVENTEEN
Happy Birthday Blues

"Pass me the balloons, love?"

"If you call me 'love' one more time you'll be using your ass to blow these up," V says, throwing him the packet.

It's fair to say Kris has met his match in the form of Veronica Donovan.

Kris smirks, loving the constant banter between them, which has been going on for hours. The past few days have been a little tense, thanks to Kris being a pain in the ass. Kris and Jasper still have their moments, but the way Kris watches Jeremy when he interacts with Jasper reveals his problem is with his father, not his brother. Jasper is just caught in the middle of this stupid rivalry—one he wishes to take no part in.

But sibling rivalry is going to have to take a backseat because today is Jeremy's birthday. Because we've acquired a small army over the course of the week, we thought it would be fun to organize the party for him.

I, of course, am taking care of the food, V and Kris are in charge of decorations, and Jasper and Lucas are to arrange entertainment. Things are going really well, and watching Jasper and Lucas joke around and be goofballs reminds me of old times. There's no denying that being around my friends has really made me question my decision to stay in New York. Nothing was ever set in stone, but I was more inclined to stay, rather than go. But now I find myself wanting nothing more than to jump on a plane and fly back to L.A. with Lucas and V.

I'm mixing the cake batter when a little hand tugs at my leg. Looking down, I see Cara sitting at my feet, gesturing with grabby hands that she wants to be picked up. I give in as I could never say no to those eyes.

"Hello, my little Moon Pie," I say, bending down and picking her up.

She coos in response, her beautiful, cheeky smile reminding me so much of V's. She reaches out, indicating that she wants the wooden spoon I was mixing with.

"How about we get you your own spoon instead?" I suggest, hunting through the drawers to find her baby cutlery.

When I find her plastic spoon, she instantly screams in excitement and I quickly give it to her, afraid she'll bite my hand off if I don't. As she sticks it into her mouth, a glob of drool runs down her chin and onto my wrist.

I laugh, shaking my head. "Normally kiddo, drooling is gross. But you can make anything look cute."

Cara coos in agreement while I chuckle and carry on mixing my batter with her sitting snugly on my hip. I'm deciding what to do next when I feel someone watching my every move. Raising my eyes, I see Jasper watching me closely. His gaze is one of utter love, and I realize he's not only watching me, but also Cara.

I never gave much thought to having a baby, that was until I thought I was going to be a mom. Jasper was so happy when he thought I was pregnant, and judging by the faraway look in his eyes, I dare say the thought still brings a tear to his eye.

"Watch out," V says into my ear as she reaches for the streamers. "I think someone is clucky."

I don't know whether she means me or Jasper, because either way, she's right.

God dammit, like I needed another complication to add to my every growing list.

I'm slipping on my little black dress when Jasper emerges from the bathroom looking good enough to eat.

He totally makes black jeans, boots, and a black shirt, with sleeves rolled up to his elbows, work. I smile when I see he's wearing his ring, claiming to the world that in his eyes, we're already married.

"Zip me up?" I ask, brushing my curled hair to one shoulder and turning my back to him.

"It would be my pleasure," he replies as I watch him in the mirror as he saunters over to me.

The moment his warm fingers caress my neck, my skin breaks out into tiny goose bumps. I watch his reflection closely and smile when he meets my gaze.

"Thank you for flying V over. This week has been perfect. I didn't realize how much I missed her," I confess.

"It's okay. I missed Lucas, too."

"Ha. So technically you only flew V over cause she's a package deal with Lucas?"

Jasper smirks, stroking the arch of my neck with the backs of his fingers.

"But seriously, I mean it, thank you," I say, leaning into his touch.

"You don't need to thank me. I like making you happy, baby."

"I know," I reply. Giving what I'm about to say some thought, I ask softly, "You didn't happen to fly V over to sway my decision to go back home, did you?"

Jasper's mouth twitches. "Would you hate me if I did?" he asks, his fingers gliding down my arm.

"No, of course not," I reply, still watching his reflection closely.

"Well, in that case, it was part of the reason. But a very small, tiny part."

We're silent for a moment, watching each other in the mirror, both waiting for the other to speak.

"Are you afraid I won't come home?" I ask, breaking the silence.

Jasper seems to weigh up my question before speaking. "No, because I'll make anywhere my home. As long as you're with me, I'll manage. Home is where the heart is, remember?"

"But would you be happy in New York?"

Jasper leans forward, kissing my shoulder. "I'm happy with you. So wherever you are, is where I'll be," he says with conviction.

I smile, shaking my head in awe. "How'd I get so lucky?"

"I ask myself that every day," he replies, returning my smile.

"You ready to do this?" I know he's a touch nervous to socialize with all of his relatives in one place.

"I am," he replies with a nod. "Thank you for being the person I want to share this with."

"Thank you for choosing me."

His eyes smolder as he gently turns me by the shoulders. "There was never a choice. I was lost from the moment I saw you."

"Well, I'm glad we're both found, found by one another," I reply, running a hand through his hair.

"I love you, Ava," he softly declares. "Whatever city, state, country, continent we are on, my feelings for you will never change."

"I know," I reply, suddenly realizing my decision is made.

"**A**nd then I said, if you want this...you're going to have pay," screams Jasper's slightly deaf grandma, who has no mouth filter.

No guessing who loves her crude stories.

"And then what happened?" asks V, eyes wide and on the edge of her seat, eagerly awaiting the punch line.

"Then I lifted up—"

"Okay, Mom," Jeremy says, interrupting her story by loudly talking over her. "How about we get you inside? It's cold."

"I'm fine out here," she stubbornly counters, shrugging his hand off her arm. "If you're cold, you go inside."

V's mouth twitches and it looks like she's found a new role model. "Can I just say, I love you, Mrs. Blackwood."

Kathy smiles broadly. "Thank you, Veruca."

I burst out laughing, almost choking on my wine, while Jeremy sighs, probably embarrassed that his eighty-two year old mother is stealing the show. The night has been a complete success, and all the guests, who I've yet to meet because there's so many of them, seem to be having a great time.

Everyone is in good spirits as the food and wine flows freely and the vibe is totally chilled. The breezy evening is warmed up by the outdoor heaters which are scattered along the decking and backyard. The warm orange glow complements the candles that are strewn everywhere.

Jasper has been quite the popular boy amongst his family as he's been carted off left, right, and center, mingling with long lost relatives who can't get enough of him. Every time he catches a break, he's lugged off in the opposite direction, and the process starts all over again. But I can tell by his smile and the way he genuinely listens to them that he's interested in what they have to say. I guess they have many years to catch up on, so what better time to do so.

He's introduced me to so many people, I can't keep track of who's who, but none of that matters because

Jasper is happy and that makes them all my favorite people.

"I can't believe that," says V, gesturing with her chin towards Kris as he approaches us, "is Jasper's brother. I mean, yes they look alike, but while Jasper is remotely annoying, Kris makes me want to drive a pencil into my ear so I don't have to listen to him talk."

"Ha, cute," Kris says, sinking into the seat beside V. "Don't deny your panties are wet for me."

Lucas sips his beer, shaking his head, not at all troubled that Kris is constantly hitting on his wife.

"If my panties are wet, it's because my vagina is crying that you're in the same room as me," she quickly counters, while we all, including Jasper's grandma, burst out laughing.

And this is the reason why Lucas isn't concerned—V can hold her own. Kris either has no comeback, or he doesn't bother rebutting because he knows whatever he throws at V, she'll hurl it back, twice as hard.

Although I'm having a blast, my mind constantly wanders, thinking about the decision I made a few hours ago. I haven't told Jasper or V, but both know something is up. Thankfully Jasper is too busy to ask what, but V doesn't have that problem, as Cara is sound asleep.

"So," she whispers into my ear. "What's going on? I can smell something brewing."

I smile as I sip my wine. Nothing gets past her. "Nothing is going on," I reply, crossing my legs. "I'm casually sitting here, drinking my merlot."

"I call bullshit," she replies, bumping me with her shoulder. "You've decided, haven't you?"

I have no idea how she does this, but I've given up trying to figure it out. "I have," I reply softly, seeing no point in lying to her.

"And?" she asks, looking at me eagerly.

"And I want to talk to Jasper first," I reply. V blows me a raspberry.

"You're no fun anymore, Ava Thompson," she playfully mocks, stealing my wine mid-sip.

"Hey! I was drinking that," I say, wiping my mouth, as it looks like I've just taken a bite out of someone's neck.

V ignores me and guzzles it down while Lucas laughs. Kris is speaking to some random blonde to his right, so I take this opportunity to grill Lucas.

"So...Lucas." I lean forward, and pin him with my stare.

"Yes," he replies, leaning backward in his chair.

"What can you tell me about Delilah Rose?" I ask, my fingers drumming on the sofa arm. "I already know she's a skanky, evil, malicious bitch, so don't bother telling me that."

V coughs up her wine, thumping her chest with her fist. "I take it back," she wheezes. "You're more fun than ever."

Lucas squirms uncomfortably in his chair, and I know I'm putting him on the spot, but I need to know what he thinks. He's Jasper's best friend and I would love to hear his take on the whole thing.

"Ava, I don't know what you want me to say," he says, nervously rearranging his backward baseball cap.

"Cut the crap, Lucas," V says, mimicking my interrogation pose. "Tell us if her panties are wet for Jasper." She looks over at Kris with disgust as she uses his phrase.

"I don't think she wears any panties," Lucas says, which earns him deep scowls from V and I.

"I'm kiddin'." He quickly raises his hands in surrender. "Do you want the truth, or—"

"Truth," I say, cutting him off.

"Well," he replies, leaning forward and interlacing his hands together. "I think she's trouble. I also think she's making a play for Jasper."

"I knew it!" I snarl, turning to look at V, who shakes her head angrily.

"Why have you not punched this whore in the throat?" she asks, glaring at Lucas.

"Firstly, babe, she's a girl—"

"That's debatable," I mumble under my breath, interrupting him.

He ignores me. "And secondly, I'd rather be on her good side than her bad."

"She *has* a good side?" I ask smartly, hating how riled up I'm getting. V laughs, smacking her thigh in amusement.

Lucas ignores us both. "Ava, you've got nothing to worry about. It's purely one sided. Jasper is so in love with you that sometimes it gets really annoying. Trust me when I say no one else exists but you."

I huff in frustration, not at Lucas' comment, but rather the fact that Jasper is so blind to this bitch's scheming. "I trust Jasper, it's her I don't trust," I say, rubbing my temples.

V rubs my back in support. "It'll be okay, babe. You're going on tour, right?"

"Yeah, but I shouldn't feel like I should have to babysit," I reply, shaking my head. "I'm so over these home-wrecking hoochies."

Both V and Lucas are silent because they know that Delilah Rose is up to no good.

"Who are these hoochies? And what are their numbers?" Kris says, leaning over V, who pushes him away.

"You're disgusting," she says, curling her lip in disgust. "I hope you get checked for VD...weekly."

"You could always check," he replies, grabbing onto his junk and raising his hips.

Thankfully this pleasant conversation is disrupted when the music is turned down and Jeremy clears his throat loudly, getting everyone's attention.

"Sorry folks," he says when the crowd mock groans. "I'll only take a minute of your time."

The group quiets down, giving Jeremy their full attention as we all stand.

"I know some of you have traveled a long way to get here, so I want to thank everybody for being here. Today is a special day, and no, it's not because it's my birthday," he says in reply to people chuckling. "It's because it's the first birthday I've spent with my son, Jasper."

Jasper is over near the table, and all eyes dart his way. He smiles broadly and gives Jeremy a thumbs up as he's no doubt feeling a touch self-conscious with all eyes focused on him. But a thumbs up is not going to suffice.

"Get over here, son." Jeremy waves him over.

Jasper looks over at me and pulls a face. I laugh at his awkwardness. "Go," I mouth with an encouraging nod.

He puts down his beer and walks over to Jeremy, running a hand through his hair. The moment he stands by his side, Jeremy wraps an arm around his shoulder and looks at him affectionately.

"Jasper, I cannot even begin to express how happy I am to have you back in my life. You're the best present a father could ever have. I look forward to spending the next fifty years with you." He hugs Jasper into his side.

Jasper smiles, looking a touch embarrassed to be the center of Jeremy's speech, but he also looks so happy to be acknowledged by a parent who loves him more than life itself. I'm completely touched by Jeremy's heartfelt admission, but I don't fail to see Kris tense up. I'm certain Jeremy will include Kris, but when Jeremy raises his glass, I have a feeling speeches are over.

"Thank you for being a part of the best night of my life. I will never forget this day for as long as I live," he concludes, raising his champagne.

Everyone raises their glasses in salute, and before I know what's happening, Jeremy's sister is wheeling out the monster birthday cake. The fifty candles flicker beautifully and everyone takes the cake's entrance as their cue to start singing. The happy birthday song is sung off-key and out of tune, but that doesn't matter because everyone is so happy to see Jeremy bursting with pride over his son. And that's the problem. Son should really be *sons*, seeing as Jeremy has two. But he only stares lovingly at Jasper, while Kris pushes through the crowd and marches down the stairs.

I'm torn with what to do because I feel sorry for him, but I continue to sing happy birthday, not wanting to cause a scene.

Jasper watches Kris charge down the stairs, but when Jeremy nudges him and says, "Help me blow out these candles, son," he has no other choice but to comply.

The guests clap loudly and whistle, demanding more speeches, but Jeremy waves them off and signals for the music to recommence. Some Top 40 song comes on and everyone rushes over to Jeremy to pass on their congratulations. Jasper takes this opportunity to break free. He jogs over to me and instantly knows what I'm going to say.

"I'll go find him," he says, looking distraught.

"I'll come too," I say, as I have a feeling he'll need the support.

We politely push our way through the crowd but are stopped every step by some eager family member or friend wanting to talk to Jasper. Jasper gives them a well-mannered brush off because at this rate, it'll be next week by the time we get to Kris.

I have no idea where he went, so Jasper and I head to the front of the house, hoping he's blowing off some steam on the front porch. He's not there, and Jasper sighs. "I'll check inside. Do you want to go look behind the garage?"

"Sure." I step up on tippy toes and give him a light kiss on the lips. "It's not your fault your dad loves you, Jasper."

I know he's blaming himself, but I won't stand here

and let him beat himself up over something he couldn't control.

"That's the problem," he replies heatedly. "As much as I appreciate it, he needs to remember he has two sons. I don't like the favoritism, especially when it makes Kris feel like the black sheep."

Just as I'm about to reply, Kris rounds the corner, looking mighty pissed off. "Oh please, spare me your pity. I don't want it. I'm used to being the black sheep," he spits out, his eyes even stormier than usual.

"Kris, bro—"

"I am *not* your bro," he says, cutting Jasper off.

Jasper doesn't argue, and allows Kris to vent.

"I'm used to you being the golden boy. I mean, I could never live up to Jeremy's expectations. I was stupid to think we could actually be a family."

"We can. We are," Jasper implores, taking a step towards. "What happened on the court, it's history."

"Don't," Kris warns, and I suddenly get a whiff of marijuana.

No guessing what he was doing behind the garage. I don't trust anyone on drugs, so I lightly tug on Jasper's hand, silently pleading with him to let it be. Kris is obviously angry, and I don't think he'll listen to reason, especially if he's high.

Kris' gaze falls to mine and Jasper's connection and he snickers. "Figures, you get it all."

"Excuse me?" Jasper says, pulling out of my grip.

"Jasper," I say, as I don't like his abrupt tone.

"You heard me," Kris replies, looking at me angrily.

"You've got it all. You've got everyone wrapped around your little finger, but I'm not fooled."

"What's Ava got to do with this?" Jasper asks, taking a step towards him. "Leave her out of it."

"Why do you get to have it all? When is it my turn?" Kris glumly says, and I immediately feel sorry for him.

The minor progress that was made over the past few days has just been shot to hell, thanks to Jeremy's love for Jasper. It shouldn't be this way, but I can't blame Kris for being a touch defensive. Jasper however, feels anything but.

"You think I have it all?" he sarcastically says. "It may seem that way, but after the shit hand that I've been dealt my entire life, it's now my turn to catch a fucking break. I'm sorry Jeremy didn't include you in his speech, but that's not my fault. Maybe if you stopped acting like a spoiled brat, he would show you the same respect as he does me. And as for Ava, you have no clue what we've been through. It may seem like roses and sunshine, but we had to work damn hard to get where we are. So I'm not going to apologize for living because I earned this."

I can't argue there.

Kris clenches his jaw as Jasper's little speech has seemed to anger him further. "Whatever, man, go back to your lavish lifestyle of being a rockstar and leave us alone. Things were so much better when Jeremy thought you were gone for good."

Ouch. I know Kris is mad, but that was a low blow.

"Lavish lifestyle?" Jasper snarls, advancing forward. "You know nothing about me and my so called lavish lifestyle."

"No, I don't, and I don't want to," Kris replies, meeting him halfway.

This is not going to end well, and I quickly run over, tying to intervene.

"Baby, stay out of this," Jasper says, almost standing toe to toe with Kris.

"Yeah, love, stay out of this," Kris says, taking a step back and looking at me mockingly.

"She is *not* your love," Jasper says from between clenched teeth.

"No, but I bet she could be. I mean, she gave *you* a chance, didn't she?" he cruelly replies, while I gasp.

"That's not fair, Kris." I shake my head. "I know you're hurting, but lashing out is not going to solve anything. I thought we were cool?"

"Why? 'Cause we played football?" he asks, laughing crossly. "It's going to take a lot more than a game of touch for us to play happy family."

Was he playing us this entire time? I thought he was happy, but is he just a really good actor, making us believe what we so desperately wanted to believe?

"Do you know what it was like living in the shadow of a ghost?" Kris snarls when Jasper and I remain silent, not knowing what to say. "No matter what I did, I was never good enough. I could never compare to the golden son."

"I'm sorry, Kris, I truly am," Jasper says, stepping forward. "I can only imagine how that made you feel, but I'm not the enemy here. Neither is Jeremy."

I know who is, but I remain quiet, allowing Jasper to continue.

"We're just trying to make up for the past," he explains, while Kris crosses his arms over his chest. "I'm sorry I wasn't there to protect you, to be the big brother I always wanted to be. I've got an older brother, too," Jasper shares. "So I know how important they are to a younger brother."

Kris scoffs, rolling his eyes, but the action doesn't deter Jasper.

"Let me be the older brother you deserve. That you've always deserved."

"You're not the problem, Jeremy is," Kris confesses as he clears his throat, seeming touched by Jasper's heartfelt confession.

"I know," Jasper replies with a nod. "But try and see it from his side. When he looks at me, he sees his ultimate failure. He's just trying to make up for lost time."

Kris shakes his head and snickers. "I get that, but he wasn't exactly father of the year material with me, either."

Jasper sighs as he rubs the back of his neck. "Okay, I'll make you a deal," he says after a moment of silence. "I'll talk to Jeremy and tell him to go easy with the man hugs."

Kris nods, indicating he's listening.

"But you gotta meet me halfway, man. Enough with the attitude, okay? We get it. You're a brooding teen."

"I'm twenty," Kris corrects quickly.

"Well, how about you start acting it?"

There is a pregnant pause and I cross my fingers behind my back, hoping this talk has finally knocked some sense into Kris.

"I'll try my best," he replies with a shrug.

"Well, that's better than no," Jasper says, smiling. "So, truce?" he asks, extending his hand, along with the olive branch I asked him to offer.

I can only hope Kris doesn't shit on it, like Jasper first suggested he would.

"Truce," he finally says, shaking Jasper's hand lightly.

"So let's go back in there and celebrate our father's birthday," Jasper suggests, while I discreetly wipe my eyes, touched that they've made amends.

Kris nods. "Okay."

The boys stand awkwardly, and although this would be the perfect moment for them to hug and express their feelings, they don't. Jasper simply reaches forward and playfully messes up Kris' hair. "Don't worry, I won't hug you. I know you'd like it too much," he teases.

Kris scoffs, but smiles. He turns to me and looks at me sheepishly. "I'm sorry for being an ass to you," he says sincerely. Just as I'm about to accept his apology, he adds with a wink, "But I'm not sorry for seeing you naked."

My hands fly up, automatically covering my chest. "Well, if that's the best apology you can give, I'll take it," I say, shaking my head. "I'm glad I made your homecoming memorable."

"You sure did." He gives me yet another seedy wink. "It's the best homecoming I've had in quite some time."

"Okay, that's enough, you pervert," I reply, laughing.

Jasper chuckles as he draws me into his side. Kris watches the action and smiles. "You're one lucky dude."

"Don't I know it." Jasper kisses the top of my head.

"Vomit," Kris says, sticking his finger down his throat.

"I'll meet you two in there. I've got a firecracker to annoy."

I chuckle, not knowing who I feel sorrier for: V or Kris.

As Kris makes his way out back, Jasper reaches for my hand and attempts to follow. But I latch onto his wrist. "Can I have a word?" I ask, feeling a surge of confidence overtake me.

Jasper cocks his head to the side, his clear blue eyes glistening in the moonlight. "Of course, baby. Is everything all right?"

I bite my lip, deciding now is the time to tell Jasper I've made my decision. "I've made my choice. About what I want to do," I clarify as Jasper remains quiet, watching me closely. "I-I love you, Jasper."

"I love you, too."

When I lower my eyes and continue biting my lip, Jasper says, "Just tell me what it is because this is scaring me more than the truth."

I raise my eyes, and when I take in the beautiful man before me, I know my decision was the right one to make. "I'm staying in New York."

Jasper looks as if my words have sucker punched him, but he nods, accepting my decision. But there's more. There's so much more.

"When we leave here and arrive back in New York, you'll pack all your things and go on tour."

"What?" Jasper says, taken aback. "Ava, I—"

But I silence him by placing my finger over his lips. "You'll pack all your things...because I'll be doing the same."

"What?"

"The get together I've organized...it's also going to be my goodbye party. I'll tie up loose ends, and once I get organized, I'll meet you in Europe, and from there, we'll fly home. Back to L.A.," I conclude, my decision feeling like a reprieve.

Jasper is silent, his inquisitive mind no doubt processing everything I've just said. "You're coming home? To L.A.?" he clarifies.

"Yes," I reply, nodding.

Jasper runs a hand through his hair as he blows out a loud breath. "Are you sure, baby? I told you, I'll follow you anywhere."

"I know, and that's what's made my decision easier. We have to make sacrifices in life, but you're one I'm not willing to make."

"I'd never make you sacrifice your career over me," he presses. "I'm happy to stay in New York. If that's what you wanted, I would support you all the way."

"I know, but there are a million other places I can work at...but there's only one you," I firmly say, my mind made up.

Jasper stares at me, his mouth agape. I know this is a lot to take in, so I remain quiet, allowing him to digest his thoughts. "I..." and he pauses, shaking his head lightly. "Baby, I love you...so much," he says, rushing over to me and wrapping me into his arms.

"I love you, too," I squeak as he lifts me off the ground, twirling me high in the air. "Put me down." I giggle, swatting his shoulder. "You'll give yourself a hernia."

He loosens his grip so I slide down his body. He holds on tight when we're eye to eye. "Thank you," he says sincerely.

When I raise an eyebrow in confusion, he explains, "Thank you for never giving up on me."

"The same could be said about you," I reply. "Seeing as I've given you enough reason to."

"So this is it?" he says, his smile blinding me with its sparkle.

"This is what?"

"This is the start to our new life. The new Jasper and Ava—2.0," he clarifies, while I chuckle.

"Yup, this is it. Are you scared?" I ask, unable to wipe my smile clean.

"No, why?"

"Because you're stuck with me for life," I say, thinking how amazing that concept really is.

Pressing our foreheads together, he whispers, "I wouldn't have it any other way."

Neither would I.

CHAPTER EIGHTEEN

Pieces of Me

The rest of the party passes by without a hitch, and as the guests begin to dwindle to none, V and I begin tidying up, not keen on facing an entire day of cleaning.

As I'm loading the dishwasher, V stands beside me, hands on hips. "Spit it out."

"Spit what out?" I ask, looking up at her as I load in the last plate.

"Haven't you learned by now that you're a terrible liar?" She drums her black nails on the countertop.

I can't help but laugh as I close the door shut. "Fine, Miss Nosy. I'm coming home. After P.O.E. finishes up in Europe, I'll be catching a flight with Jasper back to L.A."

"For good?" V asks as she stops drumming her fingernails.

"Yes. You're stuck with me forever. I don't plan on living anywhere, apart from L.A. ever again," I say, wiping my hands on a dishcloth.

V stares at me like I've just spoken to her in Norwegian. "So, this is a good thing, right? I mean, now is the time for you to tell me it's the right thing to do."

"Of course it is," V replies, her eyes wide. "I'm just... oh my god, I'm just shocked."

"You didn't think I'd come back?" I ask, watching as she turns the hoop in her lip.

"Honestly, no."

"Why?" I ask, curious as ever.

However, when she replies, I really wish I didn't ask. "'Cause you're stupid."

"Ha! Thank you," I sarcastically reply, shaking my head.

"I mean that in the nicest way possible," she amends with a smile.

I chuckle. "I don't think there *is* a nice way to call someone stupid."

"I just mean, you always seem to go about things the hard way. Coming back to L.A. is the easy way, and staying in New York, well, that's the hard way. So the fact you've chosen the easy way out surprises me," she explains, jumping up onto the counter and swinging her legs happily.

"So you don't think it's the right choice?" I ask, a little afraid of her reply.

"Of course it is," she says likes a no brainer.

"And?"

"There is no and. It's fucking awesome news. I'm just happy you're finally coming home, and with all the experience under your belt, you could pretty much work anywhere you wanted. Maybe you could open up a restaurant that only serves desserts? I mean, I know I would be there daily," she suggests, waving a cupcake at me.

I can't help but laugh, because V is right. Not about the dessert part, but the part where I could work anywhere I wanted. Suddenly, my indecision has never looked clearer, and I can't believe I didn't make the choice sooner.

"Thank you, V," I say, stealing a mini muffin from her clutches. She opens her mouth to protest, but closes it when I add, "Thank you for always being my rude and obnoxious voice of reason."

She laughs and doesn't dispute my claims. "Any time, babe. Now that you're coming back home, be prepared to hear my rude and obnoxious voice daily."

"I'm counting on it," I reply, actually looking forward to it. "I can't wait to get back to L.A. where I don't have to dodge the paparazzi on my doorstep."

V nods, making a pained face. "So you're still off the social grid?"

"Yes," I reply, leaning against the counter. "I'm afraid to check just in case some other absurd rumor is made up about us. It's funny, I always forget that Jasper is a 'rock star,'" I say, using my fingers as quotation marks. "I'm just so used to him being...I dunno, my Jasper. It's kinda weird seeing all these obsessive fans fawning all over him."

"Well, Europe should be interesting then. You've got legions of international women to fight off," V says, chuckling when I groan.

"Thanks for reminding me." Suddenly, I'm struck with a genius idea. "Come with me," I say, nodding animatedly.

"To Europe?"

"Yes, to Europe. I know Lucas' parents have been on your back to babysit Cara. So why not? What's stopping you? You've got Jane tattooing full time and looking after Ink of Queens. So..." I say, leaving the sentence hanging.

V seems to ponder over my suggestion. As her ruby lips tip into a full smile, I know she's seen the light. "You know what? Fuck it. Let's do it."

"Yeah?" I say, clapping my hands in excitement.

"Fuck yeah!" she replies, jumping down from the counter and giving me a big hug. "This is going to be so fun. But you know what? If you can swing it, do you think you could close up shop early?"

I yelp in excitement, pulling out of our embrace and cocking an eyebrow. "Are you thinking what I'm thinking?"

"Totally," V says, nodding cheekily.

"I love that your devious mind works in sync with mine," I say, referring to our silent agreement of surprising the boys by arriving earlier than I had originally planned.

V sticks out her pinky and I laugh, as this is something we've been doing since we were kids. "Pinky swear you won't spill the beans?"

Looping my pinky around hers, I reply, "I promise."

At that exact moment, the boys walk into the kitchen, hands filled with more dishes.

"More?" I ask, my eyes widening at the tower of china before me.

"I'm sorry, Ava," Jeremy says, placing tray's into the sink. "We really should have had more plastic plates and cutlery."

Pulling up my sleeves, I smile as I walk over to the

basin. "Don't worry. This is nothing compared to the dishes I'm faced with at work."

Jasper places his tableware onto the counter and leans forward, kissing my cheek. I know his action is due to the fact that I won't be faced with that reality much longer. Surprisingly, it doesn't sadden me as much as I thought it would.

"Oh, of course," Jeremy says. "I must come out and visit you one day. Kris has been pestering me for years to see the Statue of Liberty. What do you think, son?"

I turn to look at Kris, who's placing food into the refrigerator. He pauses when he hears Jeremy's suggestion, seeming to look surprised. But in true Kris form, he downplays it, not wanting to appear affected by Jeremy's effort. "Sure, whatever," he says with a shrug, sticking his head further into the fridge.

I'm not sure if Jasper has had a chance to talk to Jeremy, but either way, I'm glad Jeremy has acknowledged Kris. But sadly, unless they're planning on visiting in the next few weeks, they'll be visiting New York without me. With that thought in mind, I decide to share my news with my family—because my news is also Jasper's.

"Well, Jeremy," I say, reaching for the plug as I turn on the facets. "I'm actually moving back to L.A. We both are," I clarify, looking at Jasper who beams at my words.

"Oh, really?" Jeremy says, the shock clear on his face as he turns to Jasper.

"Yup, we're going home." He rubs my shoulder affectionately.

"Well, in that case, I've always wanted to see Hollywood Bowl. Congratulations, you two. I know wherever you live; good fortune and health will follow. I'm so thrilled for the both of you."

"Thanks, Dad," Jaspers says, smiling.

Kris slams the fridge shut, but when he sees how happy Jasper is, his frown is replaced with a half-smile. "Good work, bro. I've heard the L.A. women are a lot less uptight than New Yorkers, so I'll definitely be using your pad as my personal love nest."

Jasper chuckles, shaking his head, while both V and I groan. "Seriously, have you heard yourself speak? You sound like a complete jackass," V teasingly says as Kris flips her off.

I don't fail to see Jeremy look lovingly at the scene before him, and I too, feel a touch nostalgic, as this right here feels like a family should. My decision has never felt more right, and everything seems to finally be falling into place. Could our lives really be that simple? For now, I like to think yes, it will be.

Jeremy's birthday has been a complete success, and I suddenly realize that the best part is yet to come.

"Oh my god, Jeremy, I'm so sorry, we forgot to give you your present." I quickly dry my hands and rush over to my bag.

"Oh, Ava, please, there's no need. All of you being here was gift enough," Jeremy says, shaking his head.

But I wave him off as I find what I'm looking for. "Well, think of this as us being here, even when we're not," I say, bypassing Jasper, who has no idea what I'm about to give Jeremy.

I know Jasper and his self-doubt over getting the

'right' gift for Jeremy prevented him from getting anything at all. But I meant it when I said that Jasper is the best birthday present. Ever.

"Happy birthday, Jeremy." I hand him his gift.

He gratefully accepts and gently brushes over the silver bow which is attached to a leather bound scrap book. From the outside, it looks like a standard journal, but it's what's on the inside that makes this diary far more personal. He nervously opens the cover as all eyes are glued to him.

As he sees the first page, he gasps, his eyes darting up to reach mine. "Oh my...Ava, thank you," he says, his tone breaking with emotion.

"It's my pleasure, Jeremy."

Jasper steps forward and looks at what's caught Jeremy's complete attention. When he sees it, he too gasps, his gaze fixing on mine. "Baby," he says, completely stunned.

"I hope you don't mind." I smile. "I kinda invaded your life."

V is the next to step forward, desperate to see what it is. Jeremy however turns the book around, revealing an old polaroid. The photograph, I believe, is the only evidence that proves that Jeremy was there the day Jasper was born. It's the picture that changed Jasper's life forever. It's the picture that set him free.

"It's a photograph of Jasper and I. It was taken the day he was born," Jeremy says, tears welling in his blue eyes.

I instantly feel awful that I've made him cry. "I'm sorry. I didn't mean to make you cry."

Jasper gently touches my cheek, answering for Jeremy as he says, "They're happy tears." I nod, as this is something Jasper has said to me before.

"It's a scrap book of Jasper's life," I explain as Jeremy flicks through the pages, tears spilling down his cheeks.

"It's remarkable," he says in awe, his gaze lingering on every page, his fingers brushing over the material inside.

I've felt like quite the stalker lately, hunting through Jasper's belongings to find all the things that I've found. Photos, lyrics, poems, report cards, awards, concert stubs, whatever personal items of Jasper's I could find that I thought commemorated a milestone event, I've glued into this book so Jeremy can look at it and relive the events like he was there.

Lucky for me, Jasper brought a ton of his paperwork to NYC, not knowing how long we'd be away, so I had access to an unlimited supply of Jasper paraphernalia. Of course they're copies, as I didn't want to give the originals away. But it's amazing how they look like the real deal. It was hard keeping this a secret from him, but so worth it, now that I've seen Jeremy's face.

Kris sighs beside me, and I bump him with my shoulder. "The best is yet to come," I say, as I would never leave him out.

As Jeremy turns to the second last page, there is a photo of him, Kris and Jasper, out in the field, playing ball. I took this sneaky picture when they were too busy arguing who the better player was. From the image, one can see the pure joy and happiness radiating off their faces, reflecting what true family means. I can't believe it when I see Kris dab lightly at his eyes, but I don't make a fuss, knowing this is his time, as much as it is Jasper and Jeremy's.

As Jeremy gets to the last page, he sees that it is blank.

"That's for you to add whatever memory you wish," I explain, while Jasper smiles, his eyes filled with nothing but love.

Jeremy brushes away his tears and nods. "This right here," he says, looking around the room. "This is my greatest memory of all."

I nod, knowing he would say that.

I walk over to my bag and get out my camera. "Okay, let's make it official." I gesture with my hand for the three boys to get together.

Kris, however, surprises me as says, "Does that thing have a timer?"

"Yeah."

"Set it and come join us. All of you," he adds, looking at V, Lucas and Cara.

I don't argue and position the camera on a stool, running to and fro to ensure we're all in the shot. When we're good to go, I set it and run over, snuggling into Jasper's side. This feels so right and an idea which I thought may be corny has turned out to be a great gift after all.

The red light flashes, indicating the photograph will be taken in ten seconds. Jasper leans forward, nuzzling my neck as he whispers, "I love you so much, Ava Thompson. When we get home...I'm going to marry you."

I pull back, stunned, and Jasper takes this stolen moment to kiss me fiercely, taking my breath away with his passion. We kiss until long after the picture is taken, and only V clearing her throat loudly pries us apart.

"I'm so sorry, Jeremy. We can take another," I say embarrassed, as we've totally ruined the picture.

But he shakes his head. "No, this photo," he says, turning the camera over and showing me the screen. "Captures what this moment is all about."

As I see V's fist connecting with Kris' arm, Lucas laughing hysterically, Cara yawning, Jeremy turning over his shoulder to see what that commotion is all about, and Jasper and I pawing at one another like it's the end of the world, I know that Jeremy is absolutely right. This has captured a moment; a moment, no matter how dysfunctional, that's absolutely perfect.

CHAPTER NINETEEN
New Beginnings

"Please know that you're always welcome. My door is always open," Jeremy says, handing Jasper our bags. "You too," he adds, looking at V and Lucas, while lovingly stroking Cara's chubby cheek.

"Thank you, Jeremy," V says, leaning forward and giving him a quick hug. "I'll be there as long as this kid isn't."

Kris grabs onto his sides and laughs sarcastically while V smirks. I think he's grown on her.

The proverbial honeymoon is over and it's now time to face reality. However, a reality I was once so afraid to face is now a reality I can't wait to tackle, head on.

"See you soon, babe." V bites her lip to stop the tears.

"Don't you dare," I warn, pointing my finger at her. "If you start, then I'll never say goodbye."

She nods, sniffing away her tears. "I'll see you soon." She leaves out the part where we'll be surprising the boys while on tour.

"You betcha," I reply, throwing my arms around her and hugging her tight. "The next airport we'll be at, we'll be shedding happy tears," I whisper.

She hugs me tighter and nods. "I'll miss you. I can't wait till you come home."

"Ditto," I reply, keeping my tears at bay.

Jasper and Lucas hug, both excited that the next time they see one another, they'll be in a different country. Kris looks at me and where his face was once marred with a constant frown, it's now replaced with a constant half-smile.

"See you soon," I say, not actually sure when I'll see him again. I'm not sure if he's returning to London, but either way, I'm so happy we met.

"It was a pleasure meeting you, Ava," he says, digging his hands into his jeans pockets.

"You too," I reply, stepping forward and giving him a light hug.

I hear Jasper and Jeremy saying their goodbyes, so I pull away and give Kris a kiss on the cheek. "Maybe I'll catch ya in London?"

He smiles. "Maybe."

Jasper walks over and stands in front of Kris, nervously fiddling with the strap of his backpack. "So, kiddo...it was interesting, to say the least."

I stand off to the side, giving them some privacy, not wanting to hover.

Kris nods, his scruffy hair falling into his eyes. "Who would have thought my brother would be a bigger pain in the ass than I am?"

Jasper laughs, playfully slapping him at the back of the head. "Hey, show some respect for your elders."

"Yeah, like way, *way* elder," Kris retorts with a smile. "If you ever get sick of Grandpa, you know who to call," he adds, looking my way and giving me a wink.

I roll my eyes and laugh, knowing that Kris' way to

deal with anything remotely serious is to make a joke about it. I know he's putting off saying goodbye to Jasper, as I think he's come to see what a great person his brother truly is.

"If you're ever around our neighborhood, our door is always open," Jasper says, his sincerity clear in his tone. "And I could always use a roadie, if you're keen?"

Just as Kris opens his mouth to reply, Jasper cheekily adds, "Actually, I've seen the way you handle my gear, maybe you could watch from afar instead."

Kris' lips twitch, as do Jasper's. I'm glad they've been able to put that incident behind them.

"Either way, keep in touch, bro." Jasper extends his hand with a smile.

Kris accepts and nods. "I will. Thank you for...thank you for not being a total douche," he says, while Jasper laughs.

There's a slight pause before Kris steps forward and gives Jasper a light, loose hug. Jeremy smiles, never looking prouder, while I dab at my eyes, touched by Kris' awkward PDA.

"Later, brat," Jasper says, playfully messing up Kris' hair as he pulls out of their embrace.

"See ya, emo," he replies, his smile radiating nothing but happiness.

"Right, well, you best be off. Your planes leave soon," Jeremy says, wrapping his arm around Kris' shoulder.

Kris shrugs him off, but I can see the gesture has touched him.

Jeremy and Jasper hug once more, while I give Cara a million kisses. We wave our goodbyes, and I hold back my tears as we make our way to the terminal. I look over my shoulder and give my best friend one final smile. She blows me a kiss in return.

We walk in silence as I'm deep in thought. When we arrive back in New York, it'll be the beginning of a new and exciting future, one I can't wait to start.

"Are you okay?" Jasper asks, squeezing my hand.

Looking up to meet the love of my life's eyes, I nod. "I am. Here's to new beginnings."

"**S**top it." I chuckle while putting out the canapés.

"I. Can't. Help. It," Jasper says in between kissing my neck. "You look good enough to eat." He wraps his hands low on my waist, pulling me backwards so I can feel him growing hard against my back.

"You're so bad," I whisper, sagging against him in defeat.

"I could be, but you won't let me," he huskily says into my ear.

Biting my lip, I tell my out of control libido to cool it because now is not the time to get hot and bothered.

Things have been good-real good. We've only been back from Chicago a couple of days, but those days have been most productive, as my entire apartment is almost unrecognizable. Almost everything of Jasper's is packed and ready to be shipped back home. I couldn't be happier. I know it's bittersweet, as we have to get through the next six weeks before our new life can really begin, but I plan on flying to Europe in two weeks so we won't be apart for too long. Now that I've made my decision, I can't wait for our future to begin. I can't wait to Mrs. Ava White.

The internet is still rife with rumors about mine and Jasper's involvement. Thankfully however, the paparazzi have taken interest in another story and have stopped camping outside my door. It's still weird that Jasper and I are considered exciting enough to be 'news,' but I know the interest lies with my fiancé. He's the hot story, not me. When I finish up with Metropolis, I'll be forgotten, which suits me just fine.

"Wanna go somewhere with me?" Jasper asks, his voice oozing seduction.

"I do. I really do," I add when he slowly grinds against me. "But I can't. People will be here any minute."

"I know," he casually replies, tonguing my ear. "I'll be quick. I promise."

A low whimper slips past my lips, betraying how turned on I am. But I stand my ground. "We can't." I pull out of his clutches and turn to face him, which is a bad idea, seeing as he looks fucking amazing.

"Five minutes," he presses, his gaze dropping to the plunging neckline of my black dress.

I shake my head, my curled hair moving freely with the movement. "No. And besides"—I step in closer as the front door to Metropolis opens—"Five minutes isn't long enough."

Jasper groans, tossing his head back in sexual frustration while I giggle and continue arranging the canapés on the table.

"Hello, Ava," Sara sings as she waltzes in looking absolutely stunning in a long bohemian dress. "And Jasper," she adds, blatantly checking him out.

"Hi, Sara," he replies with a grin, discreetly shifting behind the table to hide what's happening below the belt.

But it's pointless because by the cheeky smile on her face, Sara so knows we were moments away from clearing the table and fucking like wild rabbits.

"So, is there anything I can do?" she asks, looking around the organized room.

"You can open a bottle of red," I reply, pulling out the napkins.

"Sounds like a great idea." She skips off to the kitchen.

The moment she's gone, I look over at Jasper who smirks, his dimples revealing he's up to no good. "When we get home, I plan on showing you that five minutes is more than enough. You just have to know how to utilize every second. I'll make it the best five minutes of your life. I promise," he adds while my breath catches in my throat.

His alluring promise has me cheekily whispering, "Let's make it ten."

He playfully shakes his head. "My greedy girl."

"With you...always," I reply, my gaze dropping to the front of his snug black jeans.

Jasper licks his lower lip before replying, "Fuck, at this rate, it'll be over in ten seconds."

I can't help but laugh as he subtly rearranges himself.

This was going to be a long night.

Michel stuck true to his word and got the biggest TV he could find. The monster flat screen is flickering in the background as we're all sitting around the table eating, drinking, and having a great time. My staff are stoked that I've given them the night off and treating them to an evening well deserved.

Everyone is in good spirits, everyone except Michel. He's sitting across from Jasper and I, and I can't help but notice he doesn't appear to be his usual cheery self. I'm pretty sure things ran smoothly while I was gone, as Sara filled me in on everything I missed while away. So I know his mood isn't soured because of that. All night I've felt him watch my every move, and every time Jasper has touched me, or whispered sweet nothings into my ear, I've had the odd feeling that Michel is slightly pissed.

I heed no attention to such nonsense and decide now is the time to give everyone the news I've been bursting to share, as I hope it'll cheer Michel up. I mean, my news includes him in a big way.

"Can I please have everyone's attention?" I say, tapping my knife on the side of my wine glass.

The excited voices hush and the room goes silent. All eyes focus on me. My palms suddenly become clammy and I get a terrible case of cotton mouth. I reach for my wine and take a big sip, hoping it'll offer me the courage I need.

"First." I clear my throat. "I would like to thank all of you for coming."

"Thanks for having us here." Helen raises her glass in salute.

"It's my pleasure. You guys deserve it, and it's the least I can do to show you how much I appreciate your loyalty and hard work," I say, looking down the long table of my humble employees.

Tears sting my eyes and Jasper gives my thigh a gentle, reassuring squeeze. It's the support I need. "Tonight is a celebration," I state, sniffing back my tears.

"It sure is. We survived the dragon lady," pipes up Sara from the other end of the table.

"You're absolutely right." I nod. "But we're here to celebrate something else."

I have the entire room's attention, so I take a deep breath before confessing, "We're celebrating Sara and Michel's promotion to manager."

Everyone's mouths fall open, some in shock, but most in surprise. "This is a good thing, guys," I say, trying to get them excited about my news.

"What about Faith?" Sara asks, her eyes round as saucers.

"Faith will have to undergo a ton of therapy. I don't know when, or if she'll be back," I say sadly, turning to look at Sara, who frowns, as she and Faith got along famously.

As I look at Michel, his reaction is one I wasn't expecting to see. He looks angry. "What?" he gasps, clenching his napkin in his fist. "You're stepping down?"

"No. I'm leaving," I clarify, while everyone looks at me like I've just kicked a puppy.

"Leaving?" Michel asks, shaking his head. "*Non.* Why?"

"It's time for me to go home," I reply, Michel's reaction confusing me. Shouldn't he be ecstatic that he's just been promoted to manager after being here such a short time?

"But New York is *your* home," he argues, while Jasper tenses up beside me.

He's been quiet for the most part, but I know that's about to change. "No, L.A. is," he retorts, leaning forward and resting his hands on the table.

"Is that *your* home, or hers?" he challenges, raising a perfect brow.

"It's ours," Jasper counters, his gaze never wavering.

Everyone is watching, awaiting the next move, but we're interrupted by Yolanda's annoying voice, a voice I never thought I'd be happy to hear. "Fellow foodies, tonight is a night you do not want to miss."

Someone reaches for the remote and turns it up, but my eyes are locked on Michel and Jasper, as I'm afraid their alpha dog routine is about to explode. I place my hand on Jasper's leg under the table, asking him to cool down, as I know a few of my staff are still watching with interest.

It takes him a few seconds, but I breathe out a sigh of relief as I watch his hackles settle down. He casually leans back in his seat and turns to me, smiling. "Look, you're on TV." He gestures with his head to the flat screen.

But I couldn't care less, as I want to ensure he's okay. When I don't move a muscle, my eyes silently begging him to reassure me that he's all right, he reaches forward and caresses my cheek before gently turning my head to look at the screen.

"Holy crap!" I yelp when I see the giant version of me working frantically in the kitchen.

When Jasper chuckles, my worries are forgotten for the moment because I can't get over the fact I'm on TV, looking like the roadrunner as I dart around the kitchen frantically. We all watch in silence, laughing and squeaking in excitement when we see one another busy at work.

At about ten minutes in, I can't help but notice a lot of the shots seem to focus on Michel and I, working and laughing together. The light, happy music dubbed over the top makes what we're doing look fun and easy, and the clever editing doesn't reveal the stresses that came with preparing a meal for the likes of someone like Adelia.

I suddenly get a weird feeling in the pit of my stomach, and my worry is confirmed when there is a shot of Michel and me, taken through the small window of my kitchen door as we're talking, deep in thought. The shot makes us look like we're whispering into one another's ear, but in reality I was yelling into it, as Yolanda's crew was nosily setting up shop in my kitchen.

I have no doubt she's done this on purpose, but I

continue watching, hoping the focus will soon be on the food and Adelia. When Adelia comes into frame, Yolanda's voiceover reveals that Michel is her son, a fact I know Michel didn't want to make public. When the entree is brought out by Helen, it cuts to a shot of Michel and me hugging in excitement. There was one hug shared, and I shared it with everyone at the end of the night, not just Michel, but of course they've excluded that fact.

It just gets worse from then on.

The whole segment has flashes of Michel and me working, laughing, and talking closely alongside one another, but they've cut it to look a lot more romanticized than it was.

The entire time, I'm too afraid to look at Jasper. This episode makes it appear that something other than cooking is occurring between Michel and I. They even had the gall to put in my pep talk about coming out to serve dessert as I touch his arm in reassurance.

"*Merde*," Michel utters under his breath as he runs a hand through his hair.

I look down at my watch, desperate for this nightmare to end and sigh in relief when it cuts to Yolanda standing in front of the piano. When it cuts to Jasper, I can't help but smile as the camera really does love him. He looks and sounds amazing, and I can't tear my eyes away.

When he sings the first line of the chorus, his voice suddenly mutes and Yolanda's face pops up on screen.

She's standing out in front, Metropolis' sign shining brightly behind her. She gives a glowing review, stating that Metropolis is the hottest place to eat in NYC. But when she smiles, her full tooth grin resembling a snake, I know I'm in trouble.

"Come down to Metropolis and be prepared to fall in love. I don't know what the chef puts in her spices because she certainly knows how to cast a spell." Jasper's low voice is used for the closing credits, but the image of me and Michel hugging, while Jasper is singing passionately about me makes me look like I'm running some bordello, instead of a renowned restaurant.

I can't watch anymore and neither can Jasper. He kicks back his chair and storms out. As the credits stop rolling, everyone is silent, knowing that what they just watched made me look like some unprofessional whore. I shakily reach for my wine and down the entire glass, not caring that everyone is looking for me.

"Well, yay!" Kia says, clapping half-heartedly, trying to be positive.

It sadly doesn't work and I need to get out of here before I choke. "Excuse me." I stand up and place my napkin on the table.

"Ava," Michel presses, also standing up, but I don't wait for him to continue as there's only one person I want to talk to.

Racing out back, I see that my office door is shut. "Jasper?" I say, knocking lightly. "Can I come in?"

I wait thirty seconds before I knock again. "Jasper?" But I'm greeted with silence once again. This is ridiculous, so I open the door, thankful I never got the lock fixed.

The moment I step inside, my eyes take a moment to

adjust, as its pitch black inside. Maybe I was wrong and Jasper isn't in here after all. But as my pupils get used to the dark, I see him standing with his back turned, looking out the window.

"Jasper?" I softly close the door behind me. "Are you okay?"

He still doesn't answer me.

"Please tell me what you're thinking," I beg, taking small, measured steps towards him.

I hate that he won't face me, not that I could see him anyway. But his back turned to me is so cold and detached.

"Don't let this ruin our night. It's our night to celebrate." Well, it was, until Yolanda shit on it.

He remains still, hands dug deep into his pockets, the breeze from the open window whipping his hair lightly in the wind.

"Don't be mad. Please don't be mad. You leave for Europe tomorrow. We're past this," I state, hoping I appeal to his rational side.

Silence.

The only thing filling the static is sirens and car horns.

"Jasper," I press, my voice wavering, as the silence is killing me. "Say something. Please."

I'm a few steps away, but we may as well be worlds apart, as he's giving me nothing to work with.

"I'm sorry, okay? I know it looked bad, but it's not. I love you, you big, stubborn jerk. If you can't even give me the chance to explain then—"

But I don't get a chance to finish my sentence

because Jasper spins around and charges at me in two huge strides. I'm taken off guard and almost fall over, but his hot hand shoots out and latches onto my upper arm. His fingers flex around my bicep, and as he draws me inches away from his face, I know its game on.

I leap at him the moment he lunges for me, our mouths tangling in a frantic, frenzied mess. It's an impassioned union, the past five minutes obviously weighing heavily on us both. I clutch at his t-shirt, desperately wanting to be skin to skin, but Jasper has other ideas

Pulling away quickly, he hoarsely commands, "Turn around."

I do as he asks, unsure why. My body trembles in anticipation because he doesn't touch me, but I can feel him undressing me with his eyes. Just as I'm about to beg for some kind of contact, my skin breaks out into tiny goose bumps as he glides his finger along the slope of my neck. I tilt my head to the right, giving him greater access to my skin. He traces down my arm, fingering my ring, and then continues his journey down my leg as my hands are locked against my sides. My dress is relatively short, so when he reaches the hemline he stops, sashaying backward and forward along my thigh.

My heavy breathing betrays just how turned on I am.

"Get on the sofa." His direct order has me quickly doing as he asks.

I lean forward on all fours, resting my feet on the arm of the sofa. I look over my shoulder, awaiting further instruction. My eyes have become accustomed to the dark, and as my gaze falls on Jasper's erection, I involuntarily moan in appreciation. He sees my approval and smirks. The sight is too much, so I turn back around before I combust into flames.

Moments later, I feel his fingers slither down the length of my back, stopping when they reach the hem of my dress. He grips my hip with one hand, and with the other, he slowly gathers up my dress and pulls it up, exposing my ass.

The fact he's remained relatively silent throughout this entire time, his harsh, heavy breathing the only indication that he's as turned on as me, heightens his every action, his every move, and I can't stop the low moan which passes through my parted lips. He gently slides my underwear down my legs and stops once they pool around my knees. I'm now completely bare to him and the sensation has my body trembling, eagerly anticipating his next move.

"You're so beautiful," he finally says, running a hand across the small of my back. His touch has my body bowing, begging for more.

He gently strokes over my cheek with the backs of his fingers and I arch my head backward, my long hair tickling my heated skin. He does the same to the other, and before long, I'm so damp between the legs, I feel I'm going to detonate if he doesn't touch me where I desperately want him to be.

"Such an impatient little thing." He chuckles while kneading my ass.

I gasp in surprise when I feel his pointer finger trace the crease between my globes. This is something we've never done before, and I'm a little scared to try.

"Relax, baby," he says, slowly moving his finger. But I can't.

Jasper senses my anxiety and sweeps his finger forward, running his fingertips over my wetness. I groan in desire and push backward, wanting him to go in deeper. However, I'm stunned when he glides his finger upward, rubbing my arousal over my rear.

I don't overthink it and give my body over to him because I know he'll never hurt me. As soon as I begin to relax, it suddenly begins to feel really, really good. He moves back to my soaked entrance and pumps in two fingers, his thumb lightly running over my center. I lose all control and move in sync with his skillful actions. He steadies me by placing his hand low on my hip, and with the one hand, and in one fluid motion, he sweeps back up and circles a place he's never touched before.

At first I clench, the sensation feeling foreign, but as he slowly pushes a wet finger into me, I relax, as the fullness is exactly what I need. His hand still supports my hip and I'm glad, because I'm afraid to move.

"Is this okay?" he hoarsely asks, his finger slowly gaining deeper access into the unknown.

I nod as I'm unable to speak, the feeling of pleasure is unlike anything I've felt before.

"I want to know and cherish every part of you." He pushes in deeper, bringing me closer and closer to the edge as he slides his other hand around to my center.

Before long, he's everywhere, touching and stroking me, working me over until I scream out my release. My body has never felt so full, and I'm convinced Jasper is soaked into my every pore.

He disentangles his fingers from my body, and I instantly sag forward, unable to hold up my own weight. Softly placing a hand between my shoulder blades, he gently presses my chest flat to the cushions. With the other, he scoops it under my tummy and draws my hips backward, so my butt is sitting high in the air. I hear him impatiently unzip his jeans, yanking them down his legs, before positioning himself at my entrance. I wiggle my hips, implying I'm ready, and with one fluid motion, he sinks into me, taking my breath away with his breadth.

His hisses low in this throat and waits a few seconds for my muscles to accept him before he starts moving. This position is so intense, so deep, I feel myself coming apart only after a few gentle strokes. I raise my hips up higher, the angle hitting me in just the right way.

"Fuck, baby," Jasper groans, securing my hip in his grip and placing his hand between my blades to gain deeper access.

It all feels amazing.

I turn my cheek so it rests against the sofa and grip the cushions in my fists as Jasper continues to drive into me harder and faster.

"With you...it always feels like the first time," he pants, his speed increasing, indicating he's close. "You're mine, Ava. No one else's but mine."

I wish I could reply, but I can't. My breath is saved for breathing, because I'm seconds away from passing out because everything feels so good.

I know this act is inspired by his dominance over what he saw. And to be honest, if I were in shoes, I would probably do the same.

"It's my touch you'll always remember. Always want. If ever you need reminding," he says, his hand rounding my hip to play with my core. "Just remember this."

The moment he touches me, I explode in a loud scream, and barely hear Jasper passionately say, "You're my forever and a day, baby. I love you." Seconds later, he joins me, roaring out his release.

We both collapse, too sated and numb to control our lust. Jasper's heaving chest pushes into my back, but his heavy weight is exactly what I need. What we experienced was pure love, and it was profound, and I find myself falling even more in love with Jasper every day.

After I've caught my breath and come down from my cloud, I know we have to address the Michel issue. I hate that he's an issue, but he's an issue nonetheless.

"I can't feel my legs." I chuckle, my face squished against the sofa.

"Oh, shit, sorry," Jasper says, quickly pulling out and lifting himself off of me.

I miss his weight instantly, but I manage to crawl into a half sitting position as I cover myself up. Jasper zips up his jeans and takes a seat beside me. We're both slightly breathless, and I take a moment to catch my breath before I speak.

"About tonight—"

Jasper cuts me off as he shakes his head. "There's no need to explain. I get what Yolanda was trying to do. I guess it's her way of flipping us both off."

I nod, but I still want to make clear that whatever Jasper thinks is happening between Michel and me is wrong. And after his display of dominance, I think he needs to hear it. "I love *you*, Jasper. I belong to you. I will never forget your touch," I say, referring to what he said to me earlier. "Because you'll forever be touching me. I can't forget something I crave so badly."

Jasper lowers his eyes, and I hate that I see uncertainty in them. "I wish you could come with me tomorrow. I hate leaving you behind. I hate leaving you with him."

"Hey," I coo, lifting his chin. "I'll be there before you know it. And besides, you're not leaving me with him. I'll be so busy tying up loose ends, I'll barely see him."

Jasper cocks a disbelieving eyebrow. "I find that hard to believe seeing as you'll be handing the reins over to him."

"And Sara," I add, the moonlight illuminating his unhappiness. "I won't be long. I promise."

He sighs, and once again I hate that yet another asshole has ruined our night.

"Any time spent away from you is long enough. It doesn't matter what the time frame is, it all feels like an eternity without you by my side."

His heartfelt words have me crawling towards him and climbing into his lap. I cling onto him as I rest my head against his chest. "I know the feeling," I say after a minute of silence. "But absence makes the heart grow fonder."

Jasper's steady breathing is soothing, and before long, I find my eyelids growing heavy. I could stay like this forever. He kisses the top of my head. "Without you, it feels like a piece of my heart is missing. This is the last time we're apart," he softly states, laying kisses all over me, his anguish apparent in his touch.

I sleepily nod, as I couldn't agree more. "The last time," I drowsily reply. "Nothing will ever keep us apart."

...If only I'd kept my mouth shut.

CHAPTER TWENTY

Song to Say Goodbye

Airports and I have a bittersweet relationship. They bring happiness when a loved one returns from an adventure, but they also bring sorrow, like right now, when you're faced with having to say goodbye to the love of your life.

We've been silent on the walk to the terminal, the mood somber, as the reality of being apart, hits home. Even though it won't be that long, Jasper was right—any time spent apart is long enough.

"So, this is it," I say as we reach the international gate.

"Yeah," Jasper replies, looking at the gate. "It is."

I can't even make idle chitchat because I'm afraid if I open my mouth, I'll burst into tears.

Saying goodbye to the one you love the most is one of the toughest things to do, but knowing what lies ahead when we reunite is what's getting me through.

"Have fun," I say, my voice quivering.

Jasper sighs, looking as torn as me. "I'll try, but I'll be counting down the hours until you're back in my arms."

"You won't even know I'm not there," I say, while Jasper scoffs. I don't want to taint this for him. I want him to be happy knowing I support him one hundred percent.

"This is a once in a lifetime opportunity, Jasper. Enjoy it. You deserve this."

Jasper nods, my words seeming to convince him. "Okay. I love you."

"I love you, too."

"I'll call you when I can."He knows once he hits the road, his schedule will be outta control.

"Okay," I reply, the reality of the situation hitting hard.

He takes a step forward, his boots heavy on the floor. "Come back to me soon. I'll be waiting." He rests his hand against my cheek. "Saying goodbye to you is the hardest thing I've ever had to do. No more goodbyes. Only hellos from now on," he concludes, his gentle eyes softening, revealing he's hurting just as much as I.

I can't help the tear that rolls down my cheek.

"Tears of an angel," he says, wiping it away. "No more tears, baby. Stay strong for me. Otherwise, it'll break my heart to leave you behind."

I sniff back my sorrow and try my best to smile.

"I'll see you real soon, okay?" he says, dipping down to meet my eyes.

I nod, biting the inside of my cheek to stop the tears.

"I love you so much." He wraps his arms around me, hugging me tighter than ever before.

I take in everything about him—his smell, his touch, his warmth. I store it in my memory bank and will revert to it when I'm missing him like crazy.

He's the first to pull away, but leaves his arms around me, slung low on my waist. "Goodbye, baby."

"Bye," I reply, my voice merely a soft whisper.

Letting me go, he places both warm hands against my cheeks and draws me towards him. As he places a tender kiss against my forehead, I know it's time. We're both silent, as there's nothing more to say.

I can see the anguish on his face, but he'll have to be the first to leave because my feet won't move. With one final kiss, he slowly turns his back, leaving me to my unshed tears. I watch until I can no longer see his form, and once reality kicks in, I know it's time to go.

Holding back my tears, I sprint for the exit and run to my car. I unlock my door and the moment I charge inside, I cry ugly tears. I don't know why I'm so upset. I mean, I'll see him soon. But I can't shake this ominous feeling that something bad is about to happen. And I know that something 'bad,' will most likely be in the shape of Delilah Rose.

I cry for a few minutes, not caring that I resemble a lunatic, and only when my phone dings do I stop bawling, so I can see who it is.

> Don't cry, baby. I'll see you real soon.
> Until then, check your back pocket.

The sender is Jasper.

I look around to ensure he's not watching me cry like a baby. When the coast is clear, I realize it shouldn't surprise me that he knows me so well. I quickly raise my hips off the seat so I can reach into my pocket. Feeling a soft velvet pouch, I pull it out, wondering when he had the time to put it in there without me knowing. However, putting that thought aside, I open the flap, eager to see what's inside.

As I unwrap the white tissue paper, a silver heart charm catches the sunlight. I gasp, as it's simply beautiful. A small note is inside the pouch, and when I pull it out, new tears fill my eyes.

My heart belongs to you.

The simple sentence equates to a thousand words.

I quickly type a reply, hoping I catch him before his flight.

I'll keep it safe. I promise.

Fastening the heart onto my charm bracelet, I notice it matches the bird trinket Jasper gave me for Christmas perfectly.

As the light catches the heart once again, it sparkles, just like the real thing.

The drive back to Metropolis has got me thinking about all the things I have to do to close up shop. My aim is to be gone in two weeks, but it'll be a stretch. I'll try my hardest however, because I'm already missing Jasper like crazy.

Metro is packed full, a sight I always like to see. I haven't spoken to Michel about the rubbish Yolanda produced as I was a tad preoccupied getting thoroughly worked over by Jasper. By the time we re-emerged forty-five minutes later, Michel had left.

I figured he was just as embarrassed as I was over the footage, but when I meet his narrowed gaze, I can't help but think he's pissed, rather than embarrassed.

"Hey Michel," I say casually, hoping he'll shed some light on why he's mad.

"*Bonjour*," he curtly replies, not meeting my eyes as he shoulders open the kitchen door.

It swings shut on me, which is a perfect analogy for this entire situation.

Growing a pair, I push open the door and duck my head into the kitchen. "Michel, a word," I say, not giving him time to reply as I make my way to my office.

The moment I take a seat at my desk, Michel strolls in, raising an eyebrow, indicating he's listening.

"Michel, have I done something to offend you?" I ask, not seeing the point of dancing around in circles. "I mean, even before the episode aired, I felt that you were... angry at me," I confess, pausing to find the right word.

"I'm not angry," he says, crossing his arms over his chest, contradicting his statement.

"Then what's with the attitude? I'm not sure if you heard me correctly last night, but I'm making you manager. This is a brilliant opportunity for you. One you earned all on your own. I thought you'd be happy?"

"I am, but I'd be even happier if you stayed," he replies, his lips pulling in a tight line.

"Why?" I ask, confused.

"Because as I'm sure you know, when you find someone you gel well with and are able to create the amazing dishes that we have been, it's hard to let them go," he explains honestly.

"I'm touched, I really am. But Sara is a pretty good substitute."

"*Oui*, she's good, but that's the problem. You're exceptional. You inspire me to cook. It's hard letting that go."

I know what he means. When you find someone who 'gets you' in the kitchen, you don't just cook, you create. Michel and I are a great team, but my mind is made up.

"I understand that, but it's time for me to go," I say firmly.

But Michel won't let this lie. "Go where? And do what?" he challenges.

I open my mouth but don't say anything, as I haven't thought that far ahead. Michel sees my hesitation and continues to press.

"Excuse me if I'm over stepping a line here, but that's what I thought. Who have you made this decision for? You? Or your fiancé?"

The word fiancé has never sounded so dirty.

I instantly leap to Jasper's defense. "You're right, you have overstepped a line. My decisions are mine alone. If you can't accept them, then I'm sorry. If you don't want the managing position, I'll find someone else."

Michel frowns, rubbing the back of his neck. "I've offended you. *Je suis désolé.* I just...care about you. You've been a good friend to me and given me an opportunity of a lifetime."

"So be grateful," I say with a smile. "Don't make me regret my decision."

Thankfully, Michel nods. "Okay. I'm sorry again for offending you."

"None taken."

He doesn't believe me, but he doesn't persist. "I better get back out there," he says when I make it clear this discussion is over.

I nod. "I'll look over the accounts and hopefully be able to start showing you the ropes later on today."

"*Bien*," he says and leaves.

The moment the door shuts, I let out a frustrated breath. Looking over at the stack of files on my desk, I reach for the top one, preferring to deal with one mess at a time.

Two hours later, I'm staring at the same piece of paper I was two hours ago.

Michel's comment has really gotten under my skin and I don't know why. What I decide to do with my life is none of his concern, but if I were him, I would have probably said the same thing. I know a lot of people will blame Jasper for my decision. But if they do, they don't know him at all.

"Ava?" Michel says, ducking his head around the door.

"Oh, hey," I say, looking at him over my mountain of paperwork.

"I thought you could do with a coffee break," he says, stepping into my office, both hands filled with yummy goods.

"You're a life saver." I toss my pen onto the desk and sit up higher to see what he's got.

The moment I see croissants, I clap excitedly. "You didn't bake them fresh, did you?" I ask, hoping the answer is yes.

Michel tsks at me. "As if I would offer you anything other than freshly baked croissants."

The moment he places them in front of me, I resemble Pavlov's dogs. "Gimme, gimme," I say, making grabby hands, while Michel chuckles.

"Such an impairment, little thing."

His comment reminds me of something Jasper once said, and I instantly miss him.

"So I've been told," I reply with a reminiscent smile. Looking at the two buttery pastries, I tap my chin cheekily. "I don't know what you're eating, 'cause they're both mine."

Michel laughs, taking the seat across from me and sliding me a coffee. The moment the aroma from the freshly ground coffee beans reaches my nostrils, I hum in appreciation.

"You make the best coffee, you've gotta show me your secret before I go," I say, reaching for the cup and taking a small sip.

Michel gives me a small smile which doesn't reach his eyes. "About that, I feel like an ass for saying what I did."

I go to wave him off, but he raises his hand, gesturing for me to allow him to explain. "So this," he says, sweeping toward the table. "Is my way of saying sorry. I'd also like to take you out to dinner tonight if you were free?"

Dinner? I think that may be crossing some line somewhere. I work my finger over the handle of my cup, debating what to do. I don't want to make things any weirder between us, and it is only dinner.

Michel can see me pondering over his request. "I thought we could check out Hippo's? The food guide did say they have the best steak in New York, which I find hard to believe, seeing as I think we do," he says, leaning backward in his seat and interlacing his hands behind his head.

That has me nodding in agreement because I too, think the same thing. "Sure. Did you want to go straight from work? It's Sara's turn to play boss tonight."

Michel smiles, the first genuine smile I've seen from him all day. "Perfect. What time do you think you'll be done with all that?" he asks, pointing to my tower of paperwork.

I laugh. "It's not looking like any time soon."

"Well, in that case, let's live life on the edge and leave early," he suggests, his tone playful.

Leaving early sounds like an awesome idea, seeing as Jasper will be arriving in London later on tonight, and I want to be home early just in case he calls.

"It's a—" But I stop myself before the word 'date' passes my lips. "It's a plan," I quickly correct, hoping Michel didn't notice my slip up.

As he smirks, his dimples hugging his whiskered cheeks, I so know that he did.

CHAPTER TWENTY ONE
Sleepover

"I'm not going to ask how you got us these seats." I sip my wine, looking out at the glorious view of The Hudson River.

Michel gestures that his secret is under lock and key as he zips up his lips and throws away the key.

The night is cool, thanks to the wind coming off the water, but it's so nice to be outdoors after being cooped up in the office all day. I didn't even make a dent with my paperwork, and the possibility of leaving in two weeks is starting to look grim.

That thought is the reason why my phone has taken up permanent residency on the table, as I'm missing Jasper more than ever. I don't want to miss his call, and I've tried not to check it every five seconds, but it's hard. The thought of not seeing him for two weeks was hard enough to stomach, but now the possibility of not seeing him for even longer is turning me into an insecure crybaby. Again, that insecurity stems from Delilah.

"Everything okay?" Michel asks, snapping me from my thoughts.

Shaking my head to clear it, I realize I'm being extremely rude. I'm here with Michel, not my cell. As much as it kills me, I pick it up and place it in my handbag. "Yeah, fine," I reply. "Sorry, I'm just a little distracted. Jasper lands in London soon, and I'm waiting for him to call."

Michel nods, his scruffy hair catching in the breeze. "How long is he away?"

This is the first conversation we've had about Jasper that Michel has been able to talk about him without looking like he's going to gag.

"Six weeks. Six long weeks," I add, swirling the red in my glass.

"So he's always been in a band?" he asks, leaning back in his seat casually.

"Since I've known him, yes. I really can't see him doing anything else. I mean, he's so talented at what he does, it would be a crime if he stopped."

Michel nods, looking to be deep in thought. "Yes, I've heard him on the radio, he's very good. But I guess with someone like you as his muse, he couldn't be anything but."

I know it's a compliment and normally, I wouldn't think twice about it, but after Jasper's accusations that Michel is interested in me on more than a professional level, it makes me feel a little uncomfortable. I don't make a big deal about it though, as I don't feel Michel meant it in a sleazy way.

Our appetizers arrive, quickly putting any embarrassment on the backburner because the mozzarella sticks smells divine. I snatch one up, taking a bite, but fan my mouth because it's damn hot.

Michel chuckles while shaking his head. "Don't look

too impressed, they're meant to be our competition," he whispers from behind his hand.

I shrug, happily chewing away on my fried cheesy goodness. "Competition or not," I say, waving my mozzarella stick around like a weapon. "They know how to fry up some cheese."

As Michel takes a bite, I can see he also approves.

"But I bet we kick their ass cooking a steak," I say smugly, knowing that we've got this.

I was right. Hippo's steak, although delicious, pales in comparison to ours.

Michel and I have spent the last couple of hours critiquing every dish we've ordered. It may sound a little snooty, but it can't be helped. We all compare what we know best.

I'm having a great time and the conversation is flowing freely, just like it usually does, except the past few days. This is the Michel I know—the fun, hilarious, confident man I hired. Although I haven't known him that long, the mutual respect and appreciation was there the moment I met him. This is why it saddened me when he was acting so weird around Jasper and me. I guess the instant connection just happens with some people and Michel is one of those people. I hope we can continue our friendship once I move back to L.A. because apart from getting on like a house on fire, his culinary skills are unlike anything I've ever seen before.

"Although Mother is an absolute dragon, she does know her way around the kitchen. I guess that's something I can thank her for," Michel says, raising his wine glass in salute.

"Usually, I would be speaking up in her defense, but I've seen her in action and I think dragon is a compliment," I say, wiping my mouth with a napkin after demolishing my lemon tart.

Michel is silent and I wonder if I've offended him. Just as I'm about to apologize, he bursts into fits of laughter.

"Couldn't have said it better myself," he says, still chuckling.

When our waiter discreetly places our bill on the table, I look down at my watch and gasp when I see it's almost eleven. We've been talking nonstop for the past, I don't even know how many hours, and not once did I feel bored or did the conversation run thin. I also realize I was too distracted to check my cell.

"Excuse me," I say, reaching into my handbag.

As I retrieve my cell, I check the screen but frown when I see I haven't received any text messages or calls in the past few hours.

"No word?" Michel asks, reaching into his back pocket to pull out his wallet.

"No," I say, shaking my head, trying not to sound disappointed.

"I'm sure he's just landed." He gives me a reassuring smile. "And with the sound of his hectic tour schedule, he's probably meeting up with tour managers and record labels."

He's right, and his accurate comment makes me feel better. "You're right," I say, returning his smile.

When I see he's placed a wad of cash on the table, I quickly take away a few bills and hand them back to him. "That's too much." But he waves me off, using his hands to bat away the cash.

"It's my treat," he says, finishing his wine in one big sip. "And besides, it's not every day I get to take a beautiful girl out to dinner."

"Michel," I say, about to protest, but he stands up and hands the cash to the waiter as he waltzes past.

"Next time it's on me," I stupidly say, because this was a one-off thing. It's the courteous thing to say, and universally accepted, so why do I feel guilty for saying it?

As Jasper's warnings echo in my head, I know the reason why.

"Deal," Michel says, oblivious to my internal war.

When we make our way outside, Michel curses as he checks his pockets. "*Merde.*"

"What's the matter?"

"I've left my keys at Metropolis," he says, scratching his head, looking rather embarrassed.

"That's okay, we can swing past on the way to dropping you home."

Michel usually rides the subway to work, but I'm a paranoid Los Angeleno and insisted I drive him home. No matter the time, New York is always busy, and it takes us about twenty minutes to get to Metro. Michel runs inside, promising he won't be long.

As I idle by the sidewalk, I give into my OCD and check my phone.

Still nothing.

I try and squash down my disappointment, reminding myself that Jasper is at work, and that when I'm at work, he's lucky to get a hello outta me. It just sucks, as I have a feeling this is what the next few weeks will be like. The not knowing where he is, or who's he with is what's killing me.

Thankfully, Michel comes running back to the car to distract me from my stupidity. When he opens the door, he stands outside, his arm resting above the door frame. "I can't find them," he says, explaining why he's standing outside my car.

"When did you have them last?"

"I left them where I usually keep them—in my locker. I have no idea where they could be," he says, shaking his head in bewilderment.

"Did you retrace your steps?"

"Yes," he replies, nodding. "*Désolé, Cheri*. I'll call my friend and stay the night with him and call a locksmith tomorrow."

"Okay," I say, switching off the car. I once again check my phone while Michel is on his, but I'm still faced with a blank screen.

"*Merde*, he's not answering," he says, hanging up the phone.

"Does anyone have a spare key?" I ask, trying to be helpful.

"*Non*," he replies, running a hand through his hair.

"After I found my apartment trashed, thanks to my scorned ex, I stopped handing them out."

Well, this is awkward.

Michel drums his fingers on the roof of my car, looking to be deep in thought on what to do. "I'll stay at a hotel," he says with a sigh. "I can't believe this."

This is wrong on all accounts, and I wish I'd stopped talking, but it's too late as I say, "Don't be silly. You can stay at my place."

"No, I can't impose. I've already wasted enough of your time," he says, looking frustrated with himself.

"It's okay, really," I reply, assuring him. "If you don't mind sleeping on the sofa, then the offer stands."

Michel weighs up his options, looking torn. "Are you sure?"

"Positive. Now get in, it's cold," I say, rubbing my arms.

He smiles and quickly jumps in, buckling his seatbelt. "Thank you, *Cheri*. I'll make you breakfast as my way of saying thanks."

"Deal. You know any sort of food is my weakness," I reply with a grin as I zip into traffic.

We're both quiet on the way to my apartment, the talk radio the only thing that fills the silence. I know Jasper would hate this idea, but what else was I supposed to? It's absurd him staying at a hotel, considering it's almost midnight. By the time he checks in and gets settled, he'll be up again and checking out. This is practical and it makes sense. So why am I questioning my motives?

I pull into my underground parking garage and park

in my allocated spot. "Okay, we're here," I stupidly say, seeing as it's pretty obvious.

Michel smiles and casually unbuckles his belt while I suddenly get sweaty palms. I know he shouldn't be here, but it's too late now. We ride the elevator to my floor in silence, and I fumble with my key as I try and get it in the lock. After attempt number three, it finally budges.

"Well, make yourself at home," I say, picking up scattered items on the floor as I make my way inside.

"Your home is lovely," Michel says as he glances around my small apartment.

"Thanks, it's a lot lovelier when it doesn't look like a bombsite," I reply, hands filled with my junk. "I'm in the process of culling," I say, hoping that'll explain why my living room looks like a department store. "I won't be a minute."

Scampering to my bedroom, I toss all my belongings on the floor. I'll deal with the mess tomorrow, as I've got a bigger one to deal with right now. As I walk back out, I see Michel tidying up my couch. When his fingers pass over my red bra, I charge for it like it's a stick of dynamite.

"Sorry," he says, but I can see the smile tugging at his lips.

"It's fine," I reply, not wanting to make a big deal about it. "So, here is your comfy bed for the evening." I sweep my hand toward the sofa.

"Thank you." He sits down and begins untying his shoelaces, which is my cue to get him a blanket and pillow.

"I'll be right back," I say, walking down the hallway.

As I search through my loaded linen closet, I'm

grateful my mom made me pack all this stuff. I reach for a huge fluffy blanket and two pillows, wondering if I should maybe pull out the light afghan, too. I'm not sure if he would prefer one blanket or two, so I decide to go with both and let him decide.

"Okay," I say, as I round the corner, juggling all the goods. "I didn't know what you wanted, so I grabbed—" But I pause when my gaze lands on Michel's naked chest.

My traitorous eyes decide that this scandalous vision is not enough, so I look down and see Michel's white CK boxer briefs—briefs which he fills out rather nicely.

That thought however, has me turning my back and awkwardly stammering, "I-I...you...um...sorry," I finally decide upon, closing my eyes in embarrassment.

It feels so, *so* wrong that a half-naked man other than Jasper is standing in my living room. I tried not to look, but holy shit, Michel is just as impressive unclothed as he is clothed. His broad shoulder span is bulked up with mountains of muscles which lead into a narrow, well defined waist. His eight-pack is so ridged I could scrub my laundry off of it if this were the 16th century.

Luckily it's not, as I so should not be thinking about him and his eight-pack that way—or any way for that matter. Shaking my head, I tell myself to open my eyes and turn around because every second spent with my back turned is making this situation worse.

Thankfully my legs work and they do as they're told. "Here you go." I hold out the blankets and pillows from a few feet away, as I don't want to get too close.

"*Merci,*" he says, accepting them with a smile.

He seems either oblivious or not bothered that I can't

stop staring at him. It's been such a long time since I've been this close to a barely clothed man that isn't Jasper it seems I've forgotten my manners.

Quickly averting my eyes, I know now is the time to say goodnight. "If you need anything, my room is just down the hall." Oh crap, that could be misconstrued as being totally inappropriate. So I amend as I grab my handbag and walk backwards out the room, "Actually, just make yourself at home. Bathroom's down the hall, first door to the left, and you know where the kitchen is so...goodnight."

I'm practically jogging down the hallway when I hear Michel call out, *"Bonne nuit,"* which I'm hoping means goodnight as there's no way I'm going back out there.

Quietly shutting the door behind me, I rest up against it and catch my breath. It's totally okay to sneak in a quick look, I assure myself. I mean, I'm sure Jasper is no saint. It's natural to be attracted to good looking things, not that I'm attracted to Michel. It was just a shock to see...so much of him.

I know I'm being ridiculous, so I stop being an idiot and decide to get ready for bed. Just as I'm about to slip on my pajama bottoms, my phone rings from inside my bag. I dive for it, desperate to answer it before the person, who most likely will be Jasper, hangs up.

"Hello," I say, a touch out of breath.

"Hell...o," the broken voice, who is definitely Jasper, says from the other end.

We've got a really bad line because all I can hear is static and hissing.

"Jasper?" I say, moving around the room, trying to get better reception.

"Baby?" he says after a few seconds delay.

"Jasper, I can't hear you. We've got a really bad line."

It sounds like the phone is being spun through a washing machine. I frown as he's so close, yet so far away.

"Baby? Can you hear me?" he asks and the line seems clearer.

"Yes!" I exclaim, practically bouncing on the spot in excitement. "How are you? How was your flight? I miss you."

Jasper chuckles and the sound is one I crave to hear again and again. "I'm okay. Flight was long. I bet I miss you more. Do you like your present?"

"I love it. Thank you so much. I'll never take it off," I reply, fingering the charm.

"I'm glad," he says, and the line starts to cut in and out again.

"Ugh, the line's dropping out," I say, moving around the room.

"I...know. Sorry," he says, the delay stretching out. "I'm on a pay...phone. I need to get an international SIM."

That explains the crappy line.

"I just wanted to call to say..."

"Say what?" I say, pressing the phone to my ear, afraid we've lost the line.

"I love you. And I miss you," he finishes a few seconds later.

"I love you and miss you, too," I say, tears stinging my ears.

Michel being here, and being here half nude, gives me a serious case of the guilts, so I want to tell Jasper that he is here. "Michel is here," I say, trying to sound casual because it is casual.

"Who's ear?" Jasper asks. "Baby, I can't hear you."

"Michel is here, he's staying over because he lost his keys," I say, raising my voice, hoping that he can hear me.

"I can't—" But the line goes dead before Jasper can finish his sentence.

I don't know how much of that he heard and I wait anxiously, staring at the phone, willing it to ring. It doesn't.

After waiting ten minutes, I figure he's not calling me back. I'm hoping that's because the line is bad, and not because I just told him another man is sleeping in his house.

Changing into my pajamas, I place my phone on the bedside table just in case it rings. I slip into bed and roll onto Jasper's side, as my side feels too lonely and cold without him.

CHAPTER TWENTY TWO
Watchful Eye

I wake to the delicious smell of coffee and pancakes. Jumping out of bed, I have the world's quickest shower, eager to start the day, with Michel's yummy breakfast first on my list. I throw on some jeans and a tee and I'm out the door, rubbing my hands in delight.

"You can cook me breakfast any day," I say in a singsong voice as I walk into the kitchen. I stop dead in my tracks however, when I see Michel is topless.

His back is turned to me so he can't see my face, but he replies, "I'll cook you breakfast every day if you like." There is no hint of sleaze or flirtiness in his tone, so I shrug it off as my sleep deprived brain reading into things.

After tossing and turning for what felt like hours, I finally fell asleep, but my slumber was not restful, nor do I feel refreshed. I couldn't stop thinking about Jasper. I feel foolish telling him what I did about Michel. I know we promised to be honest with one another, but my honesty could have probably waited until he could actually hear me properly. I know Jasper though, and odds are that he didn't hear me, because if he did, it would be unlike him to not call back and ask what the hell is going on.

"Would you like some?" Michel asks, interrupting me from my thoughts.

Raising my eyes, I see him standing with the coffee pot in front of me. "Coffee. Would you like some?"

"Oh, yes please."

Michel pours me a cup. I eagerly accept as I need a dose of caffeine to zap some life into me. "So, you up for learning how to play boss today? I say, sipping my liquid gold. "It's real easy," I add with a smile.

Michel happily nods. "Sure. I'll warn you though, I'm not very good with bookkeeping and remembering who to order what from. This may take all night."

"Don't worry, there's no rush," I say, when in fact, there is.

The longer Michel takes to pick this up, the longer it keeps me away from Jasper. But I don't want him to feel like there's any pressure. Running a restaurant the size of Metropolis is hard work—I should know. So I won't push Michel, but I *will* give him a gentle nudge.

"And besides, you've got Sara to fall back on if you totally suck," I add with a playful smirk.

He laughs, shaking his head as he makes his way over to the pancake stack on the counter. "Well, we better eat all these. I have a feeling it'll be a long day."

"Cheers to that," I say, raising my cup in salute.

As we eat our breakfast over light conversation, I totally forget he's sitting before me topless—just how it should be.

The moment Michel and I walk into Metropolis, I feel Sara's eagle eyes zero in on us. Michel excuses himself as he makes his way into the men's locker room, adamant to find his keys. Just as I'm about to step into the kitchen, Sara loops her arm through mine and escorts me to my office, not saying a word.

The moment she closes the door, I know what she's going to say. "Did you and Michel just come to work together?"

I nod, rounding my desk and taking a seat. "We did."

"And..." she says, crashing into the chair across from me.

"And what?" I ask, raising an eyebrow.

"And...and why? And why is he wearing the same clothes as yesterday?" she asks, rubbing her chin suspiciously.

"Is he? I hadn't noticed," I reply, refusing to meet her eyes as I shuffle through some paperwork.

"Ava, he didn't stay over, did he?" she asks, her tone disappointed.

I finally gather the courage to meet her gaze. "Yes, he did, but it's not what you think. Like really not what you think."

Sara crosses her arms, indicating she's listening.

"We went out to dinner, purely as friends," I say, raising my hand when she opens her mouth. "He lost his keys and didn't have a place to stay, so I offered him my couch. That's it."

Sara narrows a fair brow, looking unconvinced. "Jasper said this would happen."

"Excuse me?" I say, pulling back, stunned. "He said what now?"

"He asked me to keep an eye on you. Or rather, Michel," she adds when I throw my pen down in protest.

"When?"

"Um, the night of the screening. You went off to the bathroom and he asked, very discreetly I might add, if I could make sure Michel doesn't get too friendly around you. Staying over at your place seems a little too friendly to me," she confesses. I see red.

"He asked you to *babysit* me?" I say, my voice rising in anger.

"No, no, not babysit," Sara replies, waving her hands out in front of her, attempting to diffuse the situation. "Just watch out for you."

"So in other words, spy on me," I say, adding my own take on this entire conversation.

Sara shakes her head, but I can see that's kinda what he was asking her to do. "I'm not explaining myself properly. The words spy or babysit were never mentioned. He's just worried about you, Ava. He cares about you."

"Worried why? It's Michel, for Christ's sake!" I retort, unable to hold my tongue. I feel awful, as Sara is not the person who deserves my wrath. Jasper is. But he's god knows where, and lucky for him, unreachable.

"Yeah, that's kinda the point," she says, making a face like she's afraid I'll yell at her.

"I'm not following."

"Well, I think Michel likes you," she confesses. I groan.

"Not you too," I say, resting my forehead against my palms as I cradle my head in frustration.

"You can't see it, but I can. We all can."

"All?" I ask, lowering my hands.

"Yeah," she replies, biting her glossy lip.

"Great, everyone probably believes the shit they saw on TV was real."

When she doesn't reply, I want to throttle two people —Yolanda and Jasper.

"Just, I dunno, maybe no more sleepovers?" she suggests, while I rest my head on my desk, exhausted. It's only 9 a.m.

"Like I said, the sleepover was a one off, Michel lost his keys," I pointlessly explain, as she didn't believe me the first time around.

"Michel's keys were on the kitchen counter, in plain sight," she says, her voice full of accusation.

"Don't you have lunch to prepare?" I playfully say, my words muffled, as my cheek is squished against the wood grain.

I hear the chair scraping along the floor as she stands, but I don't even have the energy to raise my head and apologize for being a bitch. "Sorry, Sara," I say, again muffled.

"It's okay, Ava. We're only trying to look out for you. We—"

"Care about me. Got it."

She doesn't say anything further as she exits my

office, leaving me alone to digest what she just said. I'm not cool with Jasper, or anyone for that matter, checking up on me because as far as I'm concerned, it's spying. Jasper obviously doesn't trust me, which saddens me. Yes, I'm uneasy about this whole Delilah situation because she's a troublesome cow, while Michel is not.

My voice of reason kicks in, alerting me to the fact that it's probably the same on Jasper's end. But I still feel betrayed. I wish he would have told me. Asking my employee to spy on me while he's not here makes me look like some untrustworthy whore. And after Yolanda's spin on what goes on here, I wouldn't blame my staff for questioning who their boss really is.

I need V.

Searching blindly for my cell, I find it in my jacket pocket. Not even bothering to lift my head, I dial her number and press the phone against my ear.

"Hello, babe. Miss me already?" V's chirpy voice says.

"Yes," I blankly reply, which comes out smooshed.

V doesn't say anything, as she's probably trying to decipher why I sound weird.

"What's wrong?" She sighs. I hear her sitting down.

"Jasper is an asshole, that's what's wrong," I say, finally lifting my head. I hold onto the edge of the table as the sudden movement makes me dizzy.

"Why?"

"Because he asked Sara, my soon to be manager, to spy on me," I reply, getting angry all over again.

"Spy on you? Why? Is he afraid you're going to eat

your body weight in chocolate while he's away?" she asks, half-jokingly.

I wish I could laugh because her comment is kinda funny, but I can't. I'm too mad to laugh. "V, this isn't funny. He doesn't trust me around Michel."

"Pepe Le Pew?" she asks randomly.

I don't reply, not knowing if she's talking to me or Cara. When she remains silent, I know she's talking to me.

"Who is Pepe Le Pew?"

"*Allo ma Cherie*," V says in a horrid French accent, attempting to impersonate the Warner Bros character.

"I know who he is," I say, chuckling. "But why in god's name did you bring him up?"

"Because Michel is French, duh. And he's in lovvvve...with you," she replies, laughing at her own lame joke.

"Seriously, you too? Does the entire world except me think that Michel is in love with me?" I snap, pulling out my ponytail to massage my sore head.

"Well, to be fair, you kinda asked Lucas about Delilah, and I think if he offered to keep an eye on her, you'd jump at the chance."

When I don't say anything, she adds, "Don't be mad. I'm just saying Jasper obviously senses something threatening in Michel that you don't. Just like you wanna pull out Delilah's hair and strangle her with it."

"This is totally different. Michel and I don't have a past."

"No, but you have a present. Whatever Jasper had with Delilah is in the past, but whatever you have with

Michel is in the now. From where I stand, he's probably got a lot more ground to stand on than you do."

Great, now my best friend is ganging up on me. "You're supposed to be on my side, ya know?" I say light-heartedly.

"There shouldn't be any sides, babe. I'm just telling you what you already know. Jasper is crazy about you, and he's also crazy protective over you. So what if he asked someone to make sure no one was touching his girl? He's only doing it because he cares," she reasons gently, making me see she's right.

Although I don't agree with his methods, I guess I can understand why he did it. And V is right. I did grill Lucas over Delilah.

"You're right, V. I'm being stupid. But I still plan on giving him a piece of my mind," I say stubbornly.

"I didn't expect anything less," she replies, laughing.

"That's if I can speak to him. Have you spoken to Lucas? Jasper called last night but the line was bad," I say, pulling up Google on my laptop to see what time it is over in London.

"Yeah, same deal with Lucas. From what I could understand, their schedule is tight, so he said he'll call when he can." I hear Cara screaming in the background, which I know is V's cue to leave.

"Okay, well, thanks for the pep talk. I'll give you a call in a few days. Here's hoping I'll be one step closer to wrapping things up here," I confess. Michel appears in my doorway. "Talk soon. And V?"

"Yes, babe."

"Thank you for being the sane one."

V laughs. "I'll take that in writing," she says, and hangs up.

I gesture Michel in, as he's still waiting by my door. He steps in and holds up his finger, his keys hanging off the end of it.

"You found them?" I exclaim happily. "Where were they?" I ask, even though Sara told me she saw them in the kitchen.

"On the kitchen counter," he explains, taking a seat in front of me. "I have no idea how they ended up there."

"Weird," I reply, shaking my head.

"Tell me about it," he confirms, looking puzzled. "Anyway, thank you for letting me stay the night."

"No problem. Just, if anyone asks, you had your keys all along, okay?" I say, hinting I don't want anyone else to know he spent the night.

"*Bien sûr*," he replies with a knowledgeable nod.

"Thank you. So," I say, looking at the files piled high on my desk. "You ready?"

Michel grins, his happiness contagious. "*Oui*. Let the fun begin."

Michel wasn't joking when he said he sucked at bookkeeping. I went over all the simple stuff—twice, but nothing seemed to sink in. I'm doubtful he'll pick up on the more complex stuff in two weeks. I mean, it took me close to three months to figure out what to order from which supplier, because we deal with about eighteen different companies. Most is based on experience and trial and error, something that's hard to teach in two weeks' time.

We gave up after six grueling, frustrating hours and I know we've only just begun. I'm going to have to work closely with Michel, day in, day out, if I have any hope of leaving and meeting Jasper overseas.

I know Sara will probably be watching us like a hawk, ready to report back to Jasper if she thinks Michel has stepped out of line. I caught her out a few times, poking her head sneakily into my office to see what we were up to. After spy attempt number five, I got up and shut the door.

Michel isn't blind, and he can see the not so covert glances Sara throws our way. I know Jasper meant well, but I'm still a little ticked off he made Sara his mole because she and Michel need to work and trust one another when I'm gone. At this rate, that's not looking likely.

After an exhausting day, I've crashed early, too tired to deal with anyone other than Charlie Hunnam. Totally engrossed in his lopsided smile, I fail to hear my phone ding on the bedside table beside me. Only when it chimes a second time, reminding me I have an awaiting text, do I reach over to see who it is.

Je t'aime

The message reads.

I feel my throat tighten. The sender, who I'm presuming and hoping is Jasper, says.

> I learned a little French in school, so I know this means I love you.

> I love you more

I reply, going with my gut that it's Jasper and not someone else.

I'm hoping he got an international SIM and not using someone's phone because that would be rather embarrassing otherwise.

> Impossible. I miss you. How was your day?

I let out the breath I was holding.

> Day was okay. Trying to wrap things up. Where are you?

I mute Charlie while I wait for Jasper's response.

> Still in London. Just about to go on stage—that's why I'm texting. Guess where we're headed tomorrow?

From his initial message, I have a pretty good idea where.

> Hmm…I give up.

> LOL! I wish you were here how long 'til you think you fly over?

And that's the million dollar question. I was hoping two weeks, but that's not looking probable. But I don't want to tell Jasper that and ruin his first international show.

> I hope 2 weeks. Maybe 3.

> Okay, baby. I miss you like crazy. Gotta go. We're about to go on. I love you so much xx

> I love you too.

I wait a few minutes, but when I don't get a reply, I know he's out there on stage, living out his dream.

Sighing, I un-mute Charlie, hoping his hotness will distract me from how much I miss Jasper. And also distract me from the fact that for a split second, I didn't know who the sender of the text message was.

CHAPTER TWENTY THREE
Touch Me

I storm into Metropolis, determined to teach Michel the ropes and having at least one lesson stick. I think I dove in too fast, too quickly yesterday, just expecting him to pick it up because I know it like the back of my hand.

It doesn't help that Sara isn't Michel's number fan at the moment, because she already knows half the stuff I'm showing him. If push comes to shove, I'll show him what I can and she'll have to guide him through the bumps along the way. But I don't want to dump all the responsibilities on her, hence me sitting in my office with Michel, explaining for the tenth time how our monthly budget works.

"I'm sorry, *Cheri*," he says, the frustration clear in his tone. "I don't understand why each month differs. This would be a lot easier if it was the same amount every month."

"It would, but each month is different because..." I say, leaving the sentence so he can fill in the blanks.

However, when he looks at me with nothing but confusion in his eyes, I know I'm doomed.

"Okay, let's try something else," I suggest, trying to

stay positive because I can see that Michel is trying. "For the time being, let's stick to what you know."

"So just cooking then?" he replies with a cheeky smile.

"We all know you're a genius in the kitchen."

"Just not out of it though," he comments, running a hand through his hair.

"Hey, stop being so hard on yourself." I reach forward and rub his hand reassuringly, while he places his hand over mine.

"Thank you for being so patient with me. I really am trying."

"I know you are. But I'm going to try something different. Something, which I'm hoping, will make all the stuff that comes with running this place a little easier to understand."

Michel nods happily, and the first smile I've seen all day lights up his face. "I like the sound of that," he says, squeezing my fingers. The gesture is chaste—one friend thanking another.

"Ava, Todd just called in sick," Sara says, bursting into my office as she looks at the roster in her hand. "Who am I supposed to call?" she adds, looking up and raising both eyebrows when she sees Michel is holding my hand.

I pull back, looking totally guilty, even though we weren't doing anything wrong. But I still feel the need to fill in the silence with meaningless chatter. "We were just talking shop and I've decided that Michel is going to take over ordering from suppliers so he can understand how our monthly budget works," I say, all in one quick breath.

Sara leans against the doorjamb, crossing her arms over her chest. "Okay."

Her blunt reply reveals she's more concerned about what she just walked into, rather than my plans for Michel learning the ropes. The judgment in her eyes really ticks me off and suddenly, I'm struck with a brilliant idea.

"I'm taking the day off." I stand up and reach for the jacket off the back of my chair.

"What?" Michel and Sara say as the same time, shocked by my announcement.

"You heard me. If Metropolis has any hope of running successfully after I'm gone, then you both need to pick up the pace. You especially, Sara. You've been here a lot longer than Michel. You want this managing position, then start acting like it."

Sara pales, and she can read my annoyance instantly. "Ava, I'm sorry. I didn't mean—"

But I wave my hand, gesturing for her to stop talking. "Show Michel what you know. I'll be back tomorrow to deal with the mess."

Sara is speechless. I can see she feels awful for stepping out of line, but too bad. I won't be judged for something I haven't done.

"What about Todd?" she asks in a soft voice.

I shrug because at this precise moment, I don't give a damn. "Figure it out." I stand in front of her, waiting for her to move. She gets the hint and guiltily moves to the side.

The moment I step outside, I feel terrible for being a

right royal bitch, but I continue walking down the street, not looking back.

My impromptu day off has proven to be quite productive.

I've packed up the majority of my things, and all that remains are the bare essentials. I still don't know when I'll be able to leave, and I guess tomorrow will determine if two weeks is still a feasible time frame. It's good to know however, that once the light at the end of the tunnel shines brightly, all my stuff is packed and I'm ready to go.

I've cleaned the house, made a triple layer chocolate cake, and I'm now sitting in bed, eating that entire cake while watching some trashy TV. Sara's behavior today has fueled my anger at Jasper all over again. If he'd just let things be, none of this would be an issue and my employees would all get along.

I'm edgy, irritated, and annoyed, and this chocolate cake is doing nothing to improve my mood. I set it on the bedside table, afraid I'll puke if I take another bite. I could maybe hit the gym and try and run myself into an exhausted heap, but as the wind howls outside, I decide to take a bath instead.

The moment I step into the scalding water, my body instantly uncoils. I sink in with no intention of arising any time soon. Countless minutes pass by, and just as I'm about to fall into a sleepy bubble of paradise, my cell rings loudly.

I consider ignoring it, but then a thought hits me—what if it's work? What if something happened and they need me? As every terrible scenario bombards my now very alert brain, I blindly reach for my phone while ripping the face cloth from my face.

"Hello?" I breathlessly say, not even bothering to look at the screen to see who it is.

I wait with my heart in my throat as I'm greeted with silence.

"Hello?" I repeat when no one speaks.

Just as I'm about to pull the phone away to see who's on the other end, the husky voice of the sexiest man alive greets me. "What are you doing that's got you so breathless?"

I'm breathless for another reason now.

"I'm taking a bath," I reply matter-of-factly.

"Oh, don't be cruel," he says, groaning in need. "I miss you. How's it going? Any clue when you'll be able to leave?"

"Well," I say, my tone revealing he's in for an earful. "Maybe if you didn't ask Sara to spy on me, I'd be able to ask for her help in training Michel. At the moment, that's not going to happen because she's too busy making sure Michel doesn't breathe the same air as me."

Jasper's quiet for a few seconds, no doubt cursing that he's been sprung. "The word spy was never mentioned," he replies jokingly.

But I won't let his charm to distract me. "Whichever

way you look at it, Jasper, it all points to the fact that you don't trust me."

"Baby," he says sternly. "That's not true. It's *him*. I just wanted to make sure he kept his manners in check while I was gone, that's all. I trust you completely. I wouldn't have asked you to marry me if I didn't. I just—" He pauses. "I won't take any chances with you. And I won't apologize for loving you, Ava."

I sigh—how can I argue with reasoning like that?

"To be fair, I didn't think Sara would take it so seriously. Has she really been that bad?" he asks, while I scoff.

"Bad is putting it mildly. I think she may have been a P.I. in her former life."

Jasper chuckles.

"But seriously, doing what you did just delayed me coming to Europe. Sara now hates Michel, which makes my life ten times harder. I get why you did it, but your good intentions have forced me to spend even more time with Michel," I say, hoping I don't sound like a nag.

Jasper takes a deep breath, realizing the truth to my words "Shit. That's definitely not what I wanted. I messed up."

I can hear his sincerity, so there's no point harping on about it.

"If I was there, I'd be on my knees, begging for forgiveness," he says when I remain pensive.

His comment gives me an idea—a very *naughty* idea.

"Well, you're not here. So what other ways can you say you're sorry?" I ask, full of innuendos.

"I don't...oh," he replies, his voice dropping low.

"Are you alone?" I question when I hear hushed voices in the background.

"No, but I can be. Gimme a sec." I hear him open a door, his boots pounding across the floor as he briskly walks to his sanctuary

When a door softly closes, my heart begins beating with what I'm about to say.

"Okay, I'm alone," he says quietly, awaiting further instruction.

"Lock the door."

I hear a lock click into place.

"What are you wearing?" I ask, needing a visual so I know where to lead this.

"My white Chili Peppers tee, black jeans, and my boots," he promptly replies.

I hum low in my throat because I can picture it clearly. "Where are you?"

"My hotel room."

"Unbuckle your belt," I command, adding, "please," a second later.

His fingers quickly go to work on the buckle. I hear it being unthreaded through his belt loops, and dropping to the floor a moment later.

"If I was there, what do you think I'd do next?" I softly ask, my entire body heating at the thought.

"I think you'd run your little fingers over my hard on," he confidently replies.

"Are you hard?" I ask, surprised at my confidence.

"Like you wouldn't believe."

"Touch yourself," I say, matching his composure. "Touch yourself as if it were me touching you."

I have no idea where this surge of sexual poise has come from, but I don't question it.

"How does it feel?" I ask curiously.

"It's a poor substitute for the real thing," he says breathlessly. "But maybe you could give me something more to work with?"

I'm unsure what he means, and he senses my uncertainty. "Rub over those amazing tits of yours. Let me hear you touching them," he says, the friction over his jeans getting louder.

His forwardness stokes my passion and I quickly do as he asks. Closing my eyes, I softly touch my right breast, the soapy water providing the perfect lubrication.

"That's it, baby," he says in approval. "Now the other."

Sliding my hand across my chest, I begin stroking over my left in a slow, circular movement.

"Use both hands," he directs as if he's here with me, watching my every move.

A whimper escapes me when I brush over my nipples quickly, the sensation hitting me straight between the legs.

"Oh fuck, baby, does it feel good?" he asks, panting.

"Yes." I increase the speed and pressure.

The harder I stroke, the more unsatisfied I get. I'm burning up inside and I need more.

Jasper hears my annoyance. "Move your hand lower. To the place where I wish my head could be."

Groaning at the visual, I slide my hand down my torso, resting it below my bellybutton.

"Touch yourself. Tell me what you feel."

With hesitant fingers, I glide up and down my entrance, moaning.

"Holy shit," Jasper says as I hear his zipper lower. "Go deeper. Touch that sweet spot."

I gasp at his naughty words, but it spurs me on and I do as he says. I'm not one who usually does this, as I have Jasper to fulfil my every need, but damn, it feels good. When I slowly insert a finger, I gasp because it feels so deliciously corrupt.

I can hear Jasper working his length, his strokes getting faster and faster. "Add another finger, baby. You know I'd have two inside of you by now," he growls.

Thrusting two in, I cry out in surprise because the sensation is too much. Is this what Jasper feels when touching me? The thought has me throwing my head back and raising my hips so I can push in deeper.

"Good girl."

"Jasper," I whimper, unable to hold on much longer.

"Oh fuck, I bet you look beautiful. Are you ready to come, baby? Tell me you're ready to come," he demands, his breath uneven and winded.

His words, my hands, the vision of him pleasuring himself while verbally pleasuring me is all too much. I come so hard water sloshes over the sides of the tub and onto the floor as I thrash around, riding my wave of pleasure.

A moment later, I hear Jasper let out a drawn out, sated groan.

That was, wow...intense. Who would have thought I'd be able to do that to myself? However, as I hear

Jasper's throaty chuckle, I know my response was set off because of him.

"That was incredible. Holy shit," he pants.

"Hmm hmm," I hum in total agreement, finally opening my eyes.

"I miss you," he says, the longing clear in his voice.

Still trying to catch my breath I say, "I miss you, too."

"You know what you've done?" Jasper says, his tone light. When I remain silent, he explains. "You've set a precedent for what we're going to do every night until you're in my arms."

I laugh, my sleepy eyes slipping shut. "Okay. But next time, I'll be the one calling the shots."

CHAPTER TWENTY FOUR
Waiting

The next day, I walk into Metropolis, not knowing what to expect.

Thanks to my wicked activities with Jasper, I fell into a deep, sated sleep, and didn't rouse until my alarm went off this morning.

I haven't received any emergency phone calls, so I'm guessing that's a good sign. As I take a quick look around, I see that everything is where it should be—so far so good.

The moment I step into the kitchen, Sara comes charging towards me and throws her arms around me. "I'm so sorry," she sniffles into my hair. "I was such a bitch to you. I was out of line. Please don't hate me. I made you macaroons."

Chuckling, I pull out of her deathly grip and smile. "It's fine. I probably overreacted a touch."

"No, you didn't. I was an idiot. It'll never happen again," she says, wiping her nose with a tissue.

"I accept your apology. And I'll also accept your macaroons." She laughs, appearing relieved that she's forgiven.

"So, the place is still standing? That's a good sign," I say, looking around the kitchen for any evidence to tell me otherwise. "How'd it go yesterday?"

"After a few small...minor," she adds quickly when I look at her. "Minor hiccups, it went remarkably well."

"That's great!" I say, unable to keep the enthusiasm from my tone. "How'd Michel go?"

Sara nods, appearing to be over her 'I hate Michel' phase. "You're right. He sucks at all the bookwork stuff. But he picked up on who all the suppliers are pretty easily."

"That's awesome." I rub Sara's arm. "Metro is in good hands. Give it a few days, and you won't even need me around," I add, hoping that my words hold some truth.

Sara smiles, but I can see the uncertainty in her eyes.

"Hey, I won't leave until both you and Michel feel 100% comfortable," I affirm, meaning every single word.

"Thanks, Ava," she says, the relief replacing her fear. "So what now?"

"Now you go pamper yourself. You've earned it," I say, looking at her tired appearance. Just as she's about contradict me, I hold up my finger. "That's boss's orders."

She smiles and salutes me, and thankfully, she doesn't argue.

I'm lost in my thoughts and don't hear Michel talking to me until he's gently shaking my arm.

"*Cheri?* Is everything all right?"

I jump up, startled that I have company and Michel's hands shoot up, raised in surrender.

"Oh shit, you scared me." I put a hand to my beating heart.

Michel grins, his mouth wickedly full. "I can see that. I'm sorry," he says, lowering his hands.

When I see my knife is gripped tight in my hand, I instantly lower it, pulling a mortified face. "Oh my god, I'm the one who's sorry."

He laughs, but steps in close, while I instantly freeze. When he lowers his lips to my ear, I listen with bated breath. "I wouldn't be so quick to lower that knife."

Just as I'm about to ask him what the hell that means, in strolls Yolanda, coffee in hand.

"Good point," I whisper back. He chuckles, muting his laugh behind his hand.

"Ava, how lovely to see you," she has the nerve to say while I glare at her something wicked.

"What do you want?" I ask with a sigh. She's the last person I want to see, like ever.

"Is that any way to greet the person who is about to change your life?" she sweetly says, placing her huge sunglasses atop her head.

She sees my annoyance, and thankfully reveals why she's here. "A little birdy told me Liam Stromboli will be here, in Metropolis, for the upcoming international food festival. You do know who Liam Stromboli is, right?" she adds when I remain silent.

The reason for my silence is not caused by ignorance but rather shock. Liam Stromboli is New York's top food connoisseur. He writes up all the restaurant reviews in the *New York Times* and any place he recommends instantly becomes a hit. And to think he will be here, in my restaurant.

I know he doesn't eat at just *any* restaurant, so to have him here is a real honor. I can't help but wonder why he chose here though, as there a thousand other restaurants he probably would have chosen over Metro.

Yolanda reads my confusion. "He was extremely impressed with the little segment I produced. So, you're welcome," she arrogantly says.

"Why are you telling me this?" I ask, knowing she has an ulterior motive.

"Because I want to film his appearance. And make Metro an even bigger hit than it already is, silly," she adds when I cross my arms over my chest.

"Metropolis has already had its five minutes of fame," I say, glaring at Yolanda. "Thanks to your little *segment*, business has been great."

"Why settle for great, when you can be sold out every night for months in advance? Imagine what this would do for your career," she says, putting forth every restaurant owner's dream.

As wonderful as this all sounds, I'm not swayed. "I can't because I'm planning to be in Europe in two weeks' time." The food festival is in five weeks, and I'm planning on being long gone by then.

"Two weeks?"

"You're what?"

Michel and Yolanda talk over the other, but I ignore the piranha and focus on Michel. "Yes, you always knew I was leaving."

"But two weeks." His mouth dips into a tight frown.

"You can't, not now. Not after this opportunity," he says, pointing to Yolanda.

"You can still do it—you're manager now, remember?" I say, nodding encouragingly.

Michel looks discouraged, but he doesn't disagree.

"No, he can't," Yolanda rebuts. "The little birdy also told me Liam wants you to cook his meals. He apparently was quite impressed with you. Once again, thanks to me."

I restrain from rolling my eyes.

"You don't have to make any decisions now, just think about it," Yolanda says, making a move to leave. However, with her hand poised on the door, she turns over her shoulder and grins. "Oh, Ava. I wouldn't put a man over your career, especially a man who isn't putting you over his."

"What's that supposed to mean?" I snarl, taking a step forward.

Michel gently pulls me back, but I shrug out of his hold.

"Just check my blog and see what your boyfriend has really been up to while away," she smugly replies, turning on her heel and leaving me with so many questions.

I want to run after her and demand answers, but I know the answers lie feet away. "Can I borrow your iPad?" I ask Michel, who hesitantly hands it over.

I frantically type in Yolanda's blog address and the first picture that flashes up on the screen has me cursing in absolute rage.

"That dirty son of a bitch!"

"Did you know?"

"Know what?" V asks, yawning loudly.

"What time is it?"

"It's time to tell me if you knew my fiancé was a dirty manwhore," I reply, pacing my office.

"Your fiancé? As in Jasper White?" she asks, the shock evident in her tone.

"The one and only." I snicker, still pacing.

"The Jasper White I know is an Avawhore, yes, but certainly not a manwhore," she replies seriously.

"Well, I'm positive you'll change your mind after you turn on your computer and check out Yolanda's blog."

"Oh, that," V says casually.

"So you did know! And it didn't occur to you to tell me my boyfriend is shoving his tongue down the enemy's throat?" I bark, blowing the truth out slightly.

"Hardly." V scoffs at my dramatics.

"Whatever. Why didn't you tell me?"

"Because of the way you're acting right now."

"A picture doesn't lie. Or in this case, numerous pictures," I say, glaring at my computer screen.

"Ava, take a breather. You're acting like a damn crazy person."

"Oh, I'm sorry that I'm a little freaked. But looking at photos of my boyfriend kissing someone other than me does that!" I reply, slumping into my chair.

"He's not kissing her. He's—he's—" V's lost for words as she tries to explain why it looks like Jasper and Delilah did a lot more than sing together last night. "Okay," she finally confesses, "It does look like he's kissing Delilah's neck."

"And the next picture? What does it look like he's kissing?" I ask, jabbing at the screen angrily.

"Her ear."

"The next," I say, cringing.

"Her lips."

"And what do you think is happening in the next photograph?" I ask, hoping by some miracle, I've misread this entire scene of events.

V weighs up her response because she knows I'm about to lose my shit. "It looks like he's following her upstairs."

"To where?"

"I dunno. The bathroom?" she suggests. If only she were right.

"What do you usually find upstairs in a swanky, romantic Parisian hotel?" I ask, a glutton for pain.

"The kitchen?" V answers, omitting what we both know to be true.

"No, her bedroom," I conclude. The last picture of Delilah beckoning Jasper with her finger as she waltzes up the stairs has my mind conjuring up all sorts of vile images.

"Seriously, you need to chill," V says, concerned "You know Jasper. He would never cheat on you—especially with that skanky hoe. Just call him. I'm sure there's a reasonable explanation."

"I have tried. His cell keeps going to voicemail," I reply, beyond annoyed as I look at my phone, willing it to ring.

"They're probably in transit. His cell would be switched off or out of service. Just take a breather. Go eat some chocolate until he calls you back," V says, trying to be helpful. I sigh because this is one circumstance where chocolate can't soothe my worries.

"You going to be okay?" she asks when I don't say a word.

"I'll survive," I reply, not wanting to worry her. "I'm just pissed that smug bitch told me about this. I bet she was just dying to tell me," I add, turning my computer off as I can't stomach to look at the pictures a second longer.

"Hold up, *why* was she at Metro?" V asks, her voice rising in questioning.

Thanks to my Jasper drama, I've totally forgotten to fill V in on how this entire saga began.

"V, something really doesn't want me to leave New York." I tell her the story.

"Something, or *someone?*" she says after I'm done talking.

"Who?" I query, even though I know who.

"I think you know who. It's all a little convenient, don't you think? I find it strange that this food critic is randomly appearing," she says. "I smell a rat."

"But why?" I press.

"Because what better way to have you stay, or at least reconsider your decision, than by dangling your dream in front of your face," she replies, sure of her premise.

"No," I say, but a small part of me can't help but think that maybe she's right.

But for the moment, I gotta deal with one drama at a time, and number one is talking to Jasper.

I've tried all morning, but I've failed to get a hold of Jasper. V is most likely right and they're probably on a train, bus, or plane, headed to their next destination. I've left him a desperate voice message, pleading for him to call me back immediately. I can only hope immediately is within the next five minutes because I can't focus on anything other than him.

"Is everything all right?" Michel asks as we sit at the bar, discussing Yolanda's proposal.

I haven't given much thought to what V said about Michel being involved in this once in a lifetime opportunity. I refuse to believe he would do something like that when he knows my mind is made up.

"I'm fine, Michel," I say, spinning my cell on the bar and watching it twirl.

He doesn't buy it. "Is this about what Yolanda said?" he asks apprehensively.

I nod, unable to stop my frown.

"I hope you don't mind, but I looked."

"It's fine," I glumly reply because I would, too. "What do you think?" I ask, afraid of his response.

He sighs before replying. "I think that if what I'm

seeing in those pictures are true, then your fiancé is a *con* for kissing someone else other than you."

I don't know what a *con* is, but the way Michel snarled it, I dare say he just insulted Jasper in the worst possible way.

But he's right, the photographs *are* incriminating, and the only reason why I'm not a total mess is because they've been taken on a cell phone and the quality isn't the best. They're quite grainy and pixelated because the photos have been enlarged to show detail. Even though I know without a doubt its Jasper and Delilah, I can't say for certain that they're doing what I think they're doing, which is a good thing.

"So he hasn't called?"

I shake my head as I doodle in my notepad. "Nope. I'm stuck here, waiting for my fiancé to call, while he's god knows where, doing god knows *who*."

"*Ma Cheri*," he says. "Do you think that maybe he's not the person you thought him to be?" he asks, cocking his head to the side.

"No," I stubbornly retort, horrified to even fathom his question. "I know Jasper. He's still the same person who gave me this," I say, holding up my hand, my ring catching the light.

Michel hesitantly reaches forward, and with shaky fingers, he loops his fingers through mine. The act feels utterly wrong, so I unlatch our fingers subtly.

He frowns, but brushes it off a second later. "If I were him, I would never leave your side. Nor would I be caught in the compromising positions he has been caught in."

I want to defend him, but I can't. His position *was* compromising, and until he can explain his actions, I'm remaining tight-lipped.

"I know I haven't known you for too long, Ava, but I hate to see you frown. And lately, that's all you've been doing," he says, using his pointer to push the corner of my mouth into half a smile.

My lips tip up into a full smirk, and he returns it. "That's better. I just want you to be happy."

I nod, touched by his concern. "Thank you, Michel. I'm happy right now."

"*Bon.* Then I'm happy, too," he simply says.

There is a sudden silence between us, and I feel like his gaze is no longer completely friendly. I lower my eyes, quickly feeling guilty, even though we're not doing anything wrong. I reach for my phone, desperate to talk to Jasper because I'm a bundle of nerves, reading into things that are probably not even there. As I look at my blank screen, I can't help but sigh because he doesn't seem too desperate to want to talk to me.

Suddenly, my cell rings and I jump up. I screw up my face when I see it's not Jasper. "Hi, Yolanda," I say, unenthused.

"I thought you'd be a little happier to talk to me, seeing as I've done nothing but watch your back."

I grind my teeth, hating that she has this hanging over my head. "Look, we talk business, that's it," I bluntly say. "My private life is none of your business. We clear?"

"Crystal," she bluntly replies. "Too bad your private life has been all over the internet."

"Well, that's not your concern," I say, moments away from crying.

"Fair enough. I'm just watching your back."

I refrain from scoffing and grumbling my thought that she's sticking a knife into it, more like.

When I don't speak, she clears her throat, getting the message loud and clear. "Anyhow, I'm calling to see if you've reconsidered."

I sigh, rubbing my forehead. "No, I have not. And besides, if I were to reconsider, there is no way I would allow you to film it."

"Why not?"

"Because you made my kitchen look like a brothel!" I bark.

I'm sad things couldn't be different, because I really, really want to cook for Liam, but I just can't.

Yolanda doesn't appreciate my jab one little bit. "The camera doesn't lie, Ava."

"But you do," I hit back, ready to take her on.

"Touché," she replies, appearing surprised that I've got balls she obviously thought I lacked. We end our pleasant conversation and I hang up, more annoyed than before.

It seems the longer I stay apart from Jasper, the worse things become. He needs to call me. Like now.

CHAPTER TWENTY FIVE
Smile for Me

Two days pass, and still no word from Jasper. His silence cements his guilt, and it also brings home the fact that maybe fame and fortune has changed him.

The only thing keeping me from falling into an inconsolable mess is focusing on wrapping things up at Metro. Michel is thankfully learning the ropes, but I'm afraid this is all for nothing.

"God dammit!" I curse, throwing my spoon down in annoyance. "Why is this so gluey?" I say, voicing my thoughts aloud. "I don't get it."

"What's wrong?" Michel asks, looking at me from across the counter.

"This is wrong." I hold up my saucepan.

Michel stands on tippy toes and looks into my pan. "Oh yes, it's *very* wrong," he says, pulling a horrified face.

I'm at the stage where I'm either going to laugh or cry, and honestly, if I start with the tears, I don't think I'll ever stop.

"*Cheri?*" Michel says softly.

The moment I meet his eyes, a blob of toffee sauce hits me square in the face. "What the hell?" I shriek, half laughing, half screaming, as I wipe it off my cheek. It however gets replaced by a splash of sticky date batter, which is dripping off Michel's spoon.

As he measures me up, ready to splatter me again, I know this is war. Before he has time to react, I lift my bowl and hurl the entire contents at him. Some ends up on the wall behind him, but the majority stains his white snug tee. He looks down at his soiled clothes, his mouth agape, but suddenly, his lips tip up into a sinister grin.

"Michel," I reason, hands raised in surrender as I walk backwards. "We're even. Now put the sticky date down before someone gets hurt," I say, looking at his mixing bowl.

"*Au contraire*, it's only just begun," he says, hurling the bowl at me. I'm too slow and before I can dodge his attack, I'm caked in sticky batter.

My high-pitched squeal bounces off the kitchen walls and before I know it, we're grabbing at anything in our reach and are having a full-blown food fight. Strawberries, tomatoes, squid, anything you can think of is getting thrown through the air, and as each splatter of food colors me and my kitchen, a sense of liberation overwhelms me and it's the first time in days I've felt like myself.

"Give up!" I yell as I throw a handful of eggs before dropping low and hiding behind a counter.

"Never! I will fight till the bitter end," he says, his accent stronger than ever.

"Well, be prepared to leave this kitchen covered in every food I can find," I declare.

"Give it your best shot," he mocks, seeming unbelieving of my claims.

Taking the challenge very seriously, I raise my arm to

search the bench above me. The only thing I discover however is Michel's hand. Before I have time to pull away, he latches onto my wrist to stop me from running. He rounds the counter to pull me into a standing position.

I howl with laughter when I see he's covered in every food known to mankind. His hair is caked with shrimp, and his shirt looks like a colorful work of art. His far from impressed expression makes me laugh even harder, and before long, tears of chocolate are running down my cheeks.

It feels so good to laugh, and when he holds up a tray of lasagna, I continue cackling, not caring that I'm moments away from swimming in sauce and cheese.

"Any last words?" he says, rubbing strawberry puree from his eye.

"Bon appetite," I reply, running my finger across his cheek and scooping up the sweet sauce.

Bringing it to my lips, I suck it into my mouth, unable to resist. Before I have time to register what I've done, Michel draws me forward and stops when we're inches apart. His smoky eyes smolder as he watches me lick my finger clean. I quickly pull it out, realizing what I've just done, but his hand darts out and he grips onto my wrist, bringing my finger to his mouth.

My body begins to tremble in fear, unsure of what he's going to do. Just as he parts his lips, drawing my finger close, my cell blares loudly.

"I-I better see who that is," I stutter, subtly pulling out of his grip and reaching into my pocket to pull out my phone.

My heart feels like it weighs a thousand pounds when I see the caller is Jasper. "I've gotta take this." I frantically wipe my hand on my jeans to wipe away the goo.

"Hello?" I say as I hit the button, pressing the phone to my ear. "Jasper, can you hear me?" I ask in a panic when I'm greeted with silence.

"Baby?" he replies moments later, the relief and guilt clear in his tone. "I'm so sorry," he says, and my eyes flick to Michel, who's standing with his hip cocked against the counter, watching me closely.

"Hang on, Jasper."

"I'll be back," I say to Michel, covering the receiver with my hand.

He nods, looking unimpressed, but I'm running towards the door faster than my feet can keep up.

"*Cheri?*" he calls out, his voice sounding desperate and vacant.

I turn around slowly, afraid of what he's going to say. But he surprises me by tossing a dish cloth my way.

"Thanks," I say with a small smile. I don't give him a chance to reply because I'm charging out the door and sprinting to my office in record speed.

Closing the door, I uncover my cell and take a deep breath before talking to the man who just may break my heart. "Hi," I say. It sounds cold to even my ears.

"Hey, baby. Have I caught you at a bad time?" Jasper asks, puzzled by my detachment.

Looking down at my saturated clothes, I decide to stand. "No, it's okay. I'm just at work."

"Oh? You're opening early today?" he asks.

"No, I'm just here with Michel," I reply, seeing no reason to lie.

"Oh."

Silence.

Is he waiting for me to ask him? Or is he going to be man enough to tell me?

"I'm sorry I haven't been able to call. We're in Frankfurt, and the cell service is real shitty. And it's also been so crazy. We've got fans out here. Like real, hardcore fans who are camping outside our hotel and stuff just to get a picture with us," he explains, the happiness radiating through.

Is one of these hardcore fans the person who snapped the photos? I decide to ask him.

"Have you been online?" I question, my heart beginning to race.

"No. Like I said, the service sucks, and we don't have WIFI in our hotel, either. Why?"

Okay, I feel a touch better knowing he's been stuck in a no technology zone. But that doesn't explain why he's Delilah's new best friend.

"Well, I have been, and I've seen some interesting photos," I confess, my hand trembling as I grip the cell tighter.

"Of what?" he innocently asks.

"Of you and Delilah."

"Oh yeah? From the show?" he asks, his tone still revealing no ounce of remorse.

"No. Of you and her in a more intimate...pose," I say, feeling bile rise.

"Intimate?" Jasper asks, shocked. "That's impossible. Not to mention gross."

"I've seen them," I say, trying not to envision them again.

"Seen what exactly?" he says quickly. "I haven't done anything wrong, baby."

"Well, in these photographs, it looks like you're doing a lot wrong."

"Like what?" he prompts.

"Like you're kissing her," I reveal, unable to keep the sadness from my voice.

"Excuse me?" he says, horrified. "Not to repeat myself, but that's impossible. You don't believe that. Do you?" he adds when I remain silent.

"A picture doesn't lie, Jasper," I finally reply, wishing that it did.

"Well, neither do I," he firmly presses. "Where was this picture taken?"

"I'm not sure. It's of you and her sitting at a table, and you're leaning in close. It looks like...like you're kissing her neck. And lips," I confess, feeling myself pale.

"Well, I can assure you that did not, nor will not happen. Ever," he angrily says as I hear something getting tossed across the room.

"But I saw it," I miserably say. "I saw *you*."

"Hold up," he quickly says, as if a thought suddenly occurred to him. "Was there a spiral staircase she was walking up?"

"Yes," I gripe, my stomach twisting at the memory.

"Baby, that photo was taken for a local newspaper, who thought it would be cool to showcase the one-hundred-year-old hotel we were staying at. The photos I'm presuming you're talking about were taken at a press conference, conducted at the same hotel. It wasn't just Delilah and me; it was all the members of our bands. I sat near Delilah because that's where I was told to sit, and I'm leaning into her because the majority of the questions were asked in German, a language she's fluent in. I asked her what they meant, and she explained them to me in English. It was so loud in there, so she had to repeat herself a few times, or pull in closer so I could hear her. And when that didn't work, I had to resort to lip reading at a very close distance."

"Yeah, taken at the right moment, the pictures may be misconstrued as being intimate, but they weren't. We were in a stuffy room, filled with reporters and fans. That's it. I was tired, lost in translation, and missing you. Nothing happened. I promise."

Taking a moment to absorb everything he just said, because it's a lot to digest, I realize I have no reason to doubt him, and I was stupid to question his loyalty in the first place. His explanation makes total sense, and the sincerity in his tone cancels out any lingering doubts.

Thank. Fuck.

"I'm sorry, Jasper. I shouldn't have doubted you. It's just...they looked so—" I say, biting my lip to stop my tears of relief.

"I know, baby. I'm sorry you had to see that. And then not to hear from me, I can't even imagine how anxious you must have been. I'm so sorry," he says regretfully.

"It's okay. I'm the one who should be apologizing. I

should have known Yolanda was up to no good," I reply, angry at myself for believing her lies.

"Yolanda? Why did you talk to her?"

"She came into Metro because she wants to film another segment here," I explain, pacing the room.

"What do you mean?" he curiously asks.

I explain about Liam Stromboli, leaving out V's conspiracy theory.

"Wow!" Jasper says after I'm done explaining. "That's fucking cool. What great exposure."

"I know." I sadly add, "But I won't be here. The festival is in five weeks' time."

"Oh," he replies, understanding that if I do this, I won't be able to meet him overseas as I'd hoped to.

With teaching Michel the ropes, preparing the perfect menu, and running Metro, there's no way I'll be leaving New York any time soon.

Jasper surprises me as he says, "That's okay. You stay there. See this through."

"I wasn't going to do it."

"You have to do this, it's a great opportunity."

"I don't care," I say passionately. "Michel can take care of it. I'm still planning on leaving, Jasper. Nothing has changed."

"I know, baby. But I want you to do this," he says, his warmth and sincerity bringing tears to my eyes.

"Are you sure?" I ask. Even though this is my dream come true, I don't want it to jeopardize what Jasper and I have worked so hard for.

"Positive. Do this as your last hurrah."

The fact I've gotten his approval has made my decision all the easier.

"Thank you for understanding and for believing in me," I say, feeling so incredibly lucky to have his support and love. "There is no way I'm having Yolanda set foot in my restaurant with her camera crew ever again. I'm just going cook, and then I'm coming home," I say, wanting to assure him.

"It's fine, baby. You've believed in me since the beginning, it's only fair I return the favor."

I don't know how to address the big elephant in the room, so I decide to be blunt. "You do know this means I'll be spending a lot more time with Michel?"

"I know," he casually replies.

When I don't hear anything being smashed, I ask, "And you're okay with that?"

Jasper sighs, and I have an image of him fisting his hair. "This trust thing, it works both ways. I asked you to marry me because I trust you. I like to think you accepted because you trust me back."

"I do. I trust you completely," I affirm.

"Well, I trust you completely, too. No more doubts, okay? Only moving forward," he cleverly says. "This is only going to work if we trust one another one hundred percent."

"I know. And I do, I trust you. I'll just stay offline from now on," I confess, unable to face another miscommunication.

Jasper laughs. "So we're okay?"

"More than okay. Well, apart from missing you like

crazy, that is," I say, wishing he was here so I could hug him.

"I know the feeling," he says, the longing clear in his tone.

When I hear muffled voices in the background, Jasper sighs. "I gotta go, baby. Tony the tour manager is chewing my ass out. I love you so much. I'll try and call you as soon as I can."

I'll never get used to saying goodbye. "Okay. I miss you," I say, trying to stay strong.

"I miss you, too."

As I feel my lower lip tremble, Jasper whispers, "Smile for me. I want that to be the last image I have of you before we speak again."

I don't know how he knows, but I do as he asks. It's a lame smile, but it's the best I can muster, considering I want to cry.

"That's my girl," he says happily. "I love you so much. Bye, baby."

"Bye," I whisper, a small sob escaping me when I hear the line go dead.

I hold onto the phone, not wanting to hang up because I'm not ready to say goodbye. I stand this way for minutes, thinking over everything Jasper just said. Even though it sucks to be apart, knowing that Jasper is my reward at the end of this separation makes everything worthwhile.

Sniffing back my tears, I set my mind at the mission ahead—focusing on my last hurrah.

CHAPTER TWENTY SIX
Time after Time

The next few weeks fly by in a blur.

Playing on my mind is the fact that I should be getting ready to jet off and start my future with Jasper. Instead, I'm elbows deep in duck fat, trying to perfect my roast potatoes. I'm so incredibly nervous, but my nerves are overshadowed by the sheer excitement that I'll be serving Liam Stromboli in two weeks' time.

Michel has been a touch distant after our impromptu food fight, but he's on his A-game when we're working side by side in the kitchen, which is all that matters. Even though I don't want to admit it, the dynamics between us has shifted. I think he was disappointed when I told him Jasper and I had sorted out the Delilah situation, but I'm too afraid to read into it because I just want to leave New York with nothing but happy memories.

I'm humming to a tune on the radio, secretly hoping P.O.E. will come on because they've been getting some serious airplay. I'm so proud of them all, especially Jasper, who deserves all the recognition he's getting. He calls when he can, which isn't often, but I know this middle leg of his tour is quite intense, so I focus on finishing what I set out to because I know once I'm done, I'm done, and then nothing can keep us apart.

"How are the potatoes going?" Sara asks, strolling into the kitchen, looking just as tired as me.

"Getting there," I reply, stifling a yawn behind my hand.

"You should get some rest," Sara says, loading the dishwasher.

She's right. Metropolis closed three hours ago, but I'm still here, paranoid my menu isn't good enough for Liam.

"You're right and I will. I just want to start from scratch one more time."

Sara looks over at the counter and shakes her head. "No, go home. And that's an order. There are only so many ways you can cook potatoes," she adds, pointing to the dishes littering my kitchen.

I sigh, knowing Sara won't budge on this. "Fine, boss," I say with a smile as I untie my apron.

My cell phone chimes in my pocket, and I quickly pull it out, hopeful its Jasper.

"Hello?" I say.

"Hello, love," Kris replies smugly.

"Kris?" I say, so not expecting his call. "How are you? Is everything okay?" I quickly ask, worried something has gone wrong.

"Everything is peachy. That fiancé of yours is a slave driver, however," he replies, tongue in cheek.

"Jasper?" I ask, while Sara looks at me concerned. I mouth "Jasper's brother," and gesture with my hand that all is fine.

"Yes, the one and only. Unless you have another fiancé?" he cheekily adds, while I chuckle.

"No, one is more than enough. What did he do?"

"Well, I took him up on his offer to be his roadie while he's in Europe," he explains, and I'm overjoyed to hear this news.

"That's amazing, Kris. You can be his personal security guard and scare off all the groupies for me," I say, only half joking.

Kris cackles. "I think Jasper is doing a pretty good job of that himself. I'm surprised no one has lost an arm yet by straying too close."

Laughing, I reply, "In that case, I'm glad you're there to keep him in line."

"I sure am. So, he tells me you're preparing for some bigwig to come eat at Metro." I hear him tapping away at a computer.

"Yeah, I am. What are you doing?" I ask, curious to know what he's up to.

"Did you know I was studying to be a computer nerd while at Cambridge?" he says, still clicking away at the keys.

"No, I didn't. You were too busy being a jerk for me to ask," I reply, laughing softly.

"Fair call," he replies, not arguing. "Well, I was. Anyway, do you have access to a computer?"

"Um, yes," I reply, a touch frightened why he's asking me this. "Is everything all right?"

But he ignores me and asks, "Can you go on YouTube?"

"Sure." I sprint out of the kitchen and into my office with Sara following closely behind.

Turning on my computer, I quickly open up YouTube and wait for further instruction.

"Okay, type in Jasper White, Time after Time. You can thank me tomorrow," he ambiguously says.

"Kris?" I say, my fingers shaking as I do as he asks.

"Just trust me, Ava," he says, and I'm thankful that I do.

The moment I get a hit, I wheeze, my eyes zeroing in on the face of an angel.

"I'll leave you to it. Jasper sends his love. He's tied up in press crap, but this is his way of saying he's thinking of you always."

Before I have time to question him, the line goes dead. But I don't try and call him back because I quickly load the video, knowing that in a moment's time, I'll be brought to tears.

"Hey," the video version of Jasper says.

Both Sara and I gasp, too enthralled to speak.

"I'm going to slow things down for a minute, if that's okay by you?" he says, playfully placing a hand over his brow and looking out into the crowd. When the camcorder pans out into the audience, I nearly choke at how many people are in the crowd.

He looks so fucking hot in a white sleeveless tee, tousled hair, and black jeans. His blazing red guitar hangs loosely by his side, and as he runs his fingers up and down the microphone stand, I hear the moans of approval of every female watching this rock god do his thing.

"I love being here with each and every one of you, but there's someone I love more. She's the most important person to me and I'm missing her like crazy."

When the crowd coos and ahh's, Jasper rewards the masses of people with his trademark lopsided smirk. "In a couple of weeks, she's going to kick some serious ass. But it cuts me up that I can't be there supporting her the way she has supported me. So, this is my way of showing her that I'm thinking of her, every second of every day. Even though I'm not there with her, she can rest assured that I'll always catch her if she feels like she's about to fall. Or if she's lost, she will always find me waiting, time after time."

By this stage, my tears are clouding my vision, so I wipe them away so I can see my man.

"Ava, I love you, baby," he says, turning to look at the camera side stage. "I'll be waiting, time after time."

He picks up his guitar and starts the intro to an acoustic version of "Time after Time" by Cyndi Lauper. It's only Jasper and his guitar, playing to the crowd of roughly twenty thousand people, and it's simply beautiful. Lighters begin to flicker and sway when he gets to the chorus, putting his heart and soul into the heartfelt words.

I hear Sara sniffle beside me because the performance is simply touching and captivating. This is Jasper stripped raw and bare, and the fact it's for me has me dabbing at my teary eyes, never wanting it to end.

His voice is flawless, and when he slows down the chorus, drawing out every note, the longing to be reunited is evident in every word he sings. I can't stop myself as I reach forward and touch the screen, my fingers stroking over the face of the man I love more than life itself.

The song finishes all too soon and the crowd erupts in

a wild round of applause. The video ends with Jasper smiling, his head raised to the heavens, looking like the true angel that he is. I'm silent, powerless to speak, because nothing could compare to what I've just seen. And nothing ever will.

Jasper has made it. He's living out his dream playing to sold out crowds, who simply adore him. I can't help but think back to the first time I saw P.O.E. play at Little Sisters. I knew it then they would accomplish big things. But to be a part of it, to have Jasper sing to me in front of thousands of adoring fans reveals to me that no matter what, Jasper will always be the same person who won my heart in that little club all those nights ago.

Fame and fortune only changes a person if that person lets them, but Jasper, Jasper will always be my forever and a day. And nothing will ever change that.

CHAPTER TWENTY SEVEN
Foreign Lips

Michel and I are discussing suppliers for the hundredth time. I don't understand how yesterday he understood this perfectly, and today he's looking at me like I'm talking in Chinese.

My thoughts are put on hold however when he curses. Wondering what has caused his outburst, I look up and gulp. Adelia is sauntering into Metro, looking like she owns the place.

"*Bonjour*," she says, waving at the gob-smacked guests.

That was once my reaction, but now I can't help but wonder what she wants.

Michel looks confused as to why she's here, but he stands and greets her. "*Bonjour, Mamam.*" He kisses both her cheeks.

I stand too, and notice a bunch of paparazzi just outside my door. I will never get used to this alleged fame and fortune.

"Oh, they're here for me," Adelia says with a wave of her hand as she notices me glaring at them.

I scoff at her arrogance but don't say a word.

She picks up on both mine and Michel's surprise to

her being here, and gets to the point. "I'm here to congratulate you, Ava. And Michel," she adds, raising a brow. "When Liam told me you had organized for him to eat here for the festival, I was a little offended you didn't ask me, as I'm just as respected as he is."

What. The. Actual. Fuck?

It takes me thirty seconds to comprehend what she just said, and when I do, I turn and glare at a sheepish looking Michel, my high totally gone. *He's* the one who organized Liam's appearance? And it wasn't a chance encounter, like he led me to believe?

My mind is spinning, but I don't let on that I'm five seconds away from demanding answers because when I do, it won't be pretty.

Adelia however, can see my surprise, and she smirks. She knows I was clueless to her son's doings, and this is her way of getting back at him for asking Liam here, instead of her. She sees Metro as her meal ticket, because there are a dozen younger up and coming food connoisseurs that will soon take her place. She wants to ride the fame train as long as she can and sadly, Metropolis and I are just innocent bystanders she'll use to see that happen.

"Maybe Liam and I could do a dual review for Yolanda's show?" she suggests, confirming my suspicions.

Well, she's about to get served. "There is *no* show," I angrily state, barely containing my anger. "I will cook for Liam because I respect him. Whether he decides to review us, that's totally up to him. I'm just excited to have him here."

"Oh?" Adelia says, taken aback. "Why wouldn't you take advantage of his fame?"

Her words cut deep, as I can't help but think, is this what my life has become? Running from the paparazzi because I have a famous boyfriend, and my restaurant getting the recognition it deserves because Michel knows the right people. If so, then screw this all to hell.

"Because I don't use people the way others do," I spit out. "Thank you for the offer, Adelia, but you're yesterday's news."

She recoils, her jaw clenching, and I'm guessing no one has spoken to her that way.

"If you'll excuse me," I say, turning and heading to my office, about ready to explode.

Pacing the tiny room, I tell myself to calm down because I have a restaurant filled with customers. "So *you're* the little birdy?" I hiss, when Michel guiltily appears in the doorway.

When he remains silent, I order, "You have ten seconds to explain yourself, Michel."

He shuts the door behind him and runs a hand down his face, ready to spill the beans. "I was going to tell you, *Cheri*."

"When? Do you know how stupid I feel? I thought Liam genuinely wanted to dine here. But now I know that's not the case. Instead, you planned this entire thing. And even worse, you were in cahoots with Yolanda."

I have no doubt Michel went to Yolanda with his proposition, and she could see how it would benefit her career, as I know Liam rarely does TV appearances.

Michel lowers his eyes, ashamed, which pisses me off further.

"Why would you do that?" I ask, not understanding his motives.

"I asked him to come see what an amazing chef you are because I knew his review would be glowing. It would make Metropolis even more popular than it already is."

"I don't understand what I've got to do with this. If you wanted him here to boost your status then fine, but why involve me? Why did Yolanda tell me he'd only eat my food?"

"What I did, it was wrong. But I did it for you," he reasons, taking a step forward.

"For me? How?"

He runs a hand through his hair. "To prove that you belong here. This,"—he sweeps his hand around the room —"is you future, not following some unfaithful rockstar around the world like a groupie. You're better than that."

My mouth falls open and V's words ring loudly in my ears. "What else have you lied to me about, Michel? Tell me," I press when he lowers his eyes. "Did you play dumb when I was trying to teach you how to run this place?"

Lately, I've sensed his ignorance is staged. In the beginning, yes, I believed he was truly stumped, but now I feel like I'm being played.

Michel's guilt is reflected on his face.

"Son of a bitch! And your keys? Did you lose them? Or was that all part of your ploy?" Everything becomes clear, and I know that yes, I've been totally played.

He remains silent, looking at the floor, cementing his shame.

"I can't believe this! I'm so stupid. Jasper was right all along," I exclaim, kicking myself for ever doubting him. "Why would you think this situation would change my mind?"

Michel finally raises his eyes. "Because I thought if you became famous, you'd stay. You'd be able to accomplish your dream of seeing Metro grow."

I shake my head, disappointed that he thinks I'm driven by fame. "Being a celebrity is not a motivator, it never was. But love, it is. I love Jasper more than life itself, and nothing, not even my dreams, are worth anything if I don't have him by my side."

He appears taken aback by my honesty, but he perseveres. "You say that now, but you will regret it."

"Even if I do, that's my problem, not yours. We're friends, that's all." My comment seems to have struck a nerve because he takes a deep breath and blows it out while looking up at the ceiling.

Did he really think we were anything more than just friends?

As he marches towards me, I know the answer is yes. "I know you feel something for me."

"No, I really don't." I bump into the counter as I retreat.

"Then why does your fiancé think there is something between us?" he asks, inching closer and closer.

What's he doing? My head is spinning.

Just as I'm about to protest, Michel catches me off guard and swoops forward, kissing me hard on the lips. It's been so long since I've felt the mouth of another, apart from Jasper's, on mine, I stand stunned, frozen to the spot.

The feeling isn't unpleasant, as his lips are soft, gentle, and full. But I feel absolutely nothing and I may as well be kissing a dead fish. The experience is unlike when I kiss Jasper, as the entire world slips away, and nothing else matters when his lips are on mine.

When he attempts to part my sealed lips with his tongue, the reality of the situation hits home and every-thing comes crashing down around me. Michel's lips feel foreign, and everything about this is wrong, so very wrong.

Snapping out of my stupor, I yank away with disgust and before my mind can catch up, I slap him so hard across the face, my hand stings the moment it connects with his cheek. But the pain is worth it because I'm furious at myself for not doing it sooner.

Michel raises a hand to his reddening cheek, appearing stunned that I hit him.

"How dare you," I snarl, wiping my mouth with the back of my shaky hand. "Don't you *ever* do that again."

My temper has reached its boiling point, and as Michel reaches out to console me, I dodge his touch, afraid of what I'll do if he touches me without my permission again.

"*Cheri*, I'm sorry. I thought—"

"I don't care what you thought," I cut him off, not interested in his excuses. "I don't know who you are, Michel. And to think I defended you to everyone. What an idiot I am." I turn to run out the door

"Ava, wait!" he pleads, the panic clear in his tone.

"No, don't follow me." I put my hand out to stop him. "Just leave me alone. I don't...I can't look at you right now."

Michel's heartbroken look kills me, but what kills me more is the fact I gave him reason to believe he could kiss me...and I'd kiss him back.

CHAPTER TWENTY EIGHT
Surrendered

"I can't believe we're here," V huffs as we lug our bags up the steep stairs of The Steigenberger Hotel.

"Neither can I," I reply breathlessly, wondering how many floors are left.

It's been two days since I kissed Michel. Or as V likes to put it, Michel kissed me. Either way, his lips were where they shouldn't have been.

I feel so incredibly guilty that I didn't push him away sooner. I'll never forgive myself for it. And that's why I ran. I called V and asked how long it would take to organize a sitter for Cara because there was only one place I wanted to be. With Jasper.

I have to tell him what happened, and I don't want to do it over the phone. So, I'm climbing up the stairs to the sixteenth floor of our German hotel. I thought we'd surprise the boys, like we originally planned to do. When I checked their tour dates online, I saw their tour was extended out by three weeks, and they would be in Germany another few days. I've always wanted to visit the home of *Oktoberfest,* so I thought what better time to do so.

But now that I'm here, I'm regretting being so impulsive and figure I maybe should have called first and given Jasper a heads up.

"Oh, thank Christ," V pants when we reach our floor. "Just our luck, the elevator is out the day we arrive."

Seconding that with a grunt, we huff and puff until we make our way to our room. The moment we step inside, I dump my bags by the door, step out of my shoes, and throw myself onto the bed, face first. I plan on staying here for some time to come.

"What a great idea." V joins me and flops onto the mattress, sighing in delight.

"V," I murmur, my face pressed into the sheets. "How am I going to tell Jasper I cheated on him?"

"You didn't cheat." she states for the umpteenth time.

"Yes, I did. Someone's lips, other than my fiancé's, were on my lips."

"Did you enjoy it?" she plainly asks.

"No."

"Did you kiss him back?"

"No."

"Was there any tongue?"

"Hell no!" I screech.

"See, you didn't cheat. Just think of it as he fell and landed on your lips." V's reasoning's really don't make me feel any better.

"I should have pulled away sooner." I sigh, burying my head under my pillow.

"I think the five second rule can be applied here."

"Huh?" I ask, emerging from my soft cave.

She turns to me and smiles. "You know, you drop a bit of food on the floor, and as long as it's picked up within five seconds of being dropped, you can just brush away the dirt and pretend it never happened."

She nods, encouraging me to believe her theory excuses my behavior.

"I wish I could pretend it never happened. And besides, it was longer than five seconds," I confess, cringing.

"Longer?" V's eyes widen, confirming what an awful person I am.

Groaning, I bury my head back under my pillow. "See, I'm a dirty slut."

"Babe, no, you're not." V touches my back, persuading me to roll over before I suffocate myself.

"This is going to ruin his tour. Maybe I'll tell him after?" I say as I throw the pillow off my head.

Rolling over, I'm met by an unimpressed V. "Have you not learned that keeping secrets from Jasper just blows up into unnecessary angst? Harsh words are said. Then there's tears, and then people, i.e., you, leave. I know your intentions are good, but no, tell him what happened. He'll understand." She nods, and she's totally right, but I'm still afraid.

"I hope so."

She cocks an eyebrow. "Have I ever been wrong so far?"

Actually no, she hasn't. "See, my point exactly," she says as if reading my mind. "Now let's get ready. You've got some groveling to do."

The dark, crowded, slightly on the nose club we're at is absolutely packed. As V and I try to wedge our way through hundreds of Jasper White die-hard fans, I know the task at hand is going to be impossible to achieve without bloodshed.

"I miss being VIP," V says over her shoulder as she shoves anyone who stands in her way to the side. "Sorry. Pardon me. Coming through," she adds after a poor girl face plants into the wall.

"V, stop." I latch onto her arm. "We're never going to get up front and quite frankly, I don't want to be up there, squished among fans who are visualizing my boyfriend naked."

She shrugs and gives up, as she can probably see my point. When she backtracks, eager fans are happy to move, all too willing to take her place.

This is insane. Actually seeing all these people in one place makes all this real. I mean, I knew P.O.E. were popular, but holy shit, this is like The Beatles!

Most girls are fawning over Jasper, wearing cool 'Jasper White Groupie' shirts, which I've never seen, or buttons, or wristbands which read, 'I Surrender to Jasper White.' It's all a little surreal, but more so, it's exciting.

V points to a girl's tee and smirks. "Jasper White groupie." She reads the white block letters aloud. "How cute is the pink little Jasper?" she says, looking at the silhouetted picture of a pink man playing guitar.

"Super cute," I reply, a touch jealous.

"Ava's a green-eyed monster," V sings, not helping the situation.

"Well, it's not your man's name displayed on the bountiful chests of a hundred screaming women," I counter as we walk towards the back of the room.

"No one likes the drummer. I mean, they hit shit with sticks," V reasons with confidence.

"Lucas?" a young blonde suddenly says, obviously overhearing our conversation. "Oh my god, I *love* him. Did you see him in Paris drumming topless?" She fans herself. "I'm only here to see him. Jasper is too pretty for me. I like my men rough."

I bite my lip in humor, as I know what's about to come.

"Listen here, you little teeny bopper," V says, poking her in the chest. "That's *my* husband you're drooling over. As in *mine*. Don't touch, don't look, or you'll lose a finger and an eye."

The British girl scoffs, incredulous to V's claims. "Oh yeah, and I'm his wife, too." She rolls her eyes.

Just to add fuel to the already out of control fire, she takes off her sweater and reveals a homemade tee which reads in black text, '*Drummers Do It Better...*' She turns around to reveal, '*So Lucas, do me.*'

V's eyes almost pop out of her head, and without a second thought, she dives towards her, fingers poised and ready to claw off her shirt.

"Hey! What's your problem?" she shrieks, hands clutching her chest.

"My problem is you, you slu—"

"Okay, bye-bye, enjoy the show." Cutting V off before she blows a fuse, I turn her by her shoulders to get far, *far* away from this girl.

"I'm going to kill her. And the only thing she'll be *doing* is looking at my fist when I connect with her prissy face."

"V, calm down." I chuckle and lead her towards the bar.

Thankfully, the prospect of getting drunk overrides her need to kill.

"How can you be so calm?" She flicks her hand out and gestures to all the girls wearing Jasper's name across their chests. "I now understand what you go through every day. That was one girl I had to deal with. You've got like one hundred. A day. You deserve some kinda medal for not beating them senseless with their lip glosses and stupid signs." At that moment, a girl pushes past us with a banner three times the size of her. I hate to know what it reads.

"I dunno," I reply with a shrug. "It just comes with dating a rockstar I guess."

"Well, I hate it. I now get why animals mark their territory," she confesses while we wait in line.

"Wait." I hold up my finger. "Are you telling me you're going to pee on your husband?"

V purses her lips in thought. "Well..."

"Oh my god, you're gross!" We cackle in laughter and it feels just like old times.

We drink our way through two support bands, one of which is Roses. V and I have agreed that the only way to survive the set is to get wasted. Halfway through listening to Delilah Rose whine her way through her new single, I realize I'm already there.

"I hate her," I slur, using my glass as a gesturing tool and spilling its contents on my arm in the process.

V nods, backing me up. "I second that, sister." She clinks my glass.

Delilah, if possible, looks like an even bigger tramp than I remember. She's wearing black denim shorts which really doesn't cover much of her ass, a slinky white tank which shows off her hot pink bra, and Doc Marten boots. The only time we applaud is when they finish and get off stage.

"I'm sooooo drunk," V says, leaning against the wall.

"Oh, c'mon, the best is yet to come," I reply, playfully swishing her pigtail with my pointer.

The moment the lights dim, it's like a stampede of screaming girls competing for who can get to the front first. It's actually quite comical. Too bad it's my fiancé they're fighting each other to see.

With that thought in mind, I state, "I need another drink. You want one?"

V shakes her head, looking like she's about to barf at the mere mention of having another.

"Lightweight," I tease over my shoulder as I walk to the bar.

There's no one waiting, thanks to the die-hards waiting for P.O.E. to come onstage. I order my drink, and just as the bartender is about to tell me the total, I'm deafened by the squeals of adoring fans. The reason for their excitement saunters out, taking the stage like the rock god that he is.

"Helllllooooo, Berlin," he huskily says into the microphone.

The moment I hear his voice, I quickly toss the bartender some bills and when I get the thumbs up, I run over to V, eager to see my man do his thing. She latches onto my hand and we excitedly bounce on the spot, waiting for P.O.E. to rock the pants off everyone in this place.

"Damn, Lucas is looking fine tonight." V licks her lips as she eye fucks him and his naked chest.

I spare a second to look at him because my attention is totally focused on Jasper. He plays the part of rockstar perfectly in his ripped blue jeans, tight black tee, and navy Chucks. He sets the tongues wagging of every female in the venue as he takes a moment to look out into the crowd, his cerulean eyes revealing just how impressed he is.

"Are you ready to rock the roof off this place?" he asks, adjusting his guitar strap.

In response, everyone, including V and I, scream, and that's Jasper's cue to steal the hearts of everyone before him.

"One, two, three, four!"

He hits every note perfectly and engages with the crowd like the true showman he is. We sing along to every song, knowing each word by heart, and although we're cramped up against sweaty, screaming fans, it's kinda cool to be out here and experience what others do when seeing P.O.E. from the crowd.

V and I dance and boogie to our favorite songs, just like we would if we were at Little Sisters. It's so nice to be carefree and relaxed, and if Jasper and Lucas saw us bopping around like lunatics, they would be cackling in laughter, encouraging our idiocy.

"Are you guys having fun?" Jasper asks, running a hand through his sweaty hair as he catches his breath.

The girls yell out varied responses of, 'Yes,' 'Marry Me,' and 'I Love You.'

When a pair of underwear gets thrown on stage and lands on Jasper's microphone stand, he smirks, shaking his head mischievously. "Why, thank you." He tilts his head to the side and takes a closer look at them. "I don't think they're my size. Or color. Although, they look a perfect fit for Lucas." He picks them off the stand, and slingshots them over the drum rise. They land in Lucas' lap.

The crowd erupts in laughter and I smile, loving the usual banter between the two best friends.

"What do you guys wanna hear?" Jasper asks, cupping his ear when the audience screams out numerous song titles.

'Surrendered' is hands down a favorite, and Jasper smirks. "You wanna hear 'Surrendered?'"

The crowd goes nuts.

"Okay, can I ask for a bit of quiet?" He gestures with his hands for them to lower the noise levels, and they listen.

"This song," he commences, the bright lights making

him appear more ethereal than he really is. "Was written for someone very special to me. At the time, we were going through something deep, and I really didn't know if we'd make it or not." He frowns as if re-living the memory.

V latches onto my hand, knowing I'm seconds away from crying.

"It was the worst time of my life," he confesses with pause. "But it was also the best. I learned that if you love something and set it free, and it comes back, it's yours. And if it doesn't, well, it was never meant to be. But she did. She came back to me like never before." He smiles, the look on his face reflecting nothing but love.

The crowd ooh and ahh and I wish Jasper could see me, but I'm eaten up amongst the swarm of people.

"So this song, it's about surrendering to the one you love the most." He strums his guitar, playing the intro to the song that melts my heart time and time again.

The fact I had another man's lips on mine seventy-two hours ago makes me feel so undeserving of such a beautiful song, but I try and focus on his words because I'll deal with my shame when I have to.

V and I dance to the heartfelt lyrics, raising our arms above our heads and sway in time to the music. I'm lost in a Jasper trance, and I never want this song to end. When it does, the crowd explodes in a thunderous applause and Jasper bows playfully.

"Hot damn, I think my ovaries just exploded watching that." V howls in laughter and nudges me. "He's so getting laid tonight."

"Yes, yes he is," I reply in total agreement.

"All right, we've got one more song to play, and there's only one person who can sing it with me."

Every hand shoots up, begging that person be them, but I know who it is, and I'm seconds away from gagging. "What a way to ruin my high. I need another drink for this."

"Wait for me," V says, following me to the bar.

"Here she is...Delilah Rose!"

I turn out of curiosity, but really shouldn't have because I gag when I see her saunter on stage, giving Jasper a flirty wink.

"You know, if you ripped out her eyes, that would stop her from winking at your man."

"V!" I cackle in laughter.

"What? It's just a suggestion," she says with a shrug.

Her homicidal humor is exactly what I need and we survive the four minute duet by downing eight shots. Once they're done, I turn to look at the stage and see Delilah kissing Jasper on the cheek.

Grinding down on my jawbone, I bark, "I'm going to ram my fist down her throat if she kisses him one more time."

V stops mid-shot and passes me her drink. "Cheers to that."

Tipping my head back, I cringe the minute the toxic liquor hits my throat. But the burn is welcome because as Jasper says goodnight, I know what I have to do.

CHAPTER
TWENTY NINE
A.A

"I feel like a groupie," gripes V as we're standing by the back door, watching roadies carry equipment to parked trucks.

"Well, the fact you're the mother of Lucas' child really says otherwise," I dispute with a hiccup.

"Yeah, but they don't know that," V replies, gesturing with her head to the twenty or so fans, waiting with P.O.E. paraphernalia and cameras ready in hand.

"Who cares. I bet they don't know Lucas does that thing—"

"Sshh! Sshh! Sshh!" V cuts me off by motioning a slashing signal to her throat. "That's something I *don't* want them to know."

I laugh, knowing the feeling all too well.

My drunken brain suddenly remembers what Kris told me when I spoke to him last. "I totally forgot, but the last time I spoke to Kris, he said he was Jasper's roadie."

V laughs, holding her sides in humor. "As if he can carry anything heavy with those weedy arms."

"Well, that's what he said. Let's hope he's telling the truth."

V rolls her eyes. "Anything that comes out of Kris' mouth is a total lie."

"Hello, love."

V yelps and turns around, fists raised. When she sees Kris standing smugly before us, she thankfully lowers them. "Don't you know it's bad manners to creep up on someone?" she says, hand over her heart.

"Just like its bad manners to talk about someone behind their back," he playfully counters with a grin.

"Oh, I'm happy to divulge my hatred to your face next time," V replies in a sweet voice.

"Okay. Enough, you two." I stand between them because I know this can go on all night otherwise. "Hello, Kris." I attempt to give him a hug, but trip over my feet in the process, and he ends up catching me very ungracefully.

"Phew! How much have you had to drink?" He pulls me away at arm's length to look into my eyes.

"I dunno. I lost count after ten."

He shakes his head, chuckling at my shameful confession. "Does Jasper know you're here?"

I can't help but smirk. "Nope. I'm a surprise."

Kris rubs his hands together sinisterly. "The things I could get in exchange for you."

"Hey! I'm not a damn bargaining chip," I say, attempting to slap him, but I miss.

"No, but you're the next best thing. Here's hoping you can snap Jasper outta his pissy mood." He sighs.

His comment has me instantly worrying. "Pissy mood? Is everything okay?"

"Yeah, he's just shitty after not speaking to you for a few days. It's a running joke that he needs to go to A.A."

"What? He's drinking?" I gasp, my heart dropping into my stomach.

Kris laughs, shaking his head. "No. A.A. stands for Ava Anonymous."

V cackles, slapping her thigh. "That's a good one."

I ignore them both because all this Jasper talk makes me miss him even more. "Where is he?" I stand on tippy toes to see inside the door.

"Oh, he's already gone," he flippantly replies.

The girls around us have slowly crept closer, clueing in that we know someone on the inside. "Oh? Jasper has gone?" a girl with a thick German asks.

"Yeah, Sweetpea, they've all gone."

"How do you know?" she questions, looking at his lanyard to figure out who he is.

I know what he's going to say, even before he says it. "'Cause I'm Jasper's brother."

I roll my eyes. *Now* he's Jasper's brother. He wasn't his brother when he was smashing his guitar into tiny pieces.

Speaking of. "I hope you're handling his stuff with care?"

Kris grins, patting me on the arm. "TLC, love. Total TLC."

"Well, where are they staying?" I stupidly ask because I have fifty pairs of ears also wanting to know the answer.

He leans in close so the girls don't hear. "Meet me at the front door in fifteen minutes and we can all go together. Now beat it, you're cramping my style."

"Please don't tell me you've been playing the 'Jasper

is my brother' card to pick up chicks?" I ask, shaking my head.

He innocently pulls back, giving me big innocent doe eyes.

"You're disgusting." I playfully slap his arm and this time, I don't miss.

"What? There are a lot of desperate women out there that have needs. If they can't have the real deal, then they'll settle for Jasper's baby brother. You should be happy your fiancé is a boring little homebody," he replies, laughing when I stick my finger down my throat.

"Again, you're disgusting. But thank you for distracting them from my fiancé."

He fake sighs. "I'm talking one for the team." He kisses us on the foreheads, saying he'll meet us in fifteen.

We wait out front like instructed, and run towards the van when we see Kris high beam us, excited to finally be reunited with our boys. The moment we jump inside, Kris tosses us a six pack of beer. "Thought you'd be thirsty."

I dive into it, needing the liquid courage to tell Jasper the reason why I'm here.

"You've chosen a good night to come," he says, indicating to make a turn.

"Why?"

"'Cause we're all having drinks to celebrate how well the tour is going," he explains, while I frown.

"All the bands will be there?"

He nods.

"Great," I grumble, sinking into my seat.

"I guess you're not pleased Ms. Rose will be there?" he asks, looking at me via the rear-view mirror.

"You guessed right." His comment has me thinking. "So, I take it you've seen her throw herself at Jasper?"

"Yup." He smirks. "But the dumb bastard is so blind; he can't see her obvious play for him. But that's because he's not one bit interested in her," he adds when I feel tears prick my eyes.

"Thanks, Kris." I know he's just trying to make me feel better.

"She's persistent, but Jasper is a hard nut to crack. I think she's given up anyway, and moved onto Lucas," he says, pulling a face and looking at V over his shoulder as he stops at a red light. "I'm joking," he quickly amends when she leans forward, ready to punch him.

"You have two of the most loyal partners ever. You've got nothing to worry about."

I know his comment is meant to make me feel better, but it just highlights what an awful person I really am.

"Just stay here and listen for your cue," Kris says as we're standing outside the door to the hotel bar.

We eagerly nod, as this is kind of exciting surprising the boys, but it's also a little daunting. What happens if they're not happy to see us?

Pushing those thoughts aside, I give Kris a thumbs up.

"Okay. See you soon." He rounds the corner.

"I can't believe I'm actually excited to see my husband," V whispers, securing her ponytails. "Do I look okay?"

"You look beautiful. Lucas is going to be a salivating fool when he sees you."

"I hope so cause this mamma needs her papa bear."

And that's a visual I could so do without. "Gross." I cover my mouth to smother my laugh.

"Sshh." She chuckles, covering her lips with her pointer.

We're both extremely drunk and excited, so I'm not sure how long we can stand out here and remain undetected.

"Hey, bro," I thankfully hear Kris say. "Great show."

"Thanks, man." The moment I hear his voice, my palms begin to sweat and I feel like I'm going to faint.

"So, I've got a surprise for you."

"Oh yeah?" The surprise is clear in Jasper's voice.

"Yeah. I've brought back the hottest—well, two of the hottest chicks for you and Lucas."

There's silence and I hold my breath, afraid Jasper will say bring them on in.

"What the fuck? I'm not interested in that shit, you know that," Jasper barks angrily, while I breathe out a sigh of relief.

"Yeah, man, thanks, but I've got my beautiful wife at home. And besides, she's all the woman I can handle."

I stifle my laugh behind my hand, while V slaps me playfully.

"Are you sure? I mean, they're smoking. Like A-grade."

"Thanks, but no." Jasper's tone reveals he's seconds away from losing his shit at Kris.

"Haven't you heard, Jasper is joining the priesthood," a catty voice says.

No guessing whose.

"His little woman has had him spaded and kept his balls in her purse for a souvenir. He can't even look at another girl without fear of being reprimanded."

"Ha, very funny," Jasper chides. "I'm just not interested in looking at anyone other than her."

My heart swells while I flip Delilah off.

"Okay well, if you're sure," Kris says, cutting off the banter.

"Yeah, dude, one hundred percent sure. Just make sure you wrap up your junk. We don't want a call in nine months' time. The world can only handle one Kris Blackwood." I'm thankful to hear Jasper is back to his usual playful self.

"All right then, it's your loss. Ladies," he calls out.

V looks at me nervously and I giggle as I push her into the doorway.

"Veronica?" Lucas gasps.

"Hi, Papa Bear," she coos. I hear her Mary Janes pound on the floor as she runs over to him.

"Are you sure you don't wanna change your mind?" Kris teases Jasper. "I've heard she's got real rotten taste in men, so you're in."

Taking that as my cue, I peek my head around the

corner and my gaze lands on Jasper, who stands by the bar, his mouth agape.

"H-hi," I stutter when he continues staring at me without a word.

"Baby?" he finally says, his eyes as wide as saucers.

"Surprise," I lamely say as I step into full view.

"Ava? What?" He's lost for words, and I don't know if that's a good thing, or a bad thing. I stand rigid, unsure of what to do, but I'm also embarrassed, as all eyes are glued to our reunion.

Suddenly when he charges forward, his bright blue eyes glowing in happiness, I do what feels natural. I run towards him, wanting nothing more than to be lost in his embrace. He catches me the moment I jump into his open arms. Wrapping my legs around his waist, I cross them behind his back while throwing my arms around his neck. The moment I bury my nose into him, I inhale his heady fragrance, the fragrance which smells like home.

"What are you doing here?" he asks, squeezing me so tight I can barely breathe.

"I missed you."

"I missed you, too." He pulls out of my hold, and places both palms on my cheeks. His intense eyes scan every angle, every feature, and before long, he's placing a billion kisses on every inch of my face. But the moment we connect, nothing else matters, and the innocent reunion turns a little heated. Before I know it, Jasper's carrying me out the door.

"Where are we going?" I say breathlessly around his lips.

"I need you," is the only response I get.

He kicks open a door, pushing my back up against it as he reaches down and locks it. The moment it clicks into place, we're tearing at each other's clothes like wild animals in heat. He loosens his hold and I slide down the door, instantly dropping to my knees and frantically yanking on his belt and zipper.

"No, baby." He lifts me up by the arms. "I want to be inside of you. I need it."

With no hesitation, I push him towards the settee and he falls back, surprised by my aggression.

But as I rip the black dress off over my head and he sees me standing in nothing but a pink lace bra and thong, that surprise turns to desire and he reaches forward, pulling me towards him by the waistband of my underwear. I come willingly, unhooking my bra in the process, and the moment I'm in reach, he sucks my nipple into his warm mouth.

Whimpering, I bow backward, giving him deeper access, but it's not enough. He senses what I need and thrusts his hand down the front of my thong, feeling how swollen and needy I am. An animalistic urge passes over me and I shove him backward, licking my lips in craving. His questioning look is replaced with understanding and he rips his jeans down while I step out of my underwear and straddle him a moment later.

"Baby, let me..." He dips two fingers between us, attempting to prepare me for his delicious intrusion. But I'm more than prepared.

Guiding his tip to my entrance, I slowly lower myself onto him, allowing my muscles to welcome him home. Jasper's guttural growls spur me on and I sink further down, but suddenly, slow is not enough. Raising my hips and clutching onto his shoulders, I slam down onto him until I've taken him all.

"Oh, fuck." He places both hands low on my waist and begins rocking me backwards and forwards, encouraging me to pick up the pace.

I do as he asks and I pump my hips fiercely, arching my back so he hits me deeper and harder, and it's exactly what I need. My desperation to wash away my sins has me violently fisting his hair, while I claw my fingers into his slicked flesh, no doubt drawing blood.

"Baby, I'm not going last," Jasper pants, and I know he's moments away from coming.

But that's okay, this is all for him and instead of slowing down, I go faster and faster and faster until Jasper convulses and groans, shuddering his release into me. The sated sound is exactly what I needed to hear, and I finally slow down, attempting to catch my breath.

Jasper has other ideas however, and the moment he's spent, he stands with us still attached and then turns, dropping me down, so I'm sitting on the edge of the red velvet settee. He falls to his knees before me, scoots my hips forward and before I can question what he's doing, he buries his head between my legs. I collapse backward, his relentless mouth determined to give me the pleasure I gave him moments ago.

I open my legs wider, but it's not enough and he wants more. So he places his hand under my knee and coaxes me to throw a leg over his shoulder. To steady myself, I balance one hand behind me, while I fist the other into his hair, drawing his mouth closer to my center.

As he sucks at my core and drives his tongue into me, I explode in a silent scream.

Only when the last tremor rocks my body does Jasper pull away. I collapse in a messy, naked heap. He arises and sits next to me, drawing me into his lap so I'm cuddling into him, cocooned in his arms. We're sweaty, slick, and sated, and it's everything I wanted and more. But as my high fades, reality kicks in, and I know I'll have to tell him about Michel soon.

"I love you, baby." He strokes his fingers down my back, spreading goose bumps down my skin, awakening my body once more.

"I love you, too." Looking around for the first time since we charged in here, I see that we're in a bathroom. A very, posh, clean bathroom, but a bathroom none-theless.

"Oh my god, did we just have sex in a restroom?"

Jasper chuckles, the deep sound low and satisfied. Lifting his head from my shoulder, he looks around the room. "Yup, looks like we did."

"Holy shit, I'm a total groupie," I say while he grins, his eyes scanning down my body.

As he begins kissing my neck, revealing that we're only getting started, I breathlessly confess, "Looks like being a groupie isn't so bad after all."

CHAPTER THIRTY
The Truth Will Set You Free

The next morning while Jasper is in the shower, happily singing away, I know it's time to face the inevitable and tell him about Michel. I can't stand to lie to him for a second longer, and the reason why I haven't told him sooner is because our mouths have literally been occupied doing other things, and talking wasn't one of them. So now that we're not caught in a bubble of passion, it's time he knows why I ran.

He steps out of the bathroom wearing nothing but his tight black jeans with the top button undone. The way they sit low on his waist, his impressive V muscle on full display, reveals he's not wearing any underwear underneath.

It's so unfair. I wish we were doing anything but this, but it has to be done.

"Is everything okay?" he asks, running a hand through his wet hair.

His ring, which hangs from his necklace, catches the light, and I bite my lip, afraid how this will turn out. "Come sit with me." I pat the bed beside me.

His anxiety is clearly evident in his clenched jaw, but he does as I ask and takes a seat near me. Reaching for his hand, I nervously toy with his fingers, hoping to deliver this the best way that I can.

"Something happened in New York."

As Jasper's fingers clench into fists, I figure that probably wasn't the best lead in. "What happened?" His tone is calm, but it's the calm before the storm.

"Well..." I commence, removing my hand from his. "You know how I told you that important food critic, Liam Stromboli, is coming into Metro for the food festival?"

He nods.

"Well, it's not by chance. Michel actually arranged for him to come in."

Jasper remains composed, but the little tick under his eye reveals otherwise.

"Adelia revealed that Michel had orchestrated the entire thing. I confronted him, things got heated, and anyway—" I cut out the finer details when he looks about ready to launch off the bed in rage.

"He confessed that he spoke to Liam because he wants me to stay in New York."

"Why?" It's the only word Jasper has spoken, and it's filled with venom.

"Because," I start, lowering my eyes. "Because he thinks there's something between us, and well..."

"Well, *what*, Ava?" he asks, barely containing his temper.

"Well, I told him no, that's not true. That I love you, and, and..." I stutter, nervously fiddling with my heart charm.

"And what?" he says from between clenched teeth.

"And then...he kissed me," I whisper, covering my eyes so I can't see him hit the roof.

"He...*what?*"

"He kissed me," I repeat. When I uncover my eyes, I witness Jasper turn from red to white then back to red.

"That mother...fucker." His breathing accelerates and he jumps off the bed like it's on fire.

As I watch him pace the room, his hands interlaced behind his head, I don't know what to say. So I don't say anything.

"I..." He pauses, shaking his head. "I don't know what to say. I mean, I could say I told you so, but that doesn't make me feel any better because I should have listened to my gut and knocked him on his smug ass when I had the chance!"

"Jasper, no!" I say, leaping off the bed. I don't touch him however, and just let him cool down.

"Did you kiss him back?" he asks, coming to a stop in front of me.

"No!" I cry, my eyes widening. "I slapped him so hard I had to ice my hand when I got home."

"Good. That motherfucker," he says again, and continues pacing. "Describe the kiss."

"What?" I ask, taken aback.

"Was it long? Short? Open mouth? Closed mouth? Was there tongue?" he snarls, turning to look at me heatedly.

"It was short, closed mouth, and most definitely no tongue!"

"Did he touch you?"

"Touch me?"

"Yes, Ava. Did he put his filthy hands all over you?" He charges towards me and grips my bicep firmly.

"No, he didn't touch me," I reply, pulling out of his hold.

"Yeah, but his lips did," he retorts, his nostrils flaring.

"Yes, they did," I answer, lowering my eyes. "I'm so sorry, Jasper. That's why I came here. I needed to tell you. But I promise, nothing else happened. It's been purely professional up until then." And up until you let him sleepover and he cooked you breakfast the next morning. I tell my stupid subconscious to zip it, as this out of control inferno doesn't need any more ignition.

"I really am sorry. I should have listened to you. I'm such an idiot."

Jasper sighs, appearing to have calmed down a fraction. "You're not an idiot. You're just too trusting of the wrong people."

Again I bite my tongue.

We stand staring at one another, the tension suffocating. "I'm so angry, Ava."

"I know, I'm sorry," I pathetically repeat. "I'll say sorry for the rest of our lives. Just please don't hate me. And please don't leave me."

His face softens, and I hold back my tears. "Baby, I'm fucking furious at *him*, not you. If you hadn't told me and I'd found out, *then* I'd be pissed. But I know you and I trust you. That doesn't make me any less angry, though."

"I understand." I sniff, my heart returning to a semi-normal pace. "Thank you for believing me."

"Of course, I believe you. You trusted me when I told

you there was nothing going on between Delilah and me," he affirms, while I try not to blanch at the memory.

"I did."

He reaches forward and interlaces our fingers, playing with my ring. "Well, I trust you."

"So, what happens now?" I'm almost afraid to ask.

He blows out a frustrated breath, but I sense the worst is over. "He's lucky we're thousands of miles apart, because I would have no issues beating him to a pulp for touching what's mine." A thought suddenly occurs to him. "What happens with the festival now?"

"I won't do it."

"No, baby, no," he presses, shaking his head and clenching my hand passionately. "You're not letting this handsy asshole ruin your career. You go back and you cook up a storm for that critic so he sings your praises from the highest rooftops in New York."

"But that means I'll have to go back soon. I mean, I have to prepare."

"I know," he replies with an understanding nod.

"And you're okay with that?"

"Well, I sure as hell am not okay with you throwing away what you've worked so hard for," he firmly states, reaching for my other hand.

"I love you, you know that," I reply, stepping forward and placing his arms around me.

"You better." He smirks, and I'm happy to see him smile.

"So, I what? Go back to New York, impress the pants off Liam, and—"

"And then you come back to me," he finishes off me for.

"Okay."

"You do realize that this guy reviewing you will set your career up for life? I mean, you'll be able to work anywhere," he says, believing that Liam will like my food as much as he does.

"He might hate what I cook for him."

"Not possible," Jasper admonishes, shaking his head with a smirk.

"Are you sure?" I ask, wanting to ensure he's comfortable with me going back.

"Yes, I want you to do this," he affirms with a nod. "Promise me you will. No matter what happens, promise me you'll see this through."

"I promise. But nothing is going to happen. I mean the plan is for you to wrap up the tour, and for me to cook, and then we go back to L.A., right?"

"Yes," he replies, brushing a curl of hair behind my ear. "This way, we've both lived out our dreams, and no one loses. You asked me once what's the compromise where we both win? Well, this is the compromise. I won't feel like you've sacrificed something you love because of me, and I've toured the world, just like I've always wanted."

"You're worth any sacrifice, but I like this compromise," I say, leaning into his touch.

This is the compromise I was looking for. Things have fallen into place, and we've somehow made a shitty situation work in our favor. It's just a shame it took Michel kissing me to realize what that was.

When he clenches his jaw, I know he's thinking about what this compromise entails. "But if he touches you again, Ava, I *will* kill him. I will fly across the world, and when I'm done with him, he'll really be a Michelle."

I stifle my laugh by biting my lip.

"I'm still fuming," he states, his expression grim.

"I know. I'm sorry." I lower my eyes, still ashamed.

After a moment of silence, he says, "So show me."

"Show you what?"

"Show me how he kissed you," he clarifies, folding his arms across his chest.

"Why?" I have no idea why he would want to torture himself this way.

"'Cause if you show me, it'll stop all the explicit images in my mind. At the moment, all I can picture is him ramming his tongue down your throat," he crossly reveals, pulling a sickened face.

"That *never* happened," I stress, reaching forward and rubbing his crossed forearm.

"I know. That's why you need you to show me. It's a lot worse in my head."

I understand his motives, and I would probably be the same way if I were in his shoes. "Well, I was standing in the kitchen and I was wedged up against the counter."

"Like this?" He marches over to me, and presses me up against the dresser so I'm trapped.

"Yes."

"Then what?" he presses, the pain clear in his tone.

"Then he said, 'then why does your fiancé think there's something between us?' in response to me telling him there is nothing romantic between us."

Jasper grinds down on his jaw. "And what did you say?"

"I didn't say anything. I opened my mouth, ready to argue, but then he—"

Jasper swoops forward, pressing his lips to mine, not allowing me to finish. I stand frozen, closing my eyes and sealing my lips shut, as he did ask me to show him what I did.

After a few seconds, he pulls away and I open my eyes. "Wow, that was cold." But he's smiling from ear to ear.

"Yup, and you didn't even let me show you the best part of when I hit him."

"I bet you got him real good. These little hands sure know how to pack a punch," he says, reaching for my shaky fingers.

"So we're okay?" I ask, afraid my re-enactment has backfired, and he's ready to throw me out of his room.

Pushing our foreheads together, he nods. "We're okay. I love you with all that I am."

"Well, that's a whole lot," I whisper, and this time, when Jasper kisses me off guard, I kiss him back.

CHAPTER
THIRTY ONE
With or Without You

The next few days pass rather quickly. Between Jasper's press conferences, in-store appearances, radio interviews, and shows, I barely see him for more than five minutes at a time. I now understand why he says there's nothing glamorous about touring. The schedule is hectic and tight, and it also doesn't give him much downtime.

V and I are side stage in Prague, waiting for P.O.E. to come on. Roses just violated my eyeballs, and I never wanna be this close to Delilah and her scantily dressed ass ever again. I know she just loves the fact that she's been spending more time with Jasper than I have. But it's *my* bed he ends up in at the end of the night, not hers, and I smugly like to remind her of it every chance I get. There's been a few 'bathroom visits,' and I've made sure she knows what we're doing in there by not exactly being quiet. Immature, I know, but hey, I take great pleasure in seeing her fume.

"Are you okay?" V gestures with her head to Delilah as she jumps down from the stage to sign autographs for fans.

"Yeah, she doesn't bother me in the slightest anymore. She's so desperate for attention," I say, nearly hurling when I see her shove her boobs in some dude's face. "It's actually a little sad to watch."

"I think you mean hilarious," V amends, laughing when the dude's girlfriend slaps him in the face.

"That too. I'm secure enough within myself and my relationship to not allow her to bug me," I state proudly, realizing how I've grown.

Jasper still looks a little wound up over the whole Michel thing, not that I blame him. I know it'll take time to fully process what happened, and being in this artificial environment hasn't really given him a moment to collect his thoughts.

"Listen to you," V says with a smile. "My little Ava has grown up." She mocks me by wiping away a pretend tear.

"I have, and I'm not going to let one little tramp ruin that." I look pointedly at Delilah, who has come back on stage and in earshot.

She scowls at me, but has the good sense not to start anything because I'm ready if she does. She flicks her long hair over her shoulder and stomps offstage while V and I cackle in laughter.

It's going to be a good night.

P.O.E. has nailed their set. It saddens me to know that this will probably be the last European show I see because I've decided to head back to New York in two days' time.

I'm waiting backstage for Jasper to emerge, as I know he likes some quiet time to unwind before he faces the VIPs. It's all so dreamlike, and I never thought my life would have turned out the way it has. Jasper and I have been through so much, but it feels like we've finally jumped over all of life's hurdles, and it's all on the up from here on in.

"Walk with me, love," Kris says, grabbing my elbow and leading me towards the door.

"Where are we going?" I ask, looking over my shoulder to ensure Jasper isn't there.

"Just for a walk," he ambiguously states.

I don't argue and allow him to lead me to the green room. When we walk inside, he closes the door and stands up against it, stopping me from leaving.

"Um, what are you doing?" I ask, wondering what's gotten into him.

"I just wanted to say goodbye. Jasper told me you're headed back to New York. He also told me what that scumbag did," he confesses, his expression mirroring Jasper's when I first told him.

"Oh. So you and Jasper, you're okay?"

"Yeah, we are. It's all thanks to you and your ridiculous suggestion of playing ball."

"Hey, it got you two to talk, didn't it?" I smile, so happy to hear their relationship looks promising.

"It did. So thank you, Ava. You were right, he really is

an amazing person. I'm so lucky to have him as my brother. And I'm also lucky to have you as my future sister-in-law."

"Aw, you're going to make me cry." I chuckle, wiping my eyes.

"The next few days are going to be really tight with touring all over the place, so I wanted to say this before things got too hectic and out of control," he confesses. I can't believe this is the same Kris I met weeks ago.

"Thank you, Kris. I really don't know what to say."

He steps forward and opens his arms. "How 'bout you give your brother-in-law a hug."

"I think I can manage that." I step forward and he hugs me softly.

"He's a better man because of you, Ava. He doesn't stop smiling when you're around."

This time I do cry. "Thanks, Kris. But he's always been a better man. He's the best, with or without me. Although, I prefer with."

Kris' cell dings and he pulls out of our embrace with a grin.

"Hold up, what's going on?" I ask, tilting my head to the side.

"My work here is done," he reveals. As he opens the door, in strolls a freshly showered Jasper.

My eyes dart to Kris, who laughs. "Have fun, kids. Don't do anything that I wouldn't do."

Before I have time to reply, Jasper steps forward and gives me a quick peck on the lips. He smells amazing, and I latch onto the back of his neck to make that quick peck a long smooch. But he pulls out of my embrace, chuckling softly.

"There's plenty of time for that later."

"Later? What's happening now?"

"You'll see," he cheekily replies. "Or, you won't see." He holds up a blindfold.

"And that's my cue to get outta here," Kris says. Before he leaves, he unexpectedly bends forward and gives me a quick kiss on the cheek. "I meant what I said."

"I know. Thank you," I say, and this time, I'm the one who stands on tippy toes and kisses his cheek.

"What are you up to?" I ask Jasper as Kris closes the door behind him.

"Up to? What makes you think I'm up to anything?" he smugly replies, twirling the red blindfold from his finger.

"Well, the fact I'm about to be blinded suggests you're up to a lot."

He steps closer, his eyes turning dark and mysterious. "Have you ever disapproved of my blindfolding before?"

Thinking back, no, I guess I haven't. My cheeks heat when I remember this one particular time in the bedroom. Just the thought of what he did to my body while I was blindfolded has me stepping forward, ready to get this show on the road.

Jasper must remember it too because he disturbs my vivid thoughts by leaning forward and nibbling on my ear. "See, I told you. Nothing but pleasure comes from being blindfolded. And I know how much you like plea-sure," he whispers, his voice dripping with innuendo. "So turn around, baby, and let the fun begin."

I quickly do as he asks, barely holding back my moan. He slips it over my head, and I'm cloaked in sudden darkness.

"Okay, I'm going to guide you. Trust me, baby?"

"With my life," I reply without a second thought.

He wraps his hands around my waist a moment later, and when I hear the door open, he guides me outside.

With him at my back, I feel protected and have no fear of falling or tripping over my feet. I'm curious however to know where we're going, so I extend my hands out in front of me, hoping to feel for any clues en route to our destination.

"You okay?" His breath is warm against my neck.

"Yes." I nod. "Just curious to know where you're taking me."

"You'll know soon enough. We're coming to a staircase. There are ten steps in total."

I get a little nervous, and walk cautiously to stop myself from face planting.

"I've got you. I won't let you fall."

With his words of reassurance in mind, I lower my hands and allow the love of my life to guide me, trusting him completely. His warmth, heady scent, and strength envelope me in my own personal Jasper bubble. I never want to leave.

"Only a few more to go," he whispers into my ear, his whiskers tickling my sensitive skin.

We take it slow, but when I meet flat ground, I know we've arrived.

"Okay, baby, you can take off the blindfold." He leans over my shoulder and I hear a door creak open.

Slowly raising my hesitant fingers, I slip it off. My eyes take a moment to adjust to the dim light, but when they do, I gasp, a hand flying to my open mouth. "W-what is this?" I ask, taking in the dreamlike scene before me.

"It's for you. Come on," he says, stepping around me and offering his hand.

I accept, wanting nothing more than to step into this magical wonderland with the man of my dreams. He leads me through the outdoor restaurant, especially created for two. The stunning table is covered in traditional Czech dishes of pancakes, fruit dumplings, macaroons, and all kinds of different chocolates.

"Jasper." My voice trembles. "This is beautiful."

If the food wasn't enough, he's organized for two massive outdoor heaters to warm up the chilly night air. Their glow highlights the beauty of the thousand candles spread out as far as the eye can see. These are our only light source, and it's simply perfect.

He pulls out a chair for me and smiles. "Ms. Thompson."

"Thank you, Mr. White," I say, tucking my skirt underneath me and taking a seat.

I glance around the table, my taste buds dancing in delight.

"Coffee?" he asks, holding up a pot.

"Yes, please."

Reaching for my cup, he pours me the divine smelling caffeine, and then pours himself one also.

"This is so amazing. Thank you," I say, looking around me in awe. "Not that I'm complaining, but what did I do to deserve all this?" I sweep my hand out, indicating the perfect scene before us.

Jasper peers at me over his coffee cup, his eyes appearing crystal clear in the candlelight. "You deserve all this and more. I'm sorry I haven't had the chance to spend some quality time with you. All we seem to get are stolen moments."

"But those stolen moments are ours," I say, reaching for his hand. "I understand. This isn't a holiday, it's your job. Yes, your workplace isn't conventional, but it's still work. I knew what I was getting into the moment I said yes."

He smiles, squeezing my fingers. "Thank you for understanding. I'm glad you're here. It's been cool to have you on tour. You've been my sanity. I don't know I'll survive when you go," he confesses with a frown.

"Yeah, I've noticed your schedule is kinda insane. You look tired," I say, touching his cheek.

"I am," he admits, turning into my palm. "I'm exhausted. I'm mentally and physically drained. Going out there and giving it your all takes it out of you. It's like you're giving away a piece of your soul night after night. Having you here has made it easier to deal with the crazy. It's going to suck when you leave." He toys with my diamond, a habit he's picked up.

"I know. But just think where we'll be when we see one other again."

"We'll be home," he declares, revealing his relief.

I happily nod. "You think you'll be able to cope without your legions of adoring fans?" I tease. "You know, even rock stars have to take out the garbage."

Jasper smirks. "Baby, I'm just me. And all of this,"—he draws a circle in the air—"isn't real. But this," he concludes, running his finger over my ring once more. "*This* is real. Can you believe we've made it this far?"

"Honestly, no, I can't. I'm surprised one of us isn't rocking in some corner somewhere."

Jasper laughs. "We've survived this, baby. We can survive anything."

He's totally right. The hardships we've sustained to get where we are all seem like a distant memory, because what we have now is simply perfect.

I nod, trying to hold back my tears, because tonight is about celebrating. "What I won't survive is if those pancakes get cold," I say, tongue in cheek, as I point to the delicious looking sweets.

I lift my plate, while Jasper grins. "One or two? Actually, don't answer that," he corrects, passing me two.

He knows me so well.

After stuffing myself full, I'm eyeing the last dumpling, ticking off the reasons why I shouldn't eat it.

The night has been epic, and I'm not even sure how long we've been up here, as time doesn't exist when I'm talking to Jasper.

I cover an unprompted yawn behind my hand, while

Jasper chuckles. "Are you sleepy? Wanna head to our room?"

"Only if you want to. I'm perfectly happy to stay up here all night."

"Oh, isn't that sweet," a snide voice says from behind us.

"What do you want?" Jasper asks Delilah, as he looks over my shoulder.

"I wanted to show you something."

I can only guess what.

Her voice alone is grating on my nerves, but I won't allow her to taint my perfect evening. "If you'll excuse me." I push my chair backwards, while Jasper stands.

"Is everything all right?"

"Yeah, I'm just going to the bathroom. I'm not interested in seeing anything she has to offer," I say, hooking my thumb over my shoulder.

"I'm right here," she snarls. I can just imagine her sourpuss face.

Ignoring her, I lean over the table to give Jasper a light kiss on the lips. "I'll be right back."

"Are you sure you don't wanna stay?" she asks when I turn to face her.

"No, thank you," I reply, giving her a stiff upper lip smile.

"Suit yourself," she arrogantly sings, hands behind her back.

Holding my head up high when I walk past her, I notice a folded piece of paper in her hand, but pay no attention to it and make my way downstairs. I use the restroom and freshen up, taking as long as possible, as I'm hoping the Queen Bitch will be gone by the time I get back.

Looking into the mirror as I re-apply my lip gloss, I see my reddened cheeks have a healthy glow and my lips are sitting in a permanent smile. I know this response is because of Jasper. I'm so happy we've worked through a situation which would have probably ended in heartbreak and tears years ago.

Once I'm finished, I dart up the stairs, sighing when I see that Delilah is gone. Jasper's hands are dug deep into his pockets as he looks over the railing with his head bowed.

Unable to wait, I run over to him and wrap my arms around his waist, pressing my cheek into his back. "Miss me?" I mumble against him.

However, he doesn't reply, and his rigid stance hints that something is wrong.

"Is everything okay? Did Delilah say something to upset you?" I ask, as he was fine before I left him with her.

When the silence is drawn out, he really starts to worry me. So I press that he tells me what's wrong. "Jasper, you're scaring me. What's the matter?"

The air is filled with an uncomfortable static, and I get an ominous feeling that something awful is about to happen.

"*This* is the matter," he finally says, pulling a piece of paper from his pocket.

As he turns, I take a step back, the fury on his face revealing something is terribly wrong. I take the piece of paper he extends to me with trembling fingers, unsure what I'm about to see. Opening it with hesitation, I gasp when I see what's inside.

It's a photograph of Michel kissing me, but from this photocopied image, it looks like I'm kissing him back. I stare, stunned, as I'm sure he never touched my face. But here it is, clear as day, his hand pressed against my cheek, while the other draws me close, pressing us chest to chest.

The pose looks very intimate, and it also doesn't look like I'm struggling too hard to get away. But I know I did. I know what comes next. And so does Jasper, because I've told him the truth.

"I told you this happened," I say, turning the picture around.

He turns his head away, unable to look at the image without appearing as if he's going to be sick. "You told me *he* kissed you. You never told me *you* kissed him back."

"Because I didn't," I stress in a panic. "I know this picture makes it appear that way, but it really wasn't. You have to believe me. You *do* believe me, don't you?" I add when he continues to avoid my gaze.

"Jasper?" When he remains quiet, I know that he doesn't. "That's not fair. I believed you when you told me nothing happened between Delilah and you. Why can't you do the same for me?"

"Because nothing did happen, but that photograph," he snarls, finally meeting my eyes. "Proves that something did happen between you and...him." He eyes the paper like it's his worst enemy.

"Nothing happened!" I exclaim, hurt that he doesn't believe me. "Where did the photo come from, anyway? Delilah?"

I have no doubt the paparazzi outside my door took this incriminating picture. And knowing Yolanda, she probably owns the rights and it's plastered all over her blog. I suspect this is my payback for not doing her show.

"It doesn't matter. All that matters is why he thought he had the right to touch you. To kiss you"—his eyes closing in despair—"the way that he did. What else aren't you telling me?"

"Nothing!" I cry, but then I remember him staying at our house.

I didn't think it was a big deal, but did Michel? Has my naivety gotten me into trouble? Has my kindness inadvertently given Michel mixed signals?

Jasper can read me like a book. "What is it? There's more, isn't there?"

I should have told him, I tried to when it happened. But I never mentioned it again because it didn't matter. But it obviously mattered to Michel.

"He stayed over—once. He—"

"He what?" Jasper growls, his body stiffening, his eyes turning arctic.

"We went out for dinner, and I was going to drive him home. But he had lost his keys, so I said he could stay over," I confess, thinking how stupid I was to even suggest such a thing. "He stayed on the sofa, that's all. He never tried anything, Jasper, I promise." I reach for his arm, but he pulls away.

"How could you let him into our home? After you knew how I felt about him. After I asked you to be careful around him, Ava, how?" he demands, shaking his head angrily.

"I'm sorry." I lower my eyes, ashamed. "I didn't think of it like that. I thought I was just helping out a friend, that's all, I swear."

He scoffs, folding his arms over his chest. "I bet his story was total bullshit."

I bite my lip, wishing I had just listened to Jasper in the first place.

"God dammit!"

"I didn't...I didn't think," I stutter, knowing I fucked up.

"That's right, you didn't think. Do you know how it makes me feel to know that lying son of a bitch was in our house? Sleeping under the same roof as you?"

This is escalating rather quickly, and I need to pull it together before things get out of control. "Jasper, I'm sorry I didn't tell you. I tried, but it was the night we had the crappy connection. I didn't think to tell you after because it wasn't important."

"Another man, who you know I don't trust, sleeping in my house is very fucking important. I bet that French bastard cooked you breakfast."

I don't answer.

"Son of a bitch! I'm going to kill him," he promises, running both hands through his hair.

"Jasper, please just listen to me. This kiss," I state, holding up the piece of paper. "Meant nothing to me." I frantically tear it up, the tiny pieces littering the floor. "I'm sorry I didn't tell you about Michel staying over. I was wrong to ever allow him into our home. If I could take it back, I would.

"Yes, he cooked me breakfast, but it was his way of

saying thank you. We went to work, and that's it. I've never thought twice about it since. Please just calm down."

"I am calm!" he states. I don't bother to correct that he's currently sitting on the opposite end of calm. "I'm sick of this shit."

My heart begins kicking against my ribcage, afraid of what he means. "Sick of what?" I ask, swallowing down my nerves.

"Of people trying to come between us!" he yells, gripping both my uppers arms. "But you know what? No more."

Oh god, all the awful memories, all the awful fights we've had come flooding back, and I shake my head animatedly—this can't be happening again. But this time, I'll fight for him and won't let go.

"No more? Jasper, no—please don't do this," I beg, throwing my arms around his neck and latching on tight.

"Do what? Baby, what's the matter? Why are you shaking?" he asks, trying to loosen my death grip from around his neck.

"Please don't leave me," I reply, securing my hold, burying my face into him. "I'll do anything. Please, just don't leave me."

"Leave you? What are you talking about?" Jasper finally pries my fingers from around his nape so he can look at me.

I sniff, my body trembling in fright. "That's what you meant, isn't it? About no more. You don't want me anymore because I can't seem to stop breaking your heart. I'm sorry. I'll do anything. I'll—"

But Jasper cuts me off by pressing his lips to mine. I stand bewildered, as this is not the actions of someone who's had enough.

"You silly girl," he chides against my parted mouth. "I'm not going to leave you...I want you to marry me. As soon we get back home, I'm making you my wife. This thing with Michel, it's just cemented what I've wanted to do from the moment I gave you that ring. Maybe even before."

"M-Marry you?" I ask, confused. "I don't understand."

Jasper brushes a runaway tear from my cheek. "Do I need to list the people who have tried, but ultimately failed, to keep us apart?"

I shake my head, as I'm not interested in hearing that list, now or ever.

"We've been through so much, and you know what, we've survived. Yes, it's been a hell of a bumpy ride, but we made it. I still love you as much as I did the day I met you. And all these obstacles, they just prove to me that you and me, we're meant to be together. I'm not going to let this come between us. I mean, we've been through worse, right?" he says, a dimple hugging his cheek.

"Marry you?" I repeat softly, as it's the only thing I can vocalize right now.

"Yes. No more waiting. I know we haven't really spoken about it, but I want to marry you as soon as possible. I want to start this new chapter with you, baby. Tell me you want the same." The worry is etched across his face, as he's afraid I don't want the same thing.

I have no idea where this has come from, but the idea

of being Jasper's wife sooner, rather than later, sounds like the best fucking thing I've heard all day.

"Yes," I whisper, my eyes filling with fresh tears. "Yes. Yes. Yes. Yes a million times! Yes, I'll marry you, Jasper White."

The moment the words leave my lips, he swoops me up into his arms and twirls me around in the air. "Thank you, baby. You've just made me the happiest man in the world."

Tears are now streaming down my cheeks, but this time around, they're happy tears.

"I love you. I love you. I love you." He lowers me and kisses me with such passion he takes my breath away.

We kiss for what seems like forever, but it's not long enough, and when he pulls away, I pout, wanting more.

Jasper chuckles and thumbs my bottom lip. "No more kissing like that until you're Mrs. Ava White."

"Try and stop me," I challenge, pulling him by the scruff of his collar, while he smiles. "So, we're really doing this?"

"Yeah, we really are," he says, nodding happily. "You go back to New York, baby, you knock the socks off this connoisseur, you pack up, and then we plan our wedding."

I can't contain my shriek of excitement and Jasper laughs. "Finally, you'll forever be mine."

I shake my head, needing to clarify. Pressing our foreheads together, I whisper, "I'll always be yours, and nothing will ever change that."

CHAPTER THIRTY TWO

We'll Never Have to Say Goodbye...Just Goodnight

After a teary goodbye at the airport Jasper bid me farewell, promising that when we met again, we'll be one step closer to being husband and wife.

I have no idea how we got here, considering thirty seconds before Jasper was asking me to marry him, I feared we were moments away from breaking up. But either way, I don't care. For once, we didn't let anything, or anyone, stand in our way, and it feels so good to know we've grown.

V flew back to L.A. the day I left for New York, as she has taken her role as maid of honor very seriously and has started planning the wedding. I trust her completely, but honestly, I'm so happy to be marrying Jasper, I could get married under a circus big top and I wouldn't care.

It's now the night before I cook for Liam Stromboli, and I'm nervous as all hell. I've decided to have an early night because I know sleep won't come easily for me tonight. I also wanted to get away from Michel, who has been hovering since I returned.

I've told him that from now on, we only talk shop. He betrayed my trust, and if things with Jasper had turned out differently, then I wouldn't be speaking to him at all. I can see his guilt when I catch him watching me, but that's not my problem. He ruined our friendship the moment he stepped over the line.

Thankfully our personal problems haven't interfered with our cooking, and we've planned a killer menu to serve up for tomorrow night's dinner. Once this is over with, I can finally say I've achieved all I set out to by coming to New York. I can happily go home, excited to start the next chapter in my life.

I'm sitting in bed, chewing on my fifth Tum, as my stomach has been quite upset these past few days. My nerves are obviously getting the better of me because I can't seem to keep anything down. The only person who can make me better is a million miles away, so I do the only thing I can do when I miss Jasper—I load up YouTube to watch my video for the hundredth time today.

Just as I click on it, my cell rings and I reach for it off the bedside table.

"Hello?" As soon as I hear the pause, I know who's on the other end.

"Hi, baby."

My heart beats faster in excitement. "Hi, Jasper. How are you? Where are you? Oh, I love you, by the way."

He chuckles, the sound making me smile. "I'm okay, tired as all hell. I honestly have no idea where we are," he confesses. "But we're on our way to Italy."

"Wow, that's a long trip, right?" I say, as the last we spoke, he was in Poland.

"Yeah, it sucks. Our bus driver has been taking the long, windy roads, too. I'm convinced he has no idea where he's going half the time." I laugh, but can hear how exhausted he sounds. "We're all anxious to come home. Not long now."

Jasper and I have figured out that by the time I tie up my loose ends and he's done with the tour, we'll both be homebound at the same time, ready to start our life together. I can't wait.

"How you feeling? All set for tomorrow?"

"I'm okay. And yeah, I am. I'm going to make this meal my bitch," I reply, confidently.

"Hells yeah you are. I wish I was there, but I'll be thinking of you. Make sure Sara takes photos."

I laugh. "Photos of what?"

"Of everything. I don't wanna miss a thing."

"Okay, I'll tell her. I miss you, Jasper," I say, twisting my ring.

"I miss you too, baby. The only thing getting me through this is knowing that after I'm done, you'll be my wife."

Lucky I'm alone, as I'm pretty certain I would blind anyone with my smile. "Wife. I like the sound of that. Ava White. Has a nice ring to it, doesn't it?"

Jasper hums low in his throat. "You don't know how good it sounds. I...g...to."

"What? Jasper? You're breaking up," I say, jumping up and moving positions, just in case my cell has lost service.

"Sorry, baby, I gotta go. We're passing through tunnels."

I frown, hating that he has to go so soon. "Okay, I love you so much. I hate saying goodbye to you."

I can hear him sigh heavily. "Ava, one day soon, we'll never have to say goodbye...just goodnight. I love you, Mrs. White."

Before I can reply, the line drops out then goes dead. Although I'm sad our conversation ended so soon, his beautiful words have given me the strength to know that one day soon is within reach.

CHAPTER THIRTY THREE
The Last Hurrah

"Ava, are you okay?" Sara asks from outside the bathroom door.

My response is hurling for the second time today.

My nerves are on overdrive, and no matter how much I try and settle down, I just end up in here, barfing up the contents of my stomach.

"Um, I don't want to freak you out, but they're here."

My groan echoes off the toilet bowl, but I clamp my lips shut, as I refuse to throw up one more time. "Coming," I reply, wearily peeling myself off the bathroom floor.

Flushing the toilet, I creep toward the mirror and recoil when I see my pasty appearance. The bags under my eyes are damn scary, and I won't even touch on the state of my hair and makeup. But as Sara knocks on the door once again, I know I have no other choice but to suck it up and get out there.

Sara shrinks back when I yank open the door. I sigh, as I was hoping I didn't look as bad as I feel. "Are you going to be okay? No offense, but you look like shit."

I laugh, and it's exactly what I needed to hear to settle my nerves. "I'm fine. I'm just so stupidly nervous about this for some reason. I have no idea why. I mean, I cooked for Adelia Dupont, for Christ's sake. I can cook for Liam with my eyes closed."

Sara nods, rubbing my arm in support. "Yes, you can. And you know what? You cooked for Adelia while Yolanda was here, filming your every move. You totally nailed it, and I know you'll nail this, too. This is a piece of cake. Or a piece of pie," she adds with a smile, as we're cooking pie for dessert.

It's the pep talk I needed, and I instantly feel a touch better. "Thank you, Sara. Are you ready to cook?" I ask, watching her eyes fill with tears.

"It'll be my honor, Ava," she replies, knowing that this will probably be one of the last times we'll cook together.

Looping my arm through hers, we make our way to the kitchen, ready to prepare the last supper.

Sara, Michel, Paulo, and I sneakily watch through the kitchen window as Liam Stromboli demolishes his caramel apple pie. The way he scrapes his plate clean, I dare say he's enjoyed his meal.

The night has been a complete success, and I owe that achievement to my fellow chefs. We worked alongside one another like an orchestrated team. As I look around at the mess we've made, I know that disorder represents successful. I couldn't have done this without my friends, and regardless of what Liam thinks of the meal he just ate, I'm so proud of what we've achieved.

After I'm done gawking, I make a move to start the dreaded task of cleaning up. Metropolis is packed full, and we have a lot of plates to clean. When Michel rolls up his sleeves and makes a move to help, I'm so thankful we haven't allowed our differences to get in the way of something that could change our careers forever. We have worked alongside one another harmoniously, and that fact is something I will treasure for the rest of my life.

"Oh my god!" Helen exclaims as she rushes into the kitchen.

We all turn to see what the commotion is about, but when Liam Stromboli strolls in a moment later, we know what the fuss is all about.

Liam is a middle aged man who doesn't look as intimidating as his reputation claims him to be. With a permanent smile etched on his friendly face, he looks like someone who thoroughly loves his job. I realize the media has once again gotten it wrong.

"Ava," he says, looking over at me happily. "That meal was..."

We all hold our breaths, unsure of what he's about to say. But either way, I'm satisfied with what we served.

"Was amazing," he finishes off, while I let out a startled yelp of excitement.

"Thank you, Liam," I say, finally finding my voice. "I'm so pleased you enjoyed everything."

"It was remarkable. I will be sure to tell all of New

York what a great place Metropolis is. And also, what chefs you all are."

Sara squeaks while Paulo fists pumps. I can't stop the smile which spreads from cheek to cheek, as this is exactly the outcome I was hoping for. Jasper's words come back to me, and this is, by far, the best last hurrah ever. I really couldn't have hoped for anything else, and a tear of happiness slips down my cheek because I've done it.

I've come to New York and accomplished all I set out to, and now, now I can go home with no regrets. I can go home and start my life with the man of my dreams.

"Michel told me you're headed back to L.A.," Liam casually says.

"Yes, I am." I look over at Michel, and he smiles, the first open smile I've seen in days.

"Well, congratulations on all you've achieved. You should be really proud of your accomplishments. No matter where you cook, you'll be a success. And that's because you cook from the heart. I'm a big fan, Ms. Thompson, and I hope to try your dishes when you get settled in L.A.," he replies, while I almost trip over my feet.

"It would be my pleasure." My enormous smile hurts my cheeks.

Liam nods, gives Michel a light pat on the arm, and exits my kitchen just as smoothly as he entered it. We all stand silent, staring at the door, but the moment it sinks in that tonight was more than just a success, we all jump up and down, screeching in excitement.

"Holy shit, we did it!" I exclaim, rushing over to Sara and giving her a big hug.

She squeezes me hard and we happily bounce on the spot, unbelieving that we just knocked the socks off New York's biggest food critic.

When I come down from cloud nine, I know there's one thing I have to do. No matter our differences, Michel has acted professional and this experience could have been incredibly uncomfortable, but it hasn't been. We were able to put our personal differences aside, and in turn, we just achieved something we both should be incredibly proud of.

"Michel."

"*Oui?*" he replies, turning over his shoulder to look at me.

I walk over towards him slowly, and he freezes from dunking the pots into the sink, awaiting my next move. With slight hesitation, I step forward and hug him lightly. I don't say anything, because my actions are worth a million words. He hugs me back, the relief clear in his embrace. Although Michel and I will never be more than just friends, our friendship is one I will look back fondly on, and also, one I'll never forget.

"Congratulations, *Cheri.* You did it."

Pulling out of his hold, I correct, "We did it. We all did it." I look around me, at my amazing, incredible staff, and although leaving Metropolis is what I want, it's still bittersweet leaving all this behind.

Helen and Sara throw their arms around me, offering the support I need, and after I'm done being a senti-mental fool, I wipe away my tears and smile. "Thank you for making my job never feel like work. I'll never forget my time and Metropolis, and I most certainly will never forget my friends."

Sara dabs at her eyes, and as I look at Michel, I know that no matter what happened between us, we'll forever be grateful we met one another, and had the opportunity to cook together.

Pushing my nostalgia aside, I know there is one person I have to call.

"You come right back out here once you're done," Sara says, playfully wiggling her finger at me. "We have some serious celebrating to do. And by celebrating, I mean we need to drink that bottle of French Champagne."

She points to the Dom Perignon while I laugh. "Don't start without me."

As I make my way to my office, I'm unable to hide the skip to my step because this is the moment I've been waiting for my entire life. I have finally found my happily ever after, and I can't wait to tell my Price Charming the good news.

Sadly, my fairytale ending comes shattering down around when I reach for my cell.

I have seventy-four missed calls, and a dozen voice messages, which alerts me to the awful fact that something is terribly wrong. My fingers fumble as I desperately try to unlock my phone. The sound of my racing heart is deafening me, but until I know what's happening, I'll try my best to remain calm.

Just as I'm about to see who the caller is, my phone rings, and I see that Veronica is on the other line.

"Hello?"

Silence.

"Hello?" I repeat, my palms sweating.

"Ava?" Her hysterical tone is unlike anything I've ever heard before.

"V?" I ask, surprised.

"Oh, thank god!" she cries.

"V, what's going on?"

Silence.

I suddenly get goose bumps from head to toe. "What's the matter?"

She starts sobbing, the sound guttural and empty.

"Talk to me, please. You're scaring me," I say, my breath stuck in my throat.

"Ava..." she says, her voice quivering. "There's been an accident."

"What kind of an accident? Where are you? Are you okay? Is Cara okay?" I ask, my heart beginning to beat faster and faster.

V sobs again. "I'm packing. I'm going to Warsaw."

"Packing? Why are you going to Warsaw?" I ask, confused.

She takes three deep breaths, before revealing the worse news of my life. "P.O.E.'s tour bus was involved in an accident. The brakes malfunctioned, the bus flipped, and it hit a tree."

"Oh my god!" My trembling hand flies to my mouth. "When did this happen? Where are they? Is everyone all right?"

The only thing I hear is V's tiny sniffles.

"V, how are they?" I press, my entire body shaking.

She finally answers. "Lucas is stable. He's got a few broken bones and a mild concussion."

"Oh no, that's awful. I'm so sorry. Do you know how Jasper is?" I ask. My voice is barely above a whisper because deep down, I know something is not right. "Please, Veronica, just tell me. How's Jasper?"

I'm begging, begging her to tell me that Jasper is okay. But she doesn't.

"He's...he's...he's in a coma. They don't think he's... going to make it. I'm so sorry. I'm so sorry," she weeps, choking on her sobs.

"He's...what? I don't understand," I say, my brain unable to accept what she's just said.

"Jasper is on life support. He's showing no signs of... life."

Jasper. Coma. Life support. NO! Oh. My. God. NO!

I.

Can't.

Breathe.

"No, no, no, no, no!" I howl, shaking my head, the walls closing in on me. "That's not true. There's got to be some mistake. V, tell me there's some mistake!" I beg, drowning in my tears as I tear out my hair.

Her silence reveals the truth behind her words. I grip onto my desk, afraid I'm about to pass out.

"I'm s-sorry." She sniffs, unable to talk. "He tried to protect Kris. When they cut Jasper out of the wreck, he was draped over him like a human shield. The rescuers said he saved Kris' life. But in turn, he put his life in danger. He sacrificed himself for Kris," she cries, her voice caked in grief.

This isn't true. Fate isn't this cruel. It wouldn't take Jasper away from me before we had the chance to start our lives together. Before we had the chance to become man and wife.

A soundless scream tears from my throat and I drop the phone, my body slumping onto the floor. I'm unable to believe that my life, a life which I was finally ready to live, is a life I no longer want to live if Jasper is not by my side.

CHAPTER THIRTY FOUR

A Broken Heart

Thump.

Thump.

Thump.

"Ava, it's Sara. Open up."

Thump.

Thump.

Thump.

I groan while covering both ears with my hands, as Sara's incessant banging on my door scrambles my already pounding brain.

"Please open the door. I'm worried about you."

Thump.

Thump.

Thump.

"Stop pounding on the door," I whimper, my hands still firmly affixed to my ears.

"I'm not," Sara whispers.

Of course she is. Where is that noise coming from otherwise?

The door handle rattles as she tries to open the locked door.

But I can't open it.

The moment I open that door, she'll tell me my worst

nightmare is actually true. She'll tell me that Jasper is lying in some hospital bed somewhere in a coma, and that he might never wake up. And that's a reality I can't face. It's a reality I don't want to face.

The deafening thumping gets louder and louder. And before long, my entire body beats in sync with the frantic tone because I realize the thumping is coming from within my chest.

So this is what it feels like to have a broken heart. This is what it feels like to have my heart ripped from my chest, and all that remains is an empty shell of what it once was.

"Sara," I croak, crawling on hands and knees to open the door.

"Oh, Ava," she says, kneeling on the floor beside me as I collapse into a heap.

Brushing back my matted hair, she cries, "He's going to be okay. Jasper would never leave you this way. He's going to wake up soon."

How I wish her words were true, but I know they're empty promises. They're words one tells another when the truth is too hard to accept.

"Oh god, Sara." I cover my face with my hands and begin sobbing into them hysterically.

"Sshh, it's okay." She hugs me, but nothing she can say or do will ever make this pain go away.

"I need to g-go. I n-need to be th-there for him," I sob, raising my head, my heavy tears clouding my vision.

"Ava, stop. Calm down and breathe."

But I can't. I can't calm down. This is as calm as it

gets until I know Jasper will be all right. I don't care what the doctors think, because he has to be okay.

"I'm going to Warsaw. I need to see him. I need to tell him that I-I love him." I'm hysterical, and on the verge of hyperventilating, but I need to stop. I can't sit here crying, because crying isn't going to solve a thing.

The moment I jump up, my head spins, and I slouch against the wall for support.

"Please, just sit," Sara begs, holding onto my arm to stop me from falling.

"I can't sit. Are you fucking listening to me? Jasper is in a coma. I can't stay here while my fiancé's life—" But I can't finish the sentence.

"I understand, but I spoke to V. She told me that she's catching the earliest flight possible, and she'll be here tomorrow. Then you can both fly to Warsaw together."

"Tomorrow?" I shriek, shaking my head. "I have to go now! I need to be with him. I need to be there when he wakes up."

"I understand, Ava, but V is right. It's better if you two go together. And besides, Jeremy is trying to get him transferred to a better hospital in France. But the doctors don't want to move him. It's too dangerous."

"Jeremy is there?" I stupidly ask because of course he's there. He's Jasper's next of kin.

"I need to call him!" I push off the wall and ignore my dizziness as I pick up my cell from where I dropped it.

With shaky fingers I dial Jeremy, holding my breath until he picks up. "Hello?" he says, sounding like utter shit.

"Jeremy, it's Ava."

"Oh, Ava. Has Veronica gotten a hold of you?"

"Yes, she has. So it's true?" I ask, hearing a machine beep in the background.

"I'm afraid so." He sighs, his voice filled with fatigue.

Sniffing back my tears, I stay strong. "How is he?"

"He's...not good. The doctors are no damn help. I doubt if any of them have their medical licenses! He needs to be transferred someplace they can tell me something helpful."

"What are they telling you now?" I ask, so afraid of the answer.

He pauses, the heavy silence revealing all. "They're doubtful he'll ever regain consciousness. But how would they know? They haven't even given him a full scan. They've just hooked him up to this damn machine. They're waiting for him to die." I hear something being thrown against the wall.

I bite my cheek, as I'm moments away from breaking down. "Are you with him now?"

"Yes. I haven't left his side."

"Jeremy, I need to be there. I can't stay here."

"I understand that, Ava. But you listen to me. Jasper is no quitter. He'll pull through this, you hear me?" he says, needing me to believe his words.

I begin to sob. "Can I talk to him?"

"Of course. I'll put you on speaker phone."

A moment later everything is amplified. I can hear Jasper breathing through a tube, with a machine beeping in sync with his heart. I close my eyes, unable to picture him living through a machine this way.

"Okay, he's listening," Jeremy sadly says.

Taking a deep breath, I suck up my tears because I'm going to be strong for the man who's always been strong for me.

"Hi, Jasper. Jeremy told me what happened. I want you to know that I'm coming. Please hold on for me. Please don't give up. I've got so much I want to tell you. So much I want to show you." A single tear rolls down my cheek, but I wipe it away. "I'll be there soon. So please, hang in there for me. I love you...so much."

I can't hold back my tears any longer, and I weep, my heart tearing in two. Sara is by my side in an instant, and I allow her to comfort me because I don't know what else to do.

"Be strong, Ava. Be strong for the both of us," Jeremy says, his voice laden with tears.

"Okay. I will." I owe this to Jasper and Jeremy. "Can you let Kris know I said I'm glad he's okay?"

"Of course. I'll call you as soon as I can. Goodbye. I'll see you soon." The line goes dead.

I hold onto the phone, not wanting to hang up, not wanting to sever the only contact I have with Jasper.

Sara gently reaches for my cell and hangs up, while I stare at her, not knowing what to do next.

"Let's get you packed, okay? V will be here tomorrow evening."

I nod, too numb to even think. But the one thing I do know is that I need to get to Jasper, and I need to get to him now.

"Is it true Jasper White was involved in a bus accident?"

"Is he in a coma?"

"Do you have any comment about him being linked to Delilah Rose?"

As hard as it is to not punch these vultures in the mouth, I push my shades over my eyes and charge through the terminal with V by my side. I didn't expect the media to get wind of the news so quickly, but the moment I left Metropolis, I was hounded by the press and paparazzi.

But none of that matters because although it took us a while, we're finally on our way to Warsaw.

The moment I take my seat, a longing hits me so hard I have to bite my lip to stop the tears. V rubs my arm, but she too looks like utter shit.

I barely register we're in the air until I hear the familiar speech I've heard many times before.

"Ladies and gentlemen, the captain has turned off the Fasten Seat Belt sign so you may now move around the cabin.

"In a few moments, the flight attendants will be offering you hot or cold beverages. Now, sit back, relax, and enjoy the flight. Thank you."

Glancing at the reflection staring back at me from the window, I wonder, is this how others see me? A girl whose eyes are too big for her melancholy face. A girl whose frame is so small, her feet barely reach the sticky floor. A girl that laughs at everyone's jokes, even when she doesn't see the point of laughing at mindless nothingness. A girl whose heart has been crushed, chewed on, spat out, set on fire—and put on repeat just for fun.

Is this it? Has my life finally come full circle? Will I look back on my time in Europe as the time Jasper and I finally said goodbye? Our relationship has never been easy, but I refuse to believe this is the end.

Resting my head against the headrest, I decide to try to sleep because at the moment, nothing makes sense, and I'm afraid nothing ever will.

CHAPTER THIRTY FIVE
Lost in a Dream

A car picked us up from the airport and now we're headed through the unfamiliar streets of Poland, Warsaw bound.

I don't know what to expect, and quite frankly, I want to leave it that way. My overactive imagination has been my worst enemy, and I would rather not think and just see for myself because I'm sure the reality can't be as bad as what I'm prepared to see.

The moment we pull over in front of a huge white building, V and I unbuckle our seatbelts, yank open the door, and charge towards the entrance with no intention of stopping until we reach Jasper and Lucas' rooms.

Jeremy has told us what floor the boys are on, so we ride the elevator, annoyingly stopping at every floor. My reflection in the mirrored walls looks like absolute shit, so I run a hand through my hair, not wanting to scare Jasper when I walk through his door. That thought however, has me biting my lip because when I spoke to Jeremy last, there was no change in Jasper's condition.

I force down any negativity, because I promised myself I would be optimistic and strong. The moment we finally stop at our floor, V and I bolt out of the elevator and sprint down the long, sterile corridor.

We're looking overhead, trying to find their rooms, and V halts when she comes across Lucas'. She nervously tugs at her pigtails, and tears fill her eyes.

"Go to him, V, he's waiting," I say, giving her an encouraging smile.

"Are you sure you don't want me to come with you first?"

Her loyalty warms my heart, but I shake my head. "No, you go see your husband, and I'll go see mine." I give her a kiss on the cheek, and quickly make my way down the hall.

The moment I see the number I've been dreading, I stop and take a deep breath, unsure of what I'll see. With apprehensive fingers, I gently turn the handle and step into the unknown.

The smell is the first thing that hits me. It's so sterile and sharp, I almost cover my nose to stop myself from gagging. The next thing is the noise. The air is filled with an artificial beeping, weighed down with a heartbreaking silence, because that beeping is what's keeping the man hooked up to the machine alive.

I stop dead in my tracks because the room that I'm in is surely the wrong room. There is no way the person hooked up to the beeping apparatus can be Jasper. There is no fucking way that man is the man I love more than life itself, because that person looks more machine than man.

But when I see Jeremy sitting by the man's side, I know that is indeed my man, and that man is Jasper White.

I barely recognize him, and I close my eyes, unable to accept what I've seen.

"Hi, Ava," Jeremy says, and I hear him rise from his plastic, squeaky chair.

I keep my eyes shut tight, refusing to open them, hoping this is all a bad dream.

"Jasper has been waiting for you. I told him you were coming."

His words break my already broken heart, and with nothing left to lose, I open my eyes and face my nightmare as best I can.

My steps are measured as I walk towards Jasper's bed, afraid that the closer I get, the more real this becomes. I instantly see his head has been shaved, his trademark tousled hair is now replaced with dark, harsh stubble. His cerulean jewels are taped shut, and a tube is shoved down his throat, his cherub lips swollen and bruised. His face is barely recognizable as it's incredibly puffy. Deep cuts and abrasions, which have been stitched up, mar his perfect features.

I take in his entire form, and sigh when I see that everything below the sheets looks perfectly fine. A false sense of hope passes over me, because I know Jasper's injuries are all skin deep. The problem is not what I can see, but rather, it's what I *can't* see.

"Are you okay?" Jeremy kindly touches my arm.

I nod, although, I doubt I'll be okay ever again. "How's he eating?" I ask, my broken voice unlike mine.

"For the moment, all the doctors are concerned about is keeping him hydrated," he explains, pointing to a hanging bag, which holds clear fluid.

A tube, which is attached to the bag, runs down the side of the bed and inserts into the back of Jasper's left hand, via a needle.

"Oh." I frown, not understanding how this can be keeping him alive. But as I look at the life support machine, I know that it is keeping him alive, and not the damn saline.

"He's going to be okay, Ava," Jeremy says, obviously reading my thoughts.

"Has there been any change?" I ask, my gaze never leaving Jasper.

"No," he replies, his voice drained.

I turn to look at him and realize he's probably set up vigil by Jasper's bedside the moment he arrived. He's no doubt beat, and probably in desperate need of some air, food, and some fresh clothes. "Jeremy, I can stay with Jasper if you want to get something to eat? Or maybe stretch your legs?"

Jeremy runs a hand down his weary face. His grey whiskers reveal that he's been here a while. "Are you sure? I wouldn't mind having a shower."

"Positive. Go, I'll be here when you return."

He nods, looking unsure as he glances back at the bed.

"I'll call if there's any news. Jasper wouldn't want you camped by his bedside, ignoring your own needs," I affirm, and Jeremy smiles, knowing I'm right.

His beautiful eyes remind me so much of his son's. But I stand strong because I know if I breakdown, Jeremy will never leave.

He walks over to the bed and plants a soft kiss on

Jasper's forehead, lovingly stroking his cheek with the backs of his fingers. "I'll see you soon, son. Ava is here, and I'm sure there's a lot she wants to tell you."

He gives my brow the same treatment as Jasper's, and with one final look at Jasper, he softly closes the door behind him.

I let out the breath I was unintentionally holding, and cover my mouth to hold back my tears. Now that I'm alone with Jasper, I refuse to allow my sorrow to taint the fact the man I love more than life itself is only a few feet away.

Walking with one heavy foot in front of the other, I arrive at his bedside and take a moment to take everything in. I could collapse into an inconsolable mess, questioning why this had to happen to him. Or, I could take it in my stride and be the emotional support he needs. Be the emotional support he would be for me.

Shakily, I reach for his hand, my fingers trembling the moment I thread my fingers through his. "Hi, Jasper. I've missed you."

I'm greeted with his heavy breathing, his chest rising and falling, filling with artificial air. But I don't let that discourage me. I have to believe he can hear me.

"Guess what?" I say, never letting his hand go as I take a seat by his bedside. "Liam Stromboli loved my food. Can you believe it? Of course you can," I add with a smile, remembering the complete faith Jasper had in me.

"He also said he can't wait to try my food in L.A. So you know what that means? It means you have to wake up so we can go home. We've got so many things to do. So many things to plan," I say, tightening my fingers around his non-responsive ones. "I know you can hear me, and I don't care what these doctors say. I know you're going to be all right. I know you would never allow our story to end this way."

I bring his cool fingers to my lips, kissing them softly. "I promise I'll never leave your side. I'll always be here, waiting to tell you how much I love you."

I flick my gaze to his still face, pointlessly hoping for any signs of life. Even though he looks the same as he did the moment I walked through the door, I'll keep on trying because he *will* wake...he has to.

CHAPTER THIRTY SIX
Don't Stop Believin'

The next day, I enter Jasper's hospital room, my hands filled full.

"What have you got there?" Jeremy asks, quickly standing to help me unload my loot.

"Just a few things for Jasper," I reply, thankful when he reaches for the pile of books I'm trying to balance in one arm.

He scans through the titles I borrowed from the library and chuckles when he pulls out a tattered copy of an old Mills and Boon romance. "I don't really think Jasper would enjoy,"—he turns the book around to read the cover—"*Crimson Nights*," he concludes, blushing a crimson of his own.

I nod, dumping my iPod, DVDs, backpack, and a basket of muffins on the bedside table. "That's the plan. I'm planning on reading him out of a coma with smut," I breathlessly reply, looking at my goods.

He looks at me with a smirk, probably afraid for my sanity, but he doesn't argue.

Once Jeremy and I were kicked out after visiting hours ended, I went back to the hotel, a woman on a mission. I refuse to believe that Jasper is never going to wake, and I am going to do everything in my power to make sure he knows I am here.

I did some research on people in comas, and a lot of reports have claimed unconscious people can hear, smell, feel, and understand all that's going on around them. Even though they can't respond, they are still very aware of their environment. This gave me an idea. Even though Jasper can't talk to me, that doesn't mean I can't talk to him. And I plan on talking to him, day in, day out, until he opens his eyes and tells me to shut the hell up.

As I unravel my iPod ear buds, Jeremy watches closely, still unsure what I'm doing. I search through my playlist, and select 'Don't Stop Believin'' by Journey. I carefully slip a bud into his ear, and the other in mine. I turn the volume up, and then I push play.

"You might wanna close that door. This might get ugly," I say to Jeremy. His mouth pops open, as he's finally figured out my plans.

The moment the verse starts, I open up my lungs and this time, I'm the one to serenade Jasper. He's the one who usually sings to me, but now, it's my turn. And now that I've started, I don't plan on stopping anytime soon.

Reaching for my cell, I use it as a microphone, while Jeremy covers his mouth to mute his laughs. The sound is the best thing I've heard in days, and I pull out my ear bud, offering him to take over. He looks at me for split second, and then shrugs, before happily accepting. I jump up from the uncomfortable chair, and he takes my place.

I sing along to the chorus and shimmy to the bedside table. "Raspberry muffin?"

Jeremy nods as he hums away to Journey.

"These are Jasper's favorites," I explain, passing him one. "Speaking of favorites…"I unzip my backpack and produce Jasper's favorite Beatles shirt.

"I thought if it was okay with the doctors, we could dress him in something other than hospital gowns. I mean, I don't think he'll appreciate how much ass he's currently flashing."

Jeremy smiles as he bites into his muffin. "I'm sure it won't be a problem. These are delicious," he says around chewing. "Jasper was right. You really are the best chef in the world."

"Hardly, and besides, your son is biased." I lean forward and kiss Jasper on the cheek. It's the first time I've kissed him, and although he's not responsive, it still feels like the most natural thing in the world.

My action reminds me of something else I have hidden in my bag. "And," I say, digging through it. "He definitely needs some of this." I pull out a bottle of Aramis, Jasper's signature scent.

Opening it up, I spray some onto his neck. Unable to help myself, I lean back down and take a big whiff. It's amazing how a certain smell can bring back so many memories, and transport you back into time.

Jeremy reads my nostalgia, and gently reaches for my hand. "He can hear you. Be strong for him."

I meet his eyes and nod, wiping away my stolen tear.

Jasper wouldn't want me to mourn him. He would want me to celebrate all the times we shared together. No matter how hard this is, I'll be strong. I'll be strong for the both of us.

"Her heaving breasts and quivering thighs trembled with anticipation and oh my god, who the hell reads this smut?" I say, tossing the book over my shoulder. "I promise, the next one won't be so bad."

Hunting through my tower of books, I stop when I come across *Harry Potter*. "Yes! We're so reading this next."

Jeremy is currently talking to Jasper's doctors because he's still adamant that Jasper will receive better treatment in France. The doctors however, have made it perfectly clear they fear Jasper won't survive the trip. It's a risk we're both not willing to take, so for the moment, we're stuck in Poland until we figure out what to do.

"You need a shave." I stroke Jasper's cheek with the back of my hand.

A small piece of me dies when he doesn't respond to my touch. When I'm reading to him, or humming along to a song we're both listening to, I can almost pretend he's sleeping. But when I touch him and he doesn't react as I know he would if he were conscious, it brings home the awful fact that he's very much in a coma.

"Love?"

My gaze snaps up the moment I hear his voice. "Kris?"

He nods, hopping into the room on crutches, looking like complete shit. His face is beaten and bruised, and he has a huge dressing taped to his forehead.

I instantly jump up and rush over to him. "Here, let me help you." Placing my arm around his waist, we hobble over to the chair where he lowers himself, and hisses as he sits.

"You shouldn't be out of bed," I scold, standing in front of him. "But it's so good to see you."

I didn't get a chance to see him yesterday, as I was too immersed in the fact that Jasper was lying in a coma.

"It's good to see you, too," he replies, shuffling up and rearranging his leg so it sits comfortably. He looks over at Jasper and frowns.

"Is this the first time you've seen him?" I ask sadly.

He nods. "Yes. He just looks like he's sleeping," he says in a faraway voice, his stare never shifting.

"I know," I reply with a sigh as I look over my shoulder. The tubes, wires and cords sadly tell us otherwise.

Even though I will probably regret it, I swallow down my apprehension and say, "Tell me what happened." I know it's tough for him, but I need to know.

He closes his eyes for a painful second, and then reopens them. "I don't really remember much," he confesses. "We boarded the tour bus, just like we had done in the past, but this time, Jasper was over the moon. I asked him what was up, and he told me you guys were getting married once the tour ended."

I nod, unable to stop my smile.

"He was so happy, Ava. He was telling everybody

who would listen how he couldn't wait to make you his wife. We all gave him shit, of course, but deep down, everyone was happy for him. We were happy for you both."

My smile fades when I witness Kris' face turn dark. "A few hours in, I got up to stretch my legs, and that's when I saw Jasper was totally mesmerized by this."

He pulls down the collar of his gown and exposes a silver necklace—a necklace I know all too well.

"That's Jasper's," I gasp, launching forward and reaching for it.

Kris nods and pulls it over his head. "He said you had given him this ring." He holds up the chain, the silver ring spinning slowly. "He then asked me if I was ready to guard it with my life. I didn't understand what he meant. He clarified when he asked me to be his best man."

He offers it to me, while I accept with shaky fingers.

"Of course I said yes. I was so honored, because I know I didn't deserve it. But I promised that I wouldn't let him down." Kris frowns, tears filling his eyes. "The last thing he said to me was that I could never let him down. But that's not true—" He leaves the sentence unfinished.

I can see he's riddled with guilt, but I know Jasper would rather be where he is than see his little brother get hurt.

"This isn't your fault, Kris," I say, placing the necklace around my neck.

"Yes, it is," he protests, turning to look at the wall to hide his tears. "All I remember is the loud squeal of our brakes locking up, and then Jasper throwing himself on top of me. Jasper saved my life. He protected me without a second thought. But look where that got him." He angrily points to Jasper's immobile body. "How is that fair?"

I instantly rush over, and drop to my knees in front of him. "Stop blaming yourself. Jasper would never forgive himself if it were you in his position right now."

"I'm sorry, Ava," he cries, wiping his eyes. "It should have been me. I should be the one lying in a coma, not Jasper."

"Don't say that. Jasper wouldn't have this any other way," I affirm, gently rubbing his knee.

"I should have done more. I should have saved him." Kris' emotional scars are much more painful than his physical ones, and in time, when his external injuries eventually heal, I know his internal wounds will forever be a big gaping hole of regret.

"Don't go there, Kris. It's now your turn to be strong for Jasper." I reach down and finger the ring hanging from my neck. It gives me the strength I need to not breakdown.

He sniffs, and nods. "Nice shirt," he says, trying to lighten the mood as he looks at Jasper's tee. "You don't have a spare one, do you?"

I chuckle, grateful he's making jokes. "I just happen to have a whole wardrobe on hand." Walking over to my backpack, I search through it and pull out Jasper's tattered *One Direction* tee.

"You're not serious?" He opens his mouth in horror.

"Very." I grin, throwing it at him.

"Well, I supposed it's better than flashing my ass every time I move." He slips it over his head, and my mouth tugs up into the first smile I've had smiled in days.

We silently bask in this rare moment of joy. Let's hope it's the not the last we experience while here.

CHAPTER THIRTY SEVEN
An Unexpected Act of Kindness

One week merges into two, then three, and then four.

Week one, I read the entire *Harry Potter* series aloud, with no change from Jasper.

Week two, I play the complete discography of Jasper's favorite bands, but still no change.

Week three, I watch all five seasons of *Breaking Bad*, but to no avail.

And week four, I start all over again.

The doctors are no help, and I feel as each day passes, they look at Jasper as nothing but a lost cause, but I refuse to believe it. To them, he's just another patient, but to me, he's the person who animates my entire existence.

This past month has been the worst month of my life, and if I've ever experienced any worse, then I don't remember, because all pale in comparison to what I'm feeling right now. Watching your loved one shrivel to nothing but skin and bones is the most horrible thing you'll ever see.

I barely sleep because my nightmares haunt me to the

point of waking up in tears. I barely eat because I can't keep anything down. I'm barely alive, but I have to be brave, as I refuse to break. For once, I'm determined to be the strong one.

The last few days, a lot of people in white coats have come to examine Jasper's condition. The language barrier has proven to be an issue, but from what I can tell, his brain activity has apparently shown no response, therefore, they're hinting it's time we unplug his machine.

Jeremy and I have told them hell to the fuck no, as Jeremy is still trying to get Jasper transferred to a hospital in France. But sadly, this is one circumstance where money can't buy favors. He's begged, bribed, and yelled at doctors in France, but he's been shot down each and every time.

"Hey, babe. Did you wanna get some air?" asks V as she ducks her head into Jasper's room.

Lucas and V have flown home, but they've returned, bringing Cara with them. When Lucas told me he wasn't leaving a second time without Jasper, he was serious, as he hasn't left his side since they've returned from L.A.

"I'm okay," I reply, lowering the tattered paperback of *The Power of One*.

"I think Jasper will be okay for ten minutes."

"I don't want to leave him." I reach for his frail hand.

When she sighs, I know what's coming. Since she's been back, V has been pushing me to eat, sleep, shower, get some air, take a walk, but most importantly, let my guard down and cry. But each suggestion gets a reply of, 'Maybe later,' which means no.

"Babe, you look like shit," she finally confesses, revealing she's not leaving until I go with her.

I laugh because I know she's right. She's been poking me for weeks to try and break down my walls, but I'm afraid if I confess how I feel, I'll never stop.

"Okay, just for ten minutes." My stiff body creaks in protest as I lean forward and run my hand down Jasper's stubbled cheek. "I'll be back soon. I love you." Tucking the sheet around him, I fluff up his pillows before I leave.

The moment we step outside, I take a deep breath and savor the fresh air.

"When was the last time you ate?" V asks as we take a seat.

I knew it was coming. She's been pushing me to let go, but I can't. I have to stay strong.

"Um, yesterday. I had a banana," I reply, running my fingers though my matted hair.

"I thought so," she scolds. Hunting through her bag, she produces a wrapped sandwich.

The moment I see the tomato poking through the white bread, I cover my mouth, waving my hand out in front of me. "I can't eat that," I say, barely containing my nausea.

"You have to," she presses, shoving the sandwich in my face. "I know you don't feel like eating, but you have to. Otherwise, you'll be holed up in the room next door to Jasper. Look at you," She picks at the hem of my baggy top. "You're withering away. It's not healthy. You're not the one in a coma, Ava."

I flinch.

"I'm sorry. It's harsh, but it's true. Jasper wouldn't

want you to be this way. What do you think he'd say if he saw you punishing yourself like this?"

I know she's just trying to be a friend, but I don't want to hear it. "This is me coping with the fact my fiancé may never wake up. He's been cooped up in this shit hole for weeks, with no sign of improvement. So eating is the last thing I want to do right now," I snap, feeling my anger spike.

"I'm just trying to help."

"I know, but this is as good as it gets, because if I lose Jasper, what you see now," I say, sweeping down my body. "Is the new me."

"Jasper would want you to live your life," she bravely says, as she knows she's about to be served.

I know what she's doing, and it's finally worked. She wants me to breakdown and stop pretending that I'm all right. Well, here goes nothing. "Don't you get it? Jasper *is* my life. Without him in it, I'm just a husk of who I once was. You wouldn't understand." I need to stop the venom, but I can't. "Every night, you go home to your healthy husband and child. What do I go home to? The thought that when I wake, I might wake to the news that Jasper is dead. So don't stand here, and tell m-me," I say, choking on my words. "That he would w-want me to live my l-life." I'm suffocating on air and suddenly, tears I've tried so hard to keep away break through the floodgates, with no end in sight.

"I-I can't live without him, V. I just can't," I sob, allowing this one second of weakness.

"Oh, Ava." She throws her arms around me, while I weep into her shoulder. "It'll be okay."

"No, it won't be okay." I sniff, my eyes clouded with hot tears. "He hasn't shown any sign of improvement. I-I can't let him go."

"I know," she coos, rubbing my back.

"I wish we could move him to France. The doctors here have given up. They won't even try the alternative methods Jeremy has researched. I can't give up on him because I know he wouldn't give up on me. I can't let the best thing in my life go. I'm not ready, V. I'm not ready to say goodbye."

I bawl for minutes while V holds me, telling me that it'll be all right. But she can't promise that, no one can.

When I can speak again without it coming out as a garbled mess, I apologize. "I'm sorry. I didn't mean the things I said. I'm so happy Lucas is okay."

"I know you didn't. I'm glad you got it out. You've been too composed. You need to let it out, babe. We're here for you."

I nod, as I feel a touch better after sobbing like a baby.

"What's this about Jeremy wanting to move Jasper to France?"

I haven't gone into detail about Jeremy's plans, so I explain what he wants to do.

"So he thinks they'll be able to help him?" V asks once I'm done telling her Jeremy's idea.

"Yes," I reply, unwrapping the sandwich. "Apparently, they have the best coma ward in all of Europe. They're trying new techniques, which have great success rates."

"So why isn't he there? I'm sure money isn't an issue."

"'Cause money can't get us in. We need someone on the inside. Jasper is just another American."

V nods, and I can see her mulling over what I just said.

"What?" I ask, taking a small bite of my lunch.

But she just shakes her head. "Nothing. Just eat."

And this time, I don't argue.

Jeremy and I are sitting silently, both our spirits broken, as the specialists come and do their usual whispers and frowns, not letting on what they think.

"This is bullshit!" Jeremy says, suddenly standing up and pacing the room.

I jolt in surprise, not expecting the outburst, as I've never seen him so riled up. "What's wrong, Jeremy?"

"I can't sit here, watching my son fade away!" he screams, pointing to an almost unrecognizable Jasper.

I lower my eyes. "I know. But what can we do?"

Jeremy runs a frustrated hand through his hair—a gesture which has my heart hurting.

As I'm flicking through my unread emails, I see that my phone bill is due on the twenty-fifth of this month. I decide to set a reminder in my phone, as being over here has thrown my sense of time right off. However, when I scroll to the date, I see that the twenty-fifth has come and gone, and it's now the eighth.

It shouldn't surprise me that time is non-existent of late, because my life feels so surreal. But what *does* surprise me is when I skim through my diary, I see that I'm missing another date. A date I've missed before.

However, before I can address the issue my phone rings. I look at Jeremy and shrug, because I don't recognize the number. "Hello?"

There is a delay, before I hear, "Hello, *Cheri*."

"Michel?" I say, clearing my throat twice. "Is everything okay at Metropolis?"

"*Oui*, but I hear everything is not okay over there."

I wait for him to continue, curious to how he knows.

"Veronica, your friend, she called me," he explains.

"She what?"

"Just listen," he says when he hears the irritation in my voice. "She told me you're trying to get Jasper transferred to France."

"Yes, we are," I confirm, looking at Jeremy.

"Well, I have a friend who works for the medical board, and he was able to pull some strings. He has secured a bed for Jasper."

"He what?" I gasp, holding onto the table for support while Jeremy rushes to my side.

"They'll take him as soon as you can transport him over, but Ava...he'll need to be unplugged from his life support."

"Why?" I say, putting him onto speaker, as Jeremy looks about ready to explode.

"Because that's the only way they'll accept him. It's a new, radical treatment plan, and they'll only work with people who aren't...brain dead," he explains with pause.

I look at Jeremy, who weighs up the decision heavily. We've got an in, but at what cost? But with hope diminishing every second we wait, we know what we have to do.

"Why would you do this? Why would you help me?" I ask, not understanding his motives.

"Because you're my friend, *Cheri*. I've always wanted you to be happy. I now know that you're happiest with Jasper. And this is my way of saying sorry, Ava. I truly care for you, and I hate to see you suffer," he softly explains, not holding back.

I can't stop the tears. "Thank you, Michel. You'll never know how much this means to me."

Jeremy looks at Jasper, and then back at me. With a sad nod, we both know what has to be done. "How soon can this happen?"

"I'll make the preparations, and then I'll be in touch."

"Okay. Thank you again," I say, watching Jeremy sit and cradle his head in his hands.

"My pleasure. He'll be okay. He's in the hands of the best doctors in all of Europe."

"Well, I hope those hands can work miracles," I whisper.

When Michel remains quiet and Jeremy sags further in his seat, I know that regardless of what happens, I cannot lose faith.

CHAPTER THIRTY EIGHT

Breathe New Life into Me

Michel stuck true to his word and Jasper got clearance within two days.

The wait was excruciating, but now that I'm hours away from doing the worst thing I've ever had to do in my entire life, killing time was preferable than what I'm feeling right now. I asked the nurse if it would be okay if I bathed and dressed Jasper in his favorite clothes. She didn't object, and looked at me with nothing but pity in her eyes.

I visited the pharmacy earlier because there was something important I had to do—something which will change my life forever. But for now, I'll deal with one drama at a time.

Taking a seat near Jasper, I reach behind him and untie his ghastly hospital gown. It slips free from his shoulders and I hold back my tears when I see how skinny he's become. His shoulders, which once carried me physically and emotionally, are now emaciated with a sickly yellow tinge.

I bite down on my tongue and dip the sponge into the lukewarm wash, wringing out the water into the pan. Placing my forearm behind him, I gently push him forward and wash down his back and shoulders. Once he's cleaned, I sit him backward and he slumps forward like a raggedy doll. But I focus on what's important, and that's getting my man ready for his big day.

As I begin cleaning his sunken chest, I can feel his tender heart, a heart which never stopped loving me, barely beating underneath my shaky fingers. "Please wake up," I whisper, sniffing back my tears. "Please don't give up."

I soak the sponge and lift up his arm, washing down his flank and then back up to his fingers—fingers that used to touch me and make me feel alive. "We've come so far. This can't be the end. I just got you back."

I reach across his body and repeat the same treatment on the other side. When I get to his tattoo, I smile, remembering the day I saw it. How I wish we could go back to that time.

As I bathe his face, I linger over his closed eyes. I recall all the times I felt like no one existed but me when those intense eyes were focused my way. I then dip down to his parted mouth, ignoring the plastic tube. Running my fingers over his lips, I shiver when I reminisce on how these lips used to kiss me. How these lips used to tell me that I was the most important person in the world.

But now these lips, these eyes, these hands, this heart, this body, they're all attached to a lifeless man. Regardless, they're mine.

I work lower and bathe him all over until he's sparkling clean. Reaching for the razor, I carefully lather up his skeletal face, the face I'll love for all the days of my life. With care, I shave his stubble, remembering placing kisses on every inch of his skin, never wanting to stop.

Once he's cleanly shaven, I tenderly dry his face and apply a splash of collage behind his ears. "You smell amazing," I whisper, kissing his cheek lightly.

Reaching for his t-shirt off the chair, I slip it over his head and smile when the Little Sisters logo looks back at me. All the memories of when we first met come flooding back and I know I'm the luckiest girl alive to have lived the remarkable life I've lived with this man by my side.

Throwing off the sheet, I slip on his torn blue jeans and then slip on his scuffed Chucks. Standing back, I can't help but admire the person before me because now, now he looks like Jasper White.

Pulling my iPod from my pocket, there's one final thing I want to do. Scrolling through my playlist, I insert a bid into his ear, and then mine. I select 'New York' by Snow Patrol, and the moment it plays, I hum along to the words—words which express how I feel. Words which I hope he can hear. "Come back to me, Jasper. I miss you."

Interlacing our fingers one final time, I rest my head on his chest and close my eyes, listening to the slow, steady beating of his heart.

How does one prepare for something like this? They can't. They simply have to go on and hope it's the right choice to make.

I'm surrounded by my nearest and dearest—all of them lending me the strength I so desperately need.

We're standing around Jasper's bed, watching and waiting for the doctor's next move.

There are five doctors, two nurses, and a priest, crammed in the already overcrowded room. Nothing but despair paints their features, and I can't stand still as they talk amongst themselves. They've brought in an interpreter, who has explained what we're about to do.

But I don't need any clarification.

The elderly doctor turns and nods.

"It's time," the interpreter says.

V reaches down and squeezes my clammy hand.

The nurse pulls out a clipboard, ready to take notes. One of the doctors says something in Polish, and the interpreter explains. "He asks if you have any last words."

We're all quiet and shake our heads because there are no words to sum up how we're feeling.

The doctor doesn't need an interpreter to understand our reply. He puts on his glasses and begins removing all the wires and tubes. When they're gone, he frowns, and with one quick flick, he deactivates the switch, the switch which was keeping Jasper alive. The room, which was once filled with constant beeping, is now deathly quiet, and we all watch in anticipation, not understanding what happens next.

The doctors look at Jasper, grim expressions on their tired faces. A nurse picks up his wrist, placing two fingers over his pulse as she looks at her watch. Her lips pull into a thin line and she subtly shakes her head, looking at the doctor in charge.

Why is she shaking her head? I don't understand.

Another doctor places his stethoscope against Jasper's

still chest, his expression just as bleak as doctor number one.

"No. No. No. Not my boy. Not my baby boy!"

I still don't understand. Why is Jeremy screaming? Why is V crying? Why is Kris sagged against the wall? Why is Lucas holding back his tears?

I don't understand.

As I look around me, the scene before me is one my brain can't comprehend.

"Time of death," the doctor says in broken English, looking at his watch. "Is 10:17 a.m.," he concludes, looking at the nurse.

Death?

What's he talking about? Jasper is not...dead. He can't be.

"Oh, Ava, I'm so sorry," V sobs, throwing her arms around me.

But I stand rigid, my eyes never wavering from Jasper. He looks so peaceful without all the tubes and wires. He just looks like he's asleep.

He can't be dead.

He can't be.

"Body. Rites. Burial." These are the terms I refuse to process because they're lying. They're all fucking lying.

"Ava? Are you all right? He's dead. Jasper is...dead." These treacherous words ignite into a fiery collision, and I slap my hands over my ears as I won't listen. I refuse to believe.

"Ava, what are you doing?" But I ignore it. I ignore them all.

I lunge for Jasper, and I WILL kill anyone who

stands in my way. "Jasper, why aren't you opening your eyes? Open your eyes." I reach for his hand; it feels cool to the touch.

"Ava, he's gone," someone softly says. I vaguely feel their hand on my shoulder.

"No!" I state, gripping his fingers in mine as I roughly shrug them off. "You're lying. He's not gone. He's not gone!"

As the nurse makes a move to lift the sheet over his face, I shriek a bloodcurdling scream, as my entire world comes crashing down around me. "Don't you dare touch him! Jasper, wake up. Wake up!" I bellow, shaking his shoulders. "Wake up!"

A shudder so violent rocks through me, I almost collapse with the force—almost. A surge of adrenalin suddenly shoots through me, and nothing else, no one else exists but Jasper and me.

"You said we'd never have to say goodbye. You lied! This isn't goodbye. It can't be. You're strong, Jasper. You're the strongest person I know. Fight it. Come back to me. Please come back to me. Please, Jasper!" I howl, collapsing on top of him. "Don't leave me. You promised one day soon, we'll never have to say goodbye...just good-night. Well, I'm not saying goodbye. I never will." I weep into his chest, his skin feeling stale and cold. "No, you're not dead. You're not."

The emptiness I feel can be described as nothing I've ever felt before. Every moment, every memory, every minute, every second I've lived flashes before my eyes, and it's like a movie of my entire existence playing in fast forward. But my ending can't conclude this way. After everything we've been through, I deserve my happily ever after.

But as I clutch at Jasper's lifeless, cold hand, I know my ending is a horrible, grisly reality, one I will never be able to accept. I sob and sob and sob as I press my cheek to Jasper's, my tears painting his face.

I pray to whatever God is looking over me to please bring him back because he doesn't deserve to die. A world without Jasper White is a world I don't want to live in.

With my eyes swimming in tears, I whisper my final plea. "I need you. *We* need you." My hands fall to my belly—the belly which holds Jasper's unborn child.

V and Jeremy gasp while I softly cry. "You're going to be a daddy, Jasper."

After realizing the date, I decided to pay a visit to a pharmacy to confirm what I knew to be true. I was pregnant with Jasper's baby. And this time, there was no mistake. But now, he'll never meet the baby he so wanted to have.

However, in a blink of an eye, I'm being yanked off Jasper and thrown into the arms of Kris. There are a million foreign voices at once, and I don't know what a word of it means.

"Oh dear god," Jeremy gasps, running over to Jasper's bedside. "H-He's...breathing! He's alive!"

"He's what?" I whisper, my gaze dropping to his chest—to his slow rising chest.

"Ava, keep talking to him!" Jeremy frantically yells, waving me over with his hand.

Kris offers the support I need as he pushes me

forward, but he never leaves my back. Jasper's breath is soft and steady, and I never thought I'd be so happy to see his chest rise and fall.

My throat is raw, but with half a voice I affirm, "That's it, Jasper. Breathe. You're doing it. Everyone is here. Jeremy, Kris, Lucas and V."

"Yeah, wake the fuck up already," V sniffles in true Veronica fashion. We all gasp as Jasper's chest begins rising faster.

I reach for his hand and yelp when it's no longer cool. "His hand is warm!" I exclaim, rubbing it against my cheek. His breathing becomes deeper and heavier.

The doctors talk over the top of one another, and we all turn to the interpreter, desperate for him to explain what's going on. "Ask him to squeeze your hand if he can hear you."

I nod, quickly wiping my eyes. "Jasper, squeeze my hand if you can hear me." I loosen my grip, not wanting to miss any sign of life.

I can feel the doctors staring at his hand, waiting for him to respond.

Leaning forward, I gently kiss his cheek. "Squeeze my hand, Jasper. The sooner you squeeze it, the sooner you can get out of here and make an honest woman outta me. C'mon, baby," I say, using his term of endearment for me. "Your son and I are waiting to see those beautiful blue eyes."

Although I don't know the sex of our baby, I just know it's going to be a boy—a boy, with eyes as blue as his fathers, and a heart just as pure.

A second later, I feel the gentlest of touches, a mere flutter of butterfly wings.

"He squeezed my hand!" I cry out, spinning around to make sure they understood what I just said.

They pull out charts, cell phones, instruments, and push me aside, ready to take over.

I watch eagerly, standing on tippy toes, not wanting to miss a thing. Jeremy rushes over, throwing his arms around me. "Is it true? I'm going to be a grandpa?"

"Yes, it's true."

He squeezes me tighter, his ecstasy clear in his embrace. "Did you hear that, Kris? You're going to be an uncle." Before I know it, Kris runs over and starts squishing Jeremy and me.

"Hey, I wanna get in on that," V says, and drags Lucas over, too.

We're a hugging sandwich, and I couldn't be happier, which is ironic, seeing as moments ago, I wasn't sure how I would survive the night. We're crying, laughing, screaming, every emotion under the sun, but most of all; we're elated that Jasper is alive.

"Excuse me," the interpreter says, clearing his throat.

We pull apart, so not embarrassed for the PDA. He looks at me and smiles. "The doctor said it's a miracle. His vitals are good and they think he will survive. They are not sure of the extent of his injuries, but it's a better diagnosis than what we were faced with seconds ago."

"Tell them thank you," I say, dabbing at my eyes.

But he shakes his head. "No, they said thank *you*."

"Me?" I ask, confused.

"Yes, Mrs. White. They say you brought him back to life."

As much as I like to think it was me, I know that it was all of us. Looking around the room, I know Jasper lived for us all.

I shake my head and latch onto Kris and Jeremy's hands. "That's where you're wrong. Jasper brought *us* all back to life. He always has."

No one disagrees because Jasper White is the epicenter of our universes. He just needed a push to remind him that a world without him in it is a world that doesn't exist.

"So what happens now?" Jeremy asks eagerly.

"The doctors will organize his paperwork, and then he will be transported to France."

The radiant smile on Jeremy's face reflects the happiness I feel, and I turn to look at V. She's the one who made the call to Michel and made this possible. "Thank you for once again taking matters into your own hands."

She shrugs casually. "Someone's gotta look out for you."

I laugh, blessing her bossiness.

Once the doctors are done examining Jasper, they give us polite smiles and nods, and exit the room. I look at Jasper, fresh tears filling my eyes. It's still hard to believe that moments ago he was pronounced dead. But I don't want to think about that ever again because he's alive. And he's breathing on his own.

Kris takes a cautious step forward, reaching for Jasper's hand. "You scared us, bro. Don't you ever do that again."

We're all silent, and allow Kris to get whatever he needs off his chest.

"What you did for me...it goes to show what type of a person you are. When Ava told me about you, I didn't believe her. I mean, no one can be that real. But she was right. Thank you, thank you for saving my life."

Jeremy walks over to him and places his hand on his shoulder. The gesture is one Jasper would be so happy to see. But I know he will see it. One day soon.

So for now, even though there are no guarantees that Jasper will ever wake, we will hope and pray he will. Everyday holds the possibility of a miracle, and what I just witnessed...was the greatest miracle of all.

EPILOGUE

One Year Later

"That's it, Cara. Wrap your arm underneath his back. Good girl," I coo, bending forward and arranging her little arms.

"Look, mommy. I'm holding Racer." She beams, looking at V, who smiles.

"Yes, you are. You're such a clever little girl."

Cara's big eyes light up in excitement as she gently bends forward and kisses my baby boy on the forehead.

"Uh oh," V says, watching the exchange with a smile. "I think she's in love."

"That's okay. Their marriage has been arranged anyway. It's best they get along," I counter with a casual shrug.

V chuckles, but gets down to business a moment later. "Okay, Miss. Let's take a look at you."

I stand to full height, nervously straightening out my dress.

"You look so beautiful," she says, and bursts into tears.

"Stop crying." I sniff, gently dabbing at the corner of my eyes. "If you start, then I won't be able to stop."

She nods, but bites her lip.

Before she starts with the waterworks again, I affirm, "Let's do this."

"I'm ready when you are."

My mom gives me a final kiss and gently takes Racer from Cara. "I'll see you outside, honey. Veronica was right, you do look beautiful."

"Thanks, Mom." I hold back my tears because I've shed enough to last me a lifetime.

The day I lost Jasper White was the worst day of my life. The pain I felt seeing the person I loved more than life itself expire before my eyes compares to nothing I'll ever experience in this lifetime. But like Jasper once told me, you've got to experience sadness to appreciate happiness.

My sadness was weighed down with a wound so deep I never thought it would heal. But it did, thanks to two miracles.

The first was giving birth to a beautiful baby boy with eyes as blue as his father's. I never understood the bond between mother and child, but after seeing my son, my miracle, take his first breath, I now get it. The blood, sweat, and tears were so worth it, and my purpose in life has never been clearer. My life is now dedicated to giving my son the best possible life ever.

And that brings me to miracle number two.

"Are you ready?" V asks as walk outside.

Taking a deep breath, I nod. "I've been ready for this moment before I even knew I was ready."

"I'll be with you every step of the way."

Reaching for her hand, I squeeze her fingers. "Just

like you always have been. Thank you, Veronica. I love you."

She dabs at her eyes. "I love you, too. Let's do this."

When a slow melodic tune sounds over the outdoor sound system, V gives me a kiss on the cheek before walking gracefully down the garden path. I don't watch her descent, as I know it won't help the million butterflies fluttering around in my stomach. However, when the song subtly mutes and an intro of another takes its place, I know it's my turn to follow.

Closing my eyes and reopening them a second later, I wipe my sweaty palms on my beautiful white gown and take my first step down...the aisle.

Yes, Jasper was clinically dead for over a minute, but he's been alive for a billion minutes thereafter. It truly was a miracle, but I never expected anything less from the man who has showed me that miracles are possible.

So my miracle number two is...becoming Mrs. Jasper White.

We've been back home for roughly five months, and when I say home, I mean the new home we purchased in L.A.

Jeremy was right. The treatment in France was so much better than Poland, and within a week of Jasper's transfer, Jasper opened those cerulean jewels and told me he loved me more than life itself. However, his recovery was going to be a long process, as he had shrunken to a quarter of the size he once was. His coordination was also affected, and he had to relearn how to do the basics like use a knife and fork and walk without a limp.

But Jasper is as determined as he is amazing, and he

proved the doctors wrong once again by walking within three months of him waking up. When the doctors felt he was able to continue his treatment back home, we were on first flight back to L.A. It's been tough, and his grueling physical therapy sessions leave him tired and frustrated, but he perseveres for his family.

Our son, Racer White, was born three months ago. By the time I arrived at the hospital, he was ready to come out and say hello to his mommy and daddy, hence his name. V still curses me till this day, as her labor was long and arduous. But just like his father, Racer has been easy from day one.

I take in the love around me, as I'm surrounded by my closest friends and family. It's perfect. Jasper and I wanted something small, and with Racer being so young, we thought we'd celebrate our housewarming and wedding on the same day.

My steps are measured as I nervously walk down my garden path which is sprinkled with flowers and jewels. But when I'm halfway down, I lift my eyes and meet the loving gaze of my fiancé, soon to be husband. He looks happy, healthy, and he's all mine.

When he rewards me with his trademark dimpled smile, I totally ignore measured and run the last few steps. "You look beautiful," he whispers, stepping forward, stroking my cheek.

"So do you," I reply, admiring how he fills out his black tux.

His hair is slowly growing back, but the shorter style reveals the scar which pokes out from his hairline. He tells me his so called perfect looks are now flawed. But to me, he's perfect. He always has been.

Unable to stop myself, I throw my arms around him and smash my lips to his. A clearing of a throat and people laughing aren't a deterrent, and when Jasper kisses me back with as much passion, I doubt I'll ever be able to stop.

I eventually pull away however, when our celebrant whispers, "You're supposed to wait until *after* I pronounce you man and wife."

"I couldn't wait." I chuckle, wiping the corner of my mouth.

Jasper smirks, while Kris, who of course is best man, gags.

When the celebrant sees me looking at Jasper with nothing but love in my eyes, he smiles. "Okay, friends. Let's get this underway, so the next kiss *will be* as man and wife."

"Just one more, and then we're done," says our photographer, motioning that we're to stand closer together.

V groans while I laugh. "Suck it up. Did you forget what you put me through when you got married?"

"Did you forget what you've put me through my entire life?" she counters playfully. I can't argue with that.

We all smile for the camera, thankful when we see the final flash. Kris and V follow the photographer as he makes his way downstairs to join our guests. When I attempt to follow, Jasper stops me by softly reaching for my arm.

"We'll be right down," he says, his fingers caressing my bicep.

Both our friends turn over their shoulders, and smirk. "Uh-huh, see you in an hour."

When they're gone, Jasper takes a step forward, engulfing my body with his. "Hello, Mrs. White."

"Hello, Mr. White," I reply, unable to keep the smile off my face.

"Hmm." He hums low in his throat. "I like the sound of that."

Leaning down, he inhales deeply, smelling the slope of my neck. The action sends my skin into a frenzy and I groan.

"Wanna take a detour, and by detour, I mean our bedroom." He winks at me, and my god, he's handsome.

"Jasper." I smirk when he tugs on my hand. "We can't. People are waiting for us downstairs."

"Let them wait," he whispers, his eyes filled with mischief.

He licks his full bottom lip, leaving it wet and inviting. But I stand my ground and quickly shake my head before I lose my resolve.

"Fine," he fake sighs. "But you're not getting off so easily tonight."

I shiver, his promise leaving me achy and needy.

Just as I'm about to change my mind, his expression

turns serious, and he appears unsettled. "I actually wanted to talk to you." I raise my eyebrow, waiting for him to explain. "I've changed the song for our first dance."

"You have?" This is news to me.

"Yes."

"What is it?" I ask, curious to know why the sudden change.

"It's a surprise," he says, which is no help. He adds, "It'll explain some things I haven't been able to."

By his slight pause, I know he's referring to his time in a coma. It's something we haven't discussed in detail, as I know it's a time Jasper wishes to forget.

So I don't make a fuss and nod. "Let's do this then. And besides, I think your son will gnaw my mother's fingers off if he doesn't get fed."

Jasper lowers his eyes, his acute stare focusing on my gigantic boobs. "Like father, like son."

I shake my head and hitch up the top of my strapless silk gown, because under his gaze I feel naked.

"Mrs. White." He offers me his hand with a smile. I happily accept and we interlace fingers, making our way downstairs as man and wife.

The moment we walk outside, our loved ones turn around and clap loudly. Kris is the emcee for the evening. He quickly grabs the microphone. "Here they are. Mr. and Mrs. White!"

The clapping continues while Jasper leads me to the makeshift dance floor in the center of the garden. He spins me in a showy circle, and then pulls me back in so we're standing toe to toe.

"Ready?" He settles his hands low on my waist, while I wrap mine around his nape.

I nod, and he looks over my shoulder at the DJ.

The moment the first note sounds, I pull back, confused, not understanding why he chose this particular song—the particular song I played to him right before we got our second chance.

A bittersweet smile pulls at Jasper's lips, and he draws me in close, singing the first line of 'New York' by Snow Patrol into my ear. He holds me tight, leading me as we dance to the song which instantly brings tears to my eyes.

"You heard me?" I state, as it's more a statement, than a question.

"I heard it all," he replies softly. "You saved me, baby. It was your words, and knowing you were waiting for me, that kept me alive."

The tears instantly fall. But he's so far from the truth. "No, that's where you're wrong. *You* saved me. You always have. I was just returning the favor."

I pull away and Jasper strokes my cheek. "Even in death, I know you'll love me...forever and a day. And that fact makes me the luckiest man alive."

I don't say anything because there are no words. Jasper has confirmed what I suspected to be true all along. And if I had to do it again, I would do so in a heartbeat. We dreamily dance to the music, lost in the memories of our life together, and all the future memories we're destined to make.

"May I cut in?" Jeremy asks after the song ends.

"Sure, Dad." Jasper kisses my cheek and hands me over to his father.

As we dance to 'Easy' by Faith No More, I watch Jasper make a beeline for Racer. He lifts our son proudly in the air and kisses his rosy cheeks affectionately.

I'll never tire of seeing him this way, and Jeremy sees the adulation on my face. "I'll never be able to thank you enough for what you've done for my son."

"You don't have to thank me because *I'll* never be able to thank *you* enough for creating such a wonderful human being," I counter with a smile.

Jeremy smirks. "Okay, we'll call it even then."

I chuckle. "Sounds good to me."

We dance in silence, no doubt reflecting on the past year. "But seriously, thank you, Ava. Thank you for saving my son."

For the second time, I object. "We saved one another."

"Either way, what you did for my son, for *both* my sons, I will be indebted to you for the rest of my life."

I wipe away my tears. "I'll remind you of that when we need a babysitter."

Jeremy laughs. "Any time. My door is always open." I know he means that literally, as he just sold his home in Chicago and moved to L.A. to be closer to us. Kris is now living with Jeremy, as he's taking his role as uncle very seriously.

Yup, life is good.

I wave my dad over, who has been patiently waiting to dance with me. Jeremy and he shake hands, and Jeremy goes to join his son.

"I'm so proud of you, Princess. Your mother and I both are. You've grown into the woman we knew you'd always become."

"Thank you, Dad. That means so much to me." I rest my head against my father's shoulder, and savor this moment of pure happiness.

Once the song ends, I kiss both his cheeks, and go find my husband. I don't know if I'll ever get used to using that term. But as Jasper meets my adoring gaze, our son nestled in his arms, I know it won't take me long.

We do the rounds of thanking our guests for attending. Once we get to Michel, I smile, as there're no hard feelings between us. How can they be? If it weren't for him, I hate to think where Jasper would be. And besides, he's found his soul mate in the form of my former employee, Sara.

I still cannot believe it, considering how Sara hated his guts months ago. But grave situations change people. She finally saw what I saw in Michel the moment I met him.

"You look beautiful, *Cheri*." He kisses both my cheeks. "You're a lucky man," he says, extending his hand. "*Félicitations*."

"Thank you," Jasper says, accepting his handshake. "For everything," he adds, but doesn't elaborate.

He hasn't spoken to Michel about what he did, and Michel doesn't expect him to.

"*Ce ne était rien. Je suis heureux que vous êtes bien.*"

I have no idea what he just said, but Jasper surprisingly does, and replies in French. "*Je serai toujours redevable à vous.*"

Michel shakes his head. "*Non.* You don't owe me anything."

I don't ask what was just said, but from Michel's reply, I dare say Jasper just thanked him for saving his life.

Deciding to lighten the mood, I turn to Jasper, pursing my lips.

"What?" He smirks, tapping the end of my nose. "I picked up some French while I was over there."

We all chuckle and Sara hugs me warmly. "Congrats. I'm so happy for you both."

"Thank you, Sara. Thanks for being there." Not only at Metro, but for being there when my whole world was crumbling around me, I silently add.

"You'll be happy to know your baby—well, your other baby—is in good hands," she says while I laugh.

"I never doubted it for a second." As expected, Metropolis is the hottest place to dine. And that's all I ever hoped it would be.

I haven't even thought about what I'm going to do for work because honestly, my family is now my number one priority.

"We better keep moving," Jasper says, gently placing his hand on my lower back.

Nodding, I look at the horde of people patiently waiting to pass on their congratulations, realizing he's right.

"Save me a dance?" Michel says, slightly apprehensive.

I bend forward and kiss his cheek. "You bet I will."

After we're done mingling and thanking our guests,

we cut the cake, and before long, the best night of my life has come to an end. Sara has caught the bouquet, and if the amorous gaze passing between her and Michel are a sign of their love, I dare say she'll be following in my footsteps very soon.

The moment we bid our final guests goodbye, I kick off my heels and sigh in relief while Jasper grins. V rounds the corner with a garbage bag in hand.

"Don't you dare clean," I scold, reaching for the bag.

"I just tidied up."

"Don't be silly." I shake my head. "That's what tomorrow is for. I'll see you at 9 a.m."

She chuckles and nods.

Cara suddenly comes running into the living room with Lucas following close behind her, asking her to put on her shoes.

"Wanna see Racer," she stubbornly says, rushing over to Jasper and ignoring her father.

Jasper slowly bends down, revealing our bundle of joy in his arms.

"Say goodnight to Racer," V says as Lucas passes her Cara's shoes.

She leans forward and gently presses a kiss to his brow. "Goodnight, baby Racer. I love you. One day, I'm going to marry you."

We all pause and look at one another in shock.

"You want to be like Auntie Ava, Baby?" V asks, crouching down beside her daughter.

Cara's big green eyes widen as she nods. "Yes, Mamma. One day, I'm going to be Mrs. White, too."

Lucas laughs, making a sympathetic face at Racer.

"Good luck having this firecracker as your mother-in-law, kiddo."

We all chuckle and Jasper strokes Cara's cheek. "When you're all grown up, you'll make a beautiful bride, just like your Auntie Ava."

"And Racer will make a beautiful bride, too, Uncle Jasper," Cara innocently states.

"Yes, baby, he will," V says, unable to stop her cackle. "If he's anything like his sappy daddy, then you'll definitely be wearing the pants."

"Goodnight, Veronica." Jasper smirks, shaking his head as he stands.

She smiles, but turns serious as she looks at me. "But my brother-in-law is right. You do make a beautiful bride, babe. I'm so happy for you." She dabs at her eyes. Just as I'm about to tell her how much I love her, she adds, "Okay, enough with the sentimental crap. I'll see you tomorrow."

"Bye, V."

As I look at my friend, my best friend who has been there for me through thick and thin, I decide to add to the 'sentimental crap.' "Thank you for being there for me. Not only today, but always. I love you more than you'll ever know."

V nods, biting her lip as her eyes soften. "Ditto, Kiddo." She hugs me tight.

Jasper and Lucas fist bump as they talk about practice starting up after we're back from our honeymoon.

"I'll be there, man. But only if you're ready," Lucas says, his concern for Jasper apparent.

P.O.E. are on hiatus until further notice. The boys

didn't want to push Jasper, seeing as his recovery came first. He has been taking it slow, but the song he wrote especially for me to walk down the aisle to indicates he's back in the game.

"I'm more than ready. Later, bro."

This man amazes me every day.

They give us a final wave before driving down the driveway. We stand for a few moments, both reflecting on the events of today. I'm officially Mrs. Ava White.

And now, it's time for us to come together as man and wife.

"So," Jasper says, turning to look at me as if reading my thoughts.

"So," I parrot, marveling at how hot my husband looks with his bow tie sitting unfastened around his thick neck.

"I'm going to put this little man to bed and then—"

"And then what?" I whisper, my voice hitching in my throat.

"And then," he says, leaning in close. "I'm going to put you to bed."

I shiver in desire. "Meet me upstairs in thirty minutes?"

"I'll be there," he replies with promise, kissing me on the cheek, before walking into the kitchen to prepare a bottle for Racer.

I try to be graceful, but I charge up the stairs and commence undressing as I make my way to our bedroom. Breathing out a sigh of relief when I step out of my tight dress, I drape it over the chair and run into the bathroom to take a quick shower.

I'm done in minutes and as I'm drying off, I eye the skimpy lingerie I bought especially for tonight.

It's definitely out of my comfort zone, especially since I'm carrying my baby weight, but I suck it up (literally) as I put on the barely there garment.

Wow.

There's a lot more flesh than I remember, but I don't have time to back out because I can hear Jasper putting Racer down in the next room.

"Okay, Buddy, what song do you want Daddy to sing to you tonight?"

Racer coos and Jasper chuckles. "You got it. *Twinkle, Twinkle Little Star* it is."

Listening to Jasper sing to Racer is one of my most favorite things, but sadly, I don't have time tonight. I dart out of the bathroom and light the trillion candles I set up earlier. Just as I light the last one, the bedroom door opens and I dash into the bathroom, quietly shutting the door behind me.

I can only imagine Jasper's face as our bedroom looks picturesque licked in soft candlelight.

"Baby?" he calls out, while I barely contain my nerves.

"I'll be out in a minute," I reply through the door.

Giving myself one final pep talk, I smooth out the sheer material of my garment, my wedding band catching the light. This ring symbolizes everything we've worked so hard to achieve, and that's all the strength I need to squash down any last fears I have.

I slowly open the door and try my best to appear confident as I step out. However, when Jasper stops unbuttoning his shirt, his heated gaze raking down my near naked form, it's all the confidence I need. I take a step forward.

"Holy…" He pauses as he lingers on the transparent material between my legs. "Shit," he concludes, licking his lower lip.

I remain silent, mesmerized by what's happening in his pants. My mouth waters at the sight. "You've got way too many clothes on," I say, sauntering over to the bed. I climb on slowly, making sure my butt is raised high in the air to give Jasper a full preview of what's to come.

He growls low and when I lay back onto the pillows, I see him quickly disrobing. The sight is one I'll never tire of, but when his shirt drops to the floor, my mouth hinges open.

Inked across his upper torso is a breathtaking chest piece. A beautiful red heart sits enclosed in a birdcage. However, two bluebirds are opening the door of the cage, as if freeing the heart from its confines.

"It's beautiful," I finally manage to say, unable to tear my gaze away from the heart which is inked over the heart beating within his chest.

"I can't believe how far we've come. This,"—he rubs over the heart tattoo— "it symbolizes that my heart was broken and imprisoned before you. But now, it's free because of you. And my son."

"It's beautiful," I say again, my voice heavy with emotion.

"If you love something, set it free. If it comes back, it's yours. If it doesn't, it was never meant to be. Well, you came back, baby. Time and time again, you came back," he says, repeating the words he said to me years ago.

Crawling towards him, I stop when I reach the end of the bed. Placing my hand over his heart, I whisper, "I never left. You set me free, but I was lost without you. And now, I'm home."

He smiles and he closes his eyes, looking at total peace. "My heart belongs to you, Ava. It always has."

Wrapping a hand around his nape, I draw him forward and he comes willingly, bracing his weight on his palms as he stares into my eyes.

"So...what now?" I ask, my breath mounting in anticipation.

"Now," he replies, his cerulean jewels shining in the candlelight. "Now, we live...we live happily ever after."

"That sounds like the best plan. Like ever."

"Yup. But right now, right this second. My happily ever after is right here." He lowers his lips to mine, proving that fairytales really do come true. And this princess, she got her White prince.

Forever and a day.

ABOUT THE AUTHOR

Monica James spent her youth devouring the works of Anne Rice, William Shakespeare, and Emily Dickinson. When she is not writing, Monica runs her own business, but she always finds a balance between the two. She enjoys writing twisted AF stories, hoping to terrify her readers...just a little.

She is a bestselling author in the U.S.A., Australia, Canada, France, Germany, Israel, and the U.K. Monica James resides in Melbourne, Australia, with her Unicorn, and her three crazy cats. She is slightly obsessed with red lipstick, heels, and crime documentaries, and is that person who always runs late.

CONNECT WITH MONICA JAMES

Facebook: facebook.com/authormonicajames
Goodreads: goodreads.com/MonicaJames
Instagram: @authormonicajames
TikTok: @authormonicajames
BookBub: http://bit.ly/2E3eCIw
Amazon: https://amzn.to/2EWZSyS
Reader Group: http://bit.ly/2nUaRyi
Newsletter: https://tinyurl.com/mvjjk6k2
Patreon: https://www.patreon.com/c/AuthorMonicaJames
Shopify: https://authormonicajames.store/